DOOLIE

The Trials,
Tribulations, and Triumphs
of a 1957 Air Force Academy
Cadet

GENE DAVIS

First Edition published in 2019
First printing in 2019

Cover design by Mia Crews
Cover photo of the T-33 Shooting Star piloted by Gregory "Wired" Colyer of www.acemakerairshows.com

Cover photo taken by John Parker of air to air photos.

U.S. Air Force photo of the F-100 SuperSabre/Thunderbird from the National Museum of the United States Air Force, Dayton, Ohio

ISBN: 9781703128468

Disclaimer: The characters in this book are composites of various persons associated with the USAF Academy and the Academy Class of 1961 in the year 1957. The characters and their actions are literary extensions of real life. None of the characters represent actual characterizations of any specific individual. The historical nature of this work reflects the "Letters Home" of five individuals who were cadets at the Academy in the time period represented. The events portrayed happened, probably happened, or might have happened.

The Epilog, however, refers to persons who are members of the Class of 1961 and to accomplishments which they have achieved.

Books: Historical Fiction, Military Historical Fiction, Military Academies Historical Fiction.

FOREWORD

The military profession prizes integrity, courage, and mental, physical, and emotional toughness. On a sunny morning in early July, 1957, these qualities were about to be tested, and if lacking, indelibly imprinted upon three hundred and fourteen young men arrayed in formation on a sparse patch of asphalt outside Denver, Colorado.

The members of the third class inducted into the United States Air Force Academy had only a rudimentary grasp of what lay in store. Many would not survive that initial summer. After four grueling years, their ranks would diminish by a third for failing to meet Cadet Honor Code standards, the academic challenge, or the toughness considered essential to officership.

However, the bonds forged among the survivors would prove enduring. They became a unique band of brothers whose ties lasted through decades of individual triumph and tragedy, in war and in peace, in joy and sorrow, and yes, in sickness and in health.

No one is better qualified than Gene Davis to record the early experiences: that first summer and the nine months to follow. A skilled writer, he's deeply passionate about his subject. He chose his succinct title from Academy parlance for cadets in their freshman year.

As a survivor of that period, I found his account riveting, calling to mind so many experiences I'd forgotten while writing a personal biography. That decade-long task gave me a keen appreciation for the diligence and devotion required to take on the challenge of publishing, much less making such a novel compelling to an audience beyond the principal participants.

Gene hit upon the engaging approach of inter-weaving letters home from classmates with his own narrative of an intense socialization process designed to turn boys into men. Chronicling this unrelenting grind in excruciating detail while sustaining a keen anticipation of events in the daily *life* of a Doolie some 60 years ago is a truly remarkable achievement, but anyone who has lived through a long period of separation from family and friends can relate to it. Carry on, then, dear reader, but fasten your emotional seat belt: this is a wild ride to come.

Lee Butler, Class of 1961
General, US Air Force, Retired
Commander, Strategic Command
Last Commander, Strategic Air Command

ACKNOWLEDGMENTS

This book could not have been written without the permission of classmates Bob Heriza, Art Kerr, Terry Storm, and Ad Thompson to use information in their letters home, compiled in *Man's Flight Through Life*, edited and published by Bob. My Mother, Violet, also saved my letters. Mom was my inspiration. The letters provide the historical basis for the book. I have used literary license to produce *Doolie*, but the letters provided the fundamental story.

I, of course, sincerely appreciate Lee Butler's foreword. Our paths crossed several times during military service. Watching Lee work with Colin Powell in the Pentagon was impressive.

I wish to acknowledge the assistance of Drue DeBerry, an Air Force historian, who was kind enough to read my manuscript, provide editorial comments, and suggestions to improve the book. The Epilog is a response to Drue's recommendation to provide follow-on to the original story. I also had the benefit of Drue's wife, Betty's read through of the draft.

Classmates Bill Foster and Terry Storm helped me with line editing, comments, and format changes. Theda, Bill's wife was instrumental in editing and format changes. Theda went above and beyond. Dennis Dillon, another classmate, also made inputs to the project.

I would be remiss if I did not thank my wife, Judy, who not only did a read through with comments and corrections, but had the patience to allow me to work on writing *Doolie* – sometimes at the expense of ignoring "honey-do's." Although somewhat jealous of the fictitious girlfriend in the book, Judy provided fashion statements to help in describing Linda.

The Association of Graduate's *Register of Graduates* was helpful in tracing the careers of Classmates. The bond with Classmates; deriving from our experiences at the Academy and subsequent interactions through combat experiences, reunions, and personal visits is something special that not many are fortunate to experience.

A special thanks to Mia Crews, who is truly a professional editor and a friend from the Space Coast Writer's Guild. Without her help, the book would not have been published.

And we all feel the emotional loss of departed comrades or those with painful experiences such as Hector Negroni and Lee Butler. They are in our thoughts and prayers.

PROLOGUE

An explanation of the term "Doolie:" The Air Training Officers (ATOs) and upperclassmen used many disparaging terms for New Cadets (summer training) and Fourth Classmen (academic year). When you screwed up, you might hear yourself referred to as a "dumbsquat," "dumbsmack," "dumb-willy," or "do-willy." Classmate, Bob Heriza, in his book, *Man's Flight Through Life,* suggests the latter, do-willy, morphed into the term "Doolie," an acceptable and adopted term for Fourth Classmen. An article in the *Denver Post* indicated the original term was "Do it, Willie," which probably morphed to "do-willy," then to "Doolie."

This book is about the life of a Doolie in the class of 1961. It's a composite of experiences. Conversations are not quotes, but likely conversations. The incidents and events described happened, probably happened, or "might have happened." The events and actions however, derive from occurrences described in several sources – or to the best of my memory.

The greatest source of material for the book derived from Bob Heriza's book, *Man's Flight through Life,* a compilation of his and three other classmates' letters home. My Mom also saved my letters, providing an additional source of information. I have, however, taken some literary license to produce a coherent story.

Where possible, I have used the words from letters and statements that key Academy personnel (Superintendent, Air Officer Commanding) authored; however, in some instances – the key note talk by General White, for instance, which I could not locate – I used text that would have been spoken or written by the specific individuals.

Some names are fictitious in order to create characters without offending individuals or attributing characteristics to individuals that may not be accurate. I have used names of some departed classmates to honor them. The name Donald Leroy Davis honors my departed brother. The actions ascribed to individuals are a composite of the actions of several individuals and should not be ascribed to any particular individual, even if the real name is used.

PREFACE

July 2, 1957

I should have flown to Colorado. How silly to travel to the Air Force Academy on a train. The California Zephyr's swaying ascent of the western slope of the Sierra Nevada Mountains and the scenic passage calmed my anxiety—to a point.

Of course, neither my folks nor I could afford a plane ticket. It was tough enough getting the $42 together for the train from Sacramento to Denver.

Congressman Moss's telegram was the most exciting event of my seventeen years—more exciting than being B Football Team Captain—than being elected Class President; even more exciting than being Grant High's California Boy's State representative.

In April, I reported to nearby McClellan Air Force Base for the physical aptitude test and medical exam. Baseball conditioning made sit-ups, push-ups, and sprints "no sweat." However, I only managed six pull ups—marginal, but passing.

The medical exam went well; the flight surgeon commenting favorably on my 117 over 72 blood pressure reading. The color blindness test baffled me—until I grasped the concept of seeing numbers in the colored patterns. Once I caught on, I found enough numbers in the last five pages to pass the test.

I was concerned when Doctor Green, the dentist, called out cavities to his assistant. With a grimace, he said, "Well, young man. Looks like your teeth need considerable work."

As a single mom, and even later when she married Thaine, Mom never had a lot of money. We lived paycheck to paycheck, with beans and rice or homemade chili the meal of the day at week's end. Dental work was not high on the survival list.

Mom made an appointment with Dr. LeGrand Uffens, DDS. Dr. Uffens fixed my dental deficiencies for $192, filling the cavities and relieving my dental concern.

The family, somehow, scraped together the money for the eight cavities. My sister, Lucille and husband Elmer helped. My meager Weinstock-Lubin Department Store bus boy wages contributed. With the cavities filled, I passed my reevaluation at McClellan. The Department of the Air Force approved the paperwork. **I was in!**

Brown Palace Hotel
July 4, 1957

Dear Mom and Dad,

Well, I'm here. The train ride was almost 20 hours. What beautiful country. When it got dark in the Sierras, I went to sleep after I ate the turkey sandwiches you packed. Lucille's brownies were a treat.

I stayed in the Brown Palace Hotel (notice the stationary?), a block from the train station. I roomed with another fellow going to the Academy, Richard Milnes. My hotel bill was $3.75. We ate at a great restaurant, Lou's Steak House - a step up from Jim Denny's Hamburgers. I had a chicken fried steak.

Denver's a big city. It is pretty clean, at least the part we saw. Looks like a thriving town, lots of theaters and restaurants. It's called the "Mile High City" as the elevation is over 5,000 feet. The thin air is more noticeable than when Pa and I went hunting in the Sierras.

Tomorrow morning we'll catch a bus to take us to the Academy's temporary site at Lowry Air Force Base. The bus is supposed to be here at ten. Well, I'm really tired so think I'll hit the sack.

God Bless
Your loving son,
Don

John Stovall, a husky kid from Arizona slipped into the seat next to me. We exchanged names. "So, John, what did you do in high school; did you play football?'

"Call me Smoky, friends do. Nah, I played basketball. Did the usual: student government, newspaper, home coming committees, and, of course, basketball. I hope to make the basketball team, but I'm sure the competition will be tough. What about you?"

"I played football and baseball and did some of the other things you mentioned. I'd like to play baseball and football too, but think I'm a too slow and small for varsity football."

We snaked through downtown Denver traffic in what appeared a leftover WWII blue bus. The sides read 'United States Air Force Academy" in silver and blue lettering.

"Wow, Smoky, hope the rest of the Academy equipment is more modern than this blue beetle. My high school had newer buses."

"Well, we're just getting started. Lowry's a temporary site. You've seen pictures of the new site, haven't you?"

"Sure," I replied. "The catalog shows ultra-modern buildings against beautiful mountains and forests. I guess everything hasn't caught up to the catalog yet."

We spent the rest of the drive introducing ourselves. Ron Mueller, from Brooklyn, was an "All State" football halfback, student body, and National Honor Society Chapter president.

The other eleven had equally impressive resumes. *Boy, the competition is going to be tough, whether in sports or academics*, I thought. *Hell, as one of 20 from California and with competitive tests to get in, I should be all right. But I haven't met any slouches.*

"Wow, look at the chicks," said Terry Cloud, another bus mate. Six good-looking girls were standing outside the cyclone fence of the Academy entrance taking pictures. "I hear there are five girls' colleges and three coed colleges close by."

The girls smiled and waved as the blue beetle passed. "An upperclassman friend of mine wrote me the girls are crazy about cadets. Should be great pickin's," Terry said. From Michigan, he was obviously pleased with the Colorado scenery.

At the gate, a tall, thin man jumped on. "I'm Lieutenant Robert Hood. Welcome, Gentlemen, to the United States Air Force Academy. We'll get you signed in, sworn in, and over to the dormitories to drop off your gear. When you're settled, we'll form up at 1130 hours and go to the dining hall for lunch." He instructed the driver to proceed.

The small whitewashed building looked like an afterthought. The lettered sign over the doorway read: "US Air Force Academy Headquarters." We piled off the bus.

A six foot, trim officer in an impeccable khaki uniform, with gold leaves on the collar, a chest full of brightly colored ribbons, and pilot wings topped by a star, ushered us in. He lined us up six abreast in front of his grey metal desk.

"I am Major Shaun O'Brian. On behalf of the Superintendent, welcome to the Academy. I will administer the oath of office officially appointing you as USAFA "New Cadets.""

USAFA—for United States Air Force Academy—was my first introduction to military acronyms, a new vocabulary we would all quickly learn.

"Repeat after me: I, state your name . . ." The ceremony took three minutes. We grinned and shook hands as official New Cadets in the class of 1961.

***

3d Squadron, 1 st Group
The Air Force Cadet Wing
United States Air Force Academy
Denver, Colorado

Dear Mom and Dad,   *July 5, 1957*

   A group of friendly officers met the bus and showed us to quarters after we were sworn in by a Major O'Brian. Our quarters are World War II, two-story barracks. They smell like fresh paint. The beds are steel framed bunk beds.   It must get cold; there are two blankets and a fluffy comforter on the bed.

   Butch Rieselman, my roommate is from Kentucky. He plays tennis and swims. There are also guys from New York, New Jersey, Pennsylvania, Oregon, and Montana. We had great conversations when not stuffing our faces. Everyone bragged about sports, fishing, and girls, girls, girls.

   Tomorrow we have four hours of tests in English, math, and whatever. We draw equipment in the afternoon. The evening schedule says "study time." In a book, Fourth Class Customs, and another, Contrails, is a list of Air Training Officers with names and titles; like Squadron Commander, Element Leader, etc. We are supposed to memorize all of that by Monday.

   (Saturday evening) Wow, what tests, guess they want to know what we don't know. We're assigned class sections based on the tests. They put the smart people together and then filter on down. I'll probably be in the middle.

   There are 36 World War II barracks bordering an area known as the quadrangle; a Headquarters' "shack;" a vintage dining hall, a modern crème-colored academic building, and a grass field "parade ground" that make up the "campus."

> *There is a big athletic field near our barracks. There is a strange looking place with straw-filled dummies, held together by wire mesh. Don't know what it is, but I suppose we will find out sooner or later.*
>
> *Sunday, the Superintendent talks to us in the morning. The Superintendent is the big kahuna here, responsible for running the Academy. The Commandant is in charge of the military program. He and the Dean, who runs academics of course, are going to talk Sunday afternoon.*
>
> *Guess I'll sign off. We have to march to dinner. You can't believe how good the food is and you eat all you want.*
>
> *I'm a little lonesome for home and you all, but this looks like it's going to be quite an adventure. Write when you can. I'll be waiting for your letters.*
>
> > *God Bless*
> > *Your loving son,*
> > *Don*

Just as I finished the letter, Smokey yelled down the hall, "Hey Davis, come out and throw the football around."

"Want to go?" I asked Butch, who was looking through the pile of issued materials.

"Nah, I think I'll stay here and study some of this crap. I understand we have to know the Squadron ATO names and the Fourth Class Knowledge in *Contrails* by Monday."

"Ah, come on, we have tomorrow and Sunday. How much can they expect us to know in three days, hah! I'm going out and get a little exercise to warm up for Monday."

Terry Cloud, Ron Mueller, Ed Zompa, and Art Kerr were waiting with Smokey. I'd met all of them except Kerr. "Hi, I'm Don Davis from Sacramento, California. Where're you from?"

"I'm Art Kerr from Alaska."

Since there were only six of us, we divided into three man teams. Only the end was eligible for passes. It was touch football and there was no blocking or tackling.

The mile-high altitude took its toll. After two hours, I was beat. "Man, I'm winded," I said. "Think I'll take it to my room."

***

Sunday, after breakfast at 0800 we marched to Protestant Chapel Services. Following the service, which was relatively short, we marched to the base theater. "Marched" is probably the wrong term. We sort of ambled in a group formation.

"**Group, atten . . . tion**," called a deep, resonating voice at the back of the auditorium. "**Gentlemen, the Academy Superintendent, Major General James Briggs.**"

"Take seats," the General said. "Members of the Class of 1961, welcome. You are the cream of the crop of young men in this country. For the next year, and especially the next two months; however, you will not hear that phrase again. You have won an enviable opportunity; the competition is not over. Your Fourth Class year is your tryout."

"Damn, Butch, I thought we were in. What's this 'tryout' business?"

"Ssssh," Butch whispered. "Or you'll have a short career as a cadet."

"You must learn to follow before you can lead," General Briggs continued. "You must learn to accept responsibility before you can exercise authority. Your primary effort during Academics will be to meet academic standards. However, if that were the only objective, there would be no need for an Air Force Academy. We require more.

On Monday, you begin summer training and indoctrination into Fourth Class customs. Summer Training is an integral part of the Academy curriculum, with beginning courses in military, flying, and physical training. Of equal importance is initiation into the Air Force Cadet way of life, the Cadet Class System, and the Cadet Honor Code.

Fourth Class customs are sometimes initially misunderstood; to some, harshly demanding and restrictive. With a little understanding, a willingness to listen and follow without question, and the love of comradeship common to most men, there is more game than gall to the program."

"Not the way Terry Cloud's friend who washed out last year described it," I whispered.

"Ssssh!" Butch said again.

"Cadets are not hazed; Service Academy statues prohibit hazing. Nothing degrading is asked of a New Cadet. For 60 days you will undergo a regime of highly emphasized good manners, immediate response to command, and unquestioning recognition of authority.

Fourth Class double timing, squaring of corners, eating at attention, and reciting at meals may have little obvious purpose. But the result is a class spirit, a loyalty, and an anticipation of responsibilities and privileges that sets an Air Force Cadet apart.

You'll have Cadet Honor Code lectures telling how the code was devised, why and how it is controlled by cadets, what it means to live by the code, and consequences of violating it. The Code simply says: 'We will not lie, cheat, steal, nor tolerate among us those who do.'

I congratulate each of you for earning an Academy appointment. Beginning Monday, you will have a chance to earn the honor and privilege of being a graduate of the country's newest military academy. Good luck and God's speed."

"Group, atten . . .shun," boomed the back-of-the-theater voice. **"Dismissed**."

***

Lunch was again a delight. Marconi and cheese and fried chicken were topped off with fudge brownies and vanilla ice cream. After lunch, we again marched to the theater.

"**Group, atten . . . shun**," sang out the same sonorous voice from the morning. **"Gentlemen. Brigadier General Robert M. Stillman, the Academy Commandant of Cadets."**

"Seats, Gentlemen. It's my pleasure to welcome you as members of the Class of 1961. Many great aviation names lent their efforts to establishing the Academy. They include General Billy Mitchell, military airpower advocate, General Hubert R. Harmon, first Academy Superintendent and Charles Lindbergh, first to fly the Atlantic in a single engine aircraft. President Dwight D. Eisenhower signed the 'Air Force Academy Act' on 1 April 1954.

You will be tested to the limits of your endurance during the next eight weeks. If you fail the test, you don't belong here. You have the necessary qualifications—physical, mental, and spiritual; you need only superior motivation and fortitude to complete the journey.

You now, however, are at the bottom of a pyramid of challenging obstacles. Reaching the apex provides a regular commission as an Air Force Second Lieutenant; a rating as an Air Force Navigator, and a Baccalaureate Degree in Military Science.

Your mental attitude, especially during summer training and your year as a Fourth Classman, will determine if you 'hack' the program. If you develop strong self-discipline and lean on each other; each of you has the pre-qualifications to make it.

Prepare yourself for a conditioning course comparable to paratrooper jump school or marine boot camp. The program is rigorous and demanding. A national magazine has labeled us 'The Toughest School in America.' Tomorrow you will find out why.

You will be trained by some of the finest junior officers in the Air Force, Air Training Officers (ATOs). They were selected especially for this duty. They trained the first two classes.

Your record of accomplishments and meeting the demands of a highly competitive appointment process indicates you can be successful—if you have the desire. I wish to congratulate you on being here. Good luck."

"**Group, atten . . . tion**, You are dismissed to remain in place. You may talk."

"Damn, Davis, he sounds like a hard ass. 'If you can't hack the program, you don't belong here.' That's pretty frapping encouraging."

"Yeah, guess he's the bad cop. He's tough though. Did you read in *Contrails* he was shot down over Belgium in a B-26 and spent two years in a German Prison Camp? That's got to be a helluva lot tougher than anything we'll see."

Suddenly, a young Captain came through the top doors and said," Men, you may go to the latrine, but be back in your places in 10 minutes."

"Does he mean the men's room?" Butch asked.

***

"Group, atten . . . tion," came from the rear. A tall, young Colonel mounted the stage. **"Gentlemen, the Dean of Faculty, Colonel Robert F. McDermott."**

"Seats, please. Welcome, Class of 1961.You were selected under a "whole man" concept. You have good academic credentials and excellent leadership and interpersonal skills. During summer training, you will not see a lot of me. First, you are entirely in General Stillman's realm. You will need all your physical and mental skills to survive his program.

Secondly, we still have to shape the core academic program and enrichment studies. Unlike the other two major military academies, we're not preparing you for your first assignment, but rather for future leadership positions. You will have an equal dose of science and social sciences – with specialized courses in navigation training and military studies.

The curriculum includes liberal arts, science, and engineering courses to provide a foundation for future development. We will offer special courses for individual cadets to fulfill their academic potential. You may validate courses based on previous studies. Advanced courses in subjects such as English will award extra credits.

We do not have a one-size-fits-all curriculum as do our sister academies. We do have a core curriculum. Your first semester will consist of: Chemistry, English, Graphics, Math, Philosophy, Physical Education, Flying Training, and Military Studies. You well earn 36 credit hours your first year.[1]

I know you are all anxious to get back to your rooms to study *Contrails* and *Fourth Class Customs,* so I will close wishing you God's Speed. I hope to see all of you in September."

"Group, Atten . . . shun! Dismissed!"

---

[1] In addition to a balanced curriculum designed to provide cadets with problem solving abilities, an Academy goal was to obtain accreditation before the graduation of the first class – a goal which it achieved.

United States Air Force Academy
July 7, 1957 1900

Dear Folks,

What a weekend. We've been sworn in, assigned quarters, and roommates; issued tons of clothes, and been "briefed"—that's what they call talks by the Superintendent, Commandant, and Dean of Faculty. The Superintendent, Major General Briggs, said we're the "crème" of the crop, but there may be a lot of sour milk between now and graduation; especially the first year; especially during summer training.

The Commandant, Brigadier General Stillman, says one of the magazines calls this the "toughest school in America." Don't see how tomorrow can be tougher than the first football practice, but we'll see.

The Dean, a Colonel McDermott, says we have a core curriculum, but if you qualify you can take enrichment classes. You can also get extra credit for advanced classes.

All three of the officers have impressive combat records and have had important assignments in the Air Force.

This is going to be a great adventure. It's good to be in the start-up of a new school. Remember I was in the first new class at Rio Linda Junior High. And I was the first student body president. That was a great time. I hope this goes as well.

Well, I have some time; guess I'd better study the stuff they gave us. Who knows what tomorrow will be like?

God Bless,
Your loving son,
Don

United States Air Force Academy
July 7, 1957 2000 (8 p.m. . . .civilian time)

Dear Walt,

Thanks for the letter. It was waiting for me. I have a few minutes before lights out so thought I would write. Thanks again for the going away party. Don't know who got the beer, but that was some party. Say hello to Wayne; tell him to write. If you see Sharon, tell her it would be nice to get a perfumed letter from her.

This place is something. Food's fantastic. We've enjoyed it for three days. Had steak one night and half a chicken the next. I didn't see much of Denver; stayed in a nice hotel. The first weekend we drew uniforms, got "buzz" haircuts, took tests, got camping gear, and an Garand M1 rifle.

They measured us for New Cadet uniforms—designed by Cecil B. DeMille. Things are a little weird. They took a picture in jock straps. Said I have one shoulder lower than the other. I have to work to develop good military posture.

We also received a five-inch thick notebook of regulations. One, Air Force Cadet Regulation 11-6, spells out everything from how you put your things in your closet to how to make your bed to how to talk to an "inspecting officer." We will have a parade every week on Saturdays. We also have a "retreat parade" during the week just to take the flag down.

Talk about nitty-gritty (petty, chicken shit really). Fourth Classmen (right now I'm a New Cadet) can't have a radio until Christmas. The radio privilege is in place of going home—we'll be here for Christmas, so guess I won't see you guys until next summer.

Some sweet young things were by the gate when we came in. They looked friendly, smiling and waving. We don't get to see any girls until after the football games. Nothing like living in a monastery. Oops! They just called a formation. Have to go, more later.

Wow, great breakfast. Never had steak and eggs for breakfast before. You also have pancakes, bacon, sausage, juice, milk, and coffee. It's family style. Like when we went skiing and stopped at Mama Tyler's. Lunch is ham or chicken and mashed potatoes, and dinner is steak or something else good. All kinds of beverages . If I keep eating like this, I'll get fat.

The guys so far are great; smart, athletic, and friendly. The competition is going to be tough. The guys are all tops in their classes; all City this and all State that. Like the fellows were at Boy's State.

The Denver mile-high 5,000 feet takes getting used to. They say the conditioning program is tough, but you get in great shape. Don't know about tomorrow—I've heard it's worse than football conditioning. We'll see.

We have a little handbook called Contrails. It has neat stuff about the Academy and Air Force. We have to recite parts of it verbatim. But that isn't until tomorrow when we meet the Air Training Officers. They are lieutenants, graduates of the other academies and military schools.

They're our summer upperclassmen since there are only two classes ahead of us. We're told the upperclassmen aren't really ready to lead. Whatever, I'm sure it's going to be a better than Sac State Junior College.

My roommate, Butch, is from Kentucky. Says it's the state of fast women and beautiful horses. He said he had a beautiful, fast woman named Sue. They have been going together since the eighth grade.

Well, have to close. Tomorrow is the big day; we meet the Air Training Officers—ATOs for short. They sure keep us busy. I will miss you guys and, of course, the girls, too. Write lots and often.

Your buddy,
Don

Chapter 1

They were waiting like great white sharks circling a pod of young seals.

Monday, July 8, 1957 Day One

I threw back my covers and looked at the clock. *My God, it's five thirty.* I staggered out of bed, put on my fatigues, and walked over to shake Butch, who wasn't stirring. "Butch, rise and shine, they just sounded reveille[2]."

Butch grunted, slid out of bed, and slithered into his fatigues. We wandered out and stood casually in flight formation. There was an eerie silence in the quadrangle.

Standing 20 yards in front of us was a force of 30-some impeccably uniformed lieutenants. They stood motionless like a Phalanx of Roman soldiers ready for battle.

"Fall out and make corrections," boomed a throaty voice. The phalanx of khaki clad officers broke ranks and swarmed toward the 314 New Cadets of the Class of 1961.

"Chin in , Mister. Shoulders back. Get that gut in. Head up! Reach for Colorado" were the welcoming words of the short, razor-thin, first lieutenant Air Training Officer (ATO) who stood in front of me.

"What's your name, Dumbsquat?" Lieutenant Tatum whispered in my ear. The roar of voices cascaded down upon me from all directions in a deafening din.

"My name is Cadet Davis . . ."

"What????" screeched Tatum. **"Have you no military bearing at all, Mister?** Didn't the sergeants tell you that you are *New Cadet Davis* and that you address all officers as 'Sir'?"

"I, uh, uh . . ." I stammered. Sweat began to form and drip under my arms down the sleeve of my fatigues.

"Give me 10" barked Tatum.

I started counting, "One, two, three . . ."

"No, Dumbsquat. Ten push-ups. HIT IT!"

I dropped to the ground. After the 10 push-ups, my arms hurt; I gasped for breath; the dark circles of sweat under my arms reached halfway to my waist.

---

[2] The military call "revile," is a wakeup call. When we heard the bugle call, we were told to dress in fatigues and report in front of the building in the formations we had been using for the past three days.
"Tattoo" is a "call to quarters" meaning you should be in your quarters anticipating "taps."
Taps is the evening call for "lights out."

"OK, Mister New Cadet Davis. Spit it out. Why didn't you 'Sir' me? And the answer better be the right one."

I desperately tried to recall the approved school solutions. *Ah*, I thought, relieved. *Yes, Sir, No, Sir, No excuse, Sir!* I choose the last as the only suitable response. "No excuse, Sir," I said.

"Davis, I don't think you're going to make it through the summer," the Lieutenant said. He did a smart right face and stepped in front of my classmate, Butch.

I exhaled slowly as I heard, "**Chin in, Mister . . .**"

I wasn't sure I was going to make it through the day. I wasn't even sure I wanted to make it through the week, much less the summer.

After the 30 minute ATO "orientation"—which seemed an eternity—and roll call, we were dismissed to return to our rooms and change into physical training (PT) gear. We were ordered to shave and be back in formation in fifteen minutes.

***

We assembled by flights. Three squadrons with three flights each totaled 314 New Cadets. With only two upper classes, recently graduated West Point, Annapolis, Citadel, Virginia Military Institute, Air Force Reserve Officer Training (AFROTC), and even Aviation Cadet Officers were our surrogate upperclassmen. The ATOs would get very up close and personal with us in the next two months.

"**Come on, slackers.**" Lt. Tatum yelled, standing on the barrack's steps.

"Better hustle it up, Davis," a tall, gangling lieutenant said quietly as I stumbled down the stairs. Something about this officer's manner calmed me. His name tag read "John Payne." A shiver of joy ran through my body as I realized Payne was the name of my Element Leader.

After 20 minutes of exercise in the hot sun, a red rivulet ran down the front of my PT shirt, staining the white area under the USAFA emblem a dull, dark red. My nose was providing my T shirt with an unwanted transfusion. I expected Lt. Tatum to be all over me.

Instead, Lt. Payne came up and said, "Davis, you'd better go sit down on the grass before you bleed all over the quad and have to clean it up."

I welcomed the break and felt less trepidation when joined by at least a dozen classmates. The ATOs, whom we thought were insensitive beasts, knew it would take us at least two weeks to acclimate to the rarified Denver air.

Following PT, we double-timed to the barracks for a fire drill change into fatigues. We were harangued all the way to the dining hall by the zealous ATOs.

***

The shock continued during breakfast. I vaguely recall being bombarded by a constant series of ATO questions while trying to remember the strange terminology used to get food from the waiters to the head of the table and the ATOs. I don't remember eating anything, but I do remember a gnawing feeling in my stomach later during close order drill on the quadrangle.

Breakfast and the return to the barracks were a blur. Butch told me later we came back to the barracks, had 15 minutes to brush our teeth, go to the latrine, change to fatigues, and reform in flight formation.

For the next hour, we practiced close order drill. "This," Lt. Payne said, "is the position of attention." He stood ram rod straight, his white gloved hands at his sides, fingers curled.

"Now," he said, "you salute officers and upperclassmen. You DO NOT salute non-commissioned officers and airmen. You DO, however, acknowledge their salute with a crisp salute of your own. Your rank is between a Warrant Officer 2 and 3.

Render the salute by raising your right arm smartly, bending your arm at the elbow, with finger tips touching either your hat brim or, if uncovered, your eyebrow. Keep your arm and hand straight and your elbow at a 45 degree angle. It looks like this," he said, saluting. "When you approach a superior, you salute at six paces. Hold your salute until it is returned, then smartly return your hand to your side . . . like this!

If you approach a superior from the rear, salute and hold it, calling out, 'by your leave, Sir.' The superior may say, 'pass', or motion you to go by. Hold your salute until it is returned. If double timing, come to a walk, salute, pass, and resume double-timing.

If you approach the United States flag or if a U. S. flag is going to pass you, salute at distance of six paces and hold the salute until the flag is six paces past. If you are in a formation or work detail, the detail leader will call the group to attention and render the salute. Are there any questions? No? Good. Davis get out here, step in front of me and render a salute!"

"NO DAVIS! Get that elbow at a 45 degree angle, touch the brim of your hat, and don't cup your hand like you're fondling your girl." Payne straightened my arm and moved it to a 45 degree angle; then moved back in front of me. "Now, beat my hand down."

I did.

"Post," said Lt. Payne. *Well, at least nobody snickered.*

"Okay," Lt. Payne said. "We're going to do it by the numbers[3]: When I give the command 'present … arms', give me your best hand salute and hold it. When I say 'order

---

[3] "By the numbers:" a step at a time, often with instructors calling out a number for each step.

. . . arms' you bring your arm to your side and at attention. **'PRESENT . . . ARMS!'"** Lt. Payne boomed in a command voice. He walked the lines making corrections before he sang out, **"ORDER . . . ARMS!"** from the back of the flight.

"Right face," Payne commanded. "If you are taller than the man in front of you move up." With the tallest cadet in front, smaller guys in the rear required extremely long strides to keep up during drills and parades.

The commands "forward, march," "to-the-rear, march," "column, halt," "right and left oblique, march," "eyes, right," and "ready, front" along with "right, face," "left, face," and "about, face" were demonstrated; then executed over and over.

"No, Do-willie Davis, the other left. I realize you are fond of your roommate, but you're not supposed to be face-to-face." Lt. Payne was more subtle and controlled than other ATOs, as evidenced by the bellows and raging voices filling the quadrangle.

Following the close order drill session, Lt Payne brought the element into our room. He went through the order of articles listed in AFCR 11-6[4], demonstrating the correct location and display of each article. "That is the way your room will be for AMI[5] inspection every morning. Now let me show you a SAMI room," said Payne, readjusting my bedding to show the white collar and blanket arrangements.

After the second drill period, we had fifteen minutes to use the latrine. We straggled back into Squadron formation to march to the dining hall. ATOs chewed on us the entire way. ATO chatter was so loud, none of us realized the Academy Band was playing. We were oblivious to everything except the constant din in our ears.

***

Lunch was an entirely new experience straight out of a horror movie. "Well, Mister Davis, let's hear the Code of Conduct." I grimaced. I had drawn Lieutenant Eugene Tatum, a West Point graduate and our Flight Commander, as Table Commandant. At the head of the ten-man table, he was quizzing me on a mandatory Fourth Class Knowledge item. At Tatum's right was Lt. Richard Boyce, another West Pointer and Second Element Leader, C Flight. The two were a tag-team source of constant questions.

To cut chicken into "bite size" pieces while sitting at rigid attention on the first six inches of the chair and with your eyes "caged," (not looking up, down or sideways) was almost insurmountable. The procedure to cut a piece of meat, ground (lay down) your knife, switch the fork to your right hand, take a bite, and ground your fork and begin

[4] Air Force Cadet Regulation (AFCR) 11-6 was our barracks bible; it told us how to make the bed, how to arrange all items in our closet (hats, shoes, underwear, gloves, raincoats), and the proper New Cadet demeanor toward officers or upperclassmen during a room inspection.
[5] AMI: AM for "morning" inspection; SAMI: S for Saturday.

again was time consuming and inhibited eating. Combined with ATO questions, little time was left to eat.

In response to Lt. Tatum's demand, I stared at his stiff, starched uniform, decorated with a chest full of ribbons. Knowledge of the meaning of his ribbons would be a future challenge.

"Sir, I am an American fighting man. I serve in the forces which guard my country and our way of life. I . . .I . . ." My throat constricted and my heart began beating against my uniform. I did not remember any more.

"Well, cadet, let's hear it," prodded Tatum pointing his fork in my direction. "Don't you know the rest of it?"

"No, Sir," I replied, hoping my response would suffice.

"Why not?" asked Tatum.

"Well, Sir, I . . ." Then catching myself, said, "No Excuse, Sir!"

"You're right, Davis. You'd better have it all for me by dinner. Eat!"

***

Following a short break after lunch, we spent the afternoon marching and practicing close order drill. One of my least favorite activities, this later would seem a cakewalk – when we encountered Lt. Yeager's bayonet training class.

A physical training (PT) session, an hour lecture on US Air Force Customs and Courtesies, a second PT period, and an hour and a half hour of close order drill, all punctuated with frantic uniform changes, rounded out the afternoon schedule.

***

". . . I will never forget that I am an American fighting man, responsible for my actions, and dedicated to the principles which made my country free. I will trust in my God and the United States of America.[6]"

I paused and remained rigidly at attention. My classmates took advantage of the situation to get as many bites as possible. I anticipated a "well done" from Lt. Tatum, but he was engrossed in conversation with Lt. Boyce. Five minutes later, noticing I had stopped reciting, Lt. Tatum looked at me and softly said, "Carry On."

With the magic words of "continue what you were doing," I picked up my fork and began eating the potatoes and gravy. I snuck in four bites of chocolate pudding before Tatum pushed his chair back and said, "Dismissed."

---

[6] We were allowed to carry *Contrails* and, when not engaged in an activity or being addressed by an ATO, we could study Fourth Class Knowledge. My two senior high school play experiences came in handy for quickly memorizing the seven stanza "Code of Conduct."

After dinner, we were allowed to walk to the barracks. We were ordered to shower, report to our rooms, dress in PT gear, and wait for instruction on ordering our rooms. Lt. Payne's earlier instruction freed us to put our rooms in AMI[7] order and begin the meticulous task of creating an acceptable shoe shine.

"Lights out" was at 9 p.m. (oops, 2100 hours[8]). I didn't hear taps. I fell into a deep, black hole at "lights out" and did not move until the morning reveille blast.

***

As I awoke, I thought to myself, *what a horrible nightmare that was.*

---

[7] "AM" was for morning and the "I" for inspection.
[8] Military time, like European time, is on the 24-hour clock.

Chapter 2

The first few weeks at the Academy are devoted to an intensive basic training program . . . which equips the New Cadet physically and psychologically for his four years at the Academy. It is a period of complete readjustment to a . . . new way of life.

. . . "Forth Class Customs"

Tuesday, July 9, 1957 Day 2

"Sir, there are five minutes until first call for reveille formation. Dormitory 895 alert. There are five minutes, Sir."

Classmate Roger Stringer had the good fortune to be our first "minute caller." At the bottom of the stairs, callers "broadcast" to both floors of the dormitory.

"Butch, better get up. We only have a couple of minutes until formation." Butch had either not heard reveille or was having trouble believing, as I was, this was all real.

"I hear ya, Davis. What're they going to do, throw me out? Save me resigning?"

"Sir, there are four minutes to first call for reveille formation."

A familiar high-pitched Tatum voice rang out, **"Well Do-Willie, where's the rest of it? You left out the uniform, what's everyone supposed to do, come out naked and barefoot?**

"Sir, the uniform of the day is pajamas, bathrobes, and slippers," Roger yelled at the top of his voice.

"No, Dumbsquat. Slippers? What kind of pussy outfit you think you're in? Get it right and do all of it over!"

"Yes, Sir. No excuse, Sir. Sir, there are four minutes to first call for reveille formation. The uniform is pajamas, bathrobes, and shower clogs."

"Really," Tatum said loud enough for all of us to hear. **"Really, Mr. Stringer, how many minutes are there?"**

"Sir, there are three minutes to first call[9] for reveille formation. The uniform is pajamas, bathrobes, and shower clogs. This is the last minute to be called, Sir."

"Post[10]," Tatum said shrilly.

Butch struggled into his bathrobe. We staggered into the hallway, nearly knocking Lt. Tatum down, as he was standing right in front of our door.

---

[9] New Cadets and Fourth Classmen had to be in formation at "first call." ATOs had an additional five minutes to be in formation and harass.

[10] "Leave!"

Tatum glared. "Well Dumbsquats, nice of you to join us . . . **What are you staring at, Davis? Eyes front."**

We stood at attention on either side of our door. Tatum walked down the hall, counting. **"All accounted for on the bottom floor,"** he shouted up the stairs.

"All accounted for on the top deck," came an obvious Annapolis graduate reply. "Dismissed," hissed Tatum.

We had 15 minutes to get to the common latrine, shave, use the facility, and return to our room. We had to make our beds, sweep the floor, check the closets, and get dressed in the uniform of the day before leaving for formation.

Since we were at the end of the hall nearest formation, Butch and I decided to do the room and uniforms first and then go to the latrine for the required shave.

We struggled with hospital bed corners. Putting on fatigues also went slowly.

Sir, there are five minutes until first call for breakfast formation," rang out Roger's tense voice. **The uniform is fatigues, low quarter shoes, and fatigue caps. Dormitory 895 alert. Sir, there are five minutes."**

Everyone waited for Tatum's shrill screech; there was only silence.

"Oh, shit, Butch, we don't have time to make it to the latrine and out to formation."

"Yeah, and there's probably an ATO in the hall. Hell, let's fake it."

Butch and I hesitated to leave the room. Being in the first room in the hall and C Flight, the formation closest to us, we quickly figured out we could be in formation in less than 30 seconds – the less time in formation, the less time to be ATO bait.

Marching into the dining hall, we removed our hats, double-timed to our seats, and stood at attention behind our chairs. From the Command Section, the Adjutant made announcements – most having nothing to do with New Cadets. A Chaplin said grace. When the Table Commandant ordered, "Take seats," we scrambled to assume the New Cadet chair position and begin our table duties.

This morning, as I double-timed up the steps into the dining hall, I had a terrible sensation of being lost. Lt. Tatum's running commentary on my "sloppy" marching totally disoriented me. With my eyes on the floor, I couldn't see the numbers at the cadet end of the tables. The normal way to your table was to turn right or left on entering, then, depending on your table location, count the number of rows you passed, make a square turn, and again count rows until you arrived at your table. I had unwittingly turned the wrong way and didn't realize it until a right turn put me in a strange place.

I began to perspire and have visions of a dozen tours for being at the wrong table. It was my week to be "Cold-pilot." I could easily glide into my position at the end of the table. I cut across the rows until I felt I had covered the required ground. I stopped, made a right face and looked up. *Oh, my God, I'm at the wrong table.*

"Well, Dumbsquat, what's your name?" asked a rather unpleasant voice. The Table Commandant's name tag read: John Englehart.

"Sir, my name is New Cadet Davis!"

"Well, New Cadet Davis, did your gyro tumble[11]? Are you lost?"

"Ah, Yes, Sir."

"Where are you supposed to be, Do-willie? And who is your Table Commandant?"

"Sir, I am at Table 10 and my Table Commandant is Lt. Tatum"

"Hey, Tatum," the tall, light skinned Lieutenant yelled. "You lost one; you want me to give him a directional steer?

"Yeah," Tatum yelled. **"Send him over; I'll give him some additional navigational instruction tonight."**

"Well, New Cadet Davis, to return to base, left face, pass two tables and make a right.

As I made a left face and came to rigid attention, I looked up. Lt. Tatum was smirking. "Well, Davis, that was embarrassing, wasn't it?"

"Yes, Sir!"

"Okay, I'll consider that a lesson learned. Carry on."

As "Cold-pilot", I managed the cold drinks as they arrived at the ramp[12]. "Orange juice for the Table Commandant, Sir" I announced passing a full glass of juice to my left.

"Davis, don't you know anything?" Boyce snorted. "What are you supposed to call the orange juice?"

"I don't . . . I do not[13] know, Sir."

"Why not?"

"No excuse, Sir!"

"I'm beginning to think you're hopeless. That, New Cadet Davis, is Ti **ger** pis. That is how it will be announced, Eat."

"Yes, Sir. Ti **ger** pis for Lt. Boyce."

Jim Dickson, the "Hot pilot" on my left, ensured coffee and/or chocolate went to the head of the table. Most of us didn't drink coffee. First, it would be cold before we could drink it and, secondly, was the terror of spilling coffee on a fresh uniform.

---

[11] The attitude indicator on aircraft used gyro stabilizations. If the gyro failed, the instrument "tumbled."

[12] Table

[13] Fourth Classmen are not allowed to use contractions. They must use the full term.

The "Forward Air Controller," Bob Hertz, on my right, managed the flow of food from the waiter. Bob announced, "Sir, the main course is scrambled eggs. Scrambled eggs for the Commandant, Sir. Hot Plate, Sir.[14]"

"Dumbsmack! Do I look like the **Commandant** to you? **Who is the Commandant anyway?**" screeched Lt. Tatum.

"No sir, you do not look like the Commandant. The Commandant is Brigadier General Robert M. Stillman." (I'm sure Bob was thinking: *And probably a hell of a lot nicer than you*.)

"What's his middle name and full title?"

"Sir, his full title is Commandant of Cadets. I do not know his middle name!"

"Why not?"

"Well, Sir, I have only seen . . ."

"What, Mr. Hertz?"

"No excuse, Sir!"

"Roger[15]. You'll know his middle name and nickname by lunch time."

"Yes, Sir!!"

"Now, pass the food before everything gets cold."

As soon as the potatoes, bacon, sausage, toast, and grits were announced and passed, Lt Tatum leaned in Bob's direction. "Mr. Hertz, what's the waiter's name?"

"Uh, sir . . .?" Bob looked dismayed. He had not taken a bite of his breakfast.

Almost imperceptivity, our tall, slender, African American waiter slipped to Bob's side. "Cadet Hertz, here's yo strawberry jelly," he said extending a jar in front of Bob.

As Bob looked up to receive the jelly, he clearly saw Mr. White's name tag.

"Uh, Sir, that waiter's name is Mr. Bob White . . ."

"Mr. Hertz, is Mr. White a personal friend of yours?"

"No, Sir."

"Then don't you think you should give me his proper name?"

"Yes, Sir," Bob said flushing.

"It's Robert," whispered the waiter.

"Ah, Sir, the waiter's name is Robert White, Sir."

Tatum pretended not to hear the waiter's interjection. He smirked: "Eat!"

---

[14] This warning was primarily for classmates. If an obnoxious upperclassman was on your right or left, the warning might be "forgotten" and the hot pan passed along.

[15] "Roger" is pilot language for "understood." When responding to air traffic control instructions, for instance, the pilot will reply, "Roger." The term for ending a series of transmissions is "Roger, out," not "Roger, over and out." "Over" means an additional transmission is expected.

***

After breakfast, we returned to our rooms. Hitting the john, I finished my business there, ran to my room, grabbed my M1 rifle, and my helmet. Thank God, Roger's announcements had emphasized "with helmet and rifle." I ran out the door and double-timed to my flight position. *Damn, never thought I could do all that in fifteen minutes. Good thing a stall was empty.*

Standing in formation, I saw an ominous shadow approaching me from the left. Lt. Carl Jackson, an ATO from B flight, stopped in front of me and inspected me from the tip of my cap to the toes of my shoes. *Ah, shit*, I thought, *he's going to chew me out about my shoe shine.*

"Dumbguard, did you shave this morning?"

"I . . . ah . . .*Trying hard to remember if I had shaved, I recalled our disastrous time management before breakfast. I didn't have much of a beard at seventeen, but . . . Crap! I didn't shave.* No, Sir," I blurted, out knowing the guillotine was about to fall. "No, excuse, Sir!"

Lt. Jackson's face broke into a wry, evil-looking sneer. He took the paper name tag insert from the metal holder on my uniform.[16] Then said, "Mr. Davis, I will see you in front of your latrine with shaving gear, tooth paste, and towel at shower formation tonight."

Shower formation? What the hell is a shower formation? I asked myself.

Jackson started to leave. As he was about to pass Butch, he stopped and exclaimed, "What kind of raggedy-tag Air Force is this?" He snatched Butch's name tag and asked: "Mister Rieselman, did you shave this morning?" Butch was a year older than I and had a short but dark growth of a beard.

"Ah, . . . Ah, No, Sir!"

"Well, great. You can join Mr. Davis and me at shower formation tonight."

***

Striding out of the dorm, Lt Payne stopped in front of Butch and me. Well, Davis and Rieselman," Lt. Payne said with his semi-friendly smile, "Having a little trouble keeping your name tags in place?"

" . . . ahh Yes, Sir," we replied;, confused as to how to remedy the situation.

---

[16] Each New Cadet's summer name tag consisted of a metal holder with a removable paper insert displaying the cadet's name. To identify a cadet for "extra instruction," the ATO slipped the name tag out, providing him with the New Cadet's name and leaving a naked name tag. Each cadet was issued a stack of paper name slips for replacement.

"If you don't have name tags, how can an ATO know who he's assigning extra instruction?" Payne said with a mock, pained expression. "Get your butts in there and grab new name tags. You have 30 seconds. I suggest you put a couple in your pockets."

***

Lt Payne demonstrated to C Flight how to carry the M1 while marching. We then marched, by flight, to the academic area. As we marched, Lt. Payne counted cadence. "**Left . . . left . . . left, right, left.** All right, clowns, pick up the cadence." To our amusement, Lt. Payne began singing. The song was one we knew from watching war movies. "**Left . . . left . . . left, right, left. Oh, I had a good home when I left . . .**"

About a third of the flight responded: "**You're right!**" On the next verse, the entire flight responded in unison: "**You're right!**"

We put our rifles on the desk top as instructed. Lt. Tatum, and his element leaders, field striped (disassembled) and reassembled their M1s with a running commentary. They demonstrated, by the numbers, the way to clean and oil the rifles.

Near the end of the class, Tatum barked, "Ready, go!" We frantically disassembled, then reassembled our rifles. Dick Day finished in 3 minutes, 40 seconds, flaunting his prior Army Reserve training.

After the regular instruction, the five top cadets in the other flights were brought to our room. Cadets filled three desk rows, the rest of us observing at the sides of the room. Tatum slipped a blindfold over the "winning" cadets' heads.

"Okay, Men," said Lt. Tatum. "This will count for points in the flight competition. You will disassemble and reassemble your rifles with the blindfolds on. The first three to finish will receive ten, seven, and five points respectively. GO!"

Dick Day was first, exhibiting obvious experience and earning C Flight 10 points. Bill Gibbons, B Flight, was second, and Clay Harper, A Flight, was third.

Marching back to the barracks came with numerous ATO rifle position corrections. Instructions included "left-shoulder-arms," "right-shoulder-arms,[17]" and then "port arms," where the rifle is carried diagonally in front of you. Banging my helmet with my rifle during the exchanges threw my marching off and brought curses from "Smokey" Stovall in front of me. He didn't appreciate me stepping on his heels.

After another quick uniform change, we double-timed to the athletic field/parade grounds. Thirty each jumping jacks, squats, sit-ups, push-ups, and three laps around the parade grounds didn't start a nose bleed, but left me craving oxygen. "Take a break," yelled Lt. Tatum. Two minutes later, it was double-timing back to the dorms.

---

[17] Underclassmen carried the M1 for parades. The normal marching position was "right shoulder arms." Switching to left shoulder arms or port arms was a fatigue relieving maneuver.

***

Lunch time brought a new challenge. Instead of fatigues, the uniform of the day was "Class B Khakis.[18]" "Damn, Butch, I don't think I'll ever learn the trick of getting into khakis." Opening up the starched pant legs and shirt sleeves, I tried desperately to get the pants on without dragging them on the floor; creating smudge marks on the cuffs.

Next, I struggled with the suspenders that fasten to the sides of your shirt. The trick is to fasten the top, wind the bottom part of the suspender around your leg and hook it onto the top of your socks. I succeeded and stood upright pulling the shirt tight and tightening my socks. I walked over to the mirror to wrestle with my name tag.

Like getting into khakis, perfectly aligning my name tag on the top of the right pocket escaped me. I had already received three chewing outs for name tag alignment. Lt. Jackson, however, was the first to take the paper tag out of the holder. I wondered why we had a stack of paper name tags. Now, I knew.

The last uniform item was the blue tie. It had to be tied with a half Windsor knot, then tucked into the shirt below the third button. Having worn few ties growing up, I struggled to get the knot right. The thinner part invariably came out below the wide part in front. After four tries, I gave up and stuffed the tie into my shirt.

Grabbing the headache causing blue wheel hat, I centered it on my nose and put two fingers under the brim to create the required gap between the bridge of my nose and the visor tip. The hat bill required a shine equal to that of the shoes.

Perfect alignment of a "gig line" requires the blue belt buckle to be centered on the edge line of your shirt and zipper cover line. The belt's silver tip must be even with the silver buckle edge –impossible unless you cut the belt down to your waist size. Butch and I gave each other a last minute check then posted to formation.

Tatum was waiting by the formation. He was checking each flight member's uniform appearance. As Don Box rolled into formation, I saw Tatum pounce. "Well, Box, have you ever heard of a gig line?"

I almost laughed, in spite of myself. Don was small and wiry, like Tatum. They were eyeball to eyeball.

"Yes, Sir," answered Box, small beads of sweat popping out on his forehead.

"Then why don't you have a proper one?"

"Well, Sir, I tried to . . ."

"WHAT???"

---

[18] Each uniform had designated variations. Class A Khakis were with wheel hat, blue tie, low quarter shoes, and white gloves. The tie was tucked into the shirt. Class B Khakis was the same without gloves.

"Ah, NO EXCUSE, SIR."

"Report to my room tonight, Mr. Box, and we'll tend to that horrific gig line."

"Yes, Sir," Box replied, the Denver sun and Tatum causing a large spot of sweat to form under his khaki shirt sleeve.

Taking Tatum's lead, Lt. Payne was making his way down the element line. Stopping in front of me, he smirked as he pulled my tie from its nesting place in my shirt. "What's this, Davis? Did you learn to tie knots on a boat?"

"No, Sir," I replied getting the feeling extra instruction was in my future.

"Fortunately for you, Davis, your classmates are as bad at tying ties asyou are." He addressed the entire element: "Okay, I'll see all you Beau Brummells in my room after dinner."

***

Lunch was remarkably uneventful. As soon as the food and beverages reached the head of the table, Lt Tatum took a bite of his roast beef, looked at Hertz and said, "Well?"

"Sir, the Commandant of Cadet's name is Brigadier General Robert Morris Stillman and his nickname is 'Moose'. It is rumored he earned the nickname playing West Point football."

"And where did you get that little tidbit of information, Mister Hertz?"

"Sir, one of the West Point ATOs … ah … Air Training Officers …"

"Nice save, Hertz, eat!" The lieutenants were obviously hungry. Lt. Tatum nodded at Lt. Boyce and said, "Everyone eat." Given the respite, Bob finished half his plate.

***

Following our 30-minute rest and brush-your-teeth post lunch period, we marched to the quadrangle for another session of close order drill. Afterward, we went to the academic building. Second Classman Cadet Major Gerald Garvey, Chairman of the Wing Honor Committee, was waiting for our introduction to the Honor Code.

"Davis, **STAND UP!**" yelled Cadet Garvey, launching an eraser in my direction,

My head snapped up and I came to attention behind my desk. When my head cleared, I surmised standing behind one's chair was infinitely smarter than napping during an ATO or upperclassman's presentation.

***

"Sir, there are five minutes until shower formation," Roger's raspy voice sang out. **"The uniform is bathrobe and shower clogs, five minutes, Sir."**

I looked over at Butch. "Now what?" I knew we had to meet Lt. Jackson by the shower, but didn't know there was an actual shower formation."

"Beats me, but we'd better get into our bathrobes and clogs. Probably need a towel too. Oh, yeah. We have to take our razors too."

I peeled off my PT uniform—authorized as in-room evening wear—grabbed my robe and shower clogs and wandered into the hallway, not knowing where the shower formation formed.[19] Standing outside their doors at rigid attention, classmates had towels draped over their left arms; each held a toothbrush and the issued foot powder can in their left hands.

Lt. Payne, standing in front of the ATO room across the hall, called out. "Well, Dumb-smacks," addressing Butch and me. "Haven't you forgotten something," he said pointing to our classmates. "It pays to read *Fourth Class Customs*, you know. Save you a lot of trouble."

We scurried back into our room and frantically grabbed our foot powder. As we emerged into the hallway, the familiar high-pitched voice of Lt. Tatum rang out, **"Well, Davis and Rieselman, glad you could join the party."** Lt. Tatum moved menacingly toward us.

"Sir, may I make a statement!"

"What is it, Davis?"

"Sir, Lt Jackson said New Cadet Rieselman and I were to report to him in front of the showers for shower formation."

"Right. I'm sure you'll get excellent instruction. VMI grads know how to do it. Post!"

Butch and I stood rigidly for fifteen minutes; reciting Fourth Class Knowledge; naming our immediate chain-of-command; and being constantly told to "keep your back straight, get your chin in, and **SOUND OFF!!!**" Our backs were against the wall, with our heels on the baseboard. Lt. Jackson had conveniently supplied two pencil erasers to hold behind our necks.

"Okay, you two, hit it for 30 push-ups." Sweat popped out on our foreheads and dripped down the inside of our bathrobes. The belt holding the bathrobe came loose and left me awkwardly doing pushups. Butch had the same problem. "Okay, Dumbsquats, up and tie your bathrobes. Resume your former positions."

Just as I thought my knees were going to buckle, Lt Jackson said, "Get in there and shave. Take your showers, you have five minutes. Don't forget your teeth and foot powder. Report to Lt. Boyce at the bottom of the stairs when you finish."

"But, Lt. Jackson, Sir, Cadet Riselman and I don't have any shaving cream . . ."

"So? Try soap . . . now get in there Davis, you are down to four minutes."

Tom Walker reported to Lt. Boyce in front of me. After several missteps and corrections, Tom blurted out: "Sir, New Cadet Walker, 982K reports he has properly showered, brushed his teeth, powdered his feet, has no blisters on his feet, and has had two bowel movements in the last 24 hours, Sir![20]"

I bit my lip to keep from snickering, moved forward two steps, saluted, and gave my "latrine report." Life as a New Cadet was indeed both intriguing as well as fatiguing. Once again, I don't remember anything after I fell into bed.

---

[20] While this last statement was somewhat awkward and embarrassing for many; blisters and constipation could be serious medical conditions. ATOs used our input to determine whether a New Cadet needed to see a doctor.

Chapter 3

The stern discipline to which every fourth classman is subjected during summer training does more than develop self-control and an unflinching obedience to commands: it assists in [forming] an attitude that instills a sense of duty in each cadet that will serve him well throughout his Air Force career. . . . Contrails

Friday, July 12, 1957 The First Week

The rest of the week was a blur. Thursday and Friday duplicated Monday and Tuesday in terms of meals, drill, PT, and shower formations. Our shoes got shinier, flab melted, and we began to master Forth Class knowledge. We found the latter not sufficient. In fact, knowledge was like Sisyphus's never ending task of rolling the ball up the mountain. The more we conquered the required knowledge, the more it rolled down hill on us.

***

Wednesday afternoon, however, proved enjoyable and motivating. We bumped along in the bus that brought us to Lowry. That ride seemed eons ago. Where're we going, Butch?"

"We're going to the rifle range, Davis. That's why we have our M1s," offered Ron Mueller. Ron, kind of pudgy—I figured he wouldn't miss the 20 pounds he was going to lose—with black hair and a pronounced Brooklyn accent was definitely a New Yorker. "See that red flag? That's Maggie's drawers. Whenever Maggie's drawers are hanging out, the range is live."

"How do you know so much about ranges?" I asked.

"Ah, my ol' man is a Brooklyn cop. He took me to the range once or twice a month. I didn't shoot anything heavy though, just a 38 pistol. This should be fun."

****

BAM! BAM! . . . BAM! BAM! BAM! The staccato sound of numerous rifles slammed into my ears, producing a slight ringing—in spite of the mandatory wax ear plugs. My hand trembled slightly as I recycled the bolt. I tried to apply the BASS instruction: Breath . . . Aim . . . Sight . . . Squeeze. Significantly more powerful and louder than the 22 rifle I used to kill rats in the shed; the rifle jolted my shoulder and jumped in the air like it had bounced off a spring.

Today, we had instruction and a practice round. Targets were 200 yards away with five rings. Shots outside the three rings didn't count. Between the three and two rings scored three points. Between the two and one rings were worth four points. A bull's-eye earned five points.

I shot eight shots prone, eight sitting, eight kneeling, and eight standing – all at my own speed. Then in prone and sitting positions, I shot nine shots in 50 seconds, reloading once.

"Don't move the barrel around so much, Davis," Lt. Payne shouted over my shoulder. **"And don't anticipate the kick. You're pulling your shots off the target to the left."**

Of the 250 points, Dick Milnes shot a 229. The Squadron average was 175. I shot 169. I had two bulls-eyes, but most of my shots were scattered off to the left.

***

Saturday was a challenge. SAMI, Saturday Morning Inspection, included an in-room inspection, an in-ranks inspection, and a parade. It began after breakfast. Butch and I were putting lint from the floor into our laundry bags. Uniform of the day was khakis; with class As for the parade.

There was a loud rap on the door. Butch yelled, **"ROOM ATTEN—TION!"**

In charged Capt. Mallett, our Squadron AOC[21] with Lts. Tatum, Payne, and Boyce at his heels. The three had pencils and pads ready to take inspection notes.

"Good morning, Mr. Rieselman. Are you and Mr. Davis ready for us?"

"Good morning, Yes, Sir." Beads of perspiration formed on Butch's eyebrows.

Capt. Mallett used a small tape measure to test the width of the fold of our shirts. He ran a white glove over my second book shelf, rubbing his fingers together to detect dust. Peering into my laundry bag, he said," With all those dirty skivvies, Davis, you'll be running around naked under your fatigues next week. Wash out a few in the shower, but don't get caught drying them.[22]" Captain Mallett flipped a quarter in the middle of the blanket on my bed. "One demerit," he said, loose bed covers."

About to depart, he stopped in front of Butch's rifle rack. Pulling on the sling, he called out to Lt. Payne, "One demerit, tight rifle sling.[23]"

The heat and pressure of the in-ranks inspection produced familiar underarm wet spots as the inspection wore on. Everyone came to rigid attention as Capt. Mallett walked

---

[21] The ATOs were trainers, Air Officers Commanding (AOCs) were in charge of the Squadrons. Responsibilities included command functions from discharge boards to parent communications. They supervised the ATOs.

[22] Since everything we owned was marked with name and cadet serial number, it was almost impossible to deny ownership of "lost" articles.

[23] The "book" called for a loose sling when the M1 was stored in its rack.

the line. Cadet Larry Vacirca brought his M1 to port arms and opened the bolt. Mallett looked him up and down, then called out: "hat on crooked, no name tag" to Lt. Payne.

Capt. Mallett took the rifle from Vacirca, who at that instant buckled at the knees and slumped forward. Capt. Mallett caught Vacirca with his right arm, holding the rifle in his left. "Get this man inside to his room," Mallett ordered. Lts. Payne and Boyce assisted Vacirca to his feet and guided him toward dorm 895.

"The rest of you men, listen up. It's hot and the inspection takes time. When you parade, you will be standing at attention for at least 20 to 30 minutes. Do not lock your knees. That traps the blood and cuts off circulation. Your fate will be the same as Cadet . . . Cadet . . ." "Vacirca, someone shouted from the back rank." "Yes, Cadet Vacirca. When you are at attention, imperceptibly move your legs and flex your knees."

In front of the Squadron, Capt. Mallett said. "Men, you look presentable today. I know it's hot and we still have a parade. He repeated his flexing knees advice adding, "you should use as much salt as possible." The inspection was scheduled to last until 15 minutes before parade formation. We still had 40 minutes until parade first call. Go inside and drink a lot of water," Captain Mallett commanded. "I'll have salt tablets put in the dorms. **Dismissed**!"

***

"**Dress right, dress,**" Lt. O'Malley, the Squadron Commander, called for the sixth time. "Okay, troops, we're going to keep doing this until you figure out what a straight line is. You should only see the cadet next to you as you look right. That's how it is when standing; that's how it is when marching. We are going to win this parade, have you all got that!"

'**YES SIR**," came the simultaneous response from 3d Squadron.

"**READY, FRONT. FORWARD, MARCH**"'

ATOs filled the officer positions. They wore white gloves, but had no swords.[24] At the command of "left shoulder arms," I gladly moved my rifle to my left shoulder. The eleven pound M1 felt like 50 pounds by the end of the parade.

"**Rieselman**, use your peripheral vision. Dress up that line. You're a half a foot ahead of your classmate on the right," called out Lt. Boyce. For our initial parade, the assistant flight commanders were marching alongside the formation, calling out corrections as we moved.

"Hang in, Rieselman," someone chanted from the middle of the formation, causing a ripple of snickers to roll through the Squadron.

---

[24] Later, in cadet parades, cadet officers wore scabbards and carried sabers.

"At ease in there," growled Lt. Boyce. "Pick up the count. You look like corks bobbing on the ocean. Or worse, a gaggle of midshipmen. **Hup, two, three, four** . . ." Boyce sang out.

Brigadier General Stillman, the Commandant, was the reviewing officer. At "Officers Front, and Center," Captain Charles Gabriel, the Group Commander, saluted General Stillman in front of the reviewing stand. "Sir, I present the Class of 1961." The stands, filled with civilian and military guests, broke out in applause. Returning Captain Gabriel's salute, General Stillman commanded, "Pass in review."

General Stillman and his staff returned salutes as squadrons passed in review. *Now I know why the ATOs worked us so hard drilling and marching. I wouldn't have imagined the stands being nearly full for our first parade. Good public relations, I guess.* Apparently the ATOs thought our first parade was satisfactory. The outriggers disappeared as we marched back to the dorms. .

***

Immediately after the parade, I scrambled to the orderly room[25] to pick up mail for Dorm 895. Mail calls, one after breakfast and one after evening meal, were eagerly anticipated by New Cadets. Mail orderly was an enjoyable task. In addition for the chance to get to know classmates better, there was an unwritten rule among ATOs to not harass a mail orderly.

After the top floor, I was on my last three rooms on the bottom floor, including Butch and my room. I entered Art Kerr's room.

"Damn, Art, what are you trying to do, make the rest of us feel miserable? You have letters from three different girls, two guys, and your parents. If fact, there are a couple more letters from the same girls."

"Hell, Don, I just have good friends. Say, did you hear we lost two guys?"

"No. Haven't talked to anyone until I started delivering mail. Who were they?"

"Guy named Steve Jones walked off the bus, had lunch, collected his gear, hauled it to his room, looked at the dorm NCO and said, 'I quit.' He was gone in an hour. Then George Walkman, 1st Squadron, started losing his hearing. He went to the hospital. Word is he's out."

"Was it the rifle range?"

"Nah, he used ear plugs and everything. It's a medical problem."

"Where do you get all your information?"

---

[25] The orderly room is the nerve center for the squadron. The ATOs had duty there and it was manned 24 hours a day. Emergency phone calls, calls to the ATOs giving them instructions, and mail all came to the orderly room.

"Well, we've been doing an exchange program between the dorms. During Commander's Call, one of us sneaks into a classmate's room in the neighboring dorm. Somebody from that room comes over here. The tricky part is not getting caught. Afraid the scheme won't last much longer; damn ATOs are learning who we are and where we're supposed to be."

"Koerners your roommate, right?"

"Yeah."

"Got a letter for him; rest are yours. Stop getting so damn many letters. See ya."

"Yeah, see ya, hang tight!"

***

I pulled a real coup before dinner. As Lt. Payne appeared in front of the flight, he said, "Listen up, C Flight. I'm going to issue a challenge. The first person to beat my shoe shine will sit at ease at the evening meal. If you lose, you owe me 20 push-ups. By the way, I hear we are having lobster for dinner. Okay, who's first?"

Bob Hertz's hand shot up. Payne walked over to Hertz and stood toe to toe with him. "Gaze," said Payne, "whose shine is best?"

After 15 seconds looking at the shoes, Hertz conceded, "Sir, your shine is better."

"Right, mister. Hit it for 20. Next?"

Jim Dickson, in the second row, raised his hand.

Lt. Payne repeated the procedure with the same results. "Next?"

I raised my hand. I had worked intensely on my shoes after the parade[26] Lt. Tatum told me recently I had the best shine in the Flight.

Lt. Payne stood in front of me. With his four inch height advantage, I had to look up to speak to him. "Well, Davis, you think you are good, huh?"

"Sir, may I ask a question?"

"Shoot."

"Sir, may I challenge you to a shoe and hat brim competition.[27] If I win, my table will sit at ease for dinner; if I lose I will do 40 push-ups."

A slight, pleasant smile crossed Lt. Payne's face. "This calls for an outside judge. Lt. Miller, can you come over here for a second to judge shines?"

Lt. Miller, 2nd Squadron, studied our hat brims and shoes for at least 30 seconds. I figured the contest was rigged and I was about to get extra exercise before dinner. "Well,

---

[26] Marching in the parade grass took the shine off *your* shoes. We knew that the ATOs had two pairs of shoes shined; one for daily work and one for show.

[27] I noticed that Lt. Payne's hat brim had not had recent attention. The morning sun had slightly dulled the shine. I had re-shined my hat as well as my shoes.

I'd have to call the shoes a draw. Nice shine, Davis. But, in the hats, he's got you, Payne." I almost smirked, but knew better.

"Okay, Davis, good show. Way to look after your classmates. Your table will eat at ease, but you won't talk and will carry on normal table duties."

"**Squadron. . . Riiiight Face. Foorrward, March**," came from the front of the Squadron.

Evening meal was really different. Lt. Payne shepherded our element to his table. A third of the normal ATO cadre manned the tables. The usual cloud of tension was absent, as well as the normal 70 to 80 decibel ranting and raving of ATOs and Cadets. We all got a little nervous, remembering the silence of the first day. "At ease," said Payne softly, "no talking and get that food up here. I'm hungry."

***

After dinner, the dorm was eerily quiet. The absence of ATOs was even more noticeable than at dinner. We knew an ATO was in the dorm because Art Kerr snuck into the hall on his way to see Larry Vacirca. They had once competed against each other in a fencing tournament.

'Going somewhere, Mister Kerr?" rang out the booming voice of Lt. Boyce.

'I . . . ah. . . I . . .," stammered Kerr.

"**Mister Kerr, the only authorized destination is the latrine**," said Boyce loudly enough to be heard in the far reaches of the upper floor."

"Ah . . . Yes, Sir, Lt. Boyce," Kerr said, continuing toward the latrine area.[28]

We had been instructed the period after dinner was "Commander's Time," expected to be used for shining shoes and boots, memorizing Fourth Class Knowledge, or writing the mandatory letters home.

Butch and I picked up a trick from our classmates for napping, without messing up our beds. We simply laid out our comforter on the floor and used it for a mattress. While I wanted to write a letter to the folks; I succumbed to siren call of the comforter.

---

[28] Although not yet under the honor code, we were expected to act as if we were. Had Boyce asked Kerr where he was going, Art would have had to answer truthfully. We were starting to get the impression that all ATOs were not demons. Boyce had graciously given Art an out.

Chapter 4

Participation in cadet religious activities is an essential part of character development. Protestant, Catholic, and Jewish Services are held at the Academy; Cadets are free to worship in the faith of their choice[29] . . . At The Ramparts

Sunday, July 14, 1957, Week One

The scratching record sound over the public address system woke me before reveille blasted out its cheery greeting. I looked at the clock on my desk. *Oh, my God. The ATO in charge must have overslept—It's 0555, not 0535."*

"SIR, THERE ARE FIVE MINUTES UNTIL REVEILLE FORMATION. THE UNIFORM IS . . ." Roger's sleepy voice called out. Hmmm! *it must be right,* I thought. *And where is Lt. Tatum? That's the quietest I've heard minutes all week.*

"All right, men, listen up." Lt. Boyce sounded well rested. "Here's the routine. If you signed up for Catholic services, you'll assemble at 0745 and march to the base theater for services. Protestants will form up at 0900. Lt. Englehart will march you to the base theater. If you signed up for choir, you'll form up 45 minutes earlier than the rest of your group and march to the theater. Are there any questions?"

No one spoke. *Damn—oh it's Sunday. Darn, I'm glad I signed up for the Protestant services, even if I did sign up for the choir and have to go earlier.*

***

"All right, Gentlemen," Mr. James Roger Boyd, the Choir Director, said. "We will practice hymn 402, *A Mighty Fortress is our God,* and hymn 125, *The Airman's Hymn.* If you want to continue choir during academics, we have rehearsals on Wednesday evenings and Sunday mornings. During summer training, unfortunately, we only have this time to practice."

In the 30-minutes allotted, we made respectable sounds resembling the two selected hymns. Our sound, tentative as it was, was full and rich.

"You have chosen to test yourself in a very difficult program," began Chaplin (Colonel) John S. Bennett. "You have survived the first week; by accounts of previous classes, the most difficult you will face. The fact you have survived the first week indicates you have the fortitude and ability to survive the next four years.

Chaplain Bennett continued with a sermon on sacrifice and duty. Inspired by Chaplain Bennett's sermon and reflecting on its meaning for me, I left chapel feeling uplifted and ready to face the rest of the summer.

***

---

[29] Chapel was mandatory and the choices were Catholic, Protestant, or Jewish.

Marching to lunch, ATOs issued only necessary commands. The usual in-ranks and ramp harassment was absent. Our Table Commandant (we could join any table with an open space) told us to" keep it quiet." Several ATOs apparently had partied Saturday night and were adverse to loud noises. Except for the dormitory "duty" ATO, ATOs were scarce on Saturday evening and this morning. The lull was disconcerting; like being in the eye of a hurricane waiting for the back wall to arrive.

Commander's Time was scheduled until diner. *Time off, ha! There's still a lot in the Contrails I don't know. And when you know the routine stuff, they ask questions about airplanes or Air Force Commands or the President's Cabinet.* It was a good time; however, for writing letters home.

***

United States Air Force Academy
Sunday, July 14, 1957 Week Two

Dear Mom and Dad.

Sorry I haven't written sooner, but I literally have not had a minute to myself. It's been grueling. Chapel today was the first break we've had. I'm going to sing in the Protestant Choir.

You know, Mom, I don't follow the Catholic religion. To me, it wasn't right you were excommunicated because you got a divorce. If I were to go that way, however, no one has to explain purgatory or hell- I've been there this last week.

We had our first SAMI yesterday. SAMI stands for "Saturday AM (morning) Inspection." The ATOs come into your room, look for dirt, how clothes, shoes, and everything else is displayed; and "contraband," things you're not supposed to have, like a radio or candy.

Do you remember when I played B Team Football for Coach Pelleta? I told you I'd never done anything so hard in my life. I've found something harder. Lost seven pounds this week between calisthenics; marching; trying to eat sitting on the first six inches of my chair, and a constant stream of ATO - oh, Air Training Officers -- table questions.

About demerits: If they write up your room, uniform, or rifle; you're late for formation, don't know Fourth Class Knowledge or...

you get demerits. If you reach the demerit limit, you march tours; an hour marching carrying your 11 pound M1. (Pa can probably tell you about the M1.)

Punishments, besides tours, include pushups; special inspections, which are additional instruction with an ATO in his room; and confinements. Screw ups in physical training class result in extra laps around the field.

Special cases (Class IIIs) are for bad violations (missing a class, or sneaking out at night). You meet a Class III "officer board." During summer training, instead of Class IIIs, I think it's just "goodbye."

My roommate, Butch, and I get along well; which is good because each side of our room is ten feet long and four feet wide. We have a bed, a desk, a chair, a lamp, and a shared waste basket.

I mentioned AFCR 11-6 (Air Force Cadet Regulation). It's really nit-picky. Tells you how to hang your clothes; place the hangers with hooks to the rear and flying suit legs up in the crotch; zip the suit up from the bottom' how to make your bed and arrange your shoes under the bed; and so on ...

They inspect according to the regulation. Socks, underwear, shirts, and toilet articles go on designated shelves. You have "smiles" on the socks and cardboard "holders" in the shirts. Beds are the kicker. You <u>must</u> have clean sheets, a clean pillow case, hospital corners, and a white collar (four inches of top sheet folded back) for SAMI. The blanket must be tight enough to bounce a quarter on and have it jump in the air.

In-ranks SAMI inspections follow the room inspection; followed by a parade. Captain Mallette inspected our flight. My element leader, Lt Payne, has been keeping close tabs on Butch and me. He's really helpful and not cutting like Lt. Tatum, our Flight Commander. Lt Payne is more like a counselor. He checks to see Butch and I are "hacking the program."

Our parade yesterday was public; our first with an audience. I saw civilians (including some pretty good looking girls) and *military people in the stands. Rumor was that there were also newspaper reporters.*

For only a week of instruction and practice, we looked sharp. Of course, the ATO critiques said our lines weren't straight and we "bounced like a bunch of Navy Midshipmen" — (Naval Academy cadets.)

Before dinner yesterday, I challenged Lt. Payne to a shoe and hat brim-shine contest. You compare shoe shines to see who is best. I WON! My table sat at ease. Dinner was lobster thermidor with Tiramisu for dessert.. Our morning/afternoon classes include: "M1Care and cleaning", "Air Force Customs/Courtesies," "Cadet Honor Code," and "How to Care for Feet."

We can have one picture in our room. You should send me a good picture of Rex. How could they complain about such a good looking dog?

It almost rained on the SAMI. If it rained, we'd probably have had to report in raincoats and galoshes.

One of my classmates told me the ATOs have at least two pairs of shoes; one super shinned and a second pair for regular work periods. Some even have a pair of galoshes shoes. What a luxury to have "dress" shoes and "galoshes" shoes.

We went to the rifle range Wednesday for an "orientation shoot." We didn't get scored. (I had two bulls-eyes and three other counters — not great). It was the first time we wore boots with the fatigues. We all got chewed out for "crummy" boots. Fortunately, demerits don't really count until August.

Well, I'd better do some shoe and boot shining and hit the Contrails.

God Bless
Your loving son,
Don

"Hey, Butch, got your letter home done?" Butch had been shinning his shoes, but I noticed he put up his shoe shine equipment and was at his desk writing.

"Nah, but I'm workin' on it. Then I have to write to Sue. She and I have been going together since eighth grade. We'll probably get married after graduation."

"You gonna do your resignation letter after that?"

"Nah, I got a letter from my folks. They said I could do what I want, but with Jenny and Steve coming up for college, they don't have any money for me. So, I can get out, get a job, and maybe go to college. My Dad sent me a saying the troops used in Europe on the way to Berlin. It goes something like: *'Non illegitmus caborumdum!'*"

I took high school Latin, but the phrase's meaning escaped me. "What's it mean?"

"My Dad said it's: *'Don't let the bastards get you down.'* Good advice, huh? Anyway after the crap they threw at us this week, what else could they do to us?"

"Yeah, what?"

Chapter 5

*On the fields of friendly strife are sown the seeds that on other days
and other fields will bear the fruits of victory!*
—Gen. Douglas MacArthur, *Contrails*

Monday, July 15, 1957

The war was on again. Lt. Tatum greeted us in the hall for reveille formation. In his razor sharp uniform, he appeared reinvigorated from his weekend break.

"Well, dumbsmacks. You look rested; ready for another week of fun and games. Fall out. Be in formation in thirteen minutes."

"Sir, there are five minutes until breakfast formation. The uniform of the day is khakis, wheel hat and . . ."

"Okay. What idiot do we have this week?" screeched Lt. Tatum approaching New Cadet Don Box. "Mister, Box, where'd you get the absurd idea we were wearing khakis.?"

"Well, Sir, you are in a khaki uniform and . . ."

"Box, can you read?"

"Yes, Sir!"

"Then I suggest you turn around, read the Bulletin Board and get the uniform right." After a 10 second pause, Tatum continued, "Well, Box, why did you screw it up?"

"Well, Sir, I thought . . ."

"WHAT!"

"I . . . ah, NO EXCUSE, Sir!"

"You got that right. Get your roommate to finish calling minutes. Go get into the proper uniform. If you or your roommate are late for formation, that's three demerits. I'll see you tonight in my room for a special inspection. POST!"

I peeked out my door. Poor Don had destroyed a set of khakis from sweating profusely. Box's roommate, Terry Koonce, almost knocked Don down scrambling down the stairs, properly uniformed. Koonce began, **Sir, there are two minutes until breakfast formation. The uniform of the day is fatigues, fatigue cap, and low quarter shoes; two minutes."**

Koonce made it to formation on time. Lt. Tatum stood in front of Box's spot, tapping his foot. Box was 30 seconds late. Tatum signed a Form 10[30], unbuttoned Box's fatigue shirt and stuffed the yellow slip into his pocket. "You have permission to button your shirt, Dumbsquat." Tatum demonstrated compassion. An unbuttoned shirt was worth at least another demerit.

***

"Attention, Dormitory 895, the uniform is the physical training uniform with tennis shoes. Sir, there are five minutes until physical training formation!"

"Ah crap" I said to myself. "Butch, what's this?" I said, tearing off my fatigues and slipping them into in the laundry bag,[31] while retrieving my PT uniform.

"I don't know, but Hertz said the schedule had changed; 3d Squadron does PT while 2nd Squadron has drill, and 1st Squadron gets Weapons instruction."

Butch took part in our dorm exchange program yesterday. We'd spend an hour trading tips on specific ATOs—who was a pussy cat and whom to avoid at all costs. We also exchanged tips for beating the system, like storing uniforms in the laundry bag instead of hanging them in the closet. Butch had learned about the schedule change in Hertz's room.

"Sir, there are two minutes to physical training formation. The uniform is physical training uniform and tennis shoes. Two minutes, SIR," screeched New Cadet Box, with a hint of the onset of laryngitis.

Lt. Biernaki, a Virginia Military Institute graduate, stood on the four-foot-by-four-foot wooden PT platform. C Flight was arranged in a semi-circle in front of the platform. Lts. Clendenen and Henessey, both West Pointers, stood on either side of the platform.

"Today begins competitive athletics. We'll focus on soccer this morning, but you'll take part in soccer, softball, run track events, and participate in other sports later on. For the next five weeks, we'll have intra-squadron competition. The best squadron teams will compete in the end of summer group[32] games. Winning squadrons earn points toward the Superintendent's Trophy. How many have played soccer?"

---

[30] The Form 10 was the bane of every cadet's existence. Form 10s resulted in demerits for whatever infraction and drew "tours" at this stage. Comparable to a policeman's ticket, They were given freely.

[31] Innovation was essential to survive Cadet Regulation 11-6, Form 10s, ATOs, and tours. Putting fatigues in the laundry bag saved time. Being starched, khakis couldn't be "stuffed' in the laundry bag..

[32] The three squadrons were the New Cadet Summer League. "Group" games at the end of the summer determined the league champions.

Ten of the 32 cadets in the Flight held up their hands. Lt. Clendenen hauled a bag of balls and portable nets from the back of a blue pickup.

"O.K.," Lt. Biernaki called out. "Form three circles. We'll play kick ball."

In the groups, we learned to kick and dribble a soccer ball. After taking turns kicking the ball across the circle; we formed two lines and dribbled the ball down the field for 30 yards.

Next, we lined up for 30 yard races. ATOs noted cadet speeds. Using a portable chalk board, Lt Biernaki explained the game in detail. He split the experienced soccer players among the three teams; allocating the rest based on the "speed trials."

I ended up on team three with most of my element. Since Jack Tyler was an accomplished player, we immediately voted him captain. Being one of the slower players, I was placed at right fullback; comparable to right field in baseball.

Since 11 player teams were required and one had only 10; one person from the 11-man teams played with the short team during scrimmages. Jack was usually the extra player because he was obviously going to be a Squadron star.

We practiced from 0900 to 1115 hours. By the end of the period, we learned enough to set up 10 minute scrimmages. My team, with Jack starring, scored three times. With a couple savvy players on the line and Karl Kellerman, who wasn't a soccer player, but was tall enough to have a good reach as goalie, we blanked the other teams.

Given the athletes recruited as New Cadets, cadets quickly grasped the essentials of any sport. Serious[33] play took place. Competition was always keen. The fields of friendly strife were not always friendly, but the class began to bond in small groups as we came to know each other better. A downed player was always offered a hand up.

***

We scrambled to get out of the showers after a long PT session. ATOs prowling the halls ensured everyone took showers. Lenny Bruce, end of the hall, was half dressed in khakis when Lt. Tatum performed an "AMI inspection" of Lenny's room.

According to his roommate, Bill Moulton, Lenny was standing in his shorts when Tatum gave the one warning knock and entered the room. "Well, Mr. Bruce, going to enhance our lunch appetites with your aromatic body stench?' Tatum said.

"I . . . ah . . . I was going to . . ."

"Dumbsmack, haven't you learned anything in our first week together? **What is the proper answer?**" Tatum's high screech resounded throughout the building.

---

[33] At least one New Cadet, Ken Browning, was seriously injured in the PT program. Ken suffered a back injury and washed out of the program.

"Non-caborundum, Lenny," rang out from upstairs, reflecting the fact that Butch and I had passed on his father's philosophy to our classmates.

"NO SIR, NO EXCUSE, SIR," echoed through the hallway.

After a slight hesitation, we heard Tatum continue, **"O.K. Bruce, hit it for 20, put your khakis in the laundry bag, and hit the shower."**

Tatum walked out of room 106 in his best imitation of a Napoleonic stroll.

When the commotion died down, Butch and I scrambled into our positions before first call for lunch formation. Just as we arrived, an ominous shadow loomed in front of Butch, followed by the appearance of its owner, Lt. Jackson.

Lt. Jackson could not touch Butch, but I think he would've run his hand over Butch's face if he could. Instead he leaned to within a half inch of Butch's rammed in chin. Risking a sidewise glance, I could see Butch flinch.

"Well, Do-willie, I see we have learned how to shave. That's too bad, I kind of enjoyed our shower formation." Lt. Jackson looked at Butch's shoes hoping to find another flaw. Butch's shoes, however, were second only to mine in mirrored gleam within the flight.

Sneering, Lt. Jackson did a right face, took two steps, and did a left face. I was eyeball to eyeball with the VMI Lieutenant. His rancid tobacco breath almost gagged me. I held my breath as Lt. Jackson inspected me. Again, his gaze dropped as he eyed my shoes. His eyes widened slightly. He said, "Hummph," and walked away.

Sitting in a side chair, my scanner duties allowed me to glance up and down the table to determine if provisions; i.e., food, were needed. After the long PT session, my stomach was growling. I spotted the potatoes and gravy by my right side.

"New Cadet Hertz," asked Lt. Boyce. "What are the Air Force officer ranks?"

"Sir, I do not know."

Great, Bob keep them going, I grabbed the potatoes, piled them on my plate, and dug in. Mashed potatoes didn't require cutting, were filling, and could be quickly consumed.

"Mr. Hertz, you will know Air Force Officer Ranks and their Navy equivalents by the evening meal. Well then, Dickson, how about the Code of Conduct."

"Sir, I am an American fighting man. . . ."

I quietly reached for another helping of mashed potatoes.

***

"Attention, Dormitory 895, there are five minutes until special athletics. The uniform of the day is physical training uniform with athletic shoes. Sir, there are five minutes until physical training formation!

"What are you going to try out for, Butch?"

"Well, they're only doing football today and baseball tomorrow, so I guess I'll just do the drills. I don't really expect to get anywhere. My game's fencing."

"Fencing, how the hell did you get into that?"

"Short of it is I had an uncle who ran a fencing school. One summer when I was 10, my uncle took me in. That began my fencing career. I've got several trophies."

"Wow!" I said.

". . . two minutes, sir."

"We'd better get out there, Butch."

***

The blue beetle buses took us to the former Lowry athletic fields, appropriated for Academy use. A football practice field, a soccer field, and three baseball diamonds made up the sports complex. The buses stopped by the football field.

On the field a white haired, mid-fifties gentleman was flanked by several larger men. Fourth class table questions told us the MAN was varsity football coach, "Buck" Shaw, formerly of the San Francisco 49s.

Dressed in khaki pants and blue polo shirts, Shaw's team looked serious. The coaches names were on the front shirt pocket with "AF Academy Football" on the back.

Shaw informed us he would evaluate potential football players; assisted by his coaches, Lts. "Jug" Jenkins, Jesse Bounds, Byron Gillory, and Major Casmir Myslinski. "Okay, backs with Lt. Jenkins, quarterbacks and ends with Lt. Bounds, and linemen, including linebackers, with Major Myslinski and Lt. Gillory.

"All right, men," bellowed Myslinski, **"let's see how good the conditioning is; give me two laps around the field".** A quarter of the way around, the gaggle turned into a loose formation, and we began running at the pace used for physical training.

We all arrived in front of Myslinski together. "All right, wise guys," Myslinski said with a half smirk on his face, "impressive teamwork. Now, let's see what you can do individually."

"Give me your best speed to the 40 yard mark," Lt. Gillory said. He had a stop watch and clipboard. He wrote down the names as each group of four came up. Major Myslinski raised a starter's gun. "When you hear the gun, go. At the end, peel off to the sides and come back to the end of the line. Questions? . . . No, let's get to it."

I was about two thirds back in the group. We unconsciously lined up tallest in front. Tom Walker, Neal Roundtree, Roger Stringer, and Burke Morgan were first. I knew Roundtree and Stringer because they were in my flight. Lt. Gillory called out the names of each cadet as he lined up. I noted classmate names as they were called.

I looked across from me. "Hi, I'm Don Davis; don't think we've met."

"Hi, I'm Randy Rico. Where're you from?"

"I'm from Sacramento, California." I was concerned about talking, but the coaches appeared preoccupied with the trials. Our three ATOs assisted the coaches.

"I'm from Little Neck, New York. What'd you play?"

"Well, I was a guard and linebacker in High School. So I'll try those positions"

"Same with me. Good luck!"

"Ready, set." The gun went off and I sprang from a three point stance. Chris Dixon and Oleg Kominitsky ran beside Randy and me. Randy left all of us 10 yards behind. I was third.

As I came back to end of the line, I noticed the Superintendent, Commandant, and another Colonel, intently watching the drills.

"Wow, Randy, I know there's a lot of interest in football, but it's something when the brass turns out to watch tryouts. Do you know who the Colonel is?"

"Yeah," Randy replied. "That's Colonel Simler. He's the Director of Athletics.

"How do you know Simler?"

"He came to New York to recruit me for football. He's really a nice guy."

"Okay. Men," Myslinski said. "Let's see how much ummmph you've got. Line up by twos in front of the sleds. **Hustle!!!**"

Four football sleds rested on the 15-yard line. Randy and I paired up and hit the sled together. We drove it 10 yards. Lt. Boyce, sitting on top of the sled, provided extra incentive. We tried to dump him as Walker and Roundtree had done with Lt. Gillory.

Noise and excitement filled the bus. Even those not intending to play football were infected with the jubilant mood. As we rode along, somebody shouted out: "Hey, starting at the front, stand up, introduce yourself, and say where you're from." We did. Camaraderie was enveloping us like the mist of a genie escaping from his jug.

***

The air came out of the balloon at dinner as the unrelenting voices of the ATOs demanding Fourth Class Knowledge brought us back to earth. And we realized, from discussion on the bus, what was coming tomorrow. Anxiety built that evening as we shined shoes, boots, and hat visors and endured yet another shower formation.

Chapter 6

*Your son is completing a training program that demands fortitude
beyond the average expected of a youth of his age.*
Major General James E. Briggs, Superintendent, Letter to Parents.

Tuesday, July 16, 1957

**"Attention, Dormitory 895, the uniform of the day for drill formation is
fatigues, helmets, and combat boots, with rifles. There are five minutes until drill
formation. There are 61 days until the Acceptance Parade.[34] Five minutes, Sir."**

"Well, here we go again—rifles and helmets. What a pain in the ass. You'd think
we could do drill without the rifles," I whined to Butch.

"Hell, Davis, how could they beat some sense into your Polish head unless they
were beating on it with an M1? Nice catch at breakfast, I sure didn't know the Treasury
Secretary. And quit complaining or they'll throw you out for attitude . . ."

"Yeah, right, then I wouldn't have to resign . . ."

"And I wouldn't have to listen to you whining. Let's go!"

***

The two-hour period included routine marching, changing of rifle positions, and
practicing "eyes right" with the rifle at right shoulder arms. Jerry Strong stopped drill
dead in its tracks when he lost his rifle executing eyes right. Completely flustered, Jerry
stopped. The four cadets behind Jerry stacked up like they'd hit a wall. The flight
remained "at ease" while Jerry received 10 minutes of individual attention.

I had a foreboding when Lt. Tatum marched the flight off the quad and to the
parade ground 15 minutes before the end of the period. He commanded a flanking
movement to put us line abreast. The sun was at an 80 degree angle beating down. A
huge cumulonimbus cloud was approaching from the west. We formed three lines.

"Okay, Gentlemen, take up the position of 'high port' with your rifles. You will
hold high port and double-time to the end of the parade ground. When you reach the
other end, you will turn around and double-time back to this end maintaining high port."

"First line, ready, GO!"

---

[34] New Cadets are New Cadets until acceptance day (marked by a parade); the day you are
formally integrated into the Wing. You are then a Fourth Classman; still a Doolie, but a step above
a New Cadet.

The first line made it to the far end with only two or three stragglers. Our line stood ready with rifles at high port. "Go," shouted Tatum with a smirk on his face. The first 30 yards weren't bad, but your arms quickly began to feel the awkward rifle position. At 40 yards, I struggled to breathe. I could see a line of classmates on either side. It was all I could do to keep the rifle up until I finished.

On the third repetition of the drill, two of my classmates stumbled and fell near the far end. "Come on, Jerry. Come, on Bob," classmates at the far end yelled. "Come on!" Butch and I slowed, held our rifles in one hand, and brought Jerry to his feet.

As the third line arrived, so did a large, black thunderstorm. A bolt of lightning struck nearby, followed six seconds later by a rolling blast of thunder and rain flowing as if pouring out of a 12-inch pipe directly on us.

"Well, don't just stand there, Dumbsquats," Tatum hollered. "Bring it back and form up in flight formation."

Thoroughly soaked, we squished our way back to the edge of the quadrangle. Tatum conveniently didn't notice that no one had their rifle at high port. A second flash of lightning struck further away than the first.

"Dismissed," roared Tatum in front of the barracks. "Go inside and dry your rifles. Run oiled patches down the barrel. Clean your boots and stuff socks and tee shirts in them. Get into your PT clothes." Then, as the rain beat down, Tatum added, "PT is cancelled." His voice was almost drowned out by a clap of thunder.

As quickly as they came, the thunderstorms rolled east like tumbleweeds blowing across the prairie. The sun returned, sending steam rising from the quadrangle.

With PT cancelled, we had time to thoroughly oil and linseed our rifles. After cleaning the mud off our boots in the latrine, we reapplied wax.

The uniform for lunch included khakis and white gloves. "What the hell is that all about, Butch? That's a parade or drill competition uniform. Now what's going on?"

"BTSOM[35]!" replied Butch. "But we better get our butts out there."

The Academy Band was playing Sousa marches. Lt. Payne, on the left of the Squadron, was counting cadence. "Hup, two, three, four." Let's look sharp.

Half a block from the dining hall, Lt. O'Malley called out, "EYEEES . . . RIGHT!" Third Squadron snapped eyes right. My row was as straight as I had seen to date. The Superintendent, flanked by the Commandant and two Colonels stood to the right of an attractive, dignified older lady with salt and pepper hair.

---

[35] The polite version is "Beats the spit out of me." It is a phrase we picked up during competitive sports.

Impeccably dressed in a light summer dress, the lady had an aura of importance. I knew I knew the face, but couldn't produce a name. *Maybe, it's the Queen of England,* I thought. *"What would she be doing here? And the ATOs have not asked about the Queen of England. Of course, they don't know everything. That's it; they didn't know she was coming.*

"Mamie Eisenhower," whispered Hertz, turning his head slightly. "Pass it on."

In true save-your-skin fashion and a spirit of class esprit, I looked left and right for an ATO. Sighting none, I turned and whispered, "Mamie Eisenhower, pass it on."

When we were in place, Lt. Tatum said, "Take off your gloves, tuck them into your belt, and don't forget, Do-Willies, to put them back on afterwards."

"Sir, may I ask a question?" Bob Hertz said, gazing toward Lt Tatum.

"What is it? Dumbsmack!" Tatum replied.

"Sir, in honor of the First Lady, Mrs. Mamie Eisenhower's presence and her reviewing the noon formation, may the New Cadets eat at ease?.

Wow, Hertz. Great balls. And if nothing else, you let everybody know who our VIP is. It just might work. Good job, Bob, I thought, looking at Hertz admiringly.

"Nice try, Hertz. Stand up straight; get your chin in. Hope you aren't hungry."

"Attention to orders," rang out from the Command Section. "The officer of the day is Capt. Mallett." There was a pause. The Superintendent whispered something to the adjutant.

"In honor of our special guest today, the First Lady, Mrs. Mamie Eisenhower, New Cadets will sit at ease."

Hertz breathed a sigh of relief. Following the Chaplain's thankfully short "grace," Tatum barked, "**Sit . . . at ease**. No talking except for normal duties. Damn, we're getting soft."

"They were just afraid to let Mamie see what really goes on," retorted Boyce.

***

"Okay, Davis, first base," Coach Schwall said, hitting a sharp grounder to me at third base. I fielded the ball cleanly and shot it to first ahead of Mike Quimby hustling down the first base line. "Good throw, Davis. Okay. Second base."

I moved to my left to take the one hopper and threw a strike to Phil Street who was covering second base. The throw beat Mike by two steps. "That's enough, Davis, come on in and wait for batting practice."

Approximately 30 cadets gathered at each of the three diamonds. Those serious about baseball grabbed gloves and warmed up playing catch. Those not interested became base runners, ball shaggers, and bat boys.

Batting, fielding, running, catching, and pitching filled three hours in the afternoon sun. Memories of high school diamond glories temporarily transported me away from the harsh reality of summer training.

After I batted, getting two solid line drives in 10 pitches, and running the bases three times, I was told to watch the rest of the workout. I was amazed. Mike Quimby was batting. After two missed swings, he hit a sharp grounder toward second base. Rich Marble, playing shortstop, ranged far to his left, snagged the ball, set his feet, and threw a strike to Tom Walker at first base. Tom stretched; Mike was out by half a step.

Wow, I thought, *with guys like this—not even including the upperclassmen—fat chance I'll have making the team. Maybe I'll just pack it up; find a small college or junior college where I don't have all this crap and I can make the football or baseball team. It's really going to be shitty without sports.*

All too soon, ATO whistles blew for us to board the blue beetles.

As I was getting on the bus, Assistant Coach Conboy took me aside. Looking at his clipboard, he said, "Davis, you're a pretty good fielder. Your batting is a little weak. Your name won't come out on the list, but I'd give it another try come spring."

After the last week and a half, the encouraging words put me in a great mood.

Once again, the buses were raucous. Everyone had a story to tell; either an athletic victory or, in many cases, tales of female conquests. In fact, by the time we reached the quad, there were more of the latter than the former.

***

"What's the matter, Butch? You look like one of your lame race horses? You were good at baseball tryouts. You caught everything, your pegs were good, and you sure as hell hit better than I did."

"Yeah, that's not it, Davis[36]. The letter you brought from Sue. She says she loves me; then writes two pages about great parties, GREAT GUYS, and all the fun she's having this summer. I can't imagine the time she'll have at college when she's away from home. Damn, what am I doing here? I just want to marry Sue, have kids, and settle down in Kentucky."

"Well, she doesn't kiss you off. Didn't you say she can't wait to see you? And didn't she sign it 'love' or something like that?"

---

[36] We quickly picked up on the ATOs use of just last names. Actually, it was very natural as it was an old habit from high school sports. Coaches invariably used last names whether scolding or praising.

"Yeah, but the tone's different. She used to go on about us, the things we can do, and maybe she'd make a trip out here. I shouldn't have told her I wouldn't be home until summer. Now she gives *us* a paragraph and then goes on about the parties and her new, great friends."

"No sweat, Butch. She's having a good time to make up for not being with you."

"Sure, nice rationalizing. What the hell do you care, you don't have a girl?"

"Hell, tomorrow you won't even think about her; 'HIGH PORT AND RUN, YOU TWINKIES!'" I said, mimicking Lt. Tatum's high-pitched shriek.

Chapter 7

Your customs and courtesies, as outlined herein, establish a high standard of decorum which we want you to carry into your Air Force career as the governing agent for your official and social conduct.
Brigadier General H. R. Sullivan, Commandant of Cadets, USAFA Decorum

Wednesday July 17, 1957 Week 2

Wednesday morning was a repeat of Tuesday, except the entire three morning periods were flight drill. On Friday, the schedule called for flight drill competitions between squadrons. Later in the summer each squadron would enter its best flight in Group completion. The winner earned points for the Superintendent's Trophy given for the best summer training squadron.

The competition included an in-ranks inspection. The ATOs spent extra time with rifle inspections, both manual of arms and of the weapons themselves. Shoes and visor cap shines were closely examined. Gig lines and uniform appearance drew special attention. Every maneuver taught to date and a few new wrinkles were practiced, practiced, practiced.

"**Fooorward . . . March[37]!**" barked Lt. Payne. "**Left shoulder . . . Arms. Rieeght Shoulder . . . Arms. To the reeear . . . March. On the right oblieeque[38] . . . March. Left oblique . . . March. Flight . . . Halt. Left . . . Face. Preeesent Arms[39] Orda . . . Arms. Paaarade . . . Rest.** At ease.

Okay, men. Next period we have a march off with the other two flights. Commands will be based on a list given to me by Lt. O'Malley. Each flight has a judge on the inspection committee. Lt. O'Malley will observe and judge as well. The winning flight will be at ease for the evening meal. The best overall flight will represent 3d Squadron in Group competition. We start with 100 points. Subtractions are made for in-ranks inspection gigs, manual of arms mistakes, and drill errors. Any Questions? No? All right. We'll have a 10 minute break before the competition."

The in-ranks inspections began with A Flight. During the Manual of Arms, New Cadet Ben Johnson committed the only visible error; he lost the grip on his rifle returning

---

[37] The first part of a command is preparatory—tells you what you are going to do. After a pause comes the execution command, which says "do it.".

[38] This is a seldom used command that moves the unit on a 45 degree angle.

[39] If unarmed, a hand salute; if armed, a rifle salute—a two-step maneuver; first the rifle is brought from right shoulder arms to a 45 degree position in front of the body, then the rifle is turned vertical.

it to his side after inspection arms. The rifle slipped out of his grasp and the butt clanged against the macadam. A Flight's drill maneuvers were flawless.

B Flight aced the inspection and completed the drill portion with only a minor error when Tom Mulvey stepped on the heel of Chris Wheeler. Wheeler loudly spit out, **"Shit!"** and stumbled. Mulvey staggered, but regained his balance. Both got back in cadence.

Lt. Kavanaugh, B Flight Commander, finished the drill routine, maneuvered his flight to the edge of the quadrangle, put the flight at ease, and called New Cadet Wheeler to the front of the flight. "All right, mister. Stand up tall. Get your chin in. No matter what happens, you don't lose your cool. In combat, that will get you killed. Now, Mr. Wheeler, give me General Washington's Order to the Continental Army."

"Sir, General George Washington's order . . ."

"LOUDER, MISTER, I WANT THE WHOLE FLIGHT TO HEAR IT . . ."

"SIR, GENERAL GEORGE WASHINGTON'S ORDER TO THE CONTINENTAL ARMY IS AS FOLLOWS: The general is sorry to be informed that the foolish and wicked practice of profane cursing and swearing, a vice heretofore little known in an American Army, is growing into fashion. He hopes officers will, by example, as well as influence, endeavor to check it, and both they and the men will reflect that we can have little hope of the blessing of heaven on our arms if we insult it by our impiety and folly.

Added to this, it is a vice so mean and low that any man of sense and character despises and detests it, SIR!"

"NON-CABORUMDUM!" rang out from somewhere in the middle of C Flight.

Lt Kavanaugh ignored the outside cry. "All right, Wheeler, back in ranks."

C Flight had a good inspection. No gigs. A respectable Manual of Arms was highlighted by the glint of our rifles as we responded smartly to Lt. Payne's commands. However as the flight was moving forward on our second drill pass in front of the judges, Lt Payne gave the order, **"To the rear, March."**

Either Ken Smith misunderstood or did not hear the command. Normally at the rear of the flight, we had maneuvered so that Smith was the lead cadet in his outside element. As the flight responded to Lt. Payne's command, Smith continued marching – all by himself.

I had a horrible sense of déjà vu. *My mind flashed back to a play I was in in Memorial Auditorium in Sacramento. I was one of John Sutter's marching Indian scouts. We were fourth graders. We were to march single file across the stage three times and then exit left. On the second time across, Jay Jackson, immediately behind me, miscounted and turned five steps too soon. When*

I pivoted, I was five feet behind the others now exiting. I was quite embarrassed. I felt a great deal of empathy for Ken today.

We won the inspection and manual of arms parts of the program by a small margin, based in large measure on the outstanding condition of our M1s. Smith's solo march, however, cost us the drill competition and overall first place.

Ken, of course, felt terrible. The rest of the flight, however, told him to shake it off. We just didn't earn enough points. "Non-illegitamus-carburundum," we told him while standing at ease waiting for the results.

"Squadron, Atten-hut." From the front of the Squadron, Lt. O'Malley gave us the results. "Actually, men, you all looked good. I'm pleased with appearances and the drill skills. A Flight was the top flight. They won by a margin of two points over C Flight and four over B Flight. A Flight will sit at ease for lunch today."

The quiet surrounding the 3d Squadron tables was eerie. While B and C Flights were not given "at ease," our ATOs seemed content to enjoy their lunch. We could hear the usual din in the areas of 1st and 2nd Squadrons. The only logical explanation was Lt. O'Malley was pleased enough that he instructed the B and C Flight ATOs to ease up during lunch. While not at ease, Hertz, I, and the rest of us got our fill of fried chicken, mashed potatoes, and apple pie. Lt. Tatum informed us fried chicken, in the Southern manner, was eaten with the hands. That freed us of even the "bite size" rule.

***

"We will not lie, steal, or cheat; nor will we allow among us those who do. That, Gentlemen, is the essence of the honor code; simple, yet profound." Cadet Second Class Gerald Garvey, Class of 1959 droned on in the afternoon heat. Tired eyes drooped. Half of the members of the flight were standing behind their chairs to prevent hitting their heads on the desk when they fell asleep.

"General Hubert Harmon, the first Superintendent and General Robert M. Stillman, the first Commandant, were instrumental in guiding my class in development of the honor code. The code, however, Gentlemen, belongs to the cadets. When you are accepted into the Wing in September, you will abide by the code. It will be your code as well as of the classes of 1959 and 1960. Fashioned on the Honor Code of West Point, the USAFA Honor Code is our own.

The code is based on the need for integrity in armed forces officers. A classic Air Force example of lack of integrity is the case where a pilot is sent to destroy an enemy anti-aircraft position. If the pilot fails in his mission, but reports the position destroyed; a subsequent loss of lives over that enemy position constitutes a moral failure on the part of the officer. It clearly can be seen as a dereliction of duty.

Incidents may start with a simple white lie: 'Yes, sir, I did polish my shoes this morning, but the sun must have taken off the shine.' Such a lie may seem inconsequential, but it's the beginning of a sore that can fester into a scenario disastrous for a cadet. We do not tolerate a lie nor accept anyone who tells a lie. The penalty in either case is dismissal from the Academy."

"Sir, that means if I see a classmate lying, I have to report him?" asked Tom LaPlante.

"Yes, Mister LaPlante!"

"What if I am uncertain and wait a day or two to report what I have seen?"

"Normally, one would not wait more than a day. But, there is a consideration of reporting circumstances. It's up to the Honor Committee to make that judgment. You'll learn about procedures, the Honor Committee, and the honor process in future classes."

Despite Cadet Garvey's pedantic presentation, we were impressed with the Honor Code concept, mentally accepting that we would abide by the Code as Fourth Class Cadets. We had 10 minutes to discuss the issue before Lt. Boyce showed up to return us to the dormitory.

***

After a fire drill change into athletic gear from khakis, we double-timed to the athletic field for calisthenics. We were up to 15 repetitions of 20 exercises. As always, we took a mile warm up and finished with a two mile run around the field.

We selected one of five sports for squadron competition: soccer, softball, swimming, basketball, or gymnastics. I chose softball and was sent to Lt. Battle. We selected positions, and warmed up playing catch. The pitchers and catchers went with Lt Tatum to begin working together. The next PT period we'd go to the baseball fields and start building a team. Since no one else claimed to be a third baseman, I was assured of playing my high school position.

The inevitable laps preceded our return to the barracks, but strangely we were all in great spirits. When we started double-timing to the barracks, Lt. Payne began: "*Nellie wore a new dress, it was very thin . . .:*

C Flight responded with

"*She asked me how I liked it; I answered with a grin . . .*
Why don't you wait 'til the sun shines, Nelly?
And the clouds go drifting by.
We will be so happy, Nellie,
Don't you cry.
Down Lover's Lane we'll wander,
Sweethearts, you and I.

Oh, wait til the sun shines, Nellie,
By and By.
Why don't you wait 'til the sun shines, Nelly,
And the clouds go drifting by.
We will be so happy, Nellie,
You and I.

As we broke for the barracks and a quick shower, the entire flight gave out a loud **"Huraah!"** For the first time in two weeks no ATOs patrolled the hallways as we rushed through the showers and back to our rooms to get into khakis.

"Damn, Butch. I don't know why we wear ties, with a half Windsor, no less."

"Geeze, Davis, you still tying that thing every time. No wonder you're so slow. Just loosen the tie and stick it in the laundry bag. We have two. You can leave the other one hanging in the closet. Didn't your mother teach you anything about etiquette?"

"Sir, there is one minute until dinner formation. The uniform is khakis and wheel hat. One minute, sir!"

As Butch and I skidded into our places in formation, I caught a movement to Butch's right. A moment later, our nemesis, Lt. Jackson was clicking his heels together in front of Butch. "Aha, Mister Rieselman, you didn't shave again, did you?"

"Yes, Sir, I did shave this morning," Butch said with a tone of indignation in his voice.

"You wouldn't be lying to me now, would you, Rieselman?"

Butch was obviously perplexed. "Sir, I . . . ah . . ."

"Excuse me, Lt. Jackson," Lt. Payne said as he stepped between Butch and Lt. Jackson. Payne towered over the five-foot-ten Jackson, and the inflection in his voice indicated his displeasure. "You heard, Mr. Rieselman. He said he shaved this morning. I don't know how it is at VMI, but at the Air Force Academy, a cadet's word is accepted at face value. (I snickered at Lt. Payne's unintended pun). That's what the honor code is all about."

"Right," Jackson said, rather sheepishly. He quickly turned and walked away.

***

Immediately following our 30-minute after-dinner break, C Flight was told to form up with Class A Khakis. Marched into the ballroom of the Forth Class Club, we were told to sit down and be "at ease." Lt. Boyce, our escorting ATO, left. We all rose when Mrs. McComas came in. She invited us to sit.

"By act of Congress, when you graduate, you will be officers and gentlemen. My job is to make you gentlemen before you graduate." Smoothing her brown, grey streaked hair, Mrs. Gail McComas, the widow of an Air Force Officer, was a cross between a mother figure and the Academy's version of Emily Post.

Five-foot, six-inches tall with a pleasant figure, she had a naturally sympathetic face and demeanor. She planned, taught, and managed official cadet social functions. Like Yente, from *Fiddler on the Roof*, she was a match maker for cadets, possessing an impressive catalog of local girls interested in dating cadets.

We could not use Mrs. McComas' dating service until September; when we would be able to meet local girls. Limited facilities and the watchful eyes of upperclassmen, however; were not conducive to establishing solid relationships.

The "thrill" of meeting cadets quickly wore off after three sessions in the Fourth Class Club; drinking cokes and eating pizza, an evening at the movies, and a sanitized "good-bye" as the cadet answers to the tolling of call to quarters. Even a minor show of public affection, initiated either by the Fourth Classman or his date, resulted in a major gig, potentially leading to confinements. Confinements probably meant the end of any budding romance.

"You have been issued a copy of *Decorum*. That is our etiquette bible. No, I won't be asking Fourth Class Knowledge questions, but wouldn't put it past some ATOs or upperclassmen to use *Decorum* for table quizzing," she said with a knowing smile.

"However, you will be tested. When with young ladies, and, especially, with their parents, you are to act in a manner that reflects well upon yourself, the Academy, and the Air Force. Anytime you are in public, your behavior will be scrutinized.

We are the newest of the Academies. The newness has not worn off. Mrs. Turner, my assistant—you may call her 'Peej,' she likes that—and I will be here to answer any questions you have about protocol, social events, and yes, dating opportunities.

Each of you will fill out a card tonight with a bit of your background, interests, and religion. We are not really a dating service, but will make opportunities available to you to meet some of the fine, young women in the area. We will have social etiquette and dancing lessons from time to time, beginning in the academic year.

To ensure you get back after shower formation, I have a short movie on the local colleges put together by Public Affairs. After the movie, Lt. Boyce will return you to your dormitory."

There was a solid round of applause as Mrs. McComas left and the movie began. A movie, especially one highlighting the local female college population, provided an outstanding alternative to shower formation.

***

"Well, what'd you think of that, Butch? Our own personal match maker."

"Ah, hell, just made me think of Susan and how much I miss her. I need to go home. If I get another letter like the last one, I'm outta here."

"Yeah, sure. Don't forget your folk's letter. Good night."

I had just fallen asleep when I heard a rap at the door. I looked over at Butch's side. Butch was under the cover with his flashlight on.

Following the rap on the door, Lt. Tatum burst into the room and snatched Butch's blanket off the bed. (I pretended to be asleep to avoid jumping to attention without pajamas.)

"Well, well, Cadet Rieselman, a little after hours study on Fourth Class Knowledge?"

"Ah, no Sir, I ah . . . ah . . ."

"Writing home for money?"

"Ah, no, Sir, I was writing my girlfriend."

"I see. Well maybe we can get your mind off of your girlfriend. Get into your sweats, grab your M1 and follow me."

Butch came back into the room 40 minutes later. He was wheezing; his face was covered with sweat. Wet circles under his arms reached to his waist. "What the hell happened, Butch?"

"That SOB took me to the quadrangle; made me run 25 laps with my rifle at high port. Thought I was going to die. If I catch that bastard off base, I'll show him a thing or two."

"Calm down, Butch. It's all in the game."

"Yeah, Davis, easy for you to say. On top of everything, the jerk gave me five demerits, three for violating lights out and two for unauthorized sleeping uniform. He says it's five if they catch you sleeping in the nude. Guess what I get to do Saturday afternoon? It won't be going to the show. And you, buddy, haven't even got a tour . . ."

"Yet," I said. "Go to sleep, tomorrow's going to be another one of those days."

Chapter 8

Every cadet participates in athletic events --- for the development of a healthy competitive spirit, teamwork, and loyalty
–USAF Academy Catalog

Friday, July 19, 1957

Thursday was routine; with PT, a Customs and Courtesies Class, more high port running, and a shower formation from hell. The ATOs must have thought we were getting soft. We did 30 push-ups, five minutes of running in place, 50 sit-ups (at least they let us have a partner hold your feet down) , three more minutes of running in place and 30 more push-ups. I could hardly get through the shower, down the hall, and into bed.

Today started out great. Well, the morning was the usual routine. In the afternoon, Intra-Squadron sports competition began. Each squadron has teams in six sports. We play each squadron twice, so you need every win.

"Come on, Davis, hit the ball!" teammates called from the sideline. I stepped off the plate and looked for a sign from the third base coach. His swooping arm signal said hit away. I looked at runners at second and third. With two outs they would run on a hit ball. Behind 2-1 at the bottom of the seventh, I needed a hit or we would lose.

Like *Casey at the Bat* I faced an oh and two count—two strikes, no balls. Terry Guess, 2nd Squadron, was burning them in. But, I noticed when he threw his fast ball, he had a slight hitch just before he released the ball. I saw the hitch; I expected a fast ball over the plate.

"Craaack! went the bat as I hit the ball dead center. The ball sailed over the head of the center fielder, insuring the runner from second would score and we'd win the game. I ran to first base and turned toward my cheering classmates.

In an environment where we're constantly criticized, even small victories are uplifting. Despite the loss, the 2nd Squadron classmates on the bus were in good spirits. We swapped "war stories[40]" about our first two weeks, noting the good, the bad, and the ugly ATOs.

"How'd your meet go, Butch?" I asked as Butch came in the door.

---

[40] War stories, of course, are not battle experiences, but tales about training; later, trips abroad, or even female encounters.

"Well, it was close. They have guys who'll be on the swim team, but our four man relay team won the last race and we won the meet."

"That's great. We won the baseball game. So, overall we had a winning day.

***

"Gentlemen, a great day on the fields of friendly strife," began Lt. O'Malley. "Baseball team won 3-2. Swimming also won. The track team won by five points and the soccer team scored a 1 to nothing victory. The gymnastic team won by two points. Our only loss was in basketball. Considering 1st Squadron has all the giants, the 44 to 30 score was okay.

Obviously terrific 3d Squadron is leading in points for the Superintendent's Trophy, at least in athletics. Our standing is 5-1. First and 2nd Squadrons split their competitions; they're both 4 and 2. We still have a lot of work to do. As you know, the pistol and rifle shoots, parades, and the Group drill competition all provide points toward the trophy.

You men in 3d Squadron have the best ATO coaches in the group. They'll do everything to ensure you are competitive in all areas that count. Listen to their advice and instruction. In the end, it is up to you to win the trophy. Again, good show. Let's go to dinner."

Hmmm, Lt O'Malley didn't say anything about sitting at ease. You'd think after a day like today, we'd get some benefit for our efforts. Oh, well. Only five more weeks of this crap and we get to go out in the field. Hope I can hang in there that long.

***

Dinner introduced us to the "buck up" maneuver. We would learn that whenever the ATOs thought the program was getting too soft and we were getting too comfortable, we would get an intense period of increased pressure.

As soon as we took seats, Lt. Tatum looked at me (I wasn't in one of the serving positions) and said, "Okay, Davis, the third verse of the Air Force Song."

"Off we go into the wild blue yonder . . ."

"**STOP**!" bellowed Tatum. I asked for the third verse not the first verse. Do you think that is the start of the third verse, Dumbsmack!"

"Yeees, Sir, I said hesitantly.

"Well, you're wrong. The third verse starts: 'Off we go into the wild sky yonder.' Now, try again!"

"Yes Sir:
 Off we go into the wild sky yonder,
Keep the wings level and true.
If you'd live to be a grey-haired wonder . . .

"Davis, do New Cadets use contractions?

"Ah, no, Sir" *What in the hell is he talking about??? Oh, yeah, the song says "you'd."*
  "WELL, DO-WILLIE!"

"Yes, Sir."

If you would live to be a grey-haired wonder . . .

""Start over," Tatum hissed.

Off we go into the wild SKY yonder,

Keep the wings level and true.

If you WOULD live to be a grey-haired wonder

Keep your nose out of the blue . . ."

"DAVIS, are you sure it's 'Keep your nose out of the blue?"

Damn, what's with Tatum tonight. It's like he took Jeckle and Hyde pills and Mr. Hyde won out. "YES, SIR," I bluffed.

 "Do you have your *Contrails* with you? "

"Yes, Sir."

"Good, take it out, turn to page 150, and read me the fourth line."

I fumbled getting *Contrails* out of my pocket, but finally opened it to page 150. *Oh, Shit, the bastard's got me again.* "Keep THE nose out of the blue," I read weakly.

"Tell you what I'm going to do, Davis. Since it's Friday and the end of the week, I'm going to let you read your *Contrails* for the next 10 minutes, then correctly give me the third verse of the Air Force Song. Deal?

You son-of-a-bitch. I'm not going to get even a bite of steak tonight. "YES, SIR!" I said as sarcastically as I thought I could get away with.

"Hertz," Tatum said, turning toward Bob, who had finished his cold pilot duties. "Give me Air Marshall Douhet's quote; then MacArthur's message from the Far East.

It was obvious Tatum had given himself a refresher course on *Contrails* and was using it as his buck up weapon.

Hertz delivered Douhet's quote and loudly spit out MacArthur's quote, hoping that its message would blunt the ATO attack.

"Sorry, Mr. Hertz," Tatum said. "I didn't hear your second quote. Give it again?"

Exasperated, but sensing he shouldn't press the issue, Bob, in a normal voice, quoted MacArthur: "From the Far East I send you one single thought, one sole idea – written in red on every beachhead from Australia to Tokyo – 'There is no substitute for victory!"

Ha, I thought, *so much for the fruits of victory. All our victories got us today was grief.*

"Okay, Davis, let's have it."

" … In echelon we carry on! Nothing will (substituting for 'Nothing'll') stop the United States (for U.S.) Air Force!'

Lt. Tatum smirked. "Nice catch in the last line – Eat."

I managed a portion of mashed potatoes and gravy and a glass of Pan-thur-piss.

***

As soon as we entered the room, I threw my comforter down, dropped the pillow on it and stretched out on the floor. "Damn, Butch, can you believe dinner tonight? Tatum was all over me. Really chicken-shit stuff: 'the' for 'your' in the damn third verse of the Air Force Song. If this is supposed to be anything like the Air Force, I'm not sure it's for me. I'm going to see the Chaplin after church on Sunday. I've had enough of this crap. "

"Ah, come on, Don. It's just a game. The program's designed to get under your skin. They want to see if you can stick it out. If you really let them get to you – they win and you lose. Actually, nobody wins because they've already invested something in you and you took somebody's place who wanted to be here. So, if you give up, everybody loses."

"I don't know. Miss my folks. Miss going fishing. Miss my buddies back home."

"Hell, and you don't even have a girl to worry about. Come on, Davis. Get out of the funk. Get your butt ready for SAMI tomorrow. So far, we have the best room in the dormitory; no, in the Squadron. Let's keep it that way. We'll get a lot less grief and may even survive this chicken-shit outfit, to use your crude terminology."

Butch's genuine support and pep talk softened my distraught attitude, but I still had a strong vision of going home and enjoying familiar surroundings. Reluctantly, I turned my attention to the more immediate problem of tomorrow's SAMI, in-ranks inspection, and parade.

I piled the comforter on the floor at the end of my bed, stripped the bed, grabbed clean sheets, and put a SAMI dressing on the bed. Sitting at my desk, I opened the right hand drawer and pulled out my black stained shoe shine rag.

Chapter 9

Although each cadet will be kept fully occupied, he will be encouraged to write home frequently. . . . Letters from home . . . will be invaluable in keeping your son's spirits high during this period of adjustment to the life of a cadet.

Letter to Parents, Captain Charles S.T. Mallett, Air Officer Commanding,
3d Squadron

Sunday, July 21, 1957 Week Three

The letdown from Friday's intramural high was worse because of Friday night's "buck up" and second place in Saturday's Parade. Butch and I caught flak for our room during SAMI. We shared two demerits for "dirty wastebasket" (it was in the center of the room), two demerits each for bookshelf not properly aligned, and a demerit each for necktie on wrong hanger (me) and shorts facing wrong way in the closet (Butch).

"Great Butch, We didn't need all the demerits."

"Well, we got a break not having the in-ranks inspection; that could have really piled up the demerits. You still intend to see the Chaplain tomorrow after church?"

"I don't know. Been dreaming about flying ever since grade school at Bell Avenue Elementary. I used to watch the tugs towing P-51s and F-82s down the road on their way to Korea. Always thought flying would be neat. But, maybe I want to be a lawyer or journalist."

"What the hell is an F-82, Davis?"

"That's a twin P-51 Mustang. Sort of looks like the P-38. Right now, I'd be happy being back in good old Bell Avenue."

***

With the usual absence of ATOs, Sunday morning breakfast was good. Gazing discretely, I saw Lt. Cornelius Kelly as the Table Commandant at a Squadron table. In A Flight, Lt. Kelly was known for his sense of humor and philosophy that New Cadets should get enough to eat. His favorite Sunday trick was to have cadets tell a "non-dirty," joke. The first cadet who made him laugh was the table hero. An acceptable joke resulted in minimal conversations with the table commandant and an enjoyable meal for the New Cadets.

"Sir, may I join your table?" I asked.

Lt. Kelly squinted at my name tag. "Davis, huh! I don't know if I can let an Englishman sit at my table . . ."

"Sir, I'm an eighth Blackfoot Indian and we gave the British a bad time during the war of 1812. Also, the name Davis is Welsh, not English."

"Not sure that's true, Davis, but good story. Grab a chair."

"Davis, you seem to be a good story teller. Let's have a good clean joke."

Good grief, a clean joke? "Knock, knock!"

"Who's there?"

"If you."

"If you who?"

"If you would laugh, we could all eat."

"Ooooh," groaned Kelly. "Davis, that's so bad I couldn't stand another one. Eat."

The scrambled eggs, sausage, pancakes, and ti-ger-pis all had to be sent on turnarounds. I enjoyed my meal, but it still didn't make up for the last couple of starvation days.

***

The bright Colorado sunshine, warm temperature, and pleasant meal put me in a euphoric mood all the way back to my room. When I got there, Butch was sacked out. I decided to join him before I wrote home.

United States Air Force Academy
Sunday, July 21, 1957 1500 (3:00 p.m.)

Dear Mom and Dad,

What a week. They are still "getting us in shape." I lost another five pounds. I expect I'll lose a few more pounds on the Doolie Diet -- little food and lots of exercise. Friday our Squadron won five intramural games.

I'm having second thoughts about staying here. I can deal with it, but I wonder if I want to be something else - a lawyer or journalist. I may write to Stan Gilliam. He always gave me good advice.

Oh, yeah, we went to see Mrs. McComas, the Academy's official hostess. She gave us a book on customs and manners, etc. called *Decorum*. Mrs. McComas is going to teach us how to be gentlemen. The book has sections on "how to treat your date at a dance," "how to act at formal dinners," and going through a receiving line." How hotie totie is that? There are zingers, too. It says: ". . . keep in mind any ostentatious (whatever that means) display of public affection is taboo." How do you think the guys from Grant and Rio Linda would take that?

Not that we have to worry about girls. Other than a few hanging around the parade ground fence, we haven't seen any girls; and the guys are getting uglier every day.

Tell Pa to fix and sell my car. Anything over the cost of repairs, you can send to me. We can't have a car until first class year. Don't think my '49 Chevy will last that long. Sure do miss it and the wonderful times I had in it

By the way, I did get your three wonderful letters. I just haven't had time to answer. Keep your letters coming. They are lifesavers. Wayne finally sent me a letter. He is going into the Navy.

We've had four guys leave so far. Of the four, two resigned, one had a medical problem, and one swung at a training officer. The ATO used Judo to make the guy miss. Guess I'll stay until September and see how academics go. Besides, I haven't had my airplane rides yet. Wouldn't want to miss that.

We had football and baseball tryouts. The line coach in football said I was too small (and too slow) for football. So, I won't be playing football. The baseball coach was more encouraging. He said I could try out when the season comes. I didn't hit well. The pitchers are better than any in high school. It would be great to make the team.

Oh, to answer your question, don't send cookies. We can't have them in the room. We take them to the dining hall table. I doubt I'd ever see a cookie. ATOs love cookies. You can send me some in the fall.

There's a rumor we may be able to buy ice cream next week at the Cadet Store. I can't imagine they'd have enough – they sell pints – to take care of some 300 cadets. I'll buy at least two pints.

Guess I'd better close. I have to shine my boots. We start bayonet training tomorrow. Sounds like a peachy course. We're going to the Base Theater tonight for the movie *The Air Force Story*. Please write.

God Bless
Your loving son,
Don

I awoke with a start from a deep REM nightmare. The damp pillow from my sweating gave me a chill. In the dream, I was in football uniform. Coach Pelleta was on the side yelling, **"Get with it, Davis. Knock him on his ass!"** The "he" was Lt. Tatum in full football uniform with ribbons on his sweatshirt. Pelleta's commands were to no avail. Lt. Tatum flattened me four times. When he hit me a fifth time, I did a judo slap; but still landed on my back, knocking the wind out of me. As I jumped up, the sun through the window momentarily blinded me.

Butch's pep talk and a decent Sunday morning breakfast gave me second thoughts about quitting. After choir practice and chapel, I thought better about seeing the Chaplin. I might float the thought of quitting to the folks, but decided to stick it out a week or two more. *It's got to get better. Surely they don't want to lose all of us.*

"Sir, there are five minutes until first call for evening meal. The uniform of the day is khakis, rain coats, rain covers, and galoshes. Five minutes, Sir."

"Oh, crap," Butch said, geting his raincoat out of the closest. "If it rains, we'll have to dry our raincoats and get them back in the closet for AMI tomorrow."

"Hell, worse than that, remember what galoshes do to shoe shines?"

As we were given "forward march," rain came down as if Odin had poured giant buckets of water over the side of his cloud castle. Within minutes, we were drenched. Inside the raincoats, perspiration created our own personal saunas.

"Okay, men, fold your raincoats and put them over the back of your chairs," Lt. Payne ordered. "Don't slip on the puddles when you get up." When the chaplain finished the invocation, Lt. Payne said quietly, "Take seats. Eat."

With only one ATO, and that one being Lt. Payne, everyone got their fill of salad, baked ham, peas, carrots, and even tapioca pudding. Halfway through the meal, Cadet Hertz announced, "Sir, the ham has run out of stores. Does anyone care for more ham?" Three classmates adventurously stuck out hands. Lt. Payne looked up and nodded. "Sir, the ham is on turnaround, ETA[41] is five minutes."

Struggling with raincoats after dinner, we carefully avoided the puddles. The rain continued to fall heavily all the way back to the room; with continued sprinkles as we were marched to the base theater for this week's episode of *The Air Force Story*.

"Why do you think Sundays are so short, Butch?"

"They're designed that way so we don't get to enjoy them."

"That sure was a hellacious rain. Damn, look at my shoes."

"Yeah, bad omen. I can't imagine what next week is going to be like."

---

[41] ETA – estimated time of arrival.

Chapter 10

During Fourth Class summer training, the cadet has little time to consider himself as an individual and hence regards himself as a part of a large unit, being carried by the tide . . .Contrails

Monday, July 22, 1957 Week Three

The uniform, after breakfast, was fatigues, helmet, rifle, bayonet, and bayonet holder. We double-timed to the bayonet area with rifles in the high port position.

"**High port and hold.**" Lt. Yeager commanded as he stood in front of C Flight. We were lined up 10 abreast in front of the "strawmen," which vaguely resembled football tackling dummies. The strawmen had a net-like covering holding them together.

First we learned how to mount the bayonet on the rifle. Then we relearned the position of "high port." Yeager's high port was more extreme than Tatum's.

"Now, Gentlemen, lower your rifle to 45 degrees and advance thus." Lt. Yeager made a couple of shuffling steps, holding his rifle at the prescribed angle. "When I say 'thrust,' you'll jab the dummy's throat area." He demonstrated. "Do you understand?"

A weak chorus of "Yes, Sir" rang out.

"What a bunch of pansies. I SAID, '**DO YOU UNDERSTAND**?'"

"**YES, SIR**," came the 30 strong response.

Yeager walked the front line inspecting each cadet. He stopped and looked directly at me. *Oh, Shit,* I thought, *he's going to rip me a new one.* Instead, the solid chunk warrior pivoted and placed himself in front of Jeff, one of the Winters twins. He pulled a thread from Jeff's pocket. "**Well, mister, are you planning on starting a sewing class?**"

"**No SIR!**" Jeff replied.

"Are you Jeffrey or Jerry?" Lt. Yeager asked in lowered voice.

"Jeffrey, Sir."

Back in character, Yeager bellowed, "**YOU'D BETTER GET YOUR ACT TOGETHER, MISTER.**" And then, in a whisper, he said, "Glad to see you here, Jeff; say hello to Jerry."

Facing the flight from the wooden platform, Lt. Yeager said, "Before we begin bayonet exercises, we need to get warmed up. Take your bayonet off and put it back in its scabbard." Lt. Yeager removed his bayonet; placed it effortlessly in the scabbard.

Jim Watts was having trouble getting his bayonet back in its sheath. Noticing Jim's dilemma, Yeager hissed. "What's the matter, Dumbsmack, you bring two left hands today?"

Yeager jumped down from the platform and approached Jim, who was sweating profusely. Yeager, only 5'7" tall, looked into Jim's light blue eyes, which were on the verge of filling with tears. Jim was a 240 pound (well, at least when he arrived) 6' 3" Oklahoma all-star football player. "O.K. Mama's Boy, let's do it by the numbers," Lt. Yeager said in a raspy voice.

Lt. Yeager whipped his bayonet off his rifle; then moved to replace it in the scabbard, calling out numbers as he took each step. Jim nervously watched and imitated Yeager.

"All right, pussycat. You obviously need a little extra warm up. Place your rifle on the ground in front of you . . . **NO, DUMBSMACK**, across your body. Now, go down on the rifle, grip it, and give me 10 push-ups."

For 25 minutes, we exercised. *Damn this guy's tough. I'll bet if we drop the rifle or fall down, he'll run us through with a bayonet.*

Following warm-ups, Lt. Yeager lined us up in front of the dummies. "Now, I understand you're all brains; maxed the College Boards. Let's see if you remember what I told you 30 minutes ago. First line, advance to arm's length in front of the dummies. **THRUST AND HOLD!**"`

We took turns advancing and jabbing dummies. As the session progressed, Lt. Yeager got more worked up. When Don Miller made a half-hearted pass at the dummy, Yeager stopped the session; put Miller in front of him. "Mr. Miller, I'm your enemy. You are to slit my throat with your bayonet when I say 'thrust.'" Yeager was unarmed.

On command, Miller hesitated; made another feeble thrust, not reaching Yeager.

"I said, 'Slit my throat,' **MISTER, NOW THRUST!**" Yeager yelled, agitated. Miller thrust hard at Yeager's throat. Yeager hand parried the thrust and smacked the M1's butt into Miller's side. "If I were truly your enemy," Lt. Yeager said, "you'd be a casualty. If I were really nasty, the rifle would have found your privates. **Now, all of you, take this seriously.**"

Miller walked to the back of the formation holding his side. We attacked dummies for 20 minutes; each taking a half a dozen turns. Lt. Yeager's enthusiasm was contagious. At the end of 20 minutes, we were fired up in a manner I hadn't experienced since high school football. My classmates shared the adrenalin rush.

"All right, men. Form up on me. I want five man fronts. You will double-time four times around the practice field (a half a mile long).You will be at high port. **GO!**"

We lined up. The first group took off. We grunted like Marines with each step. We were beginning to get into good condition, but the hour's workout took its toll.

On the third circuit, 10 classmates opened a gap at the front of the group. Suddenly, several other classmates began to fall out – some collapsing onto the grass.

Yeager stepped in front of the lead group. **"WELL, DUMBSMACKS, THOSE ARE YOUR CLASSMATES BACK THER**E," yelled Lt. Yeager. **"FROM THIS POINT ON, YOU WILL NEVER, I REPEAT, NEVER LEAVE A CLASSMATE OR COMMRADE-IN-ARMS BEHIND. DO YOU UNDERSTAND?"**

A weak "Yes, Sir," came from the group.

"I SAID, DO YOU UNDERSTAND?" The veins stood out on Yeager's neck.

"YES, SIR!" came the response.

"Now, get to the back of the formation. You will NOT pass anyone. You will make sure all of your classmates cross that final finish line no matter what it takes."

Walking back toward the fallen classmates, Yeager looked at me and said, "Davis, go help Cadet LaPlante!"

"Yes, Sir," I replied. I retraced the 10 yards to Cadet LaPlante. "Come on, Tom you can make it. Let's go.[42]" I grabbed his rifle and helped him up. I felt near collapse myself. Helping LaPlante seemed to give me a second breath.

As I was completing the last pass, I came even with Jeff Winter. "Hey, Jeff," I said. "What the hell was that back there in ranks between you and Yeager?"

"Oh, he came to our college and encouraged Jerry and me to apply for the Academy. He's really a nice guy."

"Yeah, nice guy, like Jack the Ripper," I said as Jeff began to pull away from me.

Strangely, on the route back to the barracks, someone started a chorus of *Nellie Wore a Blue Dress*. We sang and double-timed in unison back to our rooms.

***

We were allowed to shower. Then, Lt. Tatum gave us five minutes to change into khakis. Next, he marched us to the academic area for another session on the honor code. C2C Garvey was not in the room when we arrived.

"Damn, Tom, did you see bayonet training is scheduled the rest of this week and next? I don't know if I can take that many more hours."

"Just think, Davis. You will be a trained killer by the end of next week. I do think it's helping to build esprit de corps in the class, don't you?"

Cadet Garvey retraced his previous instruction and let the class out early.

***

---

[42] This activity started a bonding process among class members that unified us and created friendships that have lasted over 50 years. It is a phenomenon that allows us to walk up to a classmate today and pick up a conversation we were having 30, or 40, or 50 years ago.

"Well, Davis, how did you enjoy Lt. Yeager and the bayonet program?" Lt. Tatum said with a slight smirk on his face.

"Sir, I think it is a wonderful program," I said with as much cynicism as I could muster. "I do not think I have had that much fun since high school football, Sir."

Lt .Tatum smiled. "Tell me about the falcon, Davis?"

Damn, he got me again. I don't know diddle about the falcon, except it's our mascot and a great predator. I'm really hungry too. Oh, well, here go's nothing. "Sir, the proud falcon is United States Air Force Academy's mascot. It is a great predator and an agile flyer . . ."

"Right, Davis, enough of the BS. You will tell me at dinner all about the falcon and why the Class of 1959 chose it as the Academy's mascot. Got it?

"Yes, Sir."

"Eat."

Holy cow, he let me eat and isn't bothering anyone else. They must all know what a drain bayonet class is. Guess it's sort of like fattening pigs for the slaughter.

***

"Mister Davis, where did you get those boots, in a thrift store? They're atrocious; no shine at all? Well?" Lt. Payne's shadow kept the glaring sun out of my eyes. I could see the quizzical look on his face.

We'd been surprised at the "fatigues, cap, and boots uniform" call because we were headed for "armaments/fueling instruction" in the academic building. "Sir, I polished my . . ."

"What, Dumbguard" said Payne in feigned disbelief. "What's the right answer?

"No, Sir."

"Right, now why are your boots like that?"

"No excuse, Sir . . . Sir, may I make a statement?"

"Shoot!"

"Sir, I polished my boots this morning for a half hour, but they have lost their shine and are dull even when I use the rag and after shave lotion."

"Hmmm. Yeah, That happens. Do you have matches or a lighter?"

"No, Sir."

"Drive around to my room after classes. You have to apply a flame and melt down the old wax and start all over again. Two, three days, they should be back up to speed."

Great, just the extra crap I need. Wonder if Lt. Payne can help me with the falcon thing? "Lt. Payne, Sir, may I ask a question?"

"You're just full of questions, today. Sure, shoot, Davis."

"Sir, I understand you have a mini-encyclopedia set in your room. May I borrow the section with falcons in it?"

"Ah, Tatum's falcon quiz, huh? Sure, we'll get that when you drive around."

***

Fuels and armament NCOs from the Lowry Flight Maintenance and Support sections gave us detailed instructions in refueling and rearming aircraft, both assigned and transient. The instruction was thorough and included practice in using proper checklists; performing supervision requirements; and, above all, safety provisions. We were impressed with the professionalism and knowledge of Technical Sergeant Brown and Master Sergeant Little.

***

Returning to my room with Lt. Payne's books and lighter, I set about learning about falcons. I wanted to write letters, but they would have to wait.

***

"Well, Mister Davis, tell me what you know about falcons."

"Sir, the sport of falconry dates back to around 2000 BC when Chinese nobility used falcons for hunting herons. Until the 17th Century, Peregrine Falcons were so highly prized, possession was limited to high nobility – Kings, Czars, and Popes.

There are 37 falcon varieties. The Academy uses the Peregrine Falcon, genus *Falco Peregrines,* as a mascot and in aerial demonstrations. The Peregrine Falcon weighs two pounds and has a wing span of four feet. The Academy has two Gyrfalcons, genus *Falco Rusticolus.* Gyrfalcons are larger and nearly white. They weigh three pounds and have a wing span of five feet. They tend to live and breed in the Arctic . . ."

Lt. Tatum looked up. *Damn,* I said under my breath. *I didn't think he was listening.* "What do you mean, tend to live in the Artic?"

"Well, Sir, they're found in other parts of the world, but not necessarily by preference, as with our own Gyrfalcons."

"Hmmm, Okay, continue," Lt Tatum said refocusing on his pork chops.

"The falcon is a fast-flying and powerful bird. The Peregrine is the largest falcon in the United States. Peregrines eat sea birds, other medium sized birds, and bats. The Peregrine attacks out of the sun, like a fighter pilot, and enters a high speed dive called a stoop from as high as 2500 feet. The falcon obtains speeds up to 200 miles per hour when diving on its prey, making it the fastest animal alive.

Versatile, falcons can swoop, skim the ground, or soar to catch unwary prey . . ."

"Oooh kay, Davis, enough of the BS. What were the Class of 1959's other possible choices and why the falcon?"

"Sir, the Class of 1959 considered the tiger, eagle, and falcon. The tiger, while courageous and feared by other animals, cannot fly. The eagle, while noble, is the national emblem. The class thought selecting the eagle might cause identity problems. Besides, the falcon is the fastest, most agile, and most aggressive aerial bird. It is said a diving falcon can disable a mule or a goat[43], Sir."

"You just made that last crap up, didn't you, Davis?"

I bit my lip to keep from smirking. "Yes, Sir," I answered.

"EAT!"

---

[43] The reference is, of course, to the Army Mule and the Navy Goat.

Chapter 11

You are of one cut now —new Air Force Cadets.
Time and many trials will discover the best of you.
—Major General Briggs, Superintendent
"Message of Welcome to the Class of 1961
Contrails

Friday, July 26, 1957 Week Three

United States Air Force Academy

Friday, July 26, 1957 0530

Dear Walt,

This has been the week from HELL! Monday we started bayonet training. Can't figure how we'll carry an M1 with bayonet in our fighters. If we have to bail out, I'm not going to wait around to jab the bad guys.

Yeager, our instructor', is the, meanest thing I've seen since Coach Pelleta. Hey makes Pelleta look like a cream puff. Remember the tackling drill? Pelleta put two dummies three feet apart with an opposing back and lineman. One had to be on the ground before he blew the whistle.. Bayonet training is at least 10 times harder and lasts longer.

At the end, we run two miles in fatigues, helmets, and rifles above our heads. I must be getting in shape. I made it all the way yesterday without stopping or falling. I'm down to 153 pounds; 12 pounds lighter than when I played varsity. Today, we only had six guys "fall out," that is drop to a knee. We have to help those guys, carry their rifles if necessary. Think we're getting close as a team. Like at the end of the season when you missed even Puccio.

Food's great, but sitting at attention on the front of the chair and making silly announcements like "Sir, the pancakes have been expended and are on turnaround," meaning the ATOs have eaten all the pancakes and we have to send out for more makes it hard to eat. I think I mentioned ATOs - Air Training Officers - our substitute upperclassmen.

We rarely get seconds and are happy to get half of the firsts. The waiters are pretty cool. They help us every chance they get. We fill out a form after every meal. We always put in: FAST, NEAT,

72

AVERAGE, FRIENDLY, GOOD, GOOD. The ratings are: "Speed of service," "Waiter's Appearance," "Portion," "Waiter's Attitude," "Quality of food," and "Quality of beverage." You don't bad mouth the waiter because you need him as an ally. They watch to see if you are going to be out of anything, food or beverage, and anticipate what you are going to ask for. That helps.

I gave a talk on falcons this week, especially why the First Class, the Class of 1959, chose the bird as our mascot. If anyone asks you, it's because it's the fastest, most agile of the predator birds. The falcon can dive at 200 miles per hour. We have several mascots trained to fly at football games.

You asked about the girl situation. There is none. We would be horny as hell if they didn't keep us so tired and starved we don't think about girls.. About two third of the guys have girls back home. Kind of glad I don't have anyone to worry about. Still, a female letter once in a while is nice. If you see Sandy, tell her to drop me a line. Think about her once in a while. She going to college? I'm sure she'll make out all right - literally -- wherever.

Today's Friday. So, we watch ATOs eat steak for dinner. We have Lt. Yeager again next week. Yeager is one mean SOB, but he really does motivate you. He so reminds me of Pelleta. Would want to play football for this guy; you'd be in shape and so mean even the farm boys from Lodi would run the other way (like they did last year—that was great!).

My roommate, Butch, and I have figured out the neat room thing. We don't get a lot of demerits. Demerits are negative points. When you screw up, you get demerits. Starting August, the demerits will count toward military aptitude grades. I'm surprised they don't grade your crapping style. Well, actually, you have to tell them every night whether you did a number two or not. How's that for wild. Over 30 demerits a month, you march tours . . . too many demerits, you meet an officer board and they throw you out.

Reading over this, I'm not sure I want to stay here. It's certainly a lot of crap. I'm seriously thinking about bailing out. Only trouble is, with no money I'd have to go to American River. Not my greatest ambition.

How's good old Grant High? Congratulations on winning Student Body President. Are you going with anyone? Kind of miss Linda Konowski; she was hot. Too bad she was just a sophomore. I took a lot of heat for going with her.

Well, I have combat boots to shine. If you show up at bayonet training with crummy boots, it's an extra lap. Tell somebody to write me. Love your letters. Keep them coming.

Your
Buddy,
Don

The morning started as usual, except the "no-eat' policy had slacked off. Even Hertz got a full meal. Fourth Class Knowledge was routine, nothing exotic like a falcon brief. Lt. Tatum and Lt. Boyce asked three or four questions, spread evenly around the table, then backed off. We were apprehensive, but grateful.

I think bayonet training causes such additional stress, the word is out "let them eat." We are instructed to drink two or three glasses of water. We can have no more than one cup of coffee because coffee dehydrates you.

Several classmates were severely ill after bayonet training yesterday, throwing up and feeling weak. We had a repeat this morning. We didn't leave anyone on the field, so they got to the barracks before they had a problem. Everyone, however, returned with perspiration-soaked fatigues from the eleven o'clock 90 degree heat. Two of the three downed classmates went to the hospital. Thad Tomkins was excused from the noon meal and allowed to rest in his room. The doctors diagnosed heat exhaustion.

Last night Lt. O'Malley talked about drinking a lot of water and eating salt tablets (now in a hallway dispenser). He said dehydration is a serious problem, treated by following his advice. He warned if you go to the hospital, you'll get an intravenous treatment; not fun. If you pass out, it might jeopardize your cadet career, or worse disqualify you from pilot training.

I have only been to the clinic once. When I couldn't stop my nose bleed during PT, Lt Payne sent me to the clinic. The corpsmen were great, very sympathetic. Airman Stanford stopped the bleeding. He told me to keep a piece of wet napkin under my upper lip during PT. His trick worked and I haven't been back since.

***

I don't know who the clown is that makes up our schedule. I'd like to meet him and give him a piece of my mind (what's left of it). After all the talk about water, salt, and fatigue, they schedule an hour of calisthenics before bayonet training. After changing from PT gear into fatigues, helmets, and M1s with bayonets, we double-timed to the bayonet course.

Lt. Yeager was waiting impatiently. "Good morning, Pussycats, seems the powers that be think this course is too much for you. Bullshit. You're tough. Good advice: drink water, eat salt tablets, but when you're here with me, show me what you've got. Take two laps."

We took the two laps in formation; rifles at high port.. On the second lap, Lt. Yeager, in front in full gear, was running backwards. He sped up the pace. "All right, Boys, Let's hear it." He started a chant: "C Flight! C Flight! C Flight!"

We picked up the chant: **C FLIGHT! . . . C FLIGHT! . . . C FLIGHT!"**

The scheduled hour went by quickly. Everyone put zest into rifle calisthenics. We tore viciously at the dummies. At the end of the period, we did three laps with a thunderous "C Flight" chant. No one dropped out. We chanted all the way back to the barracks; drawing quizzical looks from ATOs and other classmates alike.

***

Lunch was uneventful, which in itself made it eventful. Lt. Tatum and Lt. Boyce were engaged in a serious discussion. Snippets of their conversation indicated concern about training and means to achieve training goals while safeguarding cadets' health.

Noticing we were tuned into their discussion, even to the neglect of eating, Lt. Tatum looked at me: "O.K, Davis, third verse of the Air Force song. Following that Hertz, you can sing the fourth verse of the Star Spangled Banner."

Lt. Tatum listened intently to my rendering of the Air Force song. When Bob Hertz started the Star Spangled Banner, Jim Dickson jumped up and assumed a position of rigid attention. The rest of us followed suit and joined in the singing.

Startled, Lt. Tatum laughed, but then sensing the attention being drawn to our table, he said, "All right, idiots. Cease work, Hertz and all of you sit down and eat."

***

Sir, there are five minutes to afternoon formation. The uniform is fatigues, athletic shoes, and cap. Cadets will carry a towel, swimming suit, and jock strap. Five minutes, Sir!"

"Now what the hell?" said Butch, jumping up from his comforter.

"Damn, Butch, Don't you ever read the schedule?" I asked.

"Why," he replied, "that's what roommates are for. What gives anyway?"

"If you'd read the schedule, you'd know we have a swimming test…"

"No crap? First they march us like grunts, run us through bayonet training; now they test us to see if we'll be good swabbies. Hell, I thought I joined the Air Force . . .'"

"Stop griping. Get dressed. You'll be late for formation and I'll have to listen to you bitch Saturday about marching tours. At least it's athletic shoes so we won't scuff our boots."

"Yeah, yeah, great bunch of humanitarians we have leading us . . ."

" . . . One minute, Sir!"

"NICE TIMING, RIESELMAN," Lt. Tatum screeched as Butch slid into formation as the assembly bell sounded over the loudspeaker.

***

At the pool, we put on our swimming suits in the lockers and reported to the pool in fatigues. Upon reaching the pool, a slim lieutenant, wearing a swim suit and holding a clipboard, instructed us to form in groups of 15.

"My name is Lieutenant Allen Jennings. I, and my assistant ATOs, will administer the swimming test. I graduated from the Naval Academy in 1955. Here's the drill. You'll go in your groups with an ATO. He will assign certain exercises. If you get in trouble, raise your hands – if they are not tied – and wave them vigorously."

Oh, shit, I thought. *I swam in the Sacramento and American Rivers and the pool at Grant, but I've never had my hands tied and tried to swim. This is going to be a bitch.*

"Do not signal you're in trouble unless you really are," continued Lt. Jennings. "If you have to be rescued, you'll fail the test. If you fail the test, it will reflect on your PT grade and you will have remedial instruction. Are there any questions? No? Great, let's get started. Oh, by the way, you may NOT assist a classmate in any of the drills."

I joined my group at the base of the diving tower. The 10 meter, approximately 33 foot, Olympic size diving tower was intimidating. I wasn't particularly afraid of heights, but wasn't particularly fond on them either. I jumped from the Grant High tower once, on a dare. I knew I could do it, but wasn't exactly excited about jumping.

"All right, men," said the lanky, well-tanned Lieutenant. This exercise simulates jumping from the upper deck of a C-124 ditched in the Pacific Ocean. You'll jump from the tower and swim to the other end of the pool. A word of caution: cross your legs to protect your privates. Who's first?"

I raised my hand. "I'll go, Lt Hoist," I said somewhat hesitantly.

Lt. Hoist, a Coast Guard Academy graduate, had a smooth, casual manner, more that of a surfer than an Air Force Officer. "Okay, Davis. Have at it. Don't look back and don't look down. Look at the far end of the pool and jump?"

"Yes, Sir," I said scrambling up the ladder. I had a sense of aloneness on the platform. At the end of the concrete runway, I looked down. *Oh, Shit. What have I done?* I quickly focused on the far end of the pool, crossed my arms and legs, took a deep breath, and hurled into space with a loud "**Bonzai!**

The 33-foot fall seemed like an eternity. I hit the water and plunged near the bottom of the deep end. I begin thrashing to get to the surface and a gasp of air. The wet fatigues felt like they were made of lead. I struggled toward the surface. After another eternity, I broke the plane of the water and gulped down air.

"**Swim, Davis**," I heard Lt. Hoist shouting, "**Swim!**"

I treaded water; tried to orient myself. Spying the wall clock at the far end of the pool, I struck out for it. My legs felt like anchors as I stoked and kicked toward the wall. I heard a loud "sploooosh" behind me as Art Kerr hit the water. We weren't supposed to touch bottom, but about 20 feet into the swim, I sank to the bottom. I felt my shoes touch. My lungs were about to burst. I pushed as hard as I could, aiming toward the distant wall. When I came up I was 15 foot closer to my destination.

I lost sense of time. I just kept stroking and kicking. After my third eternity of the exercise, my hand hit something solid, concrete. Putting all my remaining energy into it, I climbed out of the pool and lay down on my back – completely exhausted.

After what seemed like 5 seconds, a command voice echoed in my ears, "Get up, Mister Davis, and back with your group." Lt. Jennings's eyes showed no compassion.

Art Kerr was already sloshing his way back to the tower. Two of our 15 had climbed the tower, then clutched. David Smith and Tom McCormick were given three minutes and a second chance to make the plunge. Neither could muster the balls to make the leap. Both were headed for remedial swimming. They were not excused from the rest of the test. They had to jump in the deep end and swim to the other end.

Two trials remained. The first in deep water simulated an injury after a crash. Your legs were tied together. You could go to the bottom and launch yourself upward and use your arms to surface and tread water. You had to "survive" for 8 minutes.

The second, in shallow water, consisted of treading water with your feet. Your hands were tied behind your back. Again, there was a 8 minute time limit.

Although swallowing what I thought was half the pool's water, I managed to survive both arm and leg tests. Although we could talk when we weren't testing, we all had such a numbing sense of fatigue we didn't want to talk. I introduced myself to several classmates, but the conversations were limited to name and home town.

Next, we were directed to form up along the side of the pool in new groups of 10. The clock read 1615. The blue comforter was definitely calling.

"Gentlemen," began Lt. Jennings, "you have five minutes to change into swim suits – don't forget the jock straps. Lay your fatigues on the benches to dry . . ." *Ha,* I thought, *we're going to slosh back to the dorm. These things will never dry* ". . . and get back out here. GO!"

"Line up, 10 abreast across the end of the pool," said Lt. Jennings. He held his clipboard and a whistle. "Crouch in a racing position at the edge of the pool. When you hear the whistle, give your best effort to the shallow end. Okay first group up." He blew the whistle and 10 bodies lurched into the pool.

Everyone made it to the far end. We lined up and "raced" back to the deep end. The three or four stragglers on the return were told to remain on the side of the pool.

This was a time when it didn't pay to be first. Fellows, Parsons, Olsen, Clarke, Carson, Takahashi, and Art Kerr finished first in their groups. As a reward, they raced against each other. Fellows and Parsons tied, followed closely by the others.

Putting on our fatigues, we marched back to the barracks leaving a trail of water from dripping uniforms and squishing shoes. The fatigues, hanging in the closet dripped onto towels placed on the closet floor.

**

Dinner was even quieter than lunch. When I took an illegal scan, I saw weariness in my classmates that matched mine. Between PT, bayonet training, and the swim test, this was our most physically hellacious day. Not only was the meal quiet; there was no shower formation that night. I later learned from a Squadron Third Classman that three or four of his classmates passed out at shower formation following a similar day. The Commandant ordered it would not happen again. I don't remember anything after returning to my room and dragging my blue comforter from the bed and throwing it on the floor.

Chapter 12

You will be tested to the limits of your endurance during the next seven weeks . . . If you fail the test, you do not belong here. You have the necessary qualifications . . . you need only superior motivation and fortitude to complete the journey . . .
BGen. Robert M. Stillman, Commandant

Saturday, July 27, 1957

"Wake up, Davis," Butch shouted. I looked bleary-eyed at the clock. It was 0430.

"Hell, Butch, it's not reveille. Why're you waking me up? I need the sleep."

This was the first time Butch had awakened me. Usually, I was his sentinel.

"Damn, Davis, it's Saturday, we have to prepare the room for SAMI."

"The hell with it, Butch. They can kick me out. I don't care, I'm beat."

"Sure you do, Davis. We've got this thing whipped. Get your ass off that comforter and help get the room ready."

Moving like a zombie, I got up and put the required SAMI white collar on my bed. I didn't change sheets since Butch and I slept on our comforters all week. The sheet looked all right to me. I carefully folded the comforter and put it on the bed.

I aligned my shower clogs, boots, and goulashes under the bed. I noticed the boots needed a shine, but thought: *What the hell, it's probably only a demerit. I can live with that.* I stuffed my still damp fatigues and the towel in the laundry bag.

I walked to the door carrying the wastebasket. I dumped the small amount of dirt in it halfway between rooms on the other side of the hall. Back in the room, I carefully put the waste basket on Butch's side of the room.

After checking the socks, jocks, and Tee shirt alignment; I moved to the closet and checked the order and neatness of hanging items. I laid out my khakis on the bed.

I saw Butch put a shine on his boots and shoes. "Come on, Butch. Good enough. I'm going to sleep in my chair. Wake me for reveille."

Next thing I remember was Butch shaking me. "Get up for reveille formation."

***

Breakfast was hellacious. Lt. Tatum nailed me for the Commandant's Staff, the President's Cabinet, and the British Prime Minister. I got half the Commandant's Staff, three cabinet members, and no Prime Minister. A near-empty stomach meant a long day. The only thing stopping me from getting up and walking out was my numbed state of exhaustion; and the fact Tatum lost interest in me and jumped all over Hertz.

***

At 0900, Lt. Tatum burst through the door. He gigged Butch for the wastebasket being eight inches on his side instead of the regulation two. I think he did that because Butch had a nearly perfect SAMI room. Tatum did his Napoleon stride to my side of room. "Good morning, Mister Davis. You look a little ragged this morning."

"Good Morning, Sir."

Tatum looked at my boots. "Good Lord, Davis, have you been on a private bivouac all night? Your boots look like they went through the Battle of the Bulge and lost." He turned to Lt. Payne. "Two demerits for disreputable boots." Staring at my sheets, he stepped in front of me. **"Davis, did you change your sheets?"** he screeched.

"No, Sir." I replied. *Crap,* I thought. *He's really going to screw me this morning. Oh, well, who gives a damn. I'm ready to leave this hell hole anyway.*

"Five demerits; unsanitary sheets," Turning abruptly, he stormed out.

I collapsed on my bed.

***

After dinner, I threw my comforter on the floor and flopped down on it.

"You all right, Davis?" Butch asked. "You don't look all that hot."

"Yeah, I'm all right. But, I think I want to get out of this crappy place."

"Oh, that'll blow over. You are just tired. Come on, let's go to the show."

"Nah, I don't feel like a show. I'm writing my folks to tell them I'm quitting."

"Get real," Butch said. "You're no better off than I am when it comes to paying for college. You'll hate being a nobody at a nobody school. This place is special. We're on the ground floor. We are making history. Come on, the show is *Wings of Eagles* with John Wayne and Maureen O'Hara. It'll get you motivated again."

"Nah, I'm going to write a letter and then get some more sleep."

"Fine, be a dunce. Can I bring you back a candy bar?"

"Yeah, that'd be great. Just don't wake me up. Leave it on top of my desk."

I slept for an hour, but was still fatigued; even my bones hurt. I hadn't felt this bad since the day after our Lodi football game -- their huge linemen were obviously just off the farm, used to throwing around bales of hay. On one play, I went down field to make a block. When. I turned there was their 300 pound middle guard coming at me. I threw a block at his knees, hoping he wouldn't fall on me. I was sure I'd have broken bones if Goliath hadn't missed me.

***

United States Air Force Academy
Saturday, July 27, 1957 1930

Dear Folks,

This week has been the week from HELL! Monday we started bayonet training. In fatigues with helmets and bayonets, we started with exercises, then made holes in straw dummies. After the dummies, we did four laps of the athletic field with rifles at "high port' - over our heads.

On Friday, we had a "survival" swimming test. We jumped off a 33 foot tower and swam to the other end wearing fatigues. I felt like a drowned rat and was so tired I could hardly move. I can't remember ever being that tired; not after football practice or even when working in the hot sun during the summer digging ditches all day as a laborer.

I fell asleep after dinner and didn't prepare well for the Saturday Morning Inspection. I got seven demerits from Lt. Tatum, worst I've done.

Lunch was O.K. Butch and I sat with a 1ST Squadron ATO. He asked a couple questions, then said, "Eat." Said we were lucky because he had a date with a Denver University girl and was saving his energy for her.

After lunch, we got our usual two Saturday shots; one for flu and a Yellow Fever shot. Boy, I really felt lousy all afternoon. The big gland under my arm is swollen; must be from the flu shot.

Dinner was quiet; two thirds of the ATOs were gone. My table commandant,. Lt. Brown, asked if anyone was from California. I said, "Yes." He said, "Good, Eat." I was so tired; I barely ate half my meal.

After this week and today, I'm seriously thinking about quitting. I'll just go to Junior College. I can work as a laborer in summer and make tuition. I'll work during the school year too at Weinstock-Lubin or a restaurant. You wouldn't mind if I stay at home, would you? I'll help with groceries, the electric bill, and stuff. There really is a lot of c____ here. I miss seeing girls, even if I don't have a girl friend at home.

I think I'll go see the Chaplin tomorrow; see what I have to do to get out. Don't worry. I'll be all right and will let you know what I'm going to do.

God Bless
Your loving son,
Don

Chapter 13

Through. . . . self-discipline is formed the fundamental attitude of never-say-die conduct and the ability to stick with a difficult task until completion
. . . Contrails

Sunday, July 28, 1957

The bright, Denver early-morning sun streamed through the window and woke me before reveille sounded. I looked over at a sound asleep Butch. My clock read 5:30, 25 minutes until the bugle call announcing the beginning of a New Cadet Sunday.

With nine hours of sleep, I felt well rested and alive. I sat at my desk, picked up my *Contrails*, then set the little white tormentor book down; thinking about the last week and my decision to quit the Academy. The thought was still strong in my mind.

What the hell am I going to do if I go home? Everyone; family, friends, Principle Curry and the rest of my Grant teachers will want to know what happened. Did I get sick? Did I get hurt? What, you just quit? That's not like you, Don. The guys will be supportive, but they won't understand. The girls certainly aren't going to be impressed; not like they would be if I were walking around in a good looking Cecil B. DeMille designed uniform.

Butch is right. I'll have to go to an ordinary school and work my butt off . I'll be just another Del Paso Heights guy. I'll never get to fly. I don't think I'm a quitter. Even when we were getting waxed in football, Walt, Wayne, and the rest of the guys never quit. What the hell, I can make it and there are some great things here. Non illegitmus caborumdum!

***

Lt. Boyce, acting Flight Commander, looked as ragged as I felt the evening before. He did a cursory walk up and down the elements, but did not stop for any individual inspections. Except for mandatory commands, he said nothing on the way to breakfast or at the table (Butch, Hertz, and I found our way to his table).

We loaded up at breakfast, aided by the visit of Tactical Air Command Commander, General Otto P. Weyland and a request from him that the New Cadets "sit at ease." In addition to two servings of pancakes, scrambled eggs, bacon, toast, and a donut, I downed two glasses of ti-ger-pis and two glasses of milk. Hertz, as Crew Chief, gave everyone dirty looks because he was so busy ordering extra food, he barely had time to eat. I was so full; I figured I would have trouble waddling back to the dorm.

***

I was standing at the Bulletin Board, checking yesterday's inspection results; a Sunday morning diversion. *Damn, I didn't get gigged for the sheets. Boots, yes; sheets, no. Lt*

Payne must have "lost" the Form 10 on the sheets. Wow! That probably saves me a tour next Saturday.

"**Davis**," Lt. Boyce's voice boomed, "what are you doing?"

I was puzzled. There was no way to answer "Yes, Sir," "No, Sir," or "No excuse, Sir." I tested the waters with "Reading the Bulletin Board, Sir."

"I can see that, Smart Ass. What are you doing between now and Chapel formation?"

"Ah, nothing, Sir."

"Good, we lost Brown last night and he was mail carrier. There is a bunch of letters left over from last night. Go to the Orderly Room, pick up the mail sack and deliver the mail!"

"Yes, Sir" *Wonder what happened to Tim Brown? Seemed like he was doing well. Not in trouble. Must have been yesterday's day from hell.*

"Yeah, Tim left along with four others; two each from 1st and 2nd Squadrons," Terry Cloud told me. "Tim got a 'Dear John' yesterday from his high school sweetheart. On top of Friday's physical bash and Saturday's inspections, he went to the BX and called home. His girl said if he came home everything'd be fine. His folks said they'd pay for college. Tim decided to hit the road. When he got to his room, Lt. Hansen, the duty ATO was waiting. Tim looked at him and said, 'Don't bother with the Form 10, I'm outa' here.'"

"How the hell do you know so much about the story?"

"Well, Tim and I were good friends from intramurals. After taps he came by and gave me the whole story. Too bad, he would have made a good cadet and officer."

"What do you know about the other four?"

"Brad Johnson went to the clinic after our swim meet and said he had been having migraine headaches, bright flashing lights and all. They're going to keep him in the clinic this week. If he insists he's having the migraines, he's gone. I think the other three just said 'stuff it' or something like that. Not the life for them."

"Damn, Terry, where do you get all your information?"

"I told you my friend Cindy in the Com's Shop hears everything. We talk a lot."

"I'm not even going to ask how. Thanks for the scoop. I'll let the others know."

***

Mr. Boyd, the Choir Director was in a good mood. We quickly ran through the three hymns of the morning: *Come, Ye Thankful People, Come; Thanks Be to Thee;* and *Now Thank We All Our God.* Mr. Boyd was pleased, which meant we got to run through the three hymns again. If Mr. Boyd were unhappy with a piece, we would spend a lot of time on that piece.

Things went so well that with the time left, Mr. Boyd started to teach us *The Air Force Hymn*, a song we would sing at every cadet Sunday service.

Chaplin Bennett also was on a roll. As if talking directly to me, he began: "I know you are feeling extremely exhausted right now. You are probably discouraged and, perhaps, even thinking of quitting. Put that out of your mind. The fact you have lasted this long means you have the necessary qualities to complete the program. Self-discipline and motivation are the only two characteristics you need to succeed at this point."

Using the story of Daniel in the Lions' Den, he continued talking about perseverance and the fact your faith can bring you through the most adverse situations.

Dear God, I prayed quietly to myself. *If this is to be my destiny, please give me the strength, the courage, and the ability to complete this program.*

Between Chaplin Bennett's uplifting sermon and the Air Force song played as the postlude, I walked out of the chapel with a spring in my step. I didn't ask for an appointment with Chaplin Bennett and my thoughts of resigning were dissipating like afternoon cumulus clouds. The bright Denver morning sun seemed to be shinning just on me.

***

 # United States Air Force Academy
Sunday, July 28, 1957 2030 hours

Dear Folks,

What a beautiful day today. The sun was out, no thunderstorms. It even cooled down a little. After a great lunch, I came back to the room and thought hard about being here and about leaving.

You probably received my last letter. Just disregard. I got some sleep and had two great Sunday meals. I really enjoyed singing in the choir and the Chaplain gave a great sermon. I thought he was talking directly to me. The sermon was about determination and perseverance.

As Butch says, it is really something to be here. We are only the third class. It is going to be special. The benefits are great, it's just we are having a hard time seeing that far ahead when every day is a challenge just to get through the day. Flying, field trips, and great social events - with real female dates—are carrots that will make being beat with a stick worthwhile. And, of course, the curriculum is one of the best in the country. And we get paid on top of everything else.

Being one of only 20 from California, I guess I have to keep up the good name of the State. And, of course, being the first appointee from good old Grant High, I guess I should give it a go.

Well I have some shoe polishing and studying to do. We have bayonet training again tomorrow and bad boot shines are always good for at least one extra mile lap. Also, we have a mandatory movie after dinner: *The Air Force Story*. You have to pay attention because ATOs always have movie questions on Monday.

Say hello to everyone. Write. Letters are a life saver. Send stamps and boodle.

God Bless
Your loving son,
Don

Chapter 14

You have won an enviable opportunity, but the competition is not over . . .
This, your Fourth Class Year, is your tryout.
. . . Contrails

Monday, August 5, 1957, Week Four

"Sir, there are five minutes until breakfast formation. The uniform is fatigues, ball cap, and boots. Five minutes, Sir." On my first try as minute caller, I mustered my best command voice. Lt. Tatum, late for the reveille formation, didn't have a chance to provide Monday morning instruction. Unfortunately, that was about to change.

"Mister Davis," Tatum said in an unusually quiet voice, "how are we this morning?"

"Very fine, Sir."

"Have we forgotten anything this morning?" he almost whispered.

Ah, shit. Now what? I thought. I mentally checked my uniform and decided it was in good shape, including a first class shine on my boots. The fire and rewax treatment had worked. "No, Sir," I said smartly.

"Dumbsquat. Don't you ever read the Bulletin Board?"

"Yes, Sir," I replied.

"About . . . face. Two steps forward . . . march. Halt! Left . . . face."

I stared at the Bulletin Board. A new memo read: To New Cadet Minute Callers: As of Monday, August 5, 1957, the Minute Caller will include the following in their call:

1. Days until Christmas Leave/Christmas
2. Days until graduation of the class of 1959
3. Days until graduation of the class of 1960
4. Days until graduation of the class of 1961
5. Days until Recognition of the Class of 1961
6. The Officer in Charge
7. The Squadron Duty Officer of the Day (for your squadron)
8. The Movie at the Cadet Theater
9. The Movie at the Base Theater

These items will be in addition to the normal uniform call.

The memo was signed by Lt. Gordon Smith, Adjutant, Air Force Cadet Wing.

"Now, Mister Davis. This morning you may face the Bulletin Board. However, You'll give all of the required information from memory at the noon formation. **Is that clear!"**

"**Yes, Sir.**" *Thank God for classmates,* I thought. Someone had written all of the required information on the memo. **Sir, there are three minutes until breakfast formation. The uniform of the day is fatigues, ball caps, and boots. There are 145 days until Christmas Leave, 149 days until Christmas. There are 680 days until the graduation of the class of 1959, 1,046 days until the graduation of the class of 1960, and 1, 417 days until the graduation of the class of 1961. The Officer in Charge is Major Bartholf. The Squadron Duty Officer is Lt. Prince. The Movie at the Cadet Theater is** *Untamed Youth* **with Mamie Van Doran. The Movie at the Base Theater is** *The Brothers Rico* **with Richard Conte.**"

"Well, Do Willie, forget anything?" Tatum said in a voice I could barely hear.

My mind raced through the list . . . *Ah, shit, I forgot Recognition Day! . . . ah! . . .* **Sir, there are 304 days until Recognition Day for the Class of 1961!**

Tatum smirked, turned, and strode away. I noticed at Tatum's side a short, medium build cadet with Third Class shoulder boards that had no rank. I called two minutes.

***

"Well, Smack, what took you so long to get in formation? The short, khaki uniformed Cadet Third Classman, who had been with Tatum, was in my face. The blue name tag, ironically, read: Short.

"Sir, I was minute caller and . . .

"**What's the right answer, Do Willie?**

"**No excuse, Sir.**" The bell for first call for breakfast rang over the loudspeaker.

"Well, hit it for 10 and see if that improves your memory."

Crap, we haven't been doing push-ups for such trivia for at least two weeks. These guys are going to be jerks. "Yes, Sir," I said, dropping to the pavement. I easily did the 10 push-ups and popped back up with a hint of a smirk on my face. The Third Classman was showing a slight paunch courtesy of beers consumed on leave.

"Wise ass, huh?" Short said. "Hit it for 10 more."

As I came to attention this time, still not breaking a sweat, I said to Short. "Sir, may I make a request?"

"Yeah, what is it, Smack?"

"Sir, may I challenge Cadet Third Class Short to a push-up contest?"

" Whaaa . . . Oh, so you think you can outdo me? Well, we shall see. You can drive around to my room tonight and we will have a few contests."

Oh, shit, I thought. *If it's just he and I in his room, I'll have hell to pay.*

"Oh, I think the contest should be right now, Cadet Short," said Lt. Payne, who had been watching the episode develop. "I'll do the counting. The push-up only counts if you go all the way down and all the way up again. Tell you what, Short, if Davis wins, you leave him alone for the rest of your assignment with us. If you win, Davis will drive around to your room tonight for a special inspection. That okay with you, Short?"

"Ah, Yes, Sir. That'll be fine." A bead of perspiration appeared on Short's forehead.

I stepped out in front of the flight and lined up beside Short.

"Ready! Assume the position", said Payne. He began count as Short and I began push-ups. "One . . . two . . . three . . . 45 . . . 46"

I was breathing regularly and had a good rhythm going. I glanced sideways at Short. He was beginning to breathe hard and had slowed down his upward thrust. "Come on, Short," Payne said, "keep up with the pace . . . 51 . . . 52 . . ."

I could see the sweat beginning to form under Short's armpits. *Hell, if nothing else, I ruined a set of his khakis. He's going to have to change. Ha!*

"Sixty-five . . . 70 . . . is that it, Short?" C3C Short, puffing heavily, hesitated on the upward movement. He strained to reach the top, then collapsed. Already at the top of my push-up, I completed another one before getting to my feet. I was breathing steadily, with perspiration under my arms. Since I was wearing fatigues, I wouldn't have to change – especially since our next class was bayonet training.

Payne looked at Short, who was red-faced and trying to catch his breath. "Well, Cadet Short, I'll have to declare New Cadet Davis the winner. Okay, Short, post for breakfast and remember the bargain."

Lt. Payne turned toward the flight. Tatum was nowhere in sight. Lt Payne assumed the Flight Commander Position. **"Flight . . . Atten . . . shun,"** He called out. Doing a smart about face, He called to the Squadron Commander: **"C Flight all present and accounted for, Sir."**

As we started to march, a voice from the back rang out, **"Non illegitmus caborumdum."**

***

A Commander's Time was scheduled after Monday's bayonet training. Butch and I had just finished our showers and were getting ready to put on khakis when Art Kerr rapped sharply on the door. Butch and I slammed to attention.

"Carry on," said Art, bouncing into the room with a smirk on his face and the mail bag.

"You, Fink. You're supposed to call out 'mail call;' not blow in like an ATO."

"You guys are too uptight. Davis, there's a letter from your folks; one from another relative; and, "ooh, la, la", a perfumed letter from some Sacramento dame named Nancy. Butch, you have a letter from your folks and two from Sweet Sue, sorry, no perfume."

"All right, wise guy," I said, "and I suppose the rest of the bag's for you."

"Well, not all, just most," Art said with a sly smile.

"So, what's happening, mailman?" asked Butch.

"Well, I heard in the orderly room that 1st and 2nd Squadrons lost two more guys each. After Friday, they said 'screw it' and bailed with the other five we lost."

"Do you know who they are? Did they all SIE[44]?"

"The names I heard were Farrow, Huffman, Mooney, and Purdue. Word is they all SIEed. They thought it was too hard. Friday was the last straw, just too much. Frankly, I enjoyed the swimming. That was great!

"Get out of here, Kerr," Butch, said making an obscene gesture.

***

Monday, Tuesday, and Wednesday were identical. Breakfast, Bayonet Training, Lunch, Protocol (learning the other services: ranks, customs, missions), Weapons Training (loading munitions, servicing oxygen systems, and filling out/reading aircraft maintenance forms) and competitive sports preparations. Then dinner, more Commanders Times, and shower formations. Whether numb from the training or just acclimated to the grueling schedule, no one seemed too affected by any part of the program.

***

Wednesday afternoon from after lunch until 1630 was devoted to intramural contests. We had a soccer match with a team from 1st Squadron. First Squadron had all the big guys. An advantage in American football, size wasn't so formidable in European football -- soccer. Ron Mueller stole the ball from Tom Walker and dribbled the ball toward 1st Squadron's goal.

"**Over here, over here!**" Jack Tyler yelled as he broke open in the middle of the field.

Mueller kicked the ball on a trajectory two feet in front of Jack. Jack trapped the ball, swept around Charlie Thomas, and booted the ball into the upper right-hand corner of the goal. Jack raised both his hands, fell to his knees, and shouted: "**Goal, Goal, GOAL!!!!**"

Reid Schaffner set up a similar run for Jack in the second half. Jack put that one in the upper left-hand corner of the goal and we had a 2 to 0 win, our sixth of the series.

Captain Mallet, our AOC, bragged at Thursday's Squadron meeting that 3d Squadron had won 17 of the 20 games in intramurals in the last three weeks. Winning

---

[44] SIE: Self-initiated elimination. Academics would be the big eliminator later in the year, but SIEs took the biggest toll during summer training.

games garnered Superintendent's Honor Squadron points; but weren't good enough for "at ease" meals. Wins did, however, provide slack in the amount of Fourth Class Knowledge asked at meals.

***

Thursday morning, after bayonet training, C Flight members returned to the rooms to deposit our rifles and helmets. We then went directly to the Blue Beetle Bus. Box lunches were on board. The typical box lunch, we discovered, contained a piece of chicken, a hardboiled egg, a ham and cheese sandwich, a turkey sandwich, potato chips, two chocolate chip cookies, mustard and mayonnaise packs and two cartons of milk.

The lunch was a veritable feast for a New Cadet. And even better, the 25 minute drive to the flight line allowed leisurely pace for eating the meal. The chatter usually present on such trips was limited as we all "chowed down."

Art Kerr sat next to me on the bus. "Hey, Davis what the hell was it with the Third Classman who chewed you out? Why was he the only one we've seen so far? That was great, though, you really made him look like an ass."

"Yeah, but Lt. Payne saved me. Short wanted to do the contest in his room. That would have been a disaster. Lt. Payne came to my side later and said: 'Good show. That was Cadet Peter Short. He was in my Summer Training Detail last year. Kind of surprised he's still here. He has a bad attitude. After the semester ended, he had two turnout exams,[45] so two weeks of study and then the exams. He busted one of the exams and was washed back to the Class of Sixty. He missed his class field trip; went on leave. When he came back, the Commandant's staff assigned him to us. He'll be with the detail until Third Class summer academics in two weeks. Don't sweat it, though. I'll make sure he keeps his word.'"

***

"Gentlemen," began Master Sergeant Little, "Pay close attention. We'll be working with JP-4 fuel, liquid oxygen, and live rockets and bombs. Safety is paramount. Pay strict attention to the checklists. First element is with me. TSgt. Brown will take second element. SSgt. Moore will take third element. Each of you will complete at least one of the assigned tasks.

---

[45] Cadets with less than a 70% average at the end of a course were offered a "turn-out" exam. After a week of study, including extra instruction, they took the retest. If they passed, they got a 70 for the course and rejoined their class. If they failed only one course, they could be "turned back" to the class behind them. If they failed two or more courses and turn-out exams, they were dismissed.

You know Sgt. Brown and me from classes. Sgt. Moore is an armament specialist and has five years in the field. He came from Hamilton Air Force Base in California on F-102s before he joined us at Lowry.

This afternoon, we have 3 F-86Fs to fuel and load with rockets. We also have an F-84F to fuel and load with bombs. You will all get a chance to have hands-on instruction and practice on the aircraft. Any questions?"

"Yes, Sir," said Art Kerr. "Do we need gloves?"

"Good question, Mister Kerr. When you are working with fuel and liquid oxygen, you need gloves. With liquid oxygen, you will also need protective aprons and eye shields. We'll have them available as required. Any other questions? No . . . good. Let's get going. Divide up by elements and follow your instructor."

As we approached the first F-86 on the line, Sgt. Little turned and asked, "What is the first thing we do before we service an aircraft?"

Art's hand shot up, "Check the maintenance record."

"That's right Cadet Kerr. In the Air Force it's the AF Form 781. Both maintenance and flight personnel check the 781 to determine aircraft status, especially the systems you will be working on." Sgt. Brown gingerly jumped up on the swept wing of the aircraft and retrieved the Form 781. "Who can tell me what a red cross means in the form?"

Denny Dillon and Art both thrust their hands in the air.

"Cadet Dillon, what does the Red X mean?"

"The Red X means that the aircraft is not safe to fly until whatever condition the X represents is cleared."

"That's correct, Mr. Dillon. How did you know that?"

"I was with the Guard for two years, Master Sergeant, working on flight line maintenance."

"Great. Then you'll be able to help classmates with procedures. There are two other red symbols you should know: the Red Dash means an inspection is due or some other action is required; a Red Diagonal means there is a maintenance discrepancy, but it will permit flight before it is corrected. If an aircraft has two radios, for instance, it may only require one for flight. That would create a red diagonal in the 781. Any questions, now?

We're lucky today. None of the aircraft have Red Xs or Red Dashes. By the way, Kerr, how do you know about the maintenance system?"

"Well, Master Sergeant, my father is in Coast Guard flight operations. He took me along many times to learn more about his work. He also gave me a few flying lessons, so I understand the concept of Red Xs and maintenance requirements."

"Great, let's get with it. These three aircraft have a time over target on the Buckley Range in three hours and twenty minutes, so we have to service and arm them properly for their mission. The F84 has a later range time, so we'll work the F-86s first. Mr. Kellerman, grab that oxygen cart, an apron, a shield, and a pair of gloves."

In two and half hours, we serviced all four aircraft. The weather was a sunny, pleasant 75 degrees. Wrestling with the carts and ammunition and the uncertainty of demanding, unfamiliar, and potentially dangerous tasks brought out the familiar uniform sweat bands.

The F-86 pilots completed their pre-flights and jumped in their respective aircraft. Sgt. Little had requested a pilot session with us, but servicing their aircraft took longer than planned. Given the advancing shadows, the pilots completed their preliminary tasks quickly and, with the assistance of Sgts. Little, Brown, and Moore, started their engines, saluted their ground team, and taxied toward runway 18.[46]

Standing in the shadow of hanger 25, we watched the startup operations with pride. The three F-86 Super Sabres took the runway together and did a three ship formation take-off.

Thirty minutes later, we watched the F-84 taxi onto the runway and apply full throttle. The Thunderjet lumbered down the runway, using at least a thousand feet more runway than the Sabres to get airborne. The roar of engines and the smell of JP4[47] drifted toward us with each takeoff.

As the F-84 reached a thousand feet above the 5,180 foot runway, the aircraft turned on an easterly heading toward the Buckley Bombing Range. We cheered as the F-84 made its climbing turn to the left. It was great to have even a small sense of our future lives.

The bus was relatively quiet on the return to the barracks, but the sense of motivation and introspection about our careers was reflected in the face of everyone on the bus.

***

On Friday, in a starched, ironed set of fatigues, Lt. Yeager stood ramrod straight in front of the formation. "Okay Wimps. High Port and two laps. Then, line up on the dummies."

---

[46] Runways are designated by compass direction. Runway 18 would face 180 degrees or south. Aircraft take off and land on runways most aligned with the prevailing wind. The wind this day was 170 degrees at eight knots.

[47] JP-4 was the jet fuel designation used to prescribe the type of fuel required for each aircraft.

Following rifle calisthenics, we stood in front of the dummies, our "enemy" for the past two weeks. We did four repetitions of "**Ready . . . Thrust,**" viciously attacking the dummies.

At the end of the 30 minute drill, Lt. Yeager called out. "Men, you will find a pile of lacrosse helmets and long, pogo sticks to your left. The first two in each line, find a helmet that fits and grab a stick.

Your limp Flight Commander is afraid you're going to damage the beautiful finishes on your M1s. Guess he thinks they're a display toy and not a killing weapon. So, here's what we'll do. You'll learn to parry and thrust using the sticks. Person nearest the dummy will thrust with the stick – SO," Yeager said, thrusting the four foot, six inch round stick as if it were a bayonetted rifle.

"First, though, we'll learn to stack rifles. If you're at a forward base and have to stand perimeter defense, this maneuver may come in handy." Yeager showed us how to stack rifles and, in the interest of time, helped put our rifles in conical shaped stacks.

After we finished stacking the rifles, Lt. Yeager said, "Mister Miller, step out here." Don was in the first row and had his helmet on. He stepped forward and faced Lt. Yeager. "I want you to thrust forward as if you were attacking the dummy. I will parry your thrust and counter attack. Normally, the counter thrust is aimed at the chest or head. You will parry and lightly, I said lightly, tap your opponent on the head. **Is that clear!!!**"

A robust, "**YES, SIR**" rang out.

"All right, Mr. Miller, are you ready?"

"**YES, SIR,**" Don replied defiantly.

Don thrust his stick at Lt. Yeager's unhelmeted head. Yeager easily parried the thrust with an almost imperceptible wrist movement. He then tapped Don's helmet a little more than slightly. Don shook his head, turned and faced Yeager, and performed a mock rifle salute with his stick. Yeager smiled, again almost imperceptibly.

We completed six repetitions of the drill. There was only one near casualty. Jeff Winters was facing Jim Watts. When Jeff thrust, Jim made the mistake of parrying downward instead of sideways. Jeff's errant stick struck Jim in the groin. Jim fell backward and doubled up. We were all suddenly aware of the jock strap and cup requirement. Jim groaned once, then stood up and got back in line, obviously not seriously injured. Yeager said nothing, but again the mystic hint of a smile crossed his face.

When we finished the routine, Lt. Yeager took us to the practice field. "Listen up," he said quietly. "Let's see what you've got. I want six laps at high port. **High Port . . . GO!**"

In flight formation, we began chanting: "**C Flight, C Flight, C Flight …**"

No one broke stride, and even though Jeff was in front, no one fell out. We finished the run and halted smartly in front of Lt. Yeager.

"Gentlemen," he began, "I had serious doubts several of you would make it through. I'm pleased you've proven me wrong. Now, what is the most important lesson you have learned in this course?"

We sang out in unison: **"LEAVE NO MAN BEHIND!"**

"That is absolutely right. Never forget it. It'll serve you well in the next four years, and later when you engage in the honorable profession of combat in defense of your country. Mr. Winters, take charge. **Non illegitmus caborumdum. Dismissed."**

The flight formed on Jeff. **"C Flight** . . . **Atten . . shun. Right** . . . **Face. Fooorward** . . . **March. DOUBLE-TIME . . . MARCH!"**

From the back of the flight came a melodious voice singing: **"Nellie wore a blue dress, it was very thin . . ."**

Chapter 15

The qualities [of character and discipline] must be so deeply installed within
the individual that no stress or strain will erase them from his personality.
—Fourth Class Customs

Sunday, August 11, 1957, Week Five

"Damn," Butch said. "I thought the ATOs were tough. They look like summer camp counselors compared to these jerk upperclassmen. We were sure we'd won today's parade, but were still smarting from the vicious corrections laid on by the assigned Second Classmen.

"Did you see Hertz? I thought he was going to bust Cadet Lieutenant Corey Green in the chops," Butch said. "Did you hear Green? 'Get that chin in, Mister. Suck up that gut. Reach for Colorado. My little five year-old brother has better posture.' We haven't had that much crap since day one. They're like lions that haven't been fed for a week; we're the raw meat."

"Yeah, if it weren't for the ATOs yanking on the upperclassmen's leashes every once in a while, I think the whole class would SIE. These guys are every bit as miserable as our friends, Lt. Jackson and C3C Short."

"Hey, Short is your friend, not mine. I didn't embarrass his ass in front of the 'New Cadets.' I'm afraid you're going to have bad blood with that dude for some time to come."

"Well, at least they can't get to us tonight. After dinner, we have Commander's Time and show privileges. I think I'll join you tonight. *Gunfight at the O.K. Corral* sounds interesting. I like Burt Lancaster. Rhonda Fleming's not hard on the eyes either. Too bad they didn't give us escort privileges."

"Yeah, and somebody to escort."

"Whoa, what's that? What about Sweet Sue? I haven't heard you screaming when you get Sue's letters, so I guess you're still good."

"Oh, I don't know. She has stopped talking about the parties, but there's something missing. Maybe it's just the damn program. I'll be glad when summer's over."

***

Monday was, Yogi Berra would say, *Deja vu* all over again, recalling the worst aspects of that first morning. The ATOs conducted reveille formation and took us to breakfast. An unpleasant surprise waited at the ramp. Two Second Class Cadets sat next to the ATO Table Commandant. Extra tables had been formed.

"Gentlemen, this is Cadet Captain James O'Rourke and this is Cadet Major Len Tillman. Cadet O'Rourke and Cadet Tillman, starting on my left, these are New Cadets, Dickson, Rieselman, Wildman, Green, Davis, Hertz, and Smith. Seats, Gentlemen."

As we sat, Cadet Tillman, in a normal voice, said, "Good morning, New Cadets. We are going to spend a lot of time together. So, I'd like to get to know you better. Starting with Mr. Smith, go around the table, repeat your name, and state your home state."

"Ah, Cadet Tillman, my name . . . "

"New Cadet Smith," interrupted Tillman, "let's get this started properly. You should begin with 'Cadet Major Tillman' or 'Sir.' Now, let's try it again."

Oh, crap, I thought. *Are we going to go through the Mickey Mouse all over again? So far the upperclassmen all seem like jerks.* I shot a quick, unauthorized glance at Lt. Tatum who was smirking slightly, but not missing a beat with his breakfast.

"Mister, Davis, eyes front," bellowed Cadet Captain O'Rourke.

Unnerved by O'Rourke's outburst, Smith stuttered: "Ah . . . Ah . . . Sir, Mm . . mmm . . . my Name is Cadet Ken Smith. I am from Cleveland, Ohio."

"Well, Cadet Smith, I didn't know they let stutterers in, but I'm glad to know you have been recognized. Is Ken your full name?

Damn, this is going to be a long breakfast; short on food. Thinking pancakes would be the most filling and long lasting, I tried to cut the stack of pancakes with my fork and get down several bites before the inquisition reached me.

"Mister Davis!" *Oh shit. I've already made another upperclassman friend.* I turned to look at Cadet Captain O'Rourke. He was about six foot two, had broad shoulders, red hair, and a crew cut. He looked like an Irish GI Joe. "Yes, Sir," I replied, half choking on the pancake.

"Mister Davis! *Damn, he's a yeller.* **Mister Davis, haven't we been taught the proper way to eat is to cut our food into bite size pieces and then place the bite in our mouth?"**

O'Rourke's condescending attitude and irritating high pitched voice hacked me. **"Yes, Sir!** I replied, hoping a forceful response would make this ATO wanabe back off.

I saw Tatum nudge O'Rourke in the ribs. O'Rourke looked mildly confused, then frowned slightly as he deciphered the message. "Well . . .er . . . ah . . . eat, Mister Davis, but I will be watching you."

Looking a little peeved at his classmate's interruption, Cadet Major Tillman said, "All right, Mister Smith, let's have it again."

"Sir, my name is New Cadet Kenneth Smith. My hometown is Cleveland, Ohio."

"You have no middle name?"

"Nooo, Sir."

"Eat!"

Without being asked, Hertz jumped in: "Sir, My Name is Robert Louis Hertz. My hometown is Baker, Oregon." The two upperclassmen appeared to be busy eating.

"**That's great, Mister Hertz,**" blasted Cadet Captain O'Rourke, "**Now, let's have the fourth verse of the Star Spangled Banner.**"

We all spontaneously put down our utensils and sat at attention. As Hertz jumped up and began to sing loudly: '*Oh! thus be it ever, when freemen shall stand Between their loved home and the war's desolation! . .*'" the rest of us rose and stood at attention. Lt. Tatum had a pained expression on his face. Cadet Tillman looked confused.

Doolies at the tables on either side of our table also stood at attention. All did an about face and directed themselves toward Hertz. The Table Commandants at those tables snickered.

"All right Hertz. **Sit down,**" commanded Tatum. All of you eat. O'Rourke, you and Tillman, finish your breakfast and post."

***

After the breakfast break, 3d Squadron was to form in fatigues, helmets, and backpacks on the quad. I had trouble finding a vacant stall. At the last minute before assembly, I was running down the hall, holding my helmet with one hand and buttoning my fatigue pants with the other. Just as the bell sounded, I skidded into formation. Standing in front of me was my new Irish upperclassman friend.

"Glad to see you made it, Davis. I'd love to give you obstacle course instruction, but unfortunately I have a class. I'll be sure to look you up at shower formation." With that O'Rourke turned and broke into a trot to join his classmates headed for the academic building.

"**Non-illegitamus-caborundum!**" rang out from the rear ranks.

"Gentlemen, we're going to work on the obstacle course all week," began Lt. Payne. "At week's end, you'll be timed and graded. Maximum time allowed is eight minutes." Lt. Payne was the Officer in Charge (OIC) of the obstacle course program; Lt. Boyce his assistant. "I'll walk you through the course, pointing out techniques to help you complete each obstacle."

Not nearly as arduous as bayonet training, the obstacle course presented a challenge nonetheless. On the first run, I had trouble leaping over the telephone poles, fell off the zigzag walk, got stuck under the three feet high barb wire crawl (my backpack got stuck when I arched my back), and could not get over the wall.

We made as many runs as possible to bring our times down. On my second try, I went through in nine minutes, forty-five seconds. *Damn, that's not going to hack it. I'll have to do a hell of a lot better or I'll bust the course.* I struggled all week. My time improved to nine minutes even; still not good enough. I banged my helmet on the wall when I jumped up. The pack also made it difficult to jump, catch hold of the top of the wall, and pull myself up and over.

On Thursday, a classmate from B Flight behind me on the run saw me struggling.

"Say, man," said Hector Javier. "Yo makin' it too hard." After the wall were the poles and a pit, then the course doubled back with the zigzag cross walk right beside the wall.

Hector tickled me with his Puerto Rican accent, but I was very attuned to his advice. If he could do the course at only five foot, seven inches, I could certainly make it. "Escusame! Listen! Just before the wall, toss your helmet and pack to the right. Jump the wall, do the poles and pit. Just before the zigzag, pick up your helmet and pack and finish the course."

"Isn't that cheating?" I asked.

"Nah," replied Hector. "Payne saw me do it and said, 'Very inventive, Hector. I know of no rule against it.'"

The last two days I practiced the Hector method. My times greatly improved.

The upperclassmen sat with us the rest of the week. Thank God, they had to attend classes. The ATOs took a benign view toward us during the meals. Or, at least, Lt. Tatum did.

We had irritating exchanges with Cadet Captain O'Rourke, who insisted on rehashing Fourth Class Knowledge, and Cadet Major Tillman, who practiced just being obnoxious, Lt. Tatum ensured we had enough to eat. He clearly considered the Second Classmen as interlopers. Occasionally he questioned Hertz or me.: "Who is the Prime Minister of England; what military agreement did he make fairly recently and with whom?" he asked me.

***

Friday, after breakfast, 3d Squadron boarded Blue Beetles for the Rifle Range. Lts. Tatum, Payne, and Boyce gave us additional M1 instruction on the correct firing positions. We sensed the ATOs' serious approach to the training and responded accordingly.

We sat in the grandstand seats 35 yards behind the firing line. Lt. Payne explained the course of fire: "As before, the target is at 200 yards. There are 250 points total. A bull's-eye is five points, between the bulls-eye and the next ring is four points, between the two and three rings is three points. There are no points outside the three ring. Any Questions?"

"Yes, Sir," said Ron Mueller standing up. "Is mud part of the course or did you program it just for us?" It had rained early that morning and the range was ankle deep in mud. The firing positions, fortunately, were packed with sawdust.

"Right, Mueller, just for you. But, that does bring up a good point. Be careful with your weapons. Not only is mud in the barrel a mess; it can be dangerous. A blocked barrel can cause the barrel to explode."

Focusing on the target and remembering Lt. Payne's instructions, I shot a 206, ranking me 14 out of 113 New Cadets in the Squadron. My best round was 43 of 45 during rapid fire. Twenty classmates shot over 200. We wouldn't know until evening where we placed against the other two squadrons, in the all-important competition for the Superintendent's trophy.

C Flight finished at 1130 hours. Just then, a 6-by truck pulled up with coolers containing box lunches on ice. "Listen up, Men," ordered Lt. Tatum. "Airman Johnson will distribute lunches to the cadets in the bottom rows. The men in the bottom row will pass the lunches to those above them. You will be at ease. There are latrines and wash basins behind the stands." Tatum gave a whimsical salute, turned, and marched off Napoleon style.

"Hey, Davis," Terry Cloud yelled from the top row. "Come on up."

"Give me a minute, be right up."

I greeted Terry with a handshake. "How've you been?"

"Good, how are you hitting 'em?"

"Well, if we're not talking about baseball, okay; if you are talking about girls; you've got to be kidding."

"What do you hear about the class?"

"Word I have is we lost seven more this week . . ."

"You amaze me. You always have good information?"

"Remember I told you my friend Cindy works in the Commandant's office. She's the daughter of a friend of my mother. I got her telephone number the first three days we were here. I sneak out to the public phone over by the theater. When we can't talk, she sends me notes through the mail disguised as a regular letter . . ."

"Blonde or brunette?"

"Redhead. Anyway, she keeps me posted about guys who bail or get booted. She's a sweetheart. When we get freed up, I'm going to date her.

We lost Jesse Phillips? He fell from the top of the obstacle course wall; dislocated his shoulder and broke some bones. Flight surgeon said six weeks to heal, so Jesse's out.

The Commandant's Board said he could wash back to the Class of 62 and start again."

"Anybody else get medical?"

"Nah, the rest were all SIEs. The two I knew were Burkowitz and Epperson. They're all from 1st and 2d Squadron. Man, the other squadrons must have murderous

ATOs. The washouts all bailed on Saturday or Sunday. I don't really understand. We've finished bayonet training. How much harder can it get?

"Aren't these box lunches great," I said changing the subject. *Damn,* I thought, *Burkowitz and Epperson were supposed to be good guys. Rico was talking about them being on the football team. If they can't make it, how in the hell am I going to last?*

"Yeah, normally I don't like cold fried chicken, but these days the chicken is like manna from heaven. The turkey sandwich is great too. The Twinkies are always a treat. And, look, today they slipped in an apple."

"Of course," I added, "the best part is we get a chance to eat it."

***

"All right you Slackers," Lt. Payne said pleasantly. "Back to some serious business, the M1 Carbine. The range rules are the same. Do not fire until told 'Commence Fire.'

Never point your weapon anywhere but down range. If you have a misfire, hold up your hand and an instructor will assist. You will use the same positions and order of fire as with the Garand. You will find the carbine is easier to handle. Therefore, I expect better scores. Form up in your morning sections."

The afternoon passed quickly. Everyone concentrated on upping their scores. A small thunderstorm delayed shooting for 20 minutes. We had no place to go (the buses were not near) and got wet. Once the Denver sun came out, we began steaming like we were in a giant sauna.

"For those without rain parkas to cover your rifles, keep the barrels pointed down so you don't get moisture in them" Lt Payne advised. The Carbines were issued only for firing. The task of cleaning the weapons fell on our friends, MSgt. Little and TSgt. Brown.

"How'd you do on the carbine?" I asked Terry? I liked Terry, even though his somewhat cocky attitude occasionally got us in trouble with the ATOs. I was sure his attitude would be noticed by upperclassmen. But Terry was also a font of information, something we sought to help expand our tiny world".

"I got a 210 with four bulls-eyes. How about you?"

"Ha! I beat ya'. I had a 215 and five bulls-eyes."

"Smart Ass. How'd the Squadron do, do you know?

"Nah, Lt. Payne said they'd post results on the Bulletin Board tonight."

Returning to quarters was strangely quiet; everyone took a sitting-up nap.

***

Our patience was severely tested until halfway through the evening meal. Practicing his worst imitation of an ATO, Cadet Cpt. O'Rourke went around the table demanding recitation of basic Fourth Class poop. He and Cadet Tillman shouted frequent corrections. Finally, Lt. Tatum said softly to the two upperclassmen, "At ease, Gentlemen." In a somewhat louder voice, he looked at me and asked, "Davis, who is the Prime Minister of Great Britain?"

"Sir," *Okay Classmates, here's my sacrifice, eat up.* "The Queen of England appointed Mr. Harold Macmillan Prime Minister in January to replace Sir Anthony Eden. He . . ."

"Who was the Queen, Davis?" interrupted Lt. Tatum.

"Sir, the Queen was Queen Elizabeth the Second." Noticing Lt. Tatum had given the two Second Classmen a stare down and gone back to eating, I continued. "At the end of January, President Eisenhower invited Macmillan to Bermuda to discuss US . . . ah, United States and British relations, which were strained over the United Kingdom's action in the Suez Canal crisis.

World War Two associates, President Eisenhower and Prime Minister Macmillan met in March. Macmillan would not agree to soften his approach toward Gamal Abdal Nasser, President of Egypt. They did agree the United States could base Thor missiles in Great Britain. The missiles, capable of reaching the Soviet Union, are under joint United States-Anglo control."

"All right, Davis, why do we care about the Suez Canal?"

"Sir, the Suez Canal allows the United States Navy to easily transfer ships between the Mediterranean and the Indian Ocean."

"Where did Eisenhower and Macmillan serve together?

"Sir, they served together in North Africa. "Good, everybody eat."

***

United States Air Force Academy

Sunday, July 28, 1957 2030 hours

Dear Mom and Dad,

Received the newspapers today. It's great to read the hometown news. Keep the Bee coming. It's good to read what's happening at home. I see that Grant is supposed to have a good football team. The sports' writers were surprised when we were second in the Sac-Joaquin Conference last year.

We had the obstacle course Friday. I got over the seven-foot wall and finished in 7 minutes and 44 seconds. I passed.

We wear fatigues with helmet and field pack for the obstacle course. You start with a sprint and jump over a two-foot hurdle. Then you jump up on a zigzag crosswalk; 10 steps later you hit the wall. A classmate showed me a trick to get over the wall. On the other side of the wall you dive for the ground and crawl under a three foot high 20 yard stretch of barbed wire.

You run through a path between two by-fours, jump across a three foot water pit. Next, you run through a maze that zigs and zags. You hit a set of monkey bars where you cross hand over hand. The final obstacle is a series of six telephone poles set two feet apart. You have to roll over them. Finally, you race 20 yards and jump another water pit just before the finish.

By the way, could you send me some 2 cent stamps, I will send postcards to my friends who haven't written. I'll send a card to Mr. Pierson, my Weinstock-Lubin boss, He was a nice guy, even if he made Walt and me scrub those humongous pots. Don't know how food tasted so good, the cook always seemed to burn the bottom of the pots. Guess that job and digging ditches as a laborer convinced me I should continue in school to get a better job.

Church is a good break from the New Cadet routine. Think I mentioned I am singing in the Protestant Choir. We only get to practice an hour before the service, but we have some good voices and we don't sound too bad. Mr. Boyd, the Music Director, is one of the few who doesn't scream at us. He's pretty demanding in getting the music right, however.

Have to close and get on my shoes. My nemesis, Lt. Jackson was loitering around our flight yesterday. I think he has it in for Butch and me. He comes around every so often and tries to find something wrong. I don't think Lt. Payne thinks too much of Lt. Jackson. Lt. Payne looks after us when Jackson is around.

God Bless
Your loving son,
Don

Chapter 16
Dear John . . ." A Letter from Home

Sunday,18 August1957, Week Six

"This place really sucks," bellowed Butch, slamming the door.

"What's the matter, Butch?" I asked, throwing the Sacramento Bee on my desk and walking over to his side.

Butch hurled himself at his bed and buried his face in his pillow. "This place sucks," he repeated. "I want to go home."

It was Monday evening; the twilight sun filtering through the window provided just enough light so I could see Butch sobbing softly into his pillow. In his left hand was a crumpled letter, most certainly from Sue, his girl back home.

When we got back to the room, the mail was on our beds. Butch grabbed his and headed for the latrine for private reading time.

"What's up," I said in my most sympathetic voice. "Last time, it was you telling me why I couldn't go home."

It's Sue," Butch said, holding the crumbled letter. "She sent me a Dear John. She says Lester Moore asked her to go steady and she said 'yes.' She still likes me a lot and wishes I were there, but it's too hard to be without company at parties. She wants to be friends. Hopes we can see each other when I come home next summer . . . I hate this place."

"Nah, Butch, you don't hate this place. If you did, you'd been gone before now. I'm sure Sue is a fine girl, but she's what, seventeen?"

"Yeah, she's like you; a September birthday. She'll be eighteen next month."

"She's young. She left the door open. Let's see the letter."

"Dear Butch," the letter began. "I've been sitting on the back porch swing thinking of you. Remember in the spring when we went to the State Fair and you won me a Kewpie Doll? She was so cute with her red dress and googlie eyes. I know the Carnie guy didn't think you could ring the bell, but I knew you could . . . and did!

"I loved going to the creek with you; it's something I will never forget . . ."

"Down by the creek?" I said.

"Never mind, jerk!" Butch answered.

"Butch, I have such sweet memories of you," the letter continued. "But, it has been so lonesome without you. I was invited to a party in July by Lester. He was so much fun. We went out several times. But, I was faithful to you. It's hard being alone; not having someone to go with on double dates.

"Anyway, he and I are both going to the University of Kentucky. Lester asked me to go steady. I said 'Yes.' As much as I miss you, I don't feel the same way as when you left. I really like Lester and obviously will see him at school. I don't want to hurt your feelings, but I don't think it's fair for you to have a commitment to me and not see other girls. So, I'm sending your ring back. I'd appreciate it if you'd send me my graduation picture. I'll give you your letter sweater this summer when I see you.

"Please write when you find time." The letter was signed: 'Fondly, Sue.'"

"Look, Butch," I said. "It's better this way. You won't have to sit here worrying what Sue is doing. You can concentrate on the program and, later, academics. Not only that, you'll have one less letter to write."

"Screw you, Davis!" Butch said sitting up on the bed and glowering at me.

"Butch, this is a great letter. Bet you can win ice cream on the 'Dear John' Board."

"What the hell is that?"

"Haven't you seen the Dear Johns on the Bulletin Board? When somebody gets a Dear John, they post it. Hertz has a committee that judges the letters at the end of the week. The winner gets a free pint of ice cream. What do you say?"

"Nah . . ."

"Come on, it'll help you get over Sue."

"Okay, but you take it down. I don't think I could put it up."

***

By Tuesday evening Butch was over the worst of his depression, aided by upperclassmen harassment. On Tuesday, Cadet Tillman assigned Butch a talk on the falcon and why the Class of 59 had chosen it as the mascot. I stole an illegal glance and saw a smirk on Lt. Tatum's face. Butch's reports were due for Wednesday's breakfast.

Tuesday evening I could tell Butch was in a really bad mood. Cadet O'Rourke and Cadet Tillman were all over him at dinner. He didn't know the movie at the base theater – like it matters to New Cadets. He managed some potatoes; the fried chicken went untouched. Lt. Tatum didn't control the upperclassmen.

***

"You S.O.B.," Butch screeched. "**You Son of a Bitch**," he repeated more emphatically.

I thought he was mad because I almost had a full meal while the upperclassmen were all over him. *C'est la guerre!* I thought.

"What the hell's the matter with you?" I asked, noticing the infamous crumpled Dear John letter in his left hand. Fortunately, we had two hours of Commander's Time. I had a feeling it was going to take the whole time to straighten things out between us.

"Oh, yeah, I forgot to tell you; in addition to being judged by the "panel," classmates are invited to critique the letter's style and content.

"Geeze, Butch, it's part of the healing process! I've even seen ATOs adding comments."

"Yeah, well, now everybody in the whole damn Squadron will be laughing at me. I even saw guys from the other flights reading it and putting comments on it."

"Butch, they won't be laughing at you unless you tell them it's you. That's why you cross out your name and your girl's. Even the committee doesn't know it's you. I had to submit the letter because the Dear John isn't supposed to submit it."

"Yeah, crap, like they won't know."

"Calm down, let me see the comments." I scanned the letter, trying hard not to smirk, snicker, or outright laugh. The long knives had done a good job. I read through the various comments:

- Dear "John" was filled in; "Let's do this right!"
- . . . sitting on the swing . . . "Looks like she wants to swing with someone else." Bet she's a real swinger, apparently not you.
- Remember in the spring . . . "Looks like your spring has sprung." "Too bad she had to 'spring' this on you; you're the one who took the 'fall.'" "Hope you don't lose the spring in your step . . . "left, right, left!"
- ". . . you won a Kewpie Doll . . . You should have kept the Kewpie Doll, at least you'd have a girl. Kewpie Dolls are more faithful than the real thing."
- . . . with her red dress and googlie eyes . . . "Wow, red dress; that's hot! 'Googlie eyes' is that anything like Doolie Eyes?" "Guess she gave you 'Cage those eyes, mister'."
- . . . I know the Carnie guy didn't think you could ring the bell . . . "Wow, you actually rang the bell? Should'a rung her bell -- you wouldn't have a Dear John." "Does Lt. Yeager know you can ring the bell?" "Ringing bells is for Annapolis crabs . . . maybe that's what rings her bell."
- . . . going to the creek with you . . . "Oh my now she thinks you are all wet." "Let's hope spring showers don't bring fall flowers . . . you'll get another letter." "Up a creek without a paddle or your girl; how sad!"
- . . . John, I have such sweet memories of you, but . . . "With Dear Johns, you always get it in the 'but.'" "'Memories,' isn't that a song? Of course, not one she is singing now."
- . . . it has been very lonesome without you . . . "Sorry, classmate, it doesn't sound like she has been very lonesome." "'Lonesome,' is that a synonym for 'Damn, John, I'm having a really great time without you'?"

- . . . "I was invited to a party in July by Lester. He was so much fun . . . "Ah, Lester the Jester is in the king's court." "Parties are made for remembering the guy you are pinned to . . ." "Lester made her laugh, or, just made her . . . hmm!"
- . . . We went out several times, but I was faithful to you . . ." "There's that 'but' again." "Like a Catholic Sister, she was having "nun" of that she says" "Dogs are faithful, girls . . .?"
- . . . It's hard being alone and not being able to even go on double dates . . . "'Hard' is Doolie summer. Of course, you're never alone." "A DOUBLE date?"
- . . . Lester asked me to go steady and I said 'Yes.'. . . "Well, it wasn't a subtle kiss off; Any questions?" "Steady as she goes; there's that Navy talk again."
- . . . . I don't want to hurt your feelings, but. . . . "Taking it in the 'but' again." "On the other hand, what the hell, there's Lester."
- . . . As much as I miss you, I don't feel the same way as when you left. "It's okay, Sweetheart, I don't feel the same as when I left either."
- . . . I don't think it's fair if you have a commitment to me and don't see other girls . . . "Especially since I have Lester to pester me!" "I presume you informed her we only 'see,' girls, we don't get to touch."
- . . . I'm sending your ring back. I'd appreciate it if you'd send me my graduation picture. I'll give you back your letter sweater this summer when I see you. . . . "You gave her your high school ring? Wow, what class!" "You let her have your letter sweater, are you crazy?" "Ahhh, you have to send her picture back. Guess you will have to display a Playboy pinup for SAMIs." "Yeah, or a picture of your dog."
- . . . Please write when you find time, Fondly . . . "Old Faithful" . . . "If you find time, I have some shoes you could help with." "Ah, yes, please write. I shall treasure your letters." 'Fondly,' rather than fondled."

Two grades, one for style; one for content, at the bottom of the letter read: Style: B; Content: B+. Both were the highest grades on the board. I assumed Butch's letter would win.

"Look, Butch, the comments aren't as bad as others I've seen. Besides, I think you'll win the pint of ice cream."

"Big frappin' deal, Davis. Doesn't really make up for anything."

"You're going to send the corrected letter back to her, aren't you?"

"What?" bellowed Butch.

"Yeah, some guys send the letters back to let the girls know the quality of their Dear Johns." I ducked as Butch's boot sailed over my head and into the wall.

Butch wouldn't talk to me the rest of the evening, even when I handed him the chit for winning and the $1.50 for a pint of ice cream. "Come on, Butch. You'll find someone here, prettier and more loyal. And she'll probably have a car." Silence.

Oh, crap. I hope he doesn't take this hard enough to SIE or worse, try to hurt himself. "Look, Butch, I have the poop on the falcons. Remember, Tatum made me do it, and Payne helped me. Here," I said, offering my file for Butch to read.

Silence, but Butch did grab the papers and slammed them down on his desk.

"Fine, Butch. You'll feel better in the morning. And I bet Sue and what's his name don't last one quarter . . ."

Silence.

***

Thursday and Friday were actually enjoyable. We took "field trips" to the hangers on the other side of Lowry. The operational side of the air base was always a good experience. We were scheduled for an orientation flight in the T-29 on Thursday, but nasty thunderstorms in the area all day made flying questionable. There was also a low cloud cover over the permanent site. And a flyby of the site was a highlight of the orientation flight.

Sergeants Little and Brown gave scheduled classes on emergency equipment and procedures. The thunderstorms, especially the lightening, however, dominated the day. To fill in, Lt. Jensen took us into Operations to show us how to prepare flight plans. Next, he explained the NOTAM[48] – Notices to Airmen – Board . The NOTAM had a series of telegram reports tacked under the names of individual airports and a section on airways. There was an entire separate section for International operations.

Major Sampson, the Weather Officer, briefed on weather patterns, including systems across the entire US. Next he focused on our area and explained the cause of the thunderstorms. These storms, he said, were caused by a stationary cold front running north to south across the area, which also caused the low-lying clouds up against the mountains. The new site was obscured. With the current weather conditions, it was unlikely, he said, we would fly today. He was optimistic about tomorrow because the low should have moved.

Major Galt, the Officer in Charge of our flights, made a decision at 1730 to cancel the flights for the day. After we put equipment away, we boarded the buses, happy we'd be too late for the evening meal in the dining hall. Major Galt ordered another box lunch for us.

---

[48] The NOTAM board details changes in airfield operations, equipment (VOR, etc.) outages, construction, and other hazards to flight. Pilots check NOTAMs before ever flight.

As we boarded the bus, I slid in beside Butch. I felt badly he was upset about posting the letter. He's a good roommate and classmate and I hated to have friction between us.

"Hey, look, Butch, I'm sorry about the letter. I was just trying to help you get over Sue. If I'd known you would take it so hard, I wouldn't have pushed you."

"Yeah, I know. It's just that Sue and I have been going together so long I'm crushed she's blowing me off."

"Yeah, I can sympathize; I had a couple of romances go wrong. None as long as yours, but still . . . I'm sorry. How about we call a truce? Want my cherry pie?"

'Nah, it's all right. We do pretty well together. Tell you what; I'll even share my pint of ice cream with you. What kind do you want?"

"Strawberry."

***

Friday was another great day. The weather cleared. The sky was a Colorado crystal clear blue. After Major Galt's crew briefing, we boarded T-29 Tail Number 55040. I grabbed a station over the wing, checked out the oxygen system as instructed, and looked at the array of instruments in front of me. I recognized the VOR , ADF , radar scope repeater and the radio/intercom controls. I buckled in and started to explore my box lunch.

The smell of kerosene and the tic-tic-tic of the propellers as they turned over were exciting and etched into my memory. *My first ride in an airplane. I've always wanted to do this. Great! We're taxiing.*

The twin engines roared as the acceleration threw us back in our seats. I punched the clock, something Lt. Jensen said was important on navigation missions. I felt the aircraft getting "lighter" as the runway markers zoomed past. Suddenly the rumble of the tires on the pavement ceased, replaced by the sound of the wheels spinning in the air. Airborne.

Lt. Jensen gathered us around the table containing his navigational equipment. We flew east and then southwest to pass by the permanent site. The ground beneath was dirt brown with an occasional green patch where Colorado late season vegetables were growing.

Lt. Jenson demonstrated how to interpret VOR and ADF needles to create intersecting azimuths to define a fix or location of the aircraft. He plotted a position and solved for ground speed and winds. His position showed our south-westerly track from his last "fix." We were about 45 minutes from the new site.

Major Galt made four passes over the Academy, two north and two south. I noted on the altimeter, he descended to five hundred feet over the 7,000 foot site elevation. The new construction was impressive, with mountains looming to the west, open space to the east bisected by a major north-south highway, rock outcroppings to the north and, barely visible, the town of Colorado Springs to the south.

Lt. Jensen pointed out the future location of the dormitories, the academic building, the dining hall, and the gym. Checkered patterns outlined athletic fields.

The mission was scheduled for four hours (Major Galt said he and Captain Jones needed four hours flying time for monthly flight pay). Major Galt climbed to 20,000 feet and requested clearance west to Grand Junction before returning to Denver.

The view over the mountains was incredible. Even this late in the year, tiny pockets of snow were visible in the heart of the Rockies. The mountains created slight turbulence as we passed over them, but their beauty muted thoughts of airsickness.

Returning to the Denver area, Major Galt and Captain Jones made several VOR and ADF approaches to Buckley Field before requesting a GCA to Lowry. We must have spent 45 minutes shooting approaches to the two airfields. Lt. Jensen showed us the approach plates for Buckley and Lowry and the necessary maneuvers to get to the fields so we could follow what the pilots were doing with the aircraft..

We landed at 1730. Major Galt gave a 10 minute debriefing. To ensure we didn't make the evening meal, Lt. Jensen, on his own initiative, taught a class on dead reckoning navigation. The class lasted 45 minutes, ensuring we'd not be back for dinner formation; making him an instant hero. Major Galt again ordered box lunches to take back to our rooms.

Butch and I enjoyed our box lunch in the room. The ATOs were at dinner, so the dormitory was quiet. "You all right, Butch?" I said, munching on my turkey sandwich.

"Yeah, I'll live. It would be nice, though, if we could do something about those jerk upperclassmen. I was getting weak from lack of food. Thank God for the box lunches. Don't worry about me, Don, I'm all right. We'd better get on the room. Good ole SAMI tomorrow."

"Yeah, thanks for the extra work trying to fix the dent in wall you caused when you threw your boot at me. Since I don't have any tools, it's a good thing the tooth paste filled the hole and is a close color to the wall paint.

***

THE ACADEMY 1957

United States Air Force Academy
Sunday, August 18, 1957

Dear Folks,

Friday, after classes, we went to the flight line. Weather was good. Major Galt was our pilot; Captain Jones his copilot. This was an orientation flight.

Several looked a little queasy when the T-29 aircraft began to shake. "It's just wind buffeting the plane," said Lt. Jensen. "it's not the airplane."

We learned about radar, VORs and ADFs, for navigation, but can also receive radio stations. Lt. Jensen had us tune our sets to 1390, the Denver station so we could listen to the news and music.

A normal cadet four hour mission usually goes to Ponca City, Oklahoma. We learned about the sextant, used to "shoot" the sun in daytime and the stars at night. The "shot" is plotted as a line on your navigation map. You try to cross three lines to make a fix - that's where you are supposed to be!

Flying is fun and interesting. On the climb out, Major Galt rolled empty beer cans down the aisle. He wasn't drinking, of course, but we all got a kick out of his "trick." It was even funnier when he began swaying the airplane in rhythm with a bawdy song he was singing on the intercom as we climbed.

We made several passes by the new site. It's just a bunch of holes in the ground. We could see the start of buildings, but it doesn't look like the pictures - yet. Can't wait to get to the permanent site; mainly because I'll be a Third Classman and through with all the 4th Class Mickey Mouse.

Only two weeks until Bivouac; three until we are accepted into the Wing. We'll have new squadrons and meet the upperclassmen. Hope mine are not the ones we have at the table. They are jerks. Heaven forbid I should have Cadet Short in my squadron. If I do, it will be a long year until recognition.

It's almost taps, so I need to hit the sack. Write lots and send stamps.

God Bless
Your loving son
Don

Chapter 17

You must learn to follow before you can lead . . .
Class Welcome; Contrails, James E. Briggs, Superintendent

Friday, August 23, 1957 Week Seven

The week began routinely. Cadets O'Rourke and Tillman said little at Monday morning breakfast. They appeared somewhat subdued. Rumor was Lt. Tatum had had a "woodshed talking to" with them. The upperclassmen had a lot to learn.

"Davis," Lt. Tatum finally said, "let's have the Academy Mission."

"Sir, the mission of the United States Air Force Academy is to provide instruction, experience, and motivation to each cadet so that he will graduate with the knowledge and qualities of leadership required of a junior officer in the United States Air Force, and with a basis for continued development throughout a lifetime of service to his country, leading to readiness for responsibilities as a future air commander."

"And in your words, tell me the essence of the Fourth Class System."

"Sir, the System teaches 'You must learn to follow before you can lead.'"

Glancing sideways, Lt. Tatum ensured the Second Classmen were listening. He looked back at me and said, "Eat."

From that point on, the relationships between the Second Classmen and the New Cadets at our table became more professional.

***

It was no secret the final drill competition was a key summer event. Third Squadron practiced two periods every morning for flight competition on Thursday. As in previous trials; A Flight was first, C Flight second, and B Flight third.

At the end of the competition, Lt. O'Malley addressed the Squadron. "You all looked good this morning. A Flight will represent us tomorrow in the competition.
 C Flights' rifles are a cut above. C Flight cadets will loan their rifles to A Flight. B Flight will assist with A Flight preparations by shining shoes and belt buckles.

You will all attend the competition to support your classmates. Winning Best Summer Squadron will benefit all of you. So, you **will win. Dismissed!**"

***

To ensure fairness, the Deputy Commandant, Colonel Benjamin Cassiday, was the competition's primary inspecting officer. Squadron and Flight Commanders also participated, with notebooks in hand, to record discrepancies.

The bright morning sun began heating the quadrangle. The forecast was for eighty-five degrees by noon. Shoe and hat brim shines would suffer by afternoon. .Standing at attention for inspection would test the self-discipline of New Cadets.

Paper slips drawn from a hat established competition order: 1st Squadron was first; 3d Squadron second; and 2nd Squadron last.

The inspection and manual of arms took nearly an hour for each flight. Colonel Cassiday stepped smartly in front of the first cadet in 1st Squadron. New Cadet Tom Bronson assumed the position of "inspection arms," bringing his rifle to a 45-degree angle in front of him and sharply driving the bolt open with his left hand.

As Colonel Cassiday looked at each cadet, he called out "crooked gig line," "crooked name tag," or some other grievous offense. Cassiday snatched the rifle from each cadet's hands; swung the rifle up toward the sun to check for lint in the barrel, brought the piece back to a 45-degree angle, and pushed it back toward the cadet.

As Cassiday made a crisp right face to move to another cadet, the inspected cadet released the bolt and brought the rifle down to his right side.

First Squadron had only five discrepancies. One was humorous, to all except George Swan. When Swan released his rifle bolt, his white glove caught in the chamber. George was perplexed. Had he acted quickly, the glitch might not have been noticed. The hesitation, however, caught Colonel Cassiday's attention. As Swan recycled his bolt, pulling out his glove, Cassiday turned to the Flight Commander and said in a loud voice and with a smile on his face: "**Put that man down for 'dirty gloves.'**"

First Squadron's marching performance was errorless. Classmates not competing sat at ease on the sidelines. I climbed into the stands next to Terry Cloud.

"Hi, Terry. You're still getting way too many letters. Half the Squadron's bitchin' about you. Some have suggested our own shower formation for you — without ATOs."

"Hey, I can't help it if I'm popular. Besides the girls are just friends, nothing serious. And the family has always been close."

"We should get together and trade stories about Wisconsin and California."

"Yeah, I'd love to, but they keep us so damn busy.   I feel like a hamster in a circular cage. Round and round and …"

"Yeah, I know. How do you think 1st Squadron did?"

"Oh, I think they were all right, but we're going to beat them. A Flight's really good at drill. Their Flight Commander gave them a scrub inspection after breakfast.

"What about manual of arms?"

"They're good. Englehart Captained the Woo Poo[49] demonstration drill team."

---

[49] USAFA term of endearment for West Point.

"Interesting! But how've you been doing, Terry?"

"Oh, hanging in there. Little behind the curve. I got to march a tour last Saturday for 'roving eyes in the mess hall.' My hard-ass Element Leader went through Aviation Cadets and is trying to prove to West Pointers he's tougher than they are. What the hell, only one more week of this crap. Bivouac should actually be fun. How about you, Davis? How are you doing?"

"I'm doing good. Butch, my roommate, and I have a straight shooter for Element Leader. Some ATO jerk from 1st Squadron tried to corner Butch with an improper question.[50] Lt. Payne stepped in and squared the other ATO away."

"Third Squadron, Atten . . . shun!" Lt. Jerry O'Malley barked. A Flight snapped to attention. Colonel Ben Cassiday, the Deputy Commandant, stepped in front of Neal Rountree -- game on. As he passed the last cadet in the flight, he had called six discrepancies. That put us one behind 1st Squadron for the in-ranks inspection.

Second Squadron, being last, was at a disadvantage. The super high-gloss of their shoes turned murky. Colonel Cassiday, known to be fair, still called out "shoe shine below standard" twice, indicating he thought those cadets had not started with a high enough standard shine. Even with the shoeshine gigs, 2nd Squadron had only seven write-ups, one more than we did.

***

Lt. Yeager stood in front of 1st Squadron looking like a full size lead soldier, perfect in every detail. **"Flight,"** sang out Yeager's booming bass voice. **"Atten . . . shun!"** Thirty New Cadets snapped to attention with a crispness that sent echoes of 60 shoes coming together rippling across the quadrangle.

"Riiiight Shoulderr . . . Arms!" "One, two, three, four" the cadets counted softly in unison. The rifles hit the cadet's right shoulders as if Yeager were counting cadence out loud. **"Leeft Shoulderr . . . Arms!"** Again the flight moved in perfect unison, with a sharp slap of the hand as the cadets returned their right hands to their sides. **"Pooortt . . . Arms!"** The rifles came to a 45-degree position in front of the cadets. Rivulets of sweat began to run down their noses. **"Preeesent . . . Arms!"** barked Lt. Yeager, turning smartly and rendering a hand salute to Colonel Cassiday. When his salute was returned, Yeager again pivoted and commanded, **"Orrder . . . Arms!"** Not one of the rifle butts hit the macadam. After a 15-second pause, Lt Yeager quietly said, "Rest."

---

[50] An improper question uses the honor code to elicit an answer from a cadet without a basis for the question. The question to Butch about shaving was okay because Lt. Johnson caught Butch not shaving; asking Butch if he was lying was an improper question.

Applause broke out around the quadrangle. Despite our loyalties, my classmates and I joined the applause. This was going to be hard to beat.

Third Squadron, A Flight, lived up to its manual of arms reputation. Not quite up to the US Marine Corps team standards. Nonetheless, all the maneuvers performed by A Flight were precise, synchronized, and flawless. I noted with pride the rifle barrels gleaming in the sun and the mirror-like shine of the stocks.

While 3d Squadron's performance may have been a shade under 1st Squadron, we definitely had an M1 appearance edge. A smattering of applause broke out as 3d Squadron finished its routine.

Second Squadron Cadets seemed slightly demoralized, like a football team that's behind 35 – 0 at the half. Nonetheless, the cadets of 2nd Squadron did a respectable routine, with no visible mistakes. They did not give up, but they knew they were not competitive with 1st and 3d Squadron performances.

As the manual-of-arms competition ended, Colonel Cassiday returned Lt. Green's salute and strode toward the dining hall. We were told the Flight Commanders and Deputy Commandant would compile the morning scores during lunch. Naturally, they did not share the results with us.

***

"Glad they gave us an hour to rest, Butch. I really feel for those guys who have to stand out there in that sun."

"Yeah, Davis. Almost makes you happy we didn't win for the Squadron. It's hard enough standing around watching those guys. Great to be able to talk to classmates for a change though. Did you hear we lost two more last week?"

"No, who were they?"

"Fellow named Jerry Miller. Understand he got a letter from his fiancé Friday afternoon. Seems he's going to be a father sooner than he planned. He walked out of the dorm, over to the Chaplain's office, and was out the gate by 2000.

The other guy was Gary Bensen, tough guy from Brooklyn. He was walking back from dinner Wednesday. One of the ATO's stopped him and gave him a tour Saturday for gazing. I guess Gary called the ATO a SOB and swung at him. Gary had a bus ticket home by 2100."

"Who was the ATO?"

"Nobody seemed to know"

"Bet you a dime it was our friend, Lt. Jackson!"

"Yeah, sounds like him."

"Sir, there are two minutes to drill competition formation. Uniform is khakis and wheel hats. GO 3D SQUADRON!!! Two minutes, Sir."

"We'd better get our butts out there, Davis. Tatum will be chomping at the bit. He really wants to win this thing. Man is he competitive."

"So do I. Understand we get some real privileges if we win."

***

For the marching competition, the order of presentation was reversed. Second 2nd Squadron was first and 1st Squadron was third, 3d Squadron remained second. As competition began, Colonel Cassiday handed the 2nd Squadron Flight Commander a sheet with detailed instructions to be given to the cadets.

"B Flight**, Atten . . .SHUN! Right Shoulder . . . Arms. Right . . .Face. Fooorward . . . March."** Lt. Glover put his flight through a series of maneuvers, including transferring the rifle from right shoulder arms to left shoulder arms. At one point, the flight halted in front of the Commandant, who had joined the Deputy Commandant for the afternoon session. The Director of Athletics, Colonel George Simlar was added as a third judge.

"Or . . . der . . .Arms! Pre . . . sent . . .Arms!" commanded Lt. Glover. General Stillman returned the salute. Lt. Glover glanced at his program sheet. **"Or . . . der . . . Arms. Rite Shoul . . . der . . . Arms! To the Reeear . . . March."** Several of the Cadets hesitated, then stepped forward on their right foot, pivoted, and marched off on their left foot. A cadet, in the rear row, however, started to step off on his left foot, caught himself and began the maneuver on his right (correct) foot. He nipped the heel of his classmate in the second row, however, causing a slight ripple in the ranks and, undoubtedly, the loss of one or two points.

"Hi, again," said Terry as I rejoined him. Terry introduced me to Roger Stringer. I knew Roger from minute calling and had delivered letters to him and his roommate.

"Ahh," I said. "Did you see that mistake? I think we can beat them," said Roger.

"Yeah, but they were pretty good," Terry said. "We can't make any mistakes."

Performing like automatons, A Flight's Cadets executed each maneuver with precision and crispness. It really was a flawless performance. This time, A Flight received a round of cheers from the sidelines. Yet, we knew from the posted morning ratings that 1st Squadron was a point ahead. Their manual of arms routine looked nearly as good as ours. So, First Squadron could beat us, but would have to be perfect.

The 1st Squadron Flight Commander presented his flight to the Commandant. If I were judging, I'd find it hard to choose between 3d and 1st Squadrons' performances.

Then it happened. With the first two squadrons, the order following present arms and order arms was right shoulder arms. The routines for each squadron had been slightly altered to prevent the last squadron having an advantage by watching the first two perform. The order to 1st Squadron following order arms, was "**Lefft shoul . . . der**

. . . **arms!"** Two of the Cadets made their first move toward right shoulder arms. They caught themselves in mid-maneuver, but the damage was done.

***

Jubilation rang throughout the dormitories. The ATOs walked through the halls congratulating us. We ran up and down chanting: **"We won, we won, we won!"** Captain Mallett, our AOC, put out the "unofficial word" we won.

Placing bets with the other squadrons, our ATOs won 10 pints of ice cream per flight for us; purchased by the losing ATOs. Pride of accomplishment and camaraderie among 3d Squadron classmates, however, was the sweet spot of the win. We had loaned A Flight our rifles. B flight classmates polished A Flight Cadets' shoes, hats, and belt buckles, giving them extra drill sessions during Commander's Times. It worked.

***

Lt. Tatum (who won a bottle of his favorite whiskey from each 1st and 2nd Squadron Flight and Squadron Commander) visited each room to take ice cream orders. At ease in the dorms, we spent time getting to know our classmates better.

Dinner was surreal. Before the meal, the Adjutant announced: "Gentlemen, the results of today's drill competition is as follows: 2nd Squadron 352 points; 1st Squadron, 356 points; and 3nd Squadron, 359[51] points. Third Squadron is the drill competition winner." Third Squadron cadets tried to raise the roof with their cheers.

Lt. Tatum commanded, "Take seats." Everyone assumed their respective roles. Pan-ther-pis and ice tea were distributed. As the initial duties were accomplished, Bob stuck out his hand and said, "Sir, may I ask a question?"

"NO! Mr. Hertz, you may not. Mr. Hertz," (Bob was to Tatum's right, just beyond Lt. Boyce) "start with the lowest officer rank in the Air Force . . . not counting Warrant Officer; then, I want New Cadet Grace to give me the next higher rank and so on around the table."

"General of the Air Force," concluded Bobbie Grace.

"Very good, men," Tatum said. "Now sit at ease."

Everyone assumed a relaxed position and smirked. This was the second time we had had a chance to relax at the table since those first three days.

"Mr. Davis," barked Tatum. I came to attention. "What was my order?"

"Sir, you said 'sit at ease.'"

"And what does that mean exactly, Mr. Davis?"

---

[51] There were a total of 400 points total for the competition. The final score represented the 400 less the number of points taken off by the judges for in ranks inspection, manual of arms, and the drill routine.

I hesitated slightly, then decided to go the whole nine yards. "Sir 'sit at ease' means we can sit normally in our chairs and converse quietly while performing our normal table duties."

"Excellent, Dumbsquat, I thought you all hadn't learned anything the last several weeks. Tell Mr. White to make sure we have 3d Squadron quality steaks at the table tonight. Carry on!"

"Yes, SIR!" I said. No one hesitated. We scooted our chairs forward and enjoyed the feeling of having our back rest on the chair for the first time in seven weeks.

***

"Attention, Dormitory 895." Lt. Tatum's piercing voice rang throughout the building. "I regret to inform you the Cadet Store is closed. We cannot deliver the ice cream tonight. It will be delivered tomorrow after dinner."

"This place sucks, Butch. I think they screwed us on purpose. I love ice cream. I think I'll see the chaplain Sunday and get out of this chicken shit place."

"Ah, come on, Davis, you keep whining you are going to see the Chaplin. Bull crap. You've been through the worst of it. No sense in quitting now. They can't make it any harder. Non Illegitmus Caborumdum."

Chapter 18

As a minimum goal, the Academy will accomplish its mission by providing each cadet with: . . . A knowledge of and an appreciation for airpower, its capabilities and limitations . . . . Contrails, 1957-1958

Monday August 26, 1957 Week Eight

The flush of winning the Group Drill Competition spilled over into the last week of scheduled summer training. Monday morning, Lt. Tatum, still elated over winning eight bottles of Chevis Regal, looked at Cadet Dickson.

"Dickson, start with the lowest Air Force officer rank. Each person to Dickson's right will give the next rank. Continue until you reach the highest rank. Go!"

"Sir, the lowest Air Force rank is Second Lieutenant."

The last rank fell on me. "Sir, Four Star General is the highest rank."

"Davis, aren't you forgetting a rank?"

"No sir. The current highest rank is Four Star General. Sir, the highest rank in World War Two was Five Star General of the Air Force. Our only Five Star General was Hap Arnold."

Tatum smirked. "Eat!" was the last word from the ATOs during the meal.

***

C2C Cadet Major Garvey opened the afternoon honor class session with the question: "What are the words of the honor code?"

Thirty hands went up. "Mr. Hertz, let's have it."

"Sir, the Honor Code states' we will not lie, steal, or cheat; nor will we allow among us those who do.'"

"Mr. Davis, explain the phrase 'nor will we allow among us those who do.'"

"Sir, the non-toleration clause means we are honor bound to report another cadet who has lied, cheated, or stolen."

"Great, but what if it's your roommate? Are you going to report him?"

"Yes, Sir. As difficult as it is, you are obligated to report him."

"'That's right. Mr. Likens, what if you overhear a Second Classman telling an officer something you know is not true, what do you do?"

"Sir, can you give me a name?" The class laughed. Cadet Garvey was not amused.

"Don't be a smart ass, Likens. An honor code violation is not a laughing matter."

"Yes, Sir. Sir, you would be required to report the incident to an Honor Representative."

"Then what?"

"Sir, the Honor Representative decides whether a probable violation has occurred. He will consult the Honor Committee to determine if an Honor Board should be convened."

"Correct! Who knows what an 'improper question is?"

I raised my hand. "What is it, Davis?"

"Sir, an improper question is when an ATO . . . ah . . . Air Training Office asks a cadet a question when he does not know the cadet did anything wrong."

"Well, that's sort of a convoluted answer. The Honor Code can't be used to enforce regulations. If there's a rumor a cadet went over the wall. An ATO cannot randomly question cadets about being absent the night before. However, can an ATO look at your shoes, and ask 'Mister, did you shine your shoes this morning?'"

Thirty voices answered, "Yes, Sir."

"That's right because he suspects you didn't shine your shoes. There is one more case to cover. It is the use of the term "All Right!" during call to quarters.

"As you know, neither officers nor upperclassman can enter your room without permission, unless, Mr. Rieselman, your flashlight shows under the door. However, during call to quarters, an officer or upperclassman may knock on a cadet's door and ask "All Right'. If only authorized cadets are in the room, one of the roommates will answer, "All Right, Sir.'"

"Sir," asked Art Kerr, "if someone is in the room who should not be, what do you do?

"Well, you can't answer 'All Right', can you?"

"No, Sir. So I guess you don't say anything."

"Correct. And you can expect a visit from the inspecting officer. Gentlemen, this is our last class for the summer. You will be under the Code when you return from Bivouac. If you ever have questions about the Honor Code, you should contact your Squadron Honor Representative. Questions? No? Well, good luck, dismissed."

***

After the usual hurried uniform change, we double-timed to the gym. Half of the Squadron watched the basketball game with 2nd Squadron; the other half went outside to watch a soccer game with 1st Squadron. These were the last scheduled games.

Starting the fourth quarter of the basketball game, we were behind by 12 points. With six minutes left, John Stackhouse pumped in a jump shot from the free throw line, making the score to 40 to 30. Smokey Stovall, 2nd Squadron stole the ball twice for layups. The 44 to 30 loss was the only one with 2nd Squadron.

Soccer was tied zero to zero with two minutes to go. First Squadron was driving for a score when Roger Stringer stole the ball. As he approached our goal, Terry Koonce moved right to block Jack's shot. Jack's line drive went to the upper left hand corner of the net. We let out a roar as the game ended: 3d Squadron 1 – 1st Squadron 0.

***

Monday dinner was a shock. Lt. Tatum and our Second Classmen were all over us. We all had a chance to recite every bit of Fourth Class Knowledge in *Contrails*. Noise thundered throughout the dining hall. We went through the Academy staff, Air Force Command commanders, and every quotation from General MacArthur to Air Marshall Douhet. The only thing missing was food.

"Damn, Butch, what was that all about?

"I'd heard this might be coming. The ATOs don't want us to forget summer training."

"Yeah, well crap, I didn't get two bites to eat."

"Oh stop whining," Butch said, as he threw me two Three Musketeers from the bottom of his laundry bag. "You'll survive."

***

Tuesday through Friday repeated Monday's inquisition. Mornings included five to ten mile marches, alternating between double-time and normal cadence. The ATOs matched us step for step. Following our forced marches, we practiced setting up tents and a bivouac area.

Breakfast, lunch, and dinner echoed the first days of summer training. The ATOs and upperclassmen were relentless. The only difference was we had access to the Cadet Store and candy bars and crackers. We wouldn't starve, but I still lost five pounds.

The afternoon classes focused on field items: sentry duty, camp cleanliness, and survival procedures. Lts. Tatum, Payne, and Boyce alternated teaching. After classes, we completed intramurals. Third Squadron swept swimming, track, and softball.

A highlight of my week was the Friday softball game. Behind 3-1 in the bottom of the seventh, I came to bat with two outs and bases loaded. I had struck out twice. On the first pitch, Terry Norris threw his fast ball. I watched the ball all the way to the bat.

"Wham!" I hit the ball in the sweet part of the bat. The ball shot into the center field gap. Sliding into third base, I saw Kerr cross home plate. WE WON. With 27 wins out of 30 in intramurals, 3d Squadron was on track to win the Superintendent's Trophy.

***

"Gentlemen," Using an overhead projector, Lt. Tatum displayed a list on the Day Room blackboard. "These are the items you'll need in your field pack. In addition to the mess kit, shaving gear, soap, a towel, and bug spray, the following items of clothing are required: three pair boot socks, two T-shirts, two pair underwear, and spare fatigue hat, shirt, and trousers."

Hertz stuck up his hand. "Sir, will that be enough underwear?"

"Come on, Hertz," Tatum said, "cowboys only had one change of underwear at most. Besides there'll be tubs with soap and hot water to wash your underwear, if it gets groady."

Lt. Payne covered the encampment area, a schedule of events, and the C Flight guard duty posting. "Safety is paramount in this exercise. On the night escape and evasion, you'll travel in pairs. Should your partner suffer an injury—not just a scratch— you will stand up and yell 'assistance.' Despite the rumors, there are no Gila monsters; well, except for a couple of the ATOs who might bite.

There are, however, rattlesnakes. You'll most likely encounter them during the day. If you hear the rattle, freeze. Look around. Determine the snake's location. If you don't challenge the rattler, he'll probably slither away. If you get bit, get immediate help from the staff. Do not move a lot. Send a classmate for help. There is a rare possibility you could encounter a rattler at night on the E&E[52] course. If you get bit, follow the procedure I just briefed. Any questions?"

Art Kerr's hand shot up. "Sir, if we kill a rattlesnake, do we get to eat it?"

"Mr. Kerr, do not attempt to kill a rattlesnake; they are much smarter and faster than you." A slight chuckle rippled through the room. "If you want to eat rattlesnake, go to the Roundup Restaurant in Denver during Christmas. They have rattlesnake, buffalo, and bear. Okay, troops, the rest of the evening is Commander's Time. Get your rooms spotless and get ready for the SAMI and parade. Let's earn that trophy for 3rd Squadron. Dismissed."

***

In anticipation of the Forward Airstrip Encampment (FASE) exercise, our final summer SAMI and parade were on Friday. The Commandant was the SAMI inspection officer.

"Missing name tag," General Stillman said. Art Kerr forgot his name tag, again. But this was only the third gig the Commandant gave 3d Squadron. After General Stillman and Lt. Tatum passed, Lt. Payne stopped in front of me. "Davis, is it true you haven't marched a tour?"

"Yes, Sir," I said with a slight smirk.

Lt. Payne took care of the smirk. "Well, Davis, you are on report for smirking in ranks. You will serve a tour on Saturday. No one gets through summer training without

---

[52] E&E – Escape and Evasion

a tour." It was Lt. Payne who smirked as he did a right face and caught up with the inspecting party.

Because of the forecast warm temperatures, the normal in-ranks and room inspections were reversed. The Commandant's inspections were causal. He did bounce a quarter on my bed and smiled when the quarter rose in the air. We had no write-ups. Lt. O'Malley smiled and flipped us a nonchalant salute as he left.

The 70 degree temperature and 100 percent cloud cover made the parade bearable. General Briggs, the Superintendent; the Commandant, General Stillman; and the Deputy Commandant, Colonel Cassiday constituted the reviewing party.

A full array of military and civilian spectators filled the stands. News of the parade was widely covered in the local press. The blue military uniforms were interspersed with bright yellows, soft pastels, and white hats and gloves. Best of all, there were numerous, young, pretty girls in the bleachers. Not gazing was difficult.

***

"Gentlemen, the Officer of the Day is Captain Braswell," began the Adjutant. "The winner of today's parade is 3d Squadron. Third Squadron is the Honor Squadron for summer training and has earned the Superintendent's Trophy."

Pandemonium broke out. All 3d Squadron's New Cadets were on their feet shouting, "**Third Squadron, Third Squadron, Hip, Hip Hooray! Hip, Hip, Hooray! Hip, Hip, Hooray.** The chant continued for five minutes. Suddenly, Lt. Tatum rapped on the table. "Gentlemen," he said with a rare true smile, **"At Ease!"**

I enjoyed the jubilation until I reported to Lt. Boyce for my tour. The uniform was fatigues, helmet, rifle, and white gloves. We marched back and forth across the quad for an hour. Permission to transfer your rifle from right shoulder to left shoulder arms and vice versa provided some relief for boredom and creeping fatigue. When finished, I felt like I was walking on live coals.

"Nellie Wore a New Dress" rang out as we marched to evening meal. Lt. Payne, as Table Commandant, ordered "at ease" as soon as we sat down. "Dispense with the table call outs," he added. "Enjoy your walk," Lt. Payne said to me with a genuine smile. We all had our fill of hamburgers, shoe string potatoes, and macaroni salad. There was a notable absence of 3d Squadron ATOs in the dining hall.

***

United States Air Force Academy
Friday, August 30 1957, 2030 hours

Dear Mom and Dad,

What an incredible week. We set a five mile hike record, won the intramural league, won a Friday parade; and, most importantly, are the summer training Honor Squadron.

I wasn't sure I'd survive this long, but things definitely are looking up. The sky is the limit (sky, Air Force, get it?). Anyway, basic summer training is over and I made it. I finished the summer with 20 demerits and one tour. The tour was a "gift" from my Element Leader, Lt. Payne who said no cadet should complete summer training without a tour.

Pa, about the car, sell it. You keep the money. We don't have a lot of use for money. We're paid $111.15, half the salary of a Second Lieutenant. But we only get 15 dollars spending money a month. Of course, there's no room and board; books are paid for; and most entertainment - dances, picnics, etc. - are free.

Speaking of uniforms, the *Denver Post* had a picture of our new Cecil B. DeMille duds in Sunday's paper. I'm including it in this letter. In addition to khakis and fatigues. Oh, and flight suits, we have a Class A Uniform, parade uniforms and a formal outfit..

In summer we'll wear khakis or blue pants with short sleeve shirts with shoulder boards. You can add a tie and blue blouse over the shirt. For the Class A uniform we wear a long sleeve shirt with tie and blouse.

The formal "mess dress" uniform is Air Force Academy blue with a blue bow tie (and gloves) and cummerbund. It's for all formal events.

The two parade uniforms - a summer in white and the winter in blue both have a high collar, like a priest's. There is a sash. Officers have a belt across the chest, a scabbard for the sword, and, of course, a sword.

Only First Classmen go without M1s. All the uniforms, except the mess dress have a garrison cap. The summer white uniform has a white cap. All uniforms use the black dress oxford shoes.

Thank you, Mom, for the long letter. I haven't received much mail for the past two weeks. Nothing makes me feel better than a nice long letter. I did get a letter from Mr. Gilliam today. It was great. He said the smartest thing to do is stay here. I'll have to see him next summer.

Let me know where I can call; either at Lucille's or your house. I'll have to call collect. I think it would be five or six dollars. I am anxious to talk to you. I have missed you and being at home. I'll call on Sunday, 8 September between 1300 and 1400 (1 p.m. to 2 p.m.) your time.

The weather has been cooler, but we still have afternoon thunderstorms. The cooler weather makes for better sleeping at night; although I am usually so tired, I sleep well.

Well, Mom, I hate to close so soon, but I have to put linseed oil on my rifle, shine my boots, and pack my ruck sack. I bought some peanuts and crackers at the Cadet Store. The ATOs didn't say we could do that, but they didn't say we couldn't. Better to ask forgiveness than permission. Too bad I can't pack a couple of pints of ice cream; that would be good.

Rumor is some of the guys will be quitting when we get back from FASE, but I'm getting pretty used to the system now and things are looking up. I think the hardest part is over, at least I hope so, but I will remember your saying: "Hope _for_ the best, but expect the worst."

God Bless. Write letters. I will enjoy them when we get back.

Your loving son, `

Don

Photo of uniforms included with letter

The Superintendent's Trophy

Chapter 19

"Halt! Who goes there?"
. . . Sentry Challenge from Army Field Manual 22-5[53]

Forward Air Strip Encampment (FASE)
Monday 2 September 1957

"HIT THE DIRT!" Lt. Tatum yelled in mock panic. Dust and small stones stirred up by the three F-86s, flying at 100 feet, peppered C Flight. We all cheered the mock strafing attack as the fighters swooped low, firing machine gun blanks. As briefed, we jumped headfirst into the gullies lining the dirt road. Our seventy pound backpacks drove us into the dirt.

"Damn, Butch," I said brushing off my fatigues. "That was something."

"Yeah," Butch answered, "I'd like it a hell of a lot better if I were the one making other people eat dust."

"Well, with luck some day you will be."

"All right, Pansies. Get back into formation. You were pretty damn slow getting off the road. Real life, half of you would be dead."

Just as the Squadron was given **"Forward, route step . . . March,"** the F-86s swooped down in front of the column with .50 caliber machine guns blazing. The fighters had climbed to 15,000 feet (10 thousand above the terrain), split-essed,[54] and realigned on 3d Squadron.

"HIT THE DIRT," screamed the ATOs.

The fighters made two more passes. Our fatigues now had enough desert grime that if we lay down along the road, we'd be perfectly camouflaged. On the last pass, six large puffs of debris rose behind the column as the Sabres' practice bombs exploded. Someone shouted, **"Air Power!"** We laughed, but hoped the urgent, evasive maneuvers were over. They were.

***

---

[53] As in many areas, the Air Force adopted procedures, manuals, and terminology of the Army, its former "parent."

[54] In a Split "S" maneuver, from a straight and level flight, the pilot rolls the aircraft inverted, applies back stick pressure, diving the aircraft into a half loop, which changes the aircraft's direction 180 degrees and places the aircraft at a lower altitude.

Following the nine mile hike to camp, we were ordered to fall out, stack arms, and put up our tents. Butch and I stood proudly by our tent as Lt. Payne began an element inspection.

"Well, Davis, you and Rieselman set for a relaxing evening in the desert?"

"Yes, Sir," we both responded.

"From what I see, you might have an unwanted visitor or two. Snakes love to crawl up next to a warm body. I'd suggest you gather rocks and weigh down the edges of your tent."

"Yes Sir," we replied and took off scouting for small boulders. We not only put rocks down, we weighted the edges with sand.

Fifteen minutes later, Lt. Payne made the rounds again. "Okay, chow hounds. Grab your mess kits and get over to the mess tent. When you finish, give your utensils a good scrub and rinse. If you get dysentery you'll miss a lot of good, clean – well perhaps not clean – fun."

The cooks outdid themselves serving steaks, baked beans, corn on the cob, and fresh baked rolls. Mixed fruit completed the menu. Drinks were pan-ther-pis and water.

"Man, this is living," Butch said, polishing off the cake and his second glass of grape juice. "I might even learn to be a cowboy with chow like this."

"Hell, Butch," I said. "You couldn't get two cows to go in the same direction."

"Oh, bull," he muttered.

"Yeah, well, you couldn't handle them either!"

***

At the Squadron assembly area, we climbed into the C Flight reviewing stands.

"Hi, Terry," I said waving as I climbed onto the top row. "How's it going?"

"Great so far. How about that meal? Wonder what we have to do to earn it?"

"Don't know, but I think we're about to find out."

Lt. Tatum jumped up on the PT platform facing the stands.

"Gentlemen," Tatum began, "We are simulating a perimeter encampment at a forward air base. You're responsible for guarding the base and your encampment[55]. There are two essential elements of guard duty: General Orders and Special Orders. The General Orders are as follows:

1. I will guard all within my post limits and quit my post only when properly relieved.
2. I will obey my special orders and perform all my duties in a military manner.

---

[55] Many of the ATOs had served in the Korean War. The Air Force and the Academy adopted Korean War experiences; thus the procedures for the cadet Forward Air Strip Encampment – FASE.

3.   I will report violations of my special orders, emergencies, and anything not in my instructions to the Officer of the Day. The Officer of the Day today will be Lt. Payne.

Special orders are posted on the Bulletin Board. They consist of the location and boundaries of your post, the guard's name, and scheduled times. You should note your successor's name. The Officer of the Day and the Senior Ranking Officer will be posted on the special orders. You must, I repeat, **must** memorize this information.

Two hour guard duty begins at taps. Relieve your classmate **ON TIME!** If you are late, you'll not only lose a friend, you'll be subject to disciplinary action.

An alert runner will wake the next shift's guards 15 minutes before shift start. Write your tent location by your name on the duty roster. Use the grid posted on the Bulletin Board. It is now 1830 hours, taps will be at 2030. **DISMISSED!"**

"Damn," I said to Terry sitting beside me. "More crap."

"Yeah, let's check the Bulletin Board. Hope my shift is tonight before fun and games begin. I hear escape and evasion night is a bitch. It'll be hell to have the duty after that. "

"Great," I said, "I got your wish. Cripes, my tour is at 3 a.m. That's my best sleeping time."

"T.S., Davis, I'll probably get mine the night after E&E."

***

"Pssst, Davis, wake up," Chris Dixon said softly. "Come on, Davis, wake up, it's 0245. You have guard duty in 15 minutes."

"Whaaa, what do you want? **Damn**, it's the middle of the night."

"Shhhhsh, you'll wake your tent mate. Hurry, they have coffee at the mess tent. But, you have to be on time."

"Okay, Okay I got it, go away."

"Not until I'm sure you're up."

"Okay, Okay." I said, crawling out of my sleeping bag and reaching for my fatigue pants. "Damn, it's cold."

"Yeah, make sure you bring your jacket . . . and don't forget your rifle."

Damn, I thought, *I sure as hell would've forgotten the M1.* "Uh, thanks, Chris."

***

"HALT, WHO GOES THERE?" I said with a quiver in my voice. It was 0330, dark, cold, and I was startled by the tall, uniformed figure emerging from the darkness. **"HALT!! WHAT IS THE PASS WORD?"**

"Friend . . . and the password is BEAT ARMY," the obscured figure said softly.

I relaxed as Lt. Payne entered the circle of light of the portable light cart.

I moved my rifle to port arms.

"Once you recognized me, Davis, why didn't you salute?"

"Sir, General Orders say a sentry required to challenge should not salute."

"Good, Davis. What are you responsible for at this post?"

"Sir, I am responsible for activity within my post and any government property in my area."

" . . . ah, and what government property is there?"

"Well, Sir, there is the light cart and . . . and . . . ah, my rifle."

"Davis, What would happen if you compromised the pass word?"

"Sir in wartime, I could be court martialed and shot."

"That'd be nasty, wouldn't it? Has there been any unusual activity on your post?"

"No, Sir, it has been quiet."[56]

"Okay. Here's a cup of coffee. Make sure you stay awake,"

In this refrigerator, who's going to sleep, I thought. Lt. Payne slipped into the darkness.

***

Reveille sounded at 0600 on Saturday. It was still dark, but advance rays from the sun crept over the eastern horizon. The titillating smell of eggs, bacon, sausage, biscuits and coffee roused us from our warm sleeping bags. I was a little groggy with only an hour's sleep after guard duty. Butch and I hurriedly slapped on our fatigues and headed for the mess tent.

"Should be a great day," Butch said. We are supposed to be on the range all day."

"Yeah, besides the 45 and 38 pistols, I hear we get to shoot at drones with machine guns."

After breakfast, we piled on the blue busses and headed for the range. The vast area east of Buckley NAS[57] held an impressive small arms range.

I cleared my 38 and put it on the barrel by my firing station. Anticipating watching B Flight fire, I went to the stands and spied Terry Cloud. "Hi, Terry, How'd you do?"

"I got a 220. I really like that revolver. How about you?"

"Ha, I beat you. Got a 222; Marksman."

"Well, that's a first. How'd you do on the 45?"

" I . . . ah . . .shot a 100. Didn't even qualify."

"Yeah, well I beat you 10 points. That SOB really kicks' But, would knock somebody down; providing you could hit him. Tuesday will be great with the 50 calibers. A Piper Cub drags a drone over the range. Wonder how many hits the Piper will take?"

"I understand it's a long cable."

---

[56] I was lucky; later in the week several ATOs dressed as aggressors challenged several posts and harassed the guards.

[57] NAS – Naval Air Station

When we finished the range, we bussed back to the Bivouac area. After checking our M1s – left stacked under the careful eyes of several ATOs – we headed to dinner. Steaks, baked potatoes, and broccoli followed by cherry pie with ice cream set us up for a great night's sleep.

***

Sunday was indeed a day of rest. Reveille was at 0700. After breakfast a group of us caught up on gossip. The word is we've lost 17 classmates from the Squadron, most SIEs[58]. "About five percent, not bad," Terry said, "considering summer training's almost over."

A huge tent was set up for Protestant services. Dressed in battle fatigues, Chaplain Bennett gave his usual stirring sermon. "Gentlemen," he concluded, "I hope your being in the beautiful setting of nature with the wind blowing free and the magnificent sunsets develop in you a consciousness that God is all around you – even in the environs of battle."

***

Monday, reveille was at 0630. After breakfast, we gathered by the wooden platform. Lt. Tatum, razor sharp in starched fatigues, gave us at ease and told us to sit on the ground.

"In your careers you are likely to encounter various survival situations. We fly and fight all over the world. From your WWII studies, you know pilots were downed in country sides, forests, waterways, and jungles. Therefore, we're going to cover a variety of escape, evasion, and survival scenarios, including desert conditions which you'll experience first-hand."

True to his word, Lt. Tatum covered the spectrum of escape, evasion, and survival possibilities. He explained dangers (including, of course, the enemy and hostile civilians as well as natural perils such as rattlesnakes, poison plants), ground navigation, and how to find edible food and "safe" water supplies.

"Tomorrow night, you'll have a chance to test your skills in a desert escape and evasion exercise" Lt. Tatum concluded.

***

At 1400 hours, 3d Squadron was bussed to a large tent. Nicknamed the "gas chamber;" but officially the "Gas Mask Exercise Tent;" the tent had an inner sealed room fed tear gas by portable tanks. "Gentlemen, in your combat duties you may encounter a poisonous gas attack," began TSgt. Green. "If there is such a threat, you must know how to protect your body and use a gas mask to avoid inhaling a potential killer gas."

[58] Self-Initiated Elimination

TSgt. Green lectured for an hour. When he finished, he and his assistant, Airman Second Class Kelly, adjusted the gas mask on our face.

"Damn, Butch, this doesn't sound like fun. I heard two guys in 1st Squadron got sick enough they had to take them back to Lowry."

"Yeah, Davis, but we know they're a bunch of wimps. This'll be a piece of cake. Speaking of which, Terry told me chocolate cake and ice cream are dessert tonight. They're also showing a movie. Can't get any better than that!"

"We'll see. Go ahead, you're next."

With a show of bravado, Butch stepped into the gas chamber. I followed him in. For safety purposes, only five cadets were in the chamber at a time so the technicians could watch everyone and get those in trouble out in a timely manner.

Although I could see Butch coughing and hacking near the exit, I was comfortable with my mask on. Halfway through the chamber, TSgt. Green motioned for me to take my mask off.

Immediately my eyes burned and I felt like I'd swallowed a sandpaper milkshake. I began to cough uncontrollably. *Crap, this is bad. I'd hate to encounter the real stuff. Now, where's the exit!* I began to panic. My eyes teared constantly; my coughing increased. I lost my sense of direction. A firm hand grabbed my arm and directed me 180 degrees from the direction I was going. "Come on, Davis, think you've had enough. Let's get you out of here."

As I excited the chamber, I was nearly doubled over from coughing. Butch, who had been outside the tent for five minutes, looked at me and started laughing, "What's the matter, Davis, trying to get a trip to the hospital?"

My stomach was still upset at diner. The food made me queasy. Butch and I wandered back to the tent. Our throats still sore from the tear gas, we didn't talk. I was still uncomfortable when I crawled into my sleeping bag. It took an hour to fall asleep.

***

Wednesday reveille sounded well after sun up. Butch and I awakened to the smell of pancakes, bacon, and coffee drifting from the mess tent. "You know what, Butch? This food's as good as we get in the dining hall," I said, wolfing down a second serving of pancakes and scrambled eggs.

"Yeah, but the difference is here you get to eat the food. I think I've put on four pounds."

"Look at it this way, you're just storing up. I'm sure food will be just a memory when we dine with the upperclassmen."

"What the hell, let's feast while we can. You know what? I'll bet you a candy bar I get more hits on the drone than you do."

"You're on," I said.

***

"All right, Cadet Davis, remember to lead the drone. Sight halfway between the plane and the drone." SSgt. Clark Yancy was instructing our flight on the 50 caliber machine gun. We practiced loading, aiming, and cooling the weapon. Our simulated foxhole was on the perimeter of the range. The gun was mounted to fire to the east.

I gripped the gun with sweaty hands. I sighted the Browning M-2 on the drone, moved the sight midway between the drone and the aircraft, and squeezed the trigger. Despite earplugs and ear muffs, the sound exploded in my ears. The gun's vibration shook my entire body. Tracer bullets arched toward the target. I shot three short bursts. The first line of tracers went beneath the drone. I was sure my second burst hit the drone. The third tracer flashes fell behind the drone as it was pulled out of range.

A short while later we learned the drone had two hits (the aircraft, thankfully, none). Airman Yancy credited me with being the only one to hit the drone. I would have bragging rights that night and a candy bar from Butch.

That afternoon we cleaned rifles, washed underwear, and waterproofed boots. There was leftover time to rest. Lt. Payne encouraged us to take a nap, if possible. Cool, fair weather and a lack of thunderstorms had blessed the Bivouac so far, but rain was forecast that night for 3d Squadron's E&E exercise.

We packed a water canteen, a small package of beef jerky, our compass, and light ponchos into our ruck sack. The ATOs warned if you ate the jerky, you're liable to drink all your water early and possibly suffer from dehydration, a serious consequence of lack of water. I decided to reserve the jerky for hard times back in the dorm. Feedback from 1st and 2nd Squadron classmates indicated the night was "a bitch."

Assembly was just after sunset. Taken to an unfamiliar area, we were grouped in threes and headed south. The only instructions were to head south and not get caught. The penalty for getting caught was not spelled out.

***

"Damn, what was that?" I whispered to Terry.

The small explosion was followed by a large star burst over our heads. The flare swung back and forth, suspended by a small parachute. We all dropped to the ground.

"Look," Butch said, "you can see the whole Squadron spread across the field."

The distinctive rasp of Lt. Tatum called out from in back of us. "You men had better keep quiet if you don't want to end up as POWs[59]."

We were about a third of the way through the eight mile course. It was 2230. I was cold and concerned about lightning flashes to our west moving in our direction.

Simultaneously with the flare explosions, machine guns pounded our ears with short, staccato bursts. We could see muzzle flashes from four positions on our right and left. Nothing but darkness lay beyond the luminous circle of the flare. At the edge of the light; however, we saw yellow flags indicating we were on course. The flags also identified a mine field.

"Shit," Terry said, as his right arm struck a trip wire. A loud explosion boomed to our right. Continuing on, we ran into a barb wire barrier. As instructed previously, Terry stretched across the roll of barbed wire so Butch and I could climb over the wire on his back. Once we crossed, we squashed the wire down to enable Terry to climb off the roll. Fifteen yards further, we encountered a barrier that required crawling under the wire for 20 yards. Set with various devices; it was impossible to prevent tripping them. Most set off explosions like large fire crackers, but several sent flares screeching into the night sky.

Just as we exited the last obstacle, someone on our left triggered a flare. Ahead we could see several large sagebrush. We ran for the bushes intending to hide on the ground behind them. I was three feet behind Terry and Butch. I was about to dive behind the bushes when two large men in Russian-looking uniforms grabbed my arms.

"Vell, what do we haf here," said one of the ATOs. I recognized the speaker as a 1st Squadron Element Leader. In his exceptionally lousy accent he continued: "We haf a prisner."

The two turned to the north when another large flare ignited. Taking advantage of the distraction, I ran. The "enemy" now turned their attention to three classmates running under the glare of the newly lit flare.

"Pssssst, Davis, over here." The Kentucky drawl of my roommate led me to Butch and Terry still lying behind the bushes.

"What did they do to you?" both asked at the same time.

"Nothing. They were distracted by another flare so I took off. They seemed more interested in catching three people than hanging onto me."

"Who were they?" asked Butch.

---

[59] Prisoners of War

"Hell, I don't know; looked like a couple of 1st Squadron ATOs in loopy Russian uniforms. Come on, I think we have a ways to go yet. Which way is south?"

Terry looked at the luminous dials on his compass. "That way," he pointed. As we continued south, several lightning flashes lit up the mountains. The cumulus clouds, looking like Japanese lanterns from the lightning, appeared to be moving our way. I heard the light rumble of thunder, but it was too indistinct to calculate the distance of the storms.

"Crap," Terry exclaimed as a bank of spotlights suddenly probed the 150 yard long open field in front of us. "Hit the dirt."

"The guys in 2nd Squadron said the drill here is to crawl across the field," said Butch. "When the spotlight nears you, lie still and they'll leave you alone. Let's go"

Reaching beyond the searchlight's sweep, we stood momentarily and brushed off the desert dust. "Damn," I said. "There goes a set of fatigues. The shirt's ripped at the elbow and the pants at the knee."

"Quit sniveling, Davis," Butch whispered. "It's 0100; judging by what Pete Trotogott told me, we still have a couple of hours to go. I'm cold, tired, and want to crawl into that luxurious sleeping bag. Let's go."

Three fourths across a large open stretch, lightning struck a hundred yards in front. We grabbed our ponchos. The sky opened up in a deluge . The rain continued for 20 minutes as we sloshed south. Muddy pools slowed our pace. "Damn,' said Terry. "Even with the water proofing, there go the boots. Sure glad the rain waited until we past the crawl exercise."

"Look," I said. Ahead on a well-lit building, a large sign read: "Friendly Territory." Unfortunately, between us and the building was a 10-foot wide canal gushing rainwater.

"Now, how in Hell are we supposed to cross that ditch," Terry said.

"Hey," I said, "look over there. There are a couple of two by eight planks."

"Right," said Butch, "but they're only seven foot long. Did you bring along some bailing wire or how is your pole vaulting?"

I'm not sure what bailing wire is, but you just gave me an idea, Butch. "Hey, look. What if we overlap the boards, use our belts to fasten them and lay them across the ditch. I think if we crawl across; the boards will hold us."

"You first, Davis. We'll stand downstream to fish you out if you fall," Terry said.

We put the boards together, creating as much overlap as possible. We cinched the boards together with our belts. I started to crawl across our improvised bridge. We feared if we walked across, our foot print would put too much pressure on the boards and they would separate. By distributing our weight, we had a chance. It worked.

"Come on you brave souls, do it!" I said.

After crossing, I said, "Terry, "bring the boards over so we can get our belts."

"Hey, said Butch," "what about guys behind us? We could leave the boards set."

"Right and get written up for 'out of uniform' -- no belts," Terry said. "Besides, the exercise is to test everybody's problem solving ability. The next guys have to figure it out."

"Hey, I saw shadows on the second floor of the building. I'll bet the ATOs are watching. Terry, grab a board and we'll toss them back to the other side," I said.

Our throws weren't elegant, but the boards did land on the other bank.

"Look," said Terry pointing to a sign with an arrow indicating south that read "No man's land." Ten yards beyond was a seven-yard wide, water-filled ditch. A rope hung from a crossbar allowing one to swing across the ditch.

"Okay, hotshot," I said to Terry, "your turn in the barrel."

Terry smirked and started across the open stretch to the ditch. Machine gun fire broke out on the left and right. Terry looked panicked as he began to run. He did not get a good swing on the rope and landed with a loud splash two feet short of the bank. Terry stood up looking like a mud-covered muskrat as he crawled up the far bank.

When we stopped laughing, I said, "Hell, how are we going to get the rope?"

"Look, Davis, isn't that a pole with a hook on it on this side of the ditch."

"Great," I said, "somebody loves us; let's go. I'll hook the rope, give it to you, then hit the deck. You get across and swing the rope back to me."

The plan worked. Butch swung across. When I hit the deck, the machine gun fire stopped. The rope came back to me and I swung across.

A large tent with mess hall personnel serving donuts and either coffee or hot chocolate awaited us. I grabbed a couple of donuts and hot chocolate. I joined Butch in another laugh as an ATO hosed the mud off Terry. Outside blue beetles waited to take us back to the encampment.

Air Training Officers at FASE

Lt. Payne checked our names on a list and said, "It's 0300. Go get on a bus. Cloud, grab a couple of towels in the bin over there. Wipe yourself off and sit on one. Don't dirty the bus."

***

"**Attention, 3d Squadron, it is 0755. There are five minutes until reveille. Today is Thursday, 5 September. The uniform is fatigues and combat boots. Cadets will form in front of their tents. When dismissed, they may go to the mess hall for breakfast.**" Roll call in front of the tents ensured no cadets were missing from the previous night's activities.

I don't know how Roger Stringer got the special duty of being a minute caller in FASE, but I was happy I didn't. I was bone tired. "Damn, Butch, get up. I'm hungry. If I have to wait for you, I'm going to be pissed".

"Oh, hell. What time is it?"

"It's 0800. Come on, you had your allotted four and a half hours sleep. **Get Up!**"

"Don't yell, I'm up"

***

Streaking from the north, three F-86s roared toward the large, wooden target 200 yards in front of the reviewing stands. A quarter of a mile from the target, the three Sabres simultaneously climbed at a 45 degree angle, releasing a 250 pound bomb from their wings. The earth shook as the bombs exploded inside a painted circle on the desert floor. Seconds after dirt and debris flew 30 feet in the air; our ears were blasted with the sound of the expositions.

"**Airpower!**" someone shouted in the stands behind me.

"Damn, Davis," how'd you like to be standing in the middle of that circle?"

"Ah . . . no thanks, Butch" I replied, rubbing my ears to ease the ringing; "but I'd sure as hell like to be sitting in one of those F-86s. What a beautiful bird."

"Ah, hell," Terry, said, "by the time we get there, they'll have something newer and hotter. Look at the F-100s the New Mexico guys are flying."

As they climbed, the Sabre Jets aligned themselves in trail at about 2,000 feet above the terrain. The first aircraft began a diving 180 degree left-hand- turn to align with the wooden target. We saw the smoke from six-fifty caliber machine guns before we heard the characteristic rat-a-tat-tat. Dirt splatted in a straight line as the pilots walked their shots toward the target. Pieces flew out of the target as the sleek bird went to full power and streaked away.

As we watched the first Sabre climb, we heard the rat-a-tat-tat of the second aircraft. Number two followed the lead's pattern and walked his bullets up the front of the wooden target. Number three followed in short order. All three were right on target.

"**Wahoo,**" shouted Terry. "You know, Davis, those are ATOs flying the 86s."

"I didn't, know," I said. "Impressive. Guess they've been doing more than baby-sitting us."

"Look," Terry said, pointing north.

Low on the horizon was a four ship formation of F-80s[60]. In the next 40 minutes, the Colorado Air National Guard "Minute Men" put on a show patterned after and rivaling the USAF Thunderbirds. In addition to the four ship rolls, the opposing head-on inverted passes, and the magnificent bomb burst finale, the fifth member of the team, a solo, did spectacular passes performing chandelles, figure eights, and a low level inverted pass.

A fire power demonstration by the New Mexico National Guard F-100s capped the afternoon's event. The F-100s worked in pairs. They employed machine guns, bombs, and rockets. The hit of the show, however, was the final two Super Sabres who lit up the field with napalm bombs. The flames spread across a path of 30 to 40 yards and burned with an intensity that turned the desert sands into glass particles.

As a closer, two F-100s made a low speed pass and went supersonic. The twin booms were ear splitting, but produced a sense of speed and power that thrilled us.

"Wow," said Terry. "Do we have to wait four years to do that?"

"I don't know, but you should ask Dick Carbon. He was qualified in the F-100. There must be a reason he came here instead of being out there."

"I talked to Dick," Terry said. "Dick's father. a general, told Dick that if he wanted to make a career of the Air Force, he should go to the Academy and get a regular commission."

The motivation for whatever lay ahead was evident in the bus ride back to the Bivouac area. Spirits were high and the camaraderie evident. We all wanted to be fighter pilots.

***

"That was one damn, fine show," Terry said, joining Butch and me. The three of us grabbed fried chicken, mashed potatoes and broccoli in our mess kits, and pan-ther-pis in our canteens. We returned to our tent area to eat.

"Yeah," I said. If they were trying to motivate us, I think they succeeded. Great FASE. I even enjoyed the E&E Exercise."

"Crap, Davis," Terry said. "That's because you didn't fall in the mud. Do you know how long it took me to get the mud off my boots; never mind putting a shine back on them? Wish they had a hole in them or something so I could get new ones."

---

[60] The F-80 "Shooting Star" was the first United States Army Air Force (USAAF) operational jet fighter. It flew in 1944, but did not see action in WWII. It had a speed of 558 mph, had six 50 caliber machine guns and could carry bombs or rockets.

"Bitch, bitch, bitch," Butch said. "If the machine gun hadn't scared you so much, you wouldn't have slipped."

"Screw you," Terry retorted. "Anyway, we were lucky. I heard Greg Jones in 2nd got bit by a rattlesnake. He went out behind his tent to take a pee and didn't see the rattler. Good thing he had his pants up. No telling where he might have been bitten."

"Right, I said, "Funny. Did you hear what we're doing tomorrow?"

"Yeah,' said Terry and Butch together.

"We get to pack up at 0500," Butch said. "After breakfast, we get on the buses and go to Lowry to fly the T-33. Man, that's great."

"After the T-Bird flight," Terry added, "we go back to the barracks and pack for the move Sunday. That'll be a real fire drill."

Just then Tattoo sounded.

We jumped up and hustled to the cleaning cans to wash our mess kits and canteens. "Boy, I'm going to sleep tonight," Terry said, heading for his tent. "See you all tomorrow."

FASE QUARTERS

C FLIGHT

Chapter 20

Oh, I have slipped the surly bounds of earth
High Flight, John Gillespie Magee

Saturday, 7 September1957 High Flight

"Canopy clear?"

"Canopy clear, sir," I responded.

"Davis, there is no 'sir' on my checklist. In flying as a crewmember, you respond without formalities. If you're in a B-47, for instance, you answer with your crew position; i.e., 'Pilot, navigator, change course to 180 degrees . . . Pilot, Roger' . . . got it?"

"Yes, Sir . . . ah . . . Roger," I said sheepishly.

Lt. O'Malley lowered and locked the canopy. He smoothly moved the throttle,[61] applying power to move off the parking spot. The blue Colorado sky stretched forever.

Lt. O'Malley went to 70% RPM[62], retarded to 55% and pressed on the right brake to track the taxiway white line leading to the runway. I ate a light breakfast. I'd heard of classmates who had lost breakfast in the cockpit on their flights. I didn't want that to happen to me.

Lt. O'Malley said to put my hands "lightly," he emphasized lightly, on the stick and the throttle and follow the movement of the rudder pedals with my feet.

"Buckley Ground, Falcon 21 taxing for takeoff, over."

"Roger, 21, Runway 14 is in use. Contact tower at the end of the runway."

***

"Buckley Tower, this is Falcon 21, ready for takeoff."

"Two-One, you are cleared onto Runway 14, cleared for takeoff. Winds calm, pressure altimeter is 29.92. Contact Denver Center on 247.5 for flight following when clear of the field."

"Roger, Buckley, Two-One rolling."

Lt. O'Malley said to set the radio/intercom on "interphone" and flip the UHF radio button to "up" to monitor radio transmissions. The interphone "hot mike" allowed communication with the pilot without changing settings or pressing the mike button.

---

[61] The T-33 has dual controls: throttles, rudders, sticks, altimeters, airspeeds, and instrumentation with individual ejection seats and oxygen systems.

[62] RPM – Revolutions per minutes. The tachometer indicated engine speed in percentage of RPM, with 100% representing specified maximum RPMs.

My heart beat increased as Lt. O'Malley released the brakes and brought the engine to 100%. As I was pushed back in my seat, I noticed the altimeter read 5,591 feet, the height of Buckley Field. I watched airspeed build and the runway makers pass faster and faster.

At 85 knots[63] I felt the stick[64] move slightly back. The movement lifted the nose wheel off the runway. The 8,000 foot remaining maker flashed by.

As the 6,000 foot marker zoomed by, I felt the 12,000 pound jet glide smoothly into the air. I noticed the airspeed at 115 knots and steadily increasing.

***

Out of the corner of my eye I saw the gear handle move. "Gear up," said Lt. O'Malley. We accelerated rapidly. The gear-up indicator lights turned green.

"Flaps up," The flap switch moved to "up" as we reached 150 knots. Lt. O'Malley placed the switch to "neutral" as the flaps melded into the wings. The ground rapidly sank away; the rugged terrain around Buckley dissolving into a patchwork of various shades of brown.

"All right, Davis, oxygen regulator normal. You have the aircraft," Lt. O'Malley said, vigorously moving the stick from side to side. "Look at your attitude indicator. Give us about two bars above the horizontal bar and establish a 160 knot climb."

"Yes, Sir," I said, switching the oxygen regulator from "100%" to "normal" with my left hand and nervously tightening my grip on the stick with my right. I instinctively continued to "Sir" Lt. O'Malley. He did not admonish me.

I quickly discovered a dead spot in the middle of the stick movement. I immediately over-controlled, causing the left wing to dip. I moved the stick right – again over-controlling. My efforts created an ever increasing oscillation, with the left wing dipping, then the right.

"Davis, you're making me airsick. I've got the aircraft." Centering the stick, Lt. O'Malley made imperceptible corrections, returning the aircraft to a wings level. "The secret is to make minor corrections; anticipate movement. Don't overdo it. You've got the aircraft.."

---

[63] Aircraft instrumentation is in "knots," from the term "nautical mile," the measure used on air and marine maps. A knot equals 1.151 miles per hour (mph). Here, the 85 knots would be 100 mph.

[64] In fighter aircraft (except the P-38) the "stick," a column between the pilots legs, controls ailerons and the elevator. Larger aircraft normally have a semi-circular "wheel" mounted on a column in front of the pilot. Rudder pedals control the rudder and also normally operate the brakes -- actuated by pressing down on the tops of the pedals.

Nervously, I took the stick and struggled to keep it centered. After about 10 minutes, I made small enough corrections to dampen the oscillations. I was pleased and excited.

***

At 20,000 feet, Lt. O'Malley shook the stick. "I've got the aircraft. Want to do some acrobatics?"

I eagerly replied, "Yes."

Lt. O'Malley reduced the power to 96%, leveled the aircraft and continued accelerating to 350 knots. "We have to go a little more to the southeast to the designated acrobatics areas before we can begin."

The ground below, mostly baron and brown, looked like a road map. An occasional car, the size of an ant, crawled along the east-west roads. The clear sky was an incredible blue. Far to the south, a contrail etched its way across sky like a chalk mark on a blue backboard.

O'Malley kept full throttle, nosed the aircraft over, and began a steep dive. "We're going to do a loop," he said. "We'll pick up airspeed, bring the nose up, and hold back pressure until we get to the top of the loop. To counter the G[65] pressure, you'll want to tighten your stomach muscles. As we come over the top we look for a section line on the field below to line up. We'll level off no lower than 10,000 feet, which is a little better than 5,000 above the ground. Ready?"

"Yes, siiiiiiirrrr," I groaned as we arched up. The G forces felt like someone pressing down on my body with a huge mattress. I tightened my stomach. At the top of the loop, there were a few seconds of negative Gs; then I felt the stick press back between my legs and the positive G's again pressing down.

We leveled at 10,000 feet at 400 knots. "You all right, Davis? You still with me?"

"Yes, Sir," I replied. I never liked carnival rides. But, this was exhilarating.

We did a quick barrel roll, followed by an aileron roll. My hand was lightly on the stick. "Now we're going to do a vertical maneuver. Okay, ready?"

"Yes, sssiiirrr." I forgot to tighten my stomach muscles. Suddenly, my vision began fading. My eyesight began collapsing into a dark circle. I felt I was falling into a deep, dark well. When my vision returned, we were inverted at 20,000 feet.

O'Malley smoothly rolled upright, wings level.

My attitude indicator was leaning to one side. I felt akin to the attitude indicator.

---

[65] Gs: the force of gravity expressed in multiples of normal G pressure (1 G) caused. Gs can be positive or negative depending on the maneuver. Aircraft have a "G Limit" so as not too overstress the aircraft.

"You okay, Davis?'

"Yes, Sir," I said, with a less enthusiasm than I wished.

"That was a Chinese Immelmann, a maneuver developed by a fighter pilot to use in combat to gain altitude and change flight direction. Okay ,let's go look at the new site. You feeling all right, Davis?"

"Yes, Sir. But my attitude indicator looks a little sick."

"Oh, yeah. That happens. Pull slowly and carefully on the knob on the upper right side of the attitude indicator. That's called caging the attitude indicator."

"Yes, Sir. That worked."

***

The Rocky Mountains loomed larger and larger as we continued our westerly heading. As we passed through 10,000 feet, Lt. O'Malley began a gentle turn to the north, leveling at 7500 feet. The towering mountains were now on our left. Passing underneath was a forested area.

"That mountain on the left is Pike's Peak. Up ahead you'll see excavations for the new site. O.K., grab the stick. I'll be on it with you because we're at 500 feet above the terrain. After we go by you can say you personally flew over the new site of the US Air Force Academy."

Our heading was 360 degrees; airspeed 250 knots. The aircraft burbled gently like a raft in light rapids. Ahead I saw cleared areas and a large number of buildings in various stages of erection. Incredible progress had been made since my T-29 fly-by.

When we zoomed overhead, many of the workmen waved. In an instant, we were again over a forested area. "I've got it, Davis," O'Malley said, rolling into a right climbing turn and advancing the power to 100%. "Well, what do you think of your future home, New Cadet?"

"That is spectacular, sir. It looks a little isolated, but it is going to be beautiful. What was that large square structure they were raising with the cranes?"

"That's the dining hall roof. The dining hall is a single open building --no middle support braces; just one giant room. It will seat the entire Wing next year. The valley construction is base housing. The Base Exchange, and Commissary sit on the ridge beyond the housing. The long, narrow east to west building is the dormitory. You could see the athletic fields, of course. The large building east of the athletic fields is the gym."

"Wow," was all I could I say.

***

On the return to Buckley, we climbed to 17,000 feet and accelerated to 400 knots. Lt. O'Malley was all business. "Denver Center, Falcon 21 is VFR, 10 minutes south of Buckley, seventeen thousand. Switching to tower, thanks for the flight following."

"Roger, Two-One, cleared to Buckley. Good Day. How's the new site going?"

"They're making progress. Good day, Out."

"Buckley Field, Falcon 21, VFR, on a 45 to Runway 14."

"Roger Two One, cleared to land. Winds south at five knots. Altimeter 30.01. Report gear down."

As we lined up on the runway at 6500 feet, O'Malley said, "Okay, Davis, get on the stick. I'll talk you through a pitch out landing." He shook the stick. "You've got it."

My heart was racing. I could feel sweat in my gloves and under my arms. "Yyyes, Sir."

We crossed the end of the runway numbers and "O'Malley said, Hard left turn, 45 degrees bank, keep the nose level with the rudder, and roll out on a heading of 320 degrees."

I moved the stick left and applied back pressure. I looked at the horizon to try to keep the aircraft level. I felt positive pressure on the stick, increasing the bank and exerting additional back pressure. There was also a positive pressure on the top rudder. As we neared 310 degrees the stick moved right with continued back pressure.

"Speed brake out." The aircraft buffeted and slowed noticeably. The throttle was advanced from the 50% O'Malley had set when we began the pitch. O'Malley called out, "Gear down, jiggle, jiggle.[66] Tower, Two-One turning final with the gear."

I felt the aircraft slow even more. I was trying to keep the aircraft and wings level, with a lot of help from O'Malley. "Okay, here's where we begin our turn to final and descent." O'Malley reduced power and increased the stick angle to the left. We moved toward the 140 degree runway heading; the altimeter decreasing toward field elevation at 350 feet a minute.

"Stay on the stick with me, but lightly," O'Malley said rolling wings level aligned with the runway. Over the end of the runway at 130 knots,

Gene with the T-33 "TBIRD"

[66] The T-33 gear handle did not always "lock" in the down position. Therefore, every pilot was taught to lower the gear handle, then jiggle it to make sure it was locked down. Thus, the call: "jiggle, jiggle."

O'Malley closed the throttle, eased back on the stick, and brought the nose wheel up. The aircraft touched down smoothly and rolled toward the second taxiway.

I realized I was holding my breath. I slowly breathed out, relishing my utter excitement at my first jet ride.

Chapter 21

Upon completion of our Fourth Class Summer Training,
the ATOs disappeared from USAFA
—US Air Force Academy Class of 1961 History—Colonel Hector Negroni

Friday 6, September1957, Transition

The bus ride to Lowry was quiet; everyone reliving their T-33 ride and wondering about life as a Fourth Classman. Summer Training was a challenge, but 245 New Cadets remained. Could we survive academics and the upperclassmen?

***

Dinner was strange. Four ATOs manned each squadron; a Squadron Commander and three Flight Commanders, with one ATO to a table. We were not at ease, but ATOs asked no questions.

***

With the absence of ATOs, Hertz, Dickson, Terry, Art, Butch, and I snuck down to the Squadron game room. The lone ATO sentinel was nowhere to be seen.

After discussing classmate departures, girls, and upper class threats, I wondered out loud, "What's that all about, the ATOs doing a Dining-In, whatever that is?"

As usual, Terry was on top of it. His father had sent him an Air Force customs book. "Cindy told me the ATOs will be at a Dining-In in their honor. ATOs, the Commandant, his staff, plus all support officers were 'invited.' i.e., ordered by the Superintendent to attend.

According to the book, the Dining-In is 'a formal dinner with strict protocol rules.' The President of the Mess, the Commandant, appointed by the Superintendent, sets up the whole thing: the schedule, menu, and entertainment. The rules are a riot, listen to this:

Etiquette for a Dinning-In

1. Thou shalt not be late.
2. Thou shalt move to the mess when thee hears the chimes; and will remain standing until seated by the President.
3. Thou shalt participate in all toasts unless thyself or thy group is being honored.
4. Thou shalt not laugh at ridiculously funny comments unless the President first shows approval by laughing.
5. Thou shalt not overindulge thyself in alcoholic beverages.
6. Thou shalt not wear an ill-fitted or discolored jacket.
7. Thou shalt enjoy thyself to the fullest."

"Where'd all the funny Bible language come from?" asked Kerr.

"That's not Bible language, it's old English, Chaucer!" Terry replied.

There's more, including how and when to toast. The first toast is 'To the Commander-in-Chief,' with a response: 'To the President.' Then, 'To the Chief of Staff,' answered with 'To the Chief of Staff.' The reply to all toasts after that is: 'Hear, hear!'"

If you mess up the toast or commit some other protocol violation, called an 'infraction of the Mess;' 'A member may be punished for violating the Mess rules,' and, get this, 'A member may also be punished for something they might have done earlier, or for no reason other than someone wants to send them to the grog bowl.'"

"Okay, oh fount of wisdom, what's a grog bowl?" asked Hertz.

"It says here: 'The Grog Bowl contains a combination of different foods/drinks and may be unsavory looking, but it is never undrinkable.' The rules for going to the Grog Bowl sound like New Cadet instructions. Listen: 'When sent to the Grog Bowl, one does the following:

Going to the Grog Bowl
1. Proceed to the Bowl in a military manner, **Squaring all corners.'**
2. Salute the Grog Bowl.
3. Fill the cup at least 1/3 full.
4. Do an about face and toast the mess stating: "TO THE MESS."
5. Drain the grog form the cup without removing it from the lips.
6. Tip the cup upside down over one's head signifying the cup is empty.
7. Do an about face, replace the cup, salute the grog, and return to your seat.
8. You may not talk during this process.'"

"A Second Class friend wrote to me about what goes on later in the party," Dickson offered. "On their European Field Trip, one of the stops was Cranwell, the Brits' Air Force Academy. After dinner, they were all sloshed. That's when they started playing games, like 'jousting' on bicycles, and 'jump the rug.'

Jousting takes place on bicycles with a two-man team. One drives the bicycle; the other is on the driver's shoulders. Mops and brooms are weapons and trash can lids, shields. Everyone gathers in a large hall where they form a circle 40 feet across. The teams start at the edge; then ride toward one another. This goes on, with winners taking on a new team. Last team standing is tournament winner and chug-a-lugs a 'pint'.[67].

---

[67] A pint is a large glass of beer.

In 'Jump the Rug,' cadets hold the edge of a large circular rug. The victim starts running in place in the middle of the rug. If the cadets are coordinated and like the guy, they let the rug down slowly, stopping short of the floor.

My friend said three classmates went to the hospital; one with a broken arm from jousting and two with injuries, fortunately just bad bruises, from the rug game."

"We'll see how many ATO walking wounded there are in the morning." Terry said, glancing at the wall clock. "Look at the time. We'd better break it up."

***

Saturday was a mixed bag of emotions. Breakfast was quiet; with many ATOs missing. We didn't see any injuries, but casualties could be among the missing ATOs. As Honor Squadron, 3d Squadron did not have SAMI; however, all hell broke loose at in-ranks inspection.

"**Well, Mister Davis, nice of you to join us**," Lt. Tatum yelled as I slid into place. Tatum was suddenly in my face. "Fat chin in, Mister. Haven't you learned anything these past two months? We obviously have been too slack with you."

I was stunned, but complied with Tatum's instructions. The din in the quadrangle rose in rapid increments. The ATOs seemed intent on bringing back memories of our first meeting. I had no trouble; however, even when Tatum screamed: "**Give me 10, Davis**. *Should I really play the role,* I thought, *and start counting to 10. Ah, they seem serious; I'd better not . . .* I simply dropped and did 10 quick push-ups with little effort and no damage to my fresh set of khakis.

Every New Cadet received at least two write-ups. Flight Commanders, accompanied by their Element Leaders, conducted the inspections.

***

The sun was bright; the air cool and crisp with a subtle scent of autumn emanating from the Aspens in the mountains to the west. As we lined up for the last summer training parade, I felt an immense sense of pride and excitement.

I marveled at the precise cadence as we marched to *The National Emblem.* As we came online, the Superintendent, Commandant, and Dean stood in front of the reviewing stands. The crowd was the largest I'd seen at a parade. Looking to my right for alignment, I saw an exactingly straight line. My classmates all had inflated chests in an obvious show of pride.

As the ATOs paused in their last "Officers Front and Center," the Superintendent announced 3d Squadron as the Summer Training Honor Squadron. When he pinned the Honor Squadron pennant on our guide-on, we shouted a loud "**HURRAH!!!**"

Major General James E. Briggs, began: "Good morning, Ladies and Gentlemen, members of the ATO corps, New Cadets of the Class of 1961. After today these young men, the Class of 1961, who have endured a rigorous summer training period, will be known as 'Fourth Classmen' of the United States Air Force Academy. They have undergone a two month stringent test of their resolve and endurance in the first step in a program to make them officers and leaders in the United States Air Force.

Key to our program to date has been the corps of Air Training Officers serving as upperclassmen for our first three classes. These outstanding Air Force lieutenants and captains have been assigned here since 1955. They took the place of the upperclassmen we lacked. After today, they will return to assignments throughout the Air Force to fill leadership positions. We appreciate their contributions and will miss them as we continue to expand.

To the Class of 1961: I congratulate you on reaching the first plateau on your journey to become US Air Force officers. You may feel pride in your accomplishments to date, but, as I mentioned in my initial briefing to you; the competition is not over. Your entire Fourth Class Year is your tryout.

Your primary effort during the next four years will be to meet academic standards; however, if that were the only objective, there would be no need for an Air Force Academy. You must also learn and demonstrate you can fulfill the obligations of command with the leadership skills, self-control under pressure, and ethical conduct true leadership demands. You will be tested in academics, perhaps like never before. You must meet the test, along with completing the continuing military requirements.

We expect you, the Class of 1961, will be the last to receive academic instruction here at Lowry. Construction of the permanent site is on schedule. The Cadet Wing will move in September of next year. You, along with the classes of 1959, 1960, and 1962, will inaugurate use of our new facilities and will have a hand in building the traditions of our newest academy.

Good luck and God's Speed."

***

"Group . . . Squadron . . . Paaa . . .rade . . . Rest," called out Cpt. Gabriel, Lt. O'Malley, and Lt. Tatum in succession. The ATOs stood in the same formation they had on that fateful first day. Flashes of the last two months whirled through my mind. I felt exultation and pride. I had endured the program at the "Toughest School in America" that many my age were not selected for nor could have completed.

As we stood in flight formation at parade rest, the element leaders proceeded to the front of their elements. Lt Payne stopped in front of me. I came to attention.

"Davis," he said, "there were some shaky moments, but Tatum and I were confident you were going to make it. By the way, you were just lucky to beat me in the shoe and hat competition. We wish you luck with the academics and especially with the upperclassmen. *'Non illegitamus caborundum'"*

Taking a set of Fourth Class shoulder boards from Lt. Boyd, Lt. Payne fixed them on my khakis. I snapped my best hand salute. Lt. Payne returned the salute. With a hint of a smile, he made a sharp right face and stepped in front of Butch.

***

Sunday morning breakfast again saw a minimum of ATOs on duty. Rumor was many had immediate assignments and requested early reporting. When we sat, Lt. Payne simply said: "Sit, eat, and do not make any boisterous noise; that includes food announcements.

***

"Thanks, Butch. You've been a great roommate. Having the best Squadron room helped minimize demerits. Hell, except for the tour Lt. Payne gave me so I wouldn't miss the experience, I didn't get any for demerits. How many did you have?"

"I had two, both thanks to Tatum. They were for 'fun,' not demerits; one was for 'gazing in ranks' and the other one was for 'not smiling' at a crummy joke he made. And, yeah, I've enjoyed having you as a roommate too, except, of course, for the damn game with the 'Dear John.' Where're you going?"

"I'm in 6th Squadron, Dorm 914. My roommate's Tom Sanders. Haven't met him yet. Think he was in 2nd Squadron. Hope he and I get along as well as we have."

***

I had just finished my shorts, t-shirts, and sock shelves when a stocky, five foot-ten, dark haired cadet walked into the room. "Hi, I'm Don Davis from California."

"Tom Sanders. I'm from Long Island," he said with a slight, New York accent.[68]

"You were in 2nd Squadron, right? I saw you in the last soccer game."

"Yeah, unfortunately you beat us, with that Jack stud's four goals."

"He's good. Jack was high school All-City in Philadelphia. He carried the team. Most of us never played soccer. I played guard and line-backer in football and third base in baseball. I started at varsity right guard my senior year. How about you?"

"I played halfback in football, but my sport's really wrestling. I wrestled in the light weight class in the State finals; second in my class. The guy I wrestled was a pound lighter, but looked 10 years older. He won on points, couldn't pin me."

---

[68] The ATOs, and later the upperclassmen, jumped on anyone with a strong accent. By the end of our first year, with a couple of notable exceptions, those with accents lost them.

"We won't have problems with physical activity between intramurals and PE classes. I'd like to play intramural football, but I hear upperclassmen have first choice. Doolies just get put on teams. You have a girl friend?"

"Nah, not really. I dated a couple of girls in high school, but didn't see the long distance thing working. Most girls I knew will probably be pregnant by the end of their college freshmen year. I don't plan on bailing out for a marriage. Think I'll just stay a bachelor after graduation; too much to do and places to see. How about you?"

"Well, I'm pretty much like you. I was dating a sophomore my last year in high school. That didn't work out. She stopped writing after the first letter. She was fifteen when I left so I wasn't too surprised. I had a couple of other girlfriends, but nothing too serious. I dated, but didn't go steady. Nonetheless, I had a great time in high school."

Butch, my summer roommate, and I talked a lot about staying or leaving. When it comes down to it, this is a special time in a special place. Besides, my folks can't afford to send me to college. I'd end up in Junior College; working my butt off to pay for school. Didn't get too many scholarship offers, but didn't really try once I got the Academy appointment. I had a Coast Guard Academy appointment too. But, I'm not sure I could pass their swimming tests."

"Know what you mean about college. I have a sister who'll be in college next year. Dad said they couldn't do both; he was pleased when I got the appointment."

"Your sister good looking?"

"Of course. I'll show you a picture when I get my stuff unpacked. You'll have to plan a trip out our way to meet her."

"I'd enjoy that. I've never been to New York."

"How're your academics?" Tom asked.

"Oh, I'll do all right in English and the Social Studies. I got mostly A's in all my subjects in high school, but my math score in the SATs was low. How about you?"

"I like math and the sciences, but struggle a little with English and writing."

"Sounds like we're a pretty good match."

"Hey, Don, how about trading sides? I'm more comfortable over there," Tom said.

"Sorry, Tom, squatter's rights. You get to be the AOC and upperclassmen buffer. Gives me a chance to hide stuff."

"O.K., fair enough. How about a cigarette?"

"Nah, thanks. I don't smoke."

***

United States Air Force Academy
Sunday, 8 September 1957 1900 hours

Dear Folks,

What an incredible feeling. We had our last formal formation with the Air Training Officers this morning. My Element Leader, Lt. John Payne, put on my Fourth Class shoulder boards. We've lost about 10% of those who started with us, but the ones who are left are great, talented guys.

At the in-ranks inspection yesterday (we got out of the room inspection because of Honor Squadron), the ATOs chewed us out like the first day. I think they don't want us to forget them - ha! Fat chance after the wonderful times we've had together. .

The noon and evening meals were at ease. I actually had adult conversations with the ATOs. Lt. Tatum asked about high school; what I wanted to do in the Air Force. I said, "be a pilot." He's going to an Air Defense F-102 Fighter Squadron at Mather. He said to look him up next summer.

We had our fill at dinner. It was steak and lobsters, potatoes and gravy, rolls, broccoli, and pineapple upside down cake. I thought of you, Mom, when they brought out the cake, since that's what you used to make for me.

The upperclassmen sign in at midnight so tomorrow will probably be like the first day with the ATOs; meaning we'll start all over again with the Mickey Mouse stuff. Academics begin on Wednesday. We've seen a few upperclassmen putting things in their rooms, but there seems to be a "hands off" policy with regard to us for the moment. They reply to "Good afternoon, Sir," but don't engage in conversation beyond that.

I have a new roommate and address. Tom Sanders, my roommate, is from Long Island. Seems like a great guy; hope we get along as well as Butch and I did. His good looking sister is a year younger than he is. I may have to make a trip to New York in the next year or two.

My new address is: CADET FOURTH CLASS Don Davis, 6th Sqdn., Dorm 914, The Air Force Cadet Wing, USAF Academy, Denver, Colorado.

Well, need to brush up on my *Contrail's poop* (cadet slang for information) and put my best shine on my shoes. Tom and I decided to go to bed early tonight. No telling what will happen tomorrow. Write lots.

God Bless
Your loving son,
Don

Chapter 22

New cadets are not "hazed" in any sense of the word; statutes governing the service academies specifically prohibit hazing."
Major General James E. Briggs, Superintendent

The Upperclassmen Return

Monday, 9 September, 1957

"Well, well, well, if it isn't Mister Davis," said the stocky Third Classman with his nose three inches from mine. "Fancy meeting you here."

Oh crap, I thought, *of eight cadet squadrons, I had to draw the one with Cadet Third Class Peter Short in it.* The morning started as expected with the Second and Third Classmen introducing themselves at the reveille formation. An intense 10 minutes of "Who are you? Where are you from? Why are you so unmilitary looking?"

"Tell me again, Davis, your full name and hometown."

"Sir, I am New Cadet Donald Leroy Davis from Sacramento, California. No excuse, **Sir!**"

"New Cadet? Dumbsquat, hit it for 20. Davis, you and me are going to have a lot of fun in good old Sixth Squadron -- as long as you're here."

The Denver heat, which had been turning into pleasant fall temperatures, was back. A fresh set of khakis was about to develop the dreaded under arm sweat circles. C3C Short was still sporting his summer beer belly. I finished the 20 pushups and snapped back to attention.

"Not too bad, Davis, but I think you can do better, let's have another . . . "

Just as Short was about to demand more pushups, the Wing Commander called out: "**Wing . . . Atten . . . shun;**" followed by the squadrons being called to attention.

Short took three quick steps to his place in the third rank of C Flight.

***

To my dismay, C3C Short displaced a classmate at my ramp. The Table Commandant, Cadet Major John Riddle, B Flight Commander, a tall, thin Georgian spoke with a southern drawl. "Gentlemen, taaake seats. Since we're all new to each other, let's go round the table and introduce ourselves. I'm Cadet Major John Riddle and from Athens, Georgia. Went to Georgia Tech for two years fore I got to this lovely place. I'm C Flight Commander. Cadet Simons . . ."

"I'm Cadet Second Class Sam Simons from Clovis, New Mexico. I'm the Squadron intramural boxing coach, so I'll be looking for recruits. I went a year to Arizona State." Simons, as indicated by two chevrons on his shoulder boards, was a Cadet Staff Sergeant.

Across the table, the muscular, six-foot blond haired Second Classman stated: "I'm Cadet Second Class, Cadet Lieutenant James Hutton from Mobile, Alabama. Went to the University for two years and played a year of football. I'm Third Element leader."

"After a year at Southern Cal, I decided I wanted to fly, so I came here. My name is Third Class Cadet George Baker and I'm from Fresno, California." Third Classmen had no rank on their shoulder boards[69].

Third Classman Frank Jones declared he was from the proud state of Texas. At five foot seven and 155 pounds he didn't look Texan. "I liked the military life at Texas A&M so much, I decided to come here. The free scholarship was a better deal."

I was amazed at the civility of the upperclassmen.

"I'm Cadet Second . . . ah …Third Class Peter Short." Short said no more.

Art Kerr began to recite: "Sir, I'm Cadet Fourth Class Art Kerr . . ."

"Mister Kerr, is Art your full name and do Fourth Classmen use contractions?" asked Cadet Major Riddle.

"No sir," Art replied. "My name is Arthur Kerr. **I am** from Washington State."

"And you have no middle name?"

Yes, Sir, . . . uh . . . I mean, No Sir. My middle name is Jeffery. Sir"

"And how did you get interested in the Academy, Kerr?" Riddle asked.

"Sir, my father is a Coast Guard Major who flies rescue helicopters. He encouraged me to come to the Academy to get a commission and go to flight school."

"Good. Mister Davis, what's your story?"

"Sir, I am Cadet Fourth Class Donald Leroy Davis from Sacramento, California. My high school counselor said the Academy offered a free college education and an Air Force commission. So, I applied to the Academy."

"Did you play any sports in high school, Mister Davis?"

"Yes, Sir, I played guard and linebacker in football and third base in baseball."

"Okay, Mister Lester, you're up."

"Sir, I am Cadet Fourth Class Jerry Levine Lester. My hometown is Attica, Indiana. I played golf in high school."

---

[69] Cadet shoulder boards are dark blue (almost black) with silver markings. Third class boards have two edge lines enclosing an ess-shaped line. Fourth Class boards had only an outboard straight line bordering the ess line.

"Great, Mister Lester. I don't think you'll have a lot of time for golf. Mister Sanders."

"Sir, my name is Cadet Fourth Class Thomas Andrew Sanders. I'm from Massapequa, New York and I competed . . ."

"You're from where, Mister Sanders?"

"Sir, I am from Massapequa."

"And where in the world is Massapequa?"

"Sir, it is on Long Island."

"Okay, Continue."

"Sir, I was just going to add I competed in wrestling in High School."

"Great," said Cadet Major Riddle. "Eat."

Before I could get a bite, C3C Short said, "Mister Davis, give me the four verses of the . . ."

"Short," Cadet Riddle said softly. "I'll let you know when you can start. Everyone, eat."

Anticipating all hell would break lose, Kerr, Lester, Sanders and I sat tall, took small bites, and ate as quickly as possible. We were stunned with no further interaction with the upperclassmen.

On the way out of the dining hall, Short stopped me.

"Well, Mister Davis, hasn't anybody taught you how to do a gig line?"

"Yes, sir," Glancing down to check that my belt buckle, the tip of the belt and the line of my trousers were in a straight line, I saw a little blue showing between the tip and the buckle.

"Well, Dumbsmack, you don't learn very well. Write me a Form 10 for a bad gig line and another for gazing. Drive them around to my room before call to quarters. Post"

"Sixth Squadron Fourth Classmen will report to the Day Room," ordered a booming voice from the bottom floor. Cadet Lieutenant Colonel Jimmy L. Jay, the Squadron Commander, ushered us into the day room and directed us to "take seats."

We sat quietly. Cadet Jay intently watched the door. At the scheduled time of 0715, Jay commanded, **"Squadron, Atten . . . tion!"**

"Sir, Sixth Squadron's Fourth Classmen present and accounted for," Jay said to Captain Arnold E. Braswell, the Squadron Air Officer Commanding (AOC).

Wow, I thought, Great. Captain Braswell was summer Second Squadron AOC. Warren Haslouer told me he was strict, but a straight shooter. He expected excellence, but made sure ATOs played by the rules, and his Doolies had a fair chance to complete summer training.

"Good morning, men!"

"Good morning, Sir," we responded in unison.

"Take seats. Today is the beginning of your second biggest challenge – Academics. I expect you to continue the excellent military performance you established during summer training. I see several familiar faces from Second Squadron. They can tell the rest of you what I expect in terms of effort and achievement.

The squadron upperclassmen are quality men who have proven themselves as cadets – or they wouldn't be here. Cadet Jay and I have had extended conversations about their role as leaders. They will enforce discipline, military customs and courtesies, and Academy regulations. They are also directed to be mentors; assisting you in meeting the standards.

I expect you, the Fourth Classmen, to excel in all areas: parades, inspections, intramurals, and academics. You will get guidance and assistance; not only from the upper classmen, but from me, the Academy staff, and the faculty as well.

Attack the rest of your Doolie year as you did New Cadet Summer and you'll participate in the Recognition Parade next spring. As our third class you will help to establish traditions. Make sure you, individually, do your part.

I have an open door policy; you may come see me on any matter: military, academic, or personal. If military or academic, you'll follow the chain of command before seeing me. On the military side, speak with your element, flight, and squadron commanders before seeing me. If someone in the chain of command is the issue, address it to the next level of command before coming to me. If it is a matter of Academy rules and regulations, go to the Squadron Commander directly. And, of course, if it's an honor question, you should go directly to your Squadron Honor Representative. Are there questions?"

Art Kerr stuck his hand up very tentatively. "Sir, when will we know the name of the Squadron Honor Representative?"

"Good question, Kerr. In the next several days, Cadet Jay and his staff will give you several briefings: on Squadron operations, on your duties, on staff positions and functions, and a thorough briefing on the honor code, its operations, and your obligations under it."

Seeing no further questions, Captain Braswell said, "Good luck, Gentlemen. With hard work and a great deal of prayer, I hope to see all of you marching in the Recognition Parade."

"Room, atten . ..tion!" Cadet Jay sang out. After Captain Braswell departed, Jay said, "At ease, gentlemen. Take Seats."

***

"As you know, I am Cadet Lt. Col. Jimmy L. Jay, Super Sixth's Squadron Commander. I won't repeat Captain Braswell's words, but I certainly endorse all he said.

It's my intent to compete for the Cadet Honor Squadron for the fall semester. That means we have to be tops in academics, athletics, and military standing. As Fourth Classmen, you will continue under the Fourth Class System, but you are a member of **my** team. **You will excel** as Fourth Classmen, but you'll be treated with dignity. You can expect assistance in all areas, including and, maybe especially, academics by me and all second and Third Classmen in the squadron.

I have reviewed your personnel records. I expect you to live up to your potential. If you have a problem with someone in the chain of command, come see me. If you have **any** thoughts of quitting, you **will** come to see me. If you have an issue involving the Honor Code, you will go privately to Cadet Major Gerald Garvey, the Squadron Honor Representative and Wing Honor Committee Chair. Any questions?"

Art Kerr's hand shot up. "Sir, how do we sign up for intramural teams?"

"We had a squadron meeting and assigned cadet coaches. Coaches will ask if you want to be on their team. Your first choice may not be available. In that case, or if you have experience in a particular sport, you may be assigned to a team.[70] More questions? No? It's 1840. You may visit with classmates until Call to Quarters."

***

"Where are you going Davis?" Tom asked already halfway into his PT gear.

"I have to see C3C Short. He nabbed me at noon; said to report to him tonight."

"Well, you'd better not dawdle; it's only 30 minutes until Call to Quarters."

"What are you doing in PT gear Davis? I told you fatigues, helmet, and M1." Short was lying on his bed with a *Playboy* magazine draped across his chest. His roommate, Peter Long, was at his desk, looking through his academic schedule.

"Ah, Sir, I don't think you specified a uniform. I assumed . . ."

"Dumbsquat, you don't assume anything. Are you calling me a liar? I specified the uniform. Write me a Form 10 for being in improper uniform."

"Ah, yes sir. Guess I didn't hear you properly."

"I guess not. However, since you are in PT gear and a push-up champ, let's see how good you are. Hit the deck and count out the push-ups."

"Seventy-two . . ." I struggled to get to the top of the pushup. ". . . 73 . . . uhhh!"

"Weak Davis You now have five minutes to get your butt downstairs and into the proper uniform."

---

[70] In reality, Fourth Classmen were assigned to teams based on upper classmen's desires, usually on teams upperclassmen did not want. In my case boxing, wrestling, and water polo were "assigned," as opposed to chosen sports.

"Now what the hell," Tom said as I sprinted into the room, threw my gym shorts on the bed, donned my fatigues, grabbed my helmet and M1, and bolted out the door.

"What are you doing, Davis?" Cadet Jay said as I almost ran over him in the hall.

"Sir, I am going to Cadet Short's room as ordered."

"Oh, Okay." Jay said with an inquisitive look on his face. "Post."

Racing down the stairs from our upstairs, end-of-the-hall room, I slid to a stop in front of Short's room in the middle of the building. I knocked twice.

"Come," Short said. He was in his blue bathrobe and black socks. He walked over, indicated I should come in and shut the door. His roommate was still at his desk.

"That was six minutes, Davis. That's worth a Form 10 for 'Late for formation.'"

"Yes, Sir," I moaned.

"O.K. Dumbsquat, let's see what you got. **Atten . . . shun. Right shoulder . . . arms. Port . . . arms**." Short returned to his bed and picked up his magazine.

Five minutes later, Short looked up. My arms felt like they were going to fall off. "Hey, Peter, you'd better let him go," Short's roommate said, "it's 1914."

"Oh, yeah . . . post Doolie."

I did a rifle salute, an about face, and scrambled out the door. I was just about to go down the corridor to my room when I heard a loud, **"You, Man, halt!!!"**

The voice belonged to C3C Ed Whiteman, Cadet in Charge of Quarters (CIC). Whiteman's reputation as a Fourth Class baiter was second only to C3C Peter Short. "What are you doing out of your room after Call to Quarters?" Whiteman asked.

"Sir, I was in Cadet Short's room . . ."

"What's the right answer, Smack?"

I was perplexed for a moment, then said, "No excuse, Sir."

"Right, Do-Willy. What's your problem; didn't Mama teach you to tell time?"

I clenched my teeth and said nothing.

"Well, here's a little present to help you remember the rules." He handed me a Form 10 from a pad that he was carrying; it read: "In hallway, out of uniform, after Call to Quarters." "Put the Form 10 in the box in the Orderly Room, then get to your room."

Chapter 23

The General Education [Academics] Program provides a Bachelor of Science Degree [through] . . . a broad, balanced education in liberal arts, science, and engineering.
—USAFA Catalog 1958-1959

Introduction to Academics
Tuesday, 10 September, 1957

Reveille blared over the PA system. I looked at my clock . . . *0545 . . . Doesn't look like academics are going to change much on the middle-of-the-night getting up.* "Hey, Tom, you awake?"

"Nah, just pretend I'm not here and go on without me."

"Yeah, great. C3C Short will write me up for not having a roommate in formation. Get your butt out of bed and get dressed."

"Sir, there are five minutes until breakfast formation. The uniform of the day is fatigues with ball cap and low quarter shoes. There are 106 days until Christmas leave. There 274 days until recognition. There are three days until the Falcons beat UCLA in football. There is one day until classes start. There are five minutes, SIR."

Terry Guess had the honor of being the first squadron minute caller. It was strange not to hear Lt. Tatum's screeching corrections. We would find, with notable exceptions, Squadron upperclassmen were reasonable people. They enforced the Fourth Class System, but as Cadet Lt. Col. Jay said, it was now more of a team effort.

Exiting the dorm, I almost ran over Cadet Jay standing on the porch. "By your leave, Sir."

"Pass, Davis. Leave yourself more time so you don't have to sprint into formation."

"Yes, Sir," I said and hurried to my spot in the first rank of C Flight.

"Well, Davis, glad to see you can make formation on time. Too bad you didn't get completely dressed," C3C Short said unbuttoning a button on my shirt. "Drive around a Form 10 before Call to Quarters tonight for uniform button unbuttoned."

"Sir . . ." before I could ask what the uniform was for special inspection, Cadet Jay called the squadron to attention and took the morning report.

***

At breakfast, the inquisition began. Cadet Major Riddle asked Tom for the Academy mission. Each Second Classmen asked similar routine questions of the four of us. Cadet Simons asked Cadet Kerr for the Academy key leaders. Kerr got away with stating the full names of the Superintendent, the Commandant, and the Dean.

C3C Short came after me with a vengeance. "Okay, Davis, let's have all four versus of the Air Force Song."

"Off we go into the Wild Blue Yonder," I began. Short stopped me numerous times, usually incorrectly, and had me go back to the beginning of a verse. Untouched, my food was getting cold. Short ordered a Form 10 for lack of Fourth class knowledge.

"Okay, Short, enough. Davis, eat!" Cadet Major Riddle said quietly, but firmly.

With less than five minutes to dismissal, I concentrated on my pancakes. They were cold, without syrup, but I could cut them into bite-size pieces and wash them down with milk.

"Wow," Tom said, "that was some harassment from Short. You really frosted him with the pushups last summer. Still, he shouldn't be on your butt like that. Here, take these peanut butter crackers. Maybe they'll hold you over 'til lunch"

"Thanks, Tom," I said throwing my comforter on the floor and stretching out.

***

The first Commander's period was squadron formations and marching. Cadet Captain Ken Thomas, Flight Commander, stepped in front of the flight. "**C Flight, right . . . face.**"

Classes were mixed throughout the flight; Element Leaders at the far right. "Except for Element Leaders, if you're taller than the man in front of you, move up." C3C Jon Bush, classmates Terry Koonce and Bill Gibbons ended up in front of me; Tom was behind me.

We drilled for 45 minutes. "All right, weinies," Thomas called out, "look to your right, dress on the person next to you. Keep cadence, don't bounce . . . **left, right, left; left, right left**." Standing in front of the Squadron, Cadet Lt. Col. Jay called out, "At ease." We relaxed in the shade in front of Barracks 914. "Okay, men, you're looking pretty good. We are going to have 45 minutes of squadron drill, including 'officers' front and center.'

The next hour, we'll have a wing formation to include parade practice. Saturday's parade is open to the public, our first appearance this fall. There may even be press there. So, work hard on keeping the lines straight, especially in the turns, and keep in cadence so we don't look like Middies.[71]

---

[71] "Middies" refers to Annapolis cadets who have the reputation – at least at West Point and now USAFA – of bouncing up and down like a bunch of "crabs" when they parade.

"**Squadron, atten . . . shun. Dress right . . . dress. Column of flights, A Flight, right turn . . . march.**" A Flight executed a right turning maneuver at the Flight Commander's call of "**A Flight . . . right turn . . . march!**" B and C flight followed as the squadron assumed a column formation. Cadet Jay guided the squadron to the quadrangle and went through the entire required parade maneuvers.

Cadet Lts. Musselman and Meyer, patrolled outside the formation offering encouragement and corrections. Lt. Meyer shouted out: "**Davis, you're a foot ahead of the man on your right. Use your peripheral vision. Straighten up that line.**"

At the end of the period, the squadron had straight lines, a good marching cadence, and the officers had mastered "Officers Front and Center."

"Okay, Men, good show," said Jay. "You look like a unit. Take a 15-minute break and be back in formation at 1015. **Dismissed**."

Parade practice was on the athletic field. Colonel Cassiday, Vice Commandant of Cadets, and Colonel Seith, Wing Operations Officer, were reviewing officers. We completed three march-ons and four "Officers' front and center." The Denver sun was streaming down with a vengeance. We would have had another march-on except three cadets passed out[72]"**Return to the cadet area and dismiss your men,**" commanded Colonel Cassiday.

"Nice shoes, Davis," C3C Short gloated looking down at my parade grass shine. "Bring a Form 10 tonight for 'shoes unpolished.'"

Lunch was a repeat of breakfast with recitations of the Code of Conduct, McArthur's Victory Quotation, and the Phonetic Alphabet. As I began to recite George Washington's message to his troops, "The general is sorry to be informed that the foolish and wicked practice of profane cursing and swearing . . ." Cadet Riddle said simply, "eat, Davis."

Again I had a gnawing sensation in my stomach. I avoided C3C Short on my way to the room. The upperclassmen had a Squadron meeting after lunch, so I marched to the Theater for a briefing by the Dean without further harassment

I vaguely remembered Colonel McDermott, the Dean, speaking to us when we first arrived. From a table dissertation, I knew he was a fighter pilot in WWII with 61 combat missions in the P-38 Lockheed Lightning. He taught at West Point. He reluctantly accepted assignment as Assistant Dean in 1954 with the Class of 1959 cadre. Given his Harvard MBA and considerable administrative skills (he served on General Eisenhower's

---

[72] To my knowledge, there was no record kept of cadets passing out, probably because "passing out' was a disqualifying event for pilot training and usually the cadet would recover almost immediately.

staff. In WWII), McDermott was selected as Acting Dean when the original Dean was relieved of duty in 1956.

We all came to attention as a voice called out, "**Gentlemen, the Dean of Cadets, Colonel Robert F. McDermott.**

"Take seats, please. Welcome again, 1961. Today, I want to tell you more about the academic program. You should be pleased; as a class you represent the top 5% of the 6,000 plus who applied to enter the Academy in your class.

The curriculum is designed to support the Academy Mission—which I know you have all memorized. A slight murmur ran through the audience. Let me repeat it for those of you who might have forgotten it. A low groan rippled through the crowd. 'The mission of the Air Force Academy is to provide instruction, experience, and motivation to each cadet so that he will graduate with the knowledge and qualities of leadership required of a junior officer in the United States Air Force, and with a basis for continued development throughout a lifetime of service to his country, leading to readiness for responsibilities as a future air commander.'

Each of you was chosen based on a whole man concept. We looked not only at high school academics; but also leadership activities, athletics, the College Entrance Exams, the Air Force Aptitude Tests, physical aptitude tests, and your medical qualification for pilot training. You were selected based on competitive scores. You have the aptitude and necessary qualities to complete this challenging program.

You have just completed 372 summer training hours: 270 hours in military training, 30 flying training hours, and 72 physical training hours. Your four years will include academic, physical, military, and flight training instruction. General Education has 140 hours. One hundred and 26 academic hours are devoted to the Airmanship program. You will earn a Bachelor of Science degree, the aeronautical rating of Navigator, and a commission as a Second Lieutenant in the Regular Air Force.

Your course of study is balanced between sciences and social studies/humanities. The objective, unlike West Point and Annapolis, is to provide you tools to resolve problems and make decisions throughout your career. This is opposed to graduating you with the technical skills required for your first duty assignment. That training will occur after graduation.

The Air Force entrance exams measured your aptitude for the Airmanship Program, physical training, and military studies. You are qualified for and expected to go to pilot training upon graduation.

Your instructors are military officers well qualified in their fields. We have military instructors for two reasons: one, to provide solid subject matter teaching and, secondly, to provide a model and mentor to prepare you for life as an Air Force officer.

I believe, like General Harmon, the first Academy Superintendent, you should receive an education allowing you to operate within our national environs, with other services, and with our allies.

Based on advanced placement tests and a Department Head's determination, you may validate a course; substituting an elective in its place. By passing an Academy test, you may validate a course to earn extra academic credits. If you have a special aptitude, the professor may accelerate your work to allow extra credit.

By maintaining a 74% average in prescribed courses, you may take overload courses the next semester. Public Affairs, Missile Technology, or English majors require an extra 17 credit hours above the prescribed load. Completing 32 specialized hours earns an Engineering Major.

You must study every day. A credit hour is 150 minutes of weekly student effort. Sixty minutes is class time and 90 minutes study time. You may receive graded reviews in every section on any given day. Initial section assignments are based on your summer testing. During the semester, you will be assigned to sections based on your performance in a given subject.

The Dean's List recognizes outstanding academic achievement. The Superintendent's list considers military and academic performances. Increased off- base privileges, by class, are rewards for making these lists. the Dean looked up from his notes. "Are there any questions?"

Art Kerr stood. "Sir, Cadet Kerr, can you tell us about the grading system?"

"Good question, Mister Kerr; I should have covered that. First, you are graded on the curve; that is, your grade is dependent on the performance of your classmates and your relationship to their performance. Our grading uses a 100 point system versus an alphabetical—A, B, C—system. Seventy percent is passing. You must maintain above a 70% average in all courses. Falling below 70% in any course you become "deficient," which will affect varsity sports participation and restrict some privileges.

Grades will be posted on the bulletin boards each week. Section changes will be posted on the bulletin board one week before they take effect. At semester end, if you fall below a 70 point grade average in any course, you will receive specialized study; followed by a "turn-out" exam. If you pass the turnout test, your grade for that course will reflect a 70 average.

If you fail the test, you may retake the course during Christmas or summer leave periods. Failing the retake, you'll meet an academic board. Based on your overall performance, you may be offered a "turn-back" to the next class. With failed retakes in more than one course, you will meet an academic board and, most likely, will be "turned out" of the Academy.

Doolie

Any other questions? No . . . good. Good luck and God's Speed."

The auditorium was quiet. *This is going to be hard. Grading on the curve might not be too bad if my classmates weren't so damn smart. I might be able to deal with academics without the Fourth Class System and that SOB Short trying to ride me out using the system.*

"Room atten . . . shun," rang out from the back of the auditorium.

***

Turkey breast for Cadet Riddle, hot plate, Sir," I said holding the platter by the edges and passing it to C3C Baker on my right.

"Pan-ther-pis for Cadet Riddle," my roommate sang out opposite me.

After the food was distributed, I heard the irritating hiss of C3C Short's voice.

"Davis, let's have the Superintendent's staff," said Short.

"Rescind that request. Mister Davis, eat. Mister Short, I'll see you in my room after dinner. Mr. Sanders, since you saw the Dean today, give me the Dean and Department Heads."

Short was glowering at me while Tom was reciting. When Tom finished, Short said, "Mister Davis, I'll see you in my room with the Form 10's after dinner."

***

United States Air Force Academy
Tuesday, 10 September 1957 2030

Dear Folks,

We just had a session with the Dean, who is really sharp. I read in a magazine he's changing the academies' education systems. He's very progressive. West Point and Annapolis leaders are not happy. Their academics are directed toward the technical and preparing their graduates for their first assignment. They don't have the academic credibility we do.

The Dean says USAFA is preparing us for problem solving and decision making as senior commanders. The course sounds tough or as he says 'challenging." I hope I don't get challenged out of here on academics.

My biggest challenge is a Third Classman who washed back from the first class. I embarrassed him in a pushup contest during summer training. He's been all over my case since we moved in. I haven't had much to eat for the past two days. If you have a chance, send a "boodle box," or two -- that's what they call a box full of goodies - cookies, candy, anything edible. Actually, I wouldn't mind a couple a week just to keep from starving.

If it keeps up, I may go to junior college after all. We're allowed 23 demerits a month. C3C Short has given me 15 or 16 already. And we haven't even had SAMI inspections. My AOC is one of the good guys. They say he's tough, but fair. My Squadron Commander, Cadet Lt. Col. Jay, also seems like a nice guy. He says we are all part of "his team." Hope he means that. If Short keeps it up, I may resign. I can't study with all the harassment.

Classes start tomorrow. I have advanced English, Math, Chemistry, Military Studies, Graphics, Philosophy, and Physical Education. Math and chemistry will be my hard courses. Fortunately, those are Tom's strong points. He says he's weak in English, so we can probably help each other. They have a saying "cooperate and graduate." Sounds good to me.

Our day is a little better. Reveille is at 0545 with breakfast formation at 0610. We finish breakfast at 0700 and walk back to the dorms (subject, however, to upperclassmen's "corrections"). We march to class (Fourth Class only) at 0745. Classes end at 1500. We have an hour to put things away and get to intramurals. Dinner is at 1800 (6:00 p.m.). Call to Quarters at 1915 (you have to be in your room, the library or some other authorized place). Taps is at 2230 (lights out). You can get lights out extended to 2330 (11:30 p.m.) if you are having academic problems.

There are three days until we play UCLA in football. The team had a good season last year going 6-1-2 with only two classes playing. UCLA will be tough, but I hope we win because then Fourth classmen get to sit at ease. I will probably go out for the Squadron intramural football team.

Hope you and Pa and Lucille are all well. Get Pa and Gene to write me a letter some time. Tell Pa thanks for fixing up the car. Please use it as necessary. If you need the money, sell it. You don't have to send me any money; I don't have much to spend it on. Although, I think I'll go to the Cadet Store this weekend if I can and stock up on crackers and things so I can survive going without meals.

Tell Walt and the other guys to keep writing. Jim Ledoux said he came by and had a good visit. Said you fed him meat loaf. I heard Walt was elected Student Body President. I'm not surprised.

I think you should have a copy of my summer grades by now. I was a little disappointed in the Physical Education grade, but a high passing 77 is fine. And of course, I liked the 90 military studies that put me 30th out of 300. The weighted average (military studies was worth twice physical education) was 85.6 which is a respectable grade, especially considering the competition.

Well guess I had better get after my shoes and hat. They always get inspected in formation. I dread dinner tonight because I am sure C3C Short will be all over me again. I might be able to take him if I could get enough to eat, but it is tough coming back to the room hungry.

God Bless
Your loving son,
Don

Chapter 24

Each cadet develops a sense of pride in his squadron which gives him a greater sense of belonging and helps to stimulate his performance in marching, athletics, and even academic studies.
Air Officer Commanding Letter to Parents

The First Day of School

Wednesday, 11 September, 1957

My Advanced English SAT score put me in the *Advanced Composition and Speech Course,* English 105. Art Kerr, Bob Hertz, Bill Gibbons, Dick Carbon, Gene Hopper, Denny Dillon, Terry Koonce, Tom Sessions, Twy Winslow, Tom Sutter and I are Section One of English 105. Most have English 101: *Composition, Speech, and Introduction to Literature.*

***

As the Section Leader, Sutter sat nearest the door to be able to call the room to attention when the instructor came in. "**Class atten . . . shun,**" Tom called out.

Five feet, ten inches tall; stocky, with dark wavy hair, Major Galt fit snugly in his tailored uniform. He wore Command Pilot Wings, a Distinguished Flying Cross with two Oak Leaf Clusters, 10 Air Medals (indicated by two silver clusters), and several Africa and Europe campaign ribbons on his uniform.

"Take seats, Gentlemen," Galt said, flashing a genuinely warm smile. "I'm Major John Galt. As a pilot, I've flown mostly bombers; B-17s in North Africa and, later, in Europe, in the Big War. I was an ace, crashed five aircraft; all shot up by the enemy."

Everyone snickered at Galt's description of his becoming an ace.

"My crew chief swore like a sailor but could make a wounded seagull fly. One morning after a particularly tough flight; including two ack-ack[73] fields and an attack by an FW-109, I came back to the aircraft after debriefing hoping for the best, but expecting the worst. 'How about it, Chief?' I asked.

Using the four-letter word for 'fornication,' he said, 'Lieutenant, the f _ _ _ en, f _ _ _ er's f _ _ _ed!'

Now if you can be as inventive and descriptive with the English language as Master Sergeant McCrory, you will excel in this class. Of course, in line with General Washington's admonition[74], we will not use profanity to express ourselves."

---

[73] Anti-aircraft batteries.
[74] Like most instructors, Major Galt had studied *Contrails*. He appreciated the military side of the house.

With the Major's somewhat ribald war story, the class visibly relaxed. Everyone slouched a little in their chairs and adopted an attentive attitude. Classrooms were windowless, had two large blackboards at the front, and enough tables and chairs to accommodate 12 TO 14.

"I'm an Assistant Professor of English with an A.B. and M.A. in English from Boston University. To get on Dean's good side, I'm enrolled in a Denver University PHD program. Okay. English 105: there will be a research paper. Begin thinking of an acceptable topic.

We have a respectable library with nearly a quarter of a million books, but you will still be limited in research material. Fortunately, there's a good representation of magazines and newspapers. The paper will be due before Christmas break. You will present progress reports every three weeks; with an outline, thesis, and a bibliography.

We'll work semantics, conference techniques, and public speaking. You'll be given several books: some as study guides; the rest for content. You need two hours preparation for each class. You will have a tentative subject for your research paper by Monday.

Okay, enough about me; let's hear about you. In addition to name, home town, and some extracurricular activities; tell us about a book you've read, a synopsis of it, and what you got out of it – all in five minutes. Mr. Sutter, you're on."

"Sir, I am C4C Sutter from Indiana. I enjoy singing and wrestling and participated in both in high school. The most intriguing book I've[75] read is *Atlas Shrugged* by Ayn Rand. The plot reflects the disintegration of America society as people increasingly become wards of the State. The State becomes a despotic entity headed by ruthless men who destroy all viable industry in the country. An unknown super hero, ironically John Galt, helps heroine Dagny Taggart escape to a secret hide-a-way. A group of industrialists who have disappeared are living in a hidden valley to escape the repressive government. The country collapses and John Galt, accompanied by Dagny, returns to society to rebuild the country.

The lesson is if we are not vigilant and a participant in our American society, the country can fall under a despotic government, causing us to lose our freedoms."

What a suck up, I thought, *picking a book with the professor's name in it, and the hero to boot. But, it was a good presentation. Competition is tough and Academics won't be easy.*

---

[75] While instructors were aware of the Fourth Class System, they were more interested in academic performance and did not delve into small corrections such as not allowing contractions in speech.

"Good presentation, Mr. Sutter. Mr. Kerr . . ." Just then the bell rang to end the period. "Okay. We'll continue introductions next class. Class . . . dismissed."

We spent the rest of the morning and afternoon finding classrooms and meeting the professors/instructors. Having Air Force Officers as teachers proved inspirational. We' hear a lot of war stories and learn about the "real" Air Force during the year.

My math instructor, Captain James Marsh, received his BS from California State Teachers College and a Master's Degree in Education from Pittsburg University.

Colonel Woodyard, Head of the Chemistry Department, taught our chemistry class. His Master of Science and Master of Arts are from Missouri University.

A West Point Graduate with a Master's Degree from Denver University, Captain Stan Gilliam taught philosophy. Philosophy should be useful since Air Force officers deal with a variety of people and situations. Another West Pointer, Lt. Englehart, was our graphics instructor.

Lunch was relatively quiet, with the upperclassmen discussing their new classes and professors. Doolies were asked one question apiece. Cadet Short occasionally looked up from eating and glared at me, but he didn't address me. I noticed he was not actively engaged in the conversations with his classmates or the Second Classmen.

***

I handed the pile of Form 10s to C3C Short and stood at attention. I was in khakis, the uniform for dinner. "Well, Dumbsmack, can't you ever get it right? Why in the hell are you in khakis? I told you fatigues, helmet, rifle, and backpack."

You SOB, you didn't specify a uniform. It's just an excuse for another Form 10.

"That'll be an "out of uniform" Form 10. Now get your butt downstairs and in the right uniform." Short's roommate looked up from his desk, started to say something, but didn't.

In the corridor, I almost ran over Cadet Jay. "Now where are you going, Davis?"

"Sir, I am changing into my field uniform; then going to Cadet Short's room."

"You know it's 1850? I saw the Form 10 for being in the hallway after Call to Quarters."

"Yes, Sir," I replied. "By your leave, Sir."

"Post, Davis," he said with a strange tone in his voice.

Going back to my room, having completed the manual of arms and unpacking and packing my backpack three times, I again met Cadet Jay.

"Now where are you going, Davis?"

"Sir, I am changing to physical training gear and going to Cadet Short's room."

"Davis, you stay in your room."

"Yes, Sir," I replied.

***

As I slipped into breakfast formation, a shadow loomed on my right. Suddenly C3C Short appeared in front of me. "Okay, brown-noser. The Squadron Commander heard your whining. We won't have any more evening get-togethers, but you've not seen the last of me."

***

Major Galt greeted us Friday morning with a pop quiz. Several of the guys were startled and moaned when the tests were handed out. Sutter and I had been conscientious and diligently done the home work, resulting in 100s for both of us.

***

Friday after dinner was something else. A huge pep rally self-generated on the quadrangle. Fourth Classmen were told to make up costumes and bring something as a noise maker. Tom and I grabbed garbage can lids from the back of the dormitory and brought bayonets to bang on them.

We went through all the cheers in *Contrails* and sang songs, including, of course, the Air Force Song. Night was falling and we prepared to go back to our rooms when Lt. Joe Yeager, our bayonet instructor, appeared on the balcony of Building 815. He began yelling one-liners that would have made General Patton proud.

The cadets—Second Classmen, Third Classmen, and Doolies—got caught up in the escalating crescendo. It looked like the Nuremburg crowds in the late 1930s. A tremendous energy surged through the Wing, egged on by increasing volume from Lt Yeager. All of a sudden a chant began: "Aurora[76], Aurora, Aurora, **Aurora, Aurora."**

Like a large flock of blackbirds, the mass began to drift from the quad toward the Dayton Street Gate, which led to Aurora. The loud, hooping crowd poured through the gate. Brandishing a bull-horn, the Officer of the Day was in hot pursuit in a Jeep.

The shouted cheers and boisterous singing of the cadet mob drowned out the OD's orders to return to barracks. The wave descended on Colfax Avenue, US-40. Traffic halted as the rally continued. Honking horns of the crowd joined the bedlam. The press arrived along with a few "bewildered" members of Aurora's finest. The policemen took no action other than to watch from the sidelines.

The OD cornered several Second Classmen and told them he was going to cancel the Saturday Open Post if the rally continued. Word of the OD's threat spread quickly. The Second Classmen began herding the renegade crowd back to the reservation.

---

[76] Aurora was the bedroom community adjacent to Lowry AFB and is in close proximity to the Academy.

Unfortunately, the cadet enthusiasm and bravado didn't get transmitted to the team in Los Angeles that night. The Academy was defeated 47-0.

***

Tom and I spent Friday evening listening to the team getting shellacked. We prepared our rooms, equipment, and shoes for our first Sixth Squadron SAMI. Saturday morning broke bright and clear, with a hint of fall in the air.

Captain Braswell led the inspection team. C Flight was the last to be inspected. Finally, there was a rap on the open door and Tom almost shouted, **"Room atten . . . shun."** Captain Braswell was quick, thorough, and efficient. He checked laundry bags for contraband or stored clean clothes. As he passed me, he looked down at my shoes. "Nice shine, Davis. Lt. Payne told me you have competitive shoes."

Starting to leave, Captain Braswell glanced at the shelves above my desk. Noticing Rex's picture, he smirked and called out, "One demerit for"… "picture not centered on the top shelf."

Tom and I gave out a big sigh of relief. "Does the regulation really say the picture has to be centered on the shelf?" Tom asked.

"No, I replied. And I saw Captain Braswell nudge the wastebasket to the center before he wrote you up for it not being in the proper positon. He was playing with us."

***

The early morning crispness vanished; heat began to build. As I stepped into ranks, the dreaded face of C3C Peter Short loomed in front of me. C Flight was nearest the barracks, so I used our summer trick to enter ranks just before First Call.

"Well, Mister Davis, I hear you did well in the room inspection. Braswell must be getting soft. The wimpy Squadron Commander was bragging on you and Sanders. Understand he thinks you have the best Squadron Doolie room. Let's see what this can do for your in-ranks inspection." With that, Short stood on my right shoe, grinding his sole into the top of my shoe.

I was horrified. I looked down at my shoe. It was a disaster.

"Oh, by the way, drive around a Form 10 for gazing. Just slip it under my door."

I had not been so devastated since my problems with the obstacle course wall. I was on the verge of crying. Standing next to me, Tom overheard the conversation between Short and me. He stole a glance at my shoe. "That bastard," said Tom. "He needs retribution."

Just then I heard Cadet Lt. Col. Jay's voice. Cadet Jay was standing on the front stoop of our building. Apparently, he had been there for a while. "Mr. Short, drive over here. Mister Short, did you just step on Mister Davis' shoe?"

"No, siirr," Short said arrogantly.

"You sure, Mister Short, you didn't step on Davis' shoe and grind yours on his?"

"Yes, Sir, I'm sure. Might've scraped the side as I passed by; didn't step on it."

You lying SOB. And you will probably get away with it too, I thought.

When Captain Braswell reached C Flight, the sun was hot. Captain Braswell inspected only every other rifle in order to finish up quickly. We still had a parade to go and he could see some cadets wavering.

I brought my M1 to inspection arms, snapping the bolt open with my left hand. Standing in front of me, Captain Braswell looked over my uniform, stopping his gaze at my rifle. *That's strange*, I thought, *he didn't even look at my shoes. But I heard him call out in First Element,* "Shoes inadequately polished". *I knew he was a stickler for good shoes.*

Without a word he pivoted, stepped in front of Tom and snatched his rifle. "Good looking piece, Sanders," Captain Braswell said.

The afternoon thunderstorms held off long enough for the 1100 parade to go on. It was the first Wing Parade with eight newly formed squadrons and three classes. The four squadrons formed two groups, positioned on either side of the Honor Guard which consisted of two cadets with M1s on either side of the United States and Academy Flag bearers.

The loud speaker system welcomed the crowd, gave instructions on rendering honors to the flag, broadcast the Superintendent's remarks – which were mercifully short – and announced the Wing and Group Staffs and Squadron Commanders as they marched on line. The home towns of the key cadet personal were also broadcast.

The reviewing party included the Superintendent, the Commandant, and the Dean. Staff and visitors completely filled the stands. The onlookers applauded as we passed in review. Good-looking girls and ladies dressed in their "Sunday best" were in attendance.

The Squadron's precision, given the short practice time together, amazed me. At "eyes right," I saw only the silhouette of the Third Classman next to me. "Officers Front and Center" with the saber flash as officers saluted the reviewing party was impressive.

The parade ended as billowing white cumulonimbus clouds started throwing shadows over the parade ground. We marched swiftly back to the barracks.

In the quadrangle, Cadet Lt. Col. Jay addressed the squadron. "Okay. Good show. Rumor has it we took first place. For upperclassmen, sign in for the Open Post is 2330. Do not let the spirt or spirits get the best of your judgment. Duty cadets, in my room at 1400.

Lunch formation is at 1300. Cadet Fourth Class Davis, I'll see you in my room right after dismissal."

Oh crap, I thought, *now what in the hell have I done!*

****

I went to the room, checked my uniform; put up my M1, gloves, and hat. I looked at my left shoe. I grabbed the shoe polish and tried to cover the ridges in the toe. *Oh crap, it's no use.* I wiped off the excess polish and scurried downstairs.

"Sir, Cadet Fourth Class Davis reporting as ordered."

"At ease, Davis," Jay said. The room was neat, except for the khaki uniform thrown on Cadet Captain DeSantis' bed. DeSantis was Jay's roommate. He had obviously changed and was already gone on the Open Post.

Cadet Jay was standing by his desk. Beside him stood a tall, thin, dark-haired Cadet Major who looked familiar. A single chair was adjacent to where I was standing.

"Davis, this is Cadet Garvey. He is the Wing Honor Committee Chair. You met him during Doolie Summer in the Honor Code Class. Have a seat."

Oh yeah, I remember almost falling asleep in his class. What the hell is this all about?

"We're here because I have a serious issue with Cadet Short. Do you recall what happened just before in-ranks-inspection?"

"Yes, Sir, I do."

"Tell Cadet Garvey what went on."

"Yes, Sir. I was in ranks when Cadet Short stepped in front of me. He said, 'I heard you did well in room inspections.' *I better leave out the part about Captain Braswell. I don't know where this is going.* "Then he said, 'Well, let's see what this can do for your in-ranks inspection.'"

"And what did that mean, Mister Davis," Garvey interrupted.

"I'm pretty sure it had to do with his stepping on my shoe, Sir."

"He stepped on YOUR SHOE?" Garvey said incredulously. Cadet Garvey glanced down at my shoe and winced. "Do you think it was intentional?"

"Yes, Sir, I do."

"Then what happened?"

"Cadet Short started to leave."

"Why didn't he get in ranks?

"Sir, he was called over to speak with Cadet Jay."

"And did you hear the conversation?"

"Yes. Sir."

"And what was said."

"Cadet Jay asked Cadet Short if he had stepped on my shoe. Cadet Short replied, 'No, Sir.'" *Actually, Short was really surly, but I'd better leave that to Cadet Jay.*

"Did Cadet Jay ask again if Short stepped on your shoe?"

"Yes, Sir, he asked Short if he was sure he didn't step on my shoe. Short answered he might have scrapped the side of my shoe, but he didn't step on it."

"Did anyone else hear the conversation between Cadets Short and Jay?"

"Yes, Sir, my roommate, Tom Sanders, heard the conversation."

"Are you sure and how would he hear it?" queried Garvey.

"Sir, Cadet Sanders stands on my left, closer to the dorm, in first element of C Flight. Cadet Jay was just in front of the portico. Tom . . . ah . . . Cadet Sanders and I discussed both my conversation with Short and Cadet Jay's conversation with Short."

Cadet Garvey looked pensive for a moment, then said, "I think that will be all, Davis. Jim, do you have anything else?"

"Yes, actually I do. Davis, you know you have 20 demerits? That's tops in the squadron. You're only allowed 23 a month. Keep that up you'll be thrown out on military aptitude."

"Yes, Sir. I knew I had a lot, but not how many. Yes, Sir, I know I can be thrown out for demerits and I'm . . . I am concerned about it."

"Okay. Post."

***

"Well," said Tom. "What was the call to the principal's office all about?"

"I'm not sure. It had to do with the episode with Short. Cadet Major Garvey, the Wing Honor Committee Chairman, was there and asked me what happened in-ranks and about the conversation between Cadet Jay and Short."

"You think they are going to do anything about it?"

"I doubt it. Hell, I'm a Doolie. Short's an upperclassman. In fact, he was a classmate of Cadets Jay and Garvey before he washed back."

"Maybe there will be justice after all. Come on, let's go over to the Club. I'll buy you a coke and a hot dog."

"Great, the food's been in Short supply!"

"Nice pun, Davis. I should make you buy your own for that one."

***

United States Air Force Academy
Sunday 15 September 1957 2010 Hours

Dear Folks,

It's been an interesting and hellacious week. My new Squadron is Super. I like the Squadron Commander. The other upperclassmen are good with one notable exception. The Third Classman I beat in the pushup contest last summer has a long memory, and is in my squadron.

C3C (C3C stands for Cadet Third Class) Peter Short has been raising hell with me since we got in the squadron. Because of him, I now have 20 demerits. We're only allowed 23 a month. Pass that and you march tours. Demerits count toward military standing. If C3C Short keeps giving me demerits, I could be thrown out on military aptitude for too many demerits.

Friday night we had a giant pep rally for the UCLA game. Everyone dressed in crazy costumes. Lt. Yeager, who taught bayonet training, got up on a balcony and started yelling and screaming. Everybody got all worked up. We went out into the little community of Aurora.

The cops were there, but didn't do anything. The Academy Officer of the Day threatened to cancel the Open Post on Saturday. The upperclassmen didn't want the Open Post cancelled. So, we all came back to listen to the radio to hear the team getting slaughtered 47-0.

On Saturday, except for one or two Second Classmen, the tables had Third Classmen Table Commandants. We didn't sit at ease but most tables were quiet. I went to another Squadron's table to avoid C3C Short.

Please send boodle boxes. We are now allowed in the Fourth Class Club, a converted airman's recreation center. When we went to the Club, I ordered a hamburger and strawberry milkshake. Haven't had a milkshake taste so good since the free ones I got as a busboy at Weinstock-Lubin.

We can only go to the Club on Saturday. Access to the Cadet Store (candy bars and moon pies) is limited. I went once last week after class, but C3C Short saw me go into the building. He was waiting when I came out. When I told him what I had, he said it was contraband and took it from me.

Our first classes were Wednesday. All our instructors are military. My English Instructor, Major Galt, went to Boston University. He flew B-17s in Africa in WWII. Major Galt has a Bachelor's Degree and a Master's Degree.

My math instructor, Captain Marsh, has a BS from California State Teachers College and a Master's from Pittsburg University. I'm in the seventh section math, out of 20 sections. I'm in the third section in Philosophy.

My Philosophy instructor, Captain Stan Gilliam has a Master's Degree from Denver University. He is really laid back. Colonel Woodyard, Head of the Chemistry Department, teaches our chemistry class. He has a Master of Science and a Master of Science in chemistry from the University of Missouri.

Lieutenant Englehart, is my Graphics instructor. In first semester in Military Studies, we will learn about Air Force Commands - Strategic Air Command, Tactical Air Command, Military Air Transport Service, etc.

For Physical Education, in addition to intramurals, we will have boxing, judo, swimming and gymnastics. These are scheduled classes, with instruction and testing in each of them.

Hope Pa is back working. Construction is so uncertain. Tell him to catch some fish for me. I'm looking forward to going out to the rice fields next summer, if I last that long here. Otherwise the fishing could be sooner.

Tom and I did pretty well in the room inspection Saturday and neither of us got written up in the in-ranks inspection, although C3C Short almost made it catastrophic for me when he stepped on my shoe. If it weren't for C3C Short, I would only have one demerit.

It was great to talk to you on the phone last night. Everyone sounded good. Glad you were all available to talk to me. I love you and miss you and wish I could be home. Have to quit now and answer a couple of letters and work on my shoe shine. I hope

I can melt it down like Lt. Payne taught me. Lucky for me, Tom smokes and has a cigarette lighter. Tomorrow we start academics in earnest.

God Bless
Your loving son,
Don

Chapter 25
We will not lie, steal, or cheat, nor allow among those who do . . .
USAFA Honor Code

An Honor Incident
Monday 16 September 1957

As we returned from breakfast, the CCQ handed me an envelope.

"Wow, impressive," Tom said. "An official Cadet Wing envelope addressed to you."

"Shut up, wise ass. It's probably a classroom change. *Right, now what the hell have I done? It's probably some of Short's work." Crap*, I thought. *This can't be good.* The note read:

USAF ACADEMY CADET WING
HONOR COMMITTEE
16 September 1957

Cadet Fourth Class Donald L. Davis
Sixth Squadron

You are directed to attend an Honor Board Meeting at 1830 hours on 16 September 1957 in the First Class Lounge.[77]

Uniform is Class A Khakis.

Do not discuss this matter with anyone.

Gerald G. Garvey
USAF ACADEMY CADET WING
HONOR COMMITTEE

I sat on my bed. *What the hell have I done?* I was shaken. I imagined the end of my cadet career.

---

[77] Although there were no First Classmen, the Lounge, in Arnold, Hall, was dedicated to First Class usage and, for now, was used by the ranking Second Class.

"You all right, Don? You look a little white around the gills. What's in the damn note?"

"I . . . uh . . . can't . . ." Just as I was about to tell Tom I couldn't discuss it with him with a rap on the door, the CCQ burst in. "Sanders?"

"Yes, sir," Tom said, coming to attention.

"I missed this earlier. Here, you have a note in a fancy envelope too."

Tom sat down on his bed, opened the sealed envelope and began to read. After he read the memo, he let out a deep breath, "Oh, shit, what's going on?"

I looked at Tom and shrugged.

***

The entire day was a haze. Major Galt passed out the pop quiz results. I didn't notice the 100% and "Good Show" scrawled across the top of the paper.

"Mister Davis, are you with us?" Major Galt asked, after calling on me twice.

"Ah . . . yes, sir, could you repeat the question?"

"Sure, what is the first thing you should do in selecting a theme topic?"

"Sir, you want to narrow the scope of the topic. You should also consider your audience and ensure that you have sufficient resources to complete the project."

"Good, Davis, but I only asked for the first item. No extra points for the other answers."

Thankfully Major Galt moved on to other classmates. As I started to leave, Major Galt stopped me. "O.K., Davis what's up? Some upperclassman raising hell with you?"

"Ah, no, Sir. It's an honor issue and I'm not supposed to discuss it."

"Ohhh-kay. But get over it. You can't perform like today and get by in academics."

"Yes, Sir," I said and slid out the door.

I busted a slide rule pop quiz in math. We were told Friday to study the *Versalog: Slide Rule Instructions:* "Description, Adjustment, Care and Manipulation of the Slide Rule; The Scales of the Slide Rule; and Multiplication and Division." Tom and I studied the material, but my brain was focused on the Honor Committee Board.

I answered the description and scales questions but drew a blank on the 10 multiplication and division problems. I knew I could do the problems—but I could not think clearly.

***

Arriving at Arnold Hall, Tom and I were directed to chairs outside the First Class Lounge. A stocky, dark haired Second Classman came out of the Lounge and approached us.

"At ease, gentlemen," Cadet Lt. Col. Zimmerman said quietly. "You Davis and Sanders?"

"Yes, Sir," Tom and I declared together.

"Sir, I am Cadet Fourth Class Davis."

"Sir, I am Cadet Fourth Class Sanders."

"Okay. You're here today to testify in the honor case of Cadet Third Class Peter Short. Remain here until called. After your testimony you'll return here. You're not to discuss anything with anyone until the trial is over. You'll not discuss any of the proceedings outside of this area. When you return to the cadet area, you'll not discuss anything you saw or heard here.

You may be recalled after testifying. At the Chairman's discretion, you may witness the Board's verdict. You may use the latrinje, it's on the left side of the entrance where you entered. Any questions?"

"No, Sir," I said, letting out what I hoped was not an obvious deep breath.

"No, Sir," said Tom. I could see he was also relieved.

We were surprised a couple of minutes later when Short's roommate, C3C Peter Long showed up. "Good evening, Cadet Long," I said.

"Good evening, men," Long said taking a seat. "Do you know what this is all about?"

"Sir, I think a Board member will brief you."

"Okay."

Cadet Zimmerman reappeared and gave Long the information given us but added, "You'll be asked to testify about your roommate's actions. Do you have a problem with that?"

"No, Sir," Long replied.

Five minutes later, Captain Braswell, accompanied by Cadet Jay, arrived. Both went into the lounge. Three minutes later, Cadet Jay came out and joined us.

"Evening, gentlemen," he said. I noticed Cadet Jay was also in Class A Khakis, complete with white gloves. "Long, you ever been involved in an Honor Board?"

"No, Sir."

"Well, it's pretty straight forward. There are five Board members, but you'll only be asked questions by the Chair. As for you Fourth Classmen, this is not a 'Yes, Sir, No, Sir, No excuse, Sir', situation. Answer the question fully and truthfully. If asked, describe any situation to the best of your recollection. Don't be nervous. You're not on trial, and there will be no retributions of any kind."

At that moment, Cadet 3C3 Short showed up. "Well, where the hell do I go for this kangaroo court," Short said cynically, addressing the question to Cadet Jay.

"Short, if I were you," Cadet Jay said, "I'd lose the attitude. The Board **can** terminate your cadet career."

"Yeah, yeah, let's just get on with it," Short said with a sneer.

"Follow me," Cadet Jay said. He escorted Short into the room and then returned.

Both Cadets Jay and Long began reading books they took from their backpacks. *Damn,* I thought. *That's a lesson; bring your books if you are waiting somewhere. You need every minute you can get to study. Should've learned that from carrying Contrails all summer.*

Cadet Jay, as an Honor Representative, had to recuse himself from this Board; since he had initiated the action against Short. "What they are doing now is setting up the Board—the five Board members seated at the head of the room, a chair for the defendant, a chair for the Honor Committee Officer in Charge, a chair for the Squadron AOC, and chairs for observers.

Mr. Short will be told of the charges and allowed to make a statement. He will have a "defense cadet" to assist him. The Defense Council, as we call him, can ask questions to assist Short with his defense. He may ask us questions.

We'll go in, provide our pertinent information, and answer questions from the Board."

"Can the defendant question witnesses?" I asked.

"Yes, but the Chair can limit the questioning, disallowing any he considers improper or not within the scope of the investigation."

"Cadet Lieutenant Colonel Jay, will you come in please," Cadet Lt. Col. Zimmerman said. The two shook hands and went into the Lounge.

Cadet Jay was in the Lounge for 20 minutes. When he came out he said, "Okay, Davis, the Board will see you now. Don't be nervous."

When I entered, I saw Cadet Short in a chair about 20 feet off to my right. Beside him was a Second Classman I did not recognize. Captain Braswell and Major Yancy, the Honor Committee AOC, were in chairs to my left.

"State your name, rank, and Squadron for the record," Cadet Garvey said.

"Sir, I am Cadet Fourth Class Donald L. Davis, Sixth Squadron."

"Do you recognize Cadet Short, seated behind you?"

"Yes, Sir," I replied.

"You ought to you little shit," Short said softly.

Cadet Garvey banged his gavel. "Mr. Short, you will not make disparaging remarks. You will be silent unless asked a question or have the floor, do you understand?"

"Yes, Siiir," Short replied snidely.

"Cadet Davis, do you recall the events of Saturday, the 14th of September at in-ranks?"

"Yes, Sir," I said with a slight quiver. I could feel sweat forming in my doubled-up hands and under my arms. *Cadet Jay said there'd be no retribution, but I'd better be careful what I say.*

"Good, please tell the Board, in as much detail as you can, what happened."

Oh, hell. Here goes. "Yes, Sir. I was standing in ranks when C3C Short came and stood in front of me. He made a comment about hearing our room, my roommate's and mine, was the best Squadron Doolie room. 'Well,' he said, 'let's see how you do with this in the in-ranks inspection.' Then he stepped on my left shoe and turned his shoe on top of mine."

"And you think it was deliberate, and when he said, 'Let's see how you do with this in the in-ranks inspection,' he meant he was going to step on your shoe?"

"Yes, Sir, I do."

Not too subtly, Short said to his Cadet Defense Assistant (CDA): "Ask Dumbsquat if it isn't possible he just hadn't shined his shoes and was making up this story for the inspection."

Cadet Garvey glared at Short. "Mister Short, you may have your question answered, but you will refer to Cadet Davis as 'Mister Davis' or 'Cadet 4C Davis.' Is that clear?"

Again, the snide, "Yes Siiir."

"Mister Davis," the CDA posed, "were your shoes not in inspection order and did you make up the story about Mr. Short as an excuse for poorly-shined shoes?"

"No, Sir. In fact, Captain Braswell had commented on the quality of my shoes during the room inspection." The CDA returned to his seat beside Short.

"What happened next, Mister Davis?" queried Cadet Garvey.

"Sir, the Squadron Commander, Cadet Lt Col. Jay, called Mister Short over to his side. He asked Cadet Short if he had stepped on my shoe. Cadet Short said 'No.' Cadet Jay asked again. Short replied, 'I might have scraped the side of his shoe when I left, but I didn't step on it.'"

"What happened next?"

"Cadet Lt. Col. Jay walked in front of me, looked at my shoe and groaned."

"Did anyone else hear the conversation between Cadets Short and Jay?"

"Yes, Sir, my roommate, C/4C Tom Sanders, heard the conversation.'

"Are you sure? How would he hear it?" asked Garvey.

"Sir, Cadet Sanders is on my left in first element of C Flight near where Cadet Lt. Col. Jay was standing. Tom said he heard my conversation with Cadet Short and Cadet Jay's conversation with Short."

"Any other questions?" Cadet Garvey looked up and down the table and then at Short and his CDA. "O.K. Cadet Davis, wait outside. We will call you if there are further questions."

"Yes, Sir," I said and returned to my chair outside the Lounge.

"How did it go?" Tom asked.

"It was pretty straight forward. You'll see."

Cadet Long and Tom, in turn, were called into the hearing. I knew why Tom was there but didn't understand why Cadet Long was involved.

Both returned without discussing their testimony, as instructed. There was a 20-minute lapse. "The Board is considering its decision," offered Cadet Jay.

Five minutes later, Cadet Zimmerman appeared. "Mister Long and Mister Sanders, you're dismissed. Remember not to discuss anything you've seen or heard here. Cadet Jay and Cadet Davis, you are invited to hear the recommendations of the Board because of your direct involvement. You may not speak or insert yourselves into the proceedings. Understood?"

"Right, Charley," Cadet Jay said responding to his classmate.

"Yes, Sir," I said.

The room was quiet and somber. We were directed to two chairs behind Cadet Short.

"Mister Short, come forward," began Cadet Garvey. "Cadet Short, it is the opinion of the Board that you in fact did commit, on Saturday, 14 September, 1957, an honor violation in that you stepped on Cadet Davis' shoe, then lied to your Squadron Commander, saying you had not stepped on Davis' shoe. There is sufficient evidence from the testimony of fellow cadets that the events did occur as described.

The Board recommends your status as a cadet at the United States Air Force Academy be terminated, subject to the Superintendent's approval of the Board findings. You will be notified of the Superintendent's decision in the morning.

You should gather your belongings and be prepared to out-process in the morning. You will be provided transportation to your home of record or any other location you desire within the Continental United States. Would you like to say anything, Mister Short?"

"Yeah, I would. This isn't over. As I said before, this is a kangaroo court. The Supe will hear from my old man. I'm sure your decision will be overturned."

"Thank you, Mister Short. Your comments are noted. You are dismissed and will return to your room. You will attend meals only after the Wing is dismissed. This Board is closed."

Cadet Short stormed out of the room. Someone outside reported he went immediately to the pay phone in the lobby and made a call.

"Wow, Sir, what was that about Mister Short's father?" I asked Cadet Jay.

"Short's father is a Two Star General at TAC[78] Headquarters at Langley Air Force Base. When Short was about to wash out on academic and military standing, his father, a classmate of General Briggs, called the Superintendent. General Briggs reversed the Military Review Board's finding of dismissal and had Short washed back a class."

"Do you think that will happen again?"

"I don't think so. His father is a West Point graduate and understands the Honor Code. I'm sure he'll call the Superintendent, but I don't think he will try to get his son off this time."

Just then Cadet Zimmerman approached me. "Cadet Davis, may I speak to you alone for a minute," he said gesturing toward a corner of the room.

"Yes, Sir," I replied. *Now what have I done? Cadet Jay said no retributions.*

"Look, Davis, Cadet Long's testimony indicated Cadet Short was probably hazing you beyond the bounds of Academy directives. You have a right to ask for a harassment investigation. However, Cadet Garvey and I feel Short is an anomaly. We think an investigation would bring unwarranted and unfavorable criticism of the Academy's Fourth Class System.

One reason we wanted you to sit in on the findings was for you to feel Mister Short had received adequate punishment.

Of course, if asked about Cadet Short's treatment of you, you must be truthful. Major Yancy and Captain Braswell heard the testimony also, but we believe they will not raise the issue.

Cadet Garvey and I ask you not initiate an investigation into Short's hazing. You may do so, but the result would be the same—the dismissal of Short from the Academy."

"Yes, Sir, I understand. If Mister Short were allowed to stay, I would consider discussing the hazing with Cadet Jay. But if Mister Short goes, as far as I am concerned, the issue is resolved."

"Good, Davis, go back to your room and study. We can't lose you on academics."

"Yes, Sir," I said heading toward the door.

I walked slowly back to the dorm. I was elated until I began thinking about my situation.

---

[78] TAC – Tactical Air Command with Headquarters at Langley AFB, Virginia

Mister Short—I like the idea Short is no longer entitled to be called "cadet"—hopefully, will be discharged tomorrow. He still has me screwed though; I have all those demerits and that's going to put me way down in military standing. I'll probably get enough more to walk tours, or worse get thrown Out. That SOB!!!!

Chapter 26

Physical education develops the courage, initiative, stamina,
and physical skill required of an officer who will lead others . . .
USAFA Catalog

Gymnastics

Thursday, 19 September 1957

The rest of the week flew by. On Thursday, I was assigned to Cadet Captain Ken Thomas' table along with Dickson, Hertz, and Kerr. Cadet Jay said he wanted all Squadron cadets to switch tables to get to know each other. Fair and equitable, Cadet Thomas believes Fourth Class Knowledge should be limited to 10 minutes after the food arrives.

Tennis Team Manager and C Flight Commander, Cadet Thomas seemed more academic than athletic. The meal began with the standard introductions. The other Second Classmen at the table were: Cadet Robert Low from Massachusetts, and Cadet Joseph DeSantis from New Jersey. Valmore Bourque, John McClatchy, and John Bush, Third Classmen, were from Pennsylvania, Ohio, and Nevada respectively.

***

Thursday brought a new challenge; two hours of physical training classes, scheduled in the afternoon. After lunch, we began our newest adventure – Gymnastics.

Gymnastics was more challenging than the obstacle course and equally potentially hazardous to one's cadet career. The high-roofed temporary Academy gym had wood floors, retractable basketball hoops, and collapsible wall seating.

Blue wrestling-type mats covered the floor. Lt. Robert M. Sullivan, the Academy Gymnastics Coach and OIC [79] of this program, was our first instructor.

"Okay, men, listen up," Lt. Sullivan began. "Today you'll be introduced to basic gymnastics' exercises: Floor Exercise, Rings, Parallel Bars, Rope Climb, Trampoline, Pommel Horse, and High Bar. Given many are new to gymnastics, we'll use appropriate safety devices. This is the Pommel Horse," Lt. Sullivan said, walking to an oblong pillow-looking leather device sitting on a single column. He chalked his hands. "A typical exercise involves single and double leg work. You can do straddles—a leg on each side of the horse or you can do circular rotations with the legs kept closely together above the horse. Dismount is accomplished by either swinging your body over the horse or jumping to the floor from a handstand.

[79] OIC – Officer in Charge

Mounting the horse, Lt. Sullivan swung one leg over, swung back and forth, then rose to a handstand. From the handstand, he lowered into a straddle position. He powered above the horse and made three circular moves. Rising again to a handstand, he smoothly dismounted on the right side.

"Okay," said Lt. Sullivan, "who has competed in gymnastics before?"

Cadet Paul O'Reilly raised his hand.

"Great, O'Reilly," Lt. Sullivan said, "show your classmates how it's done."

Paul (nicknamed "PR") chalked his hands. Gracefully, he replicated Sullivan's routine. Scanning name tags, Lt. Sullivan looked at me. "Okay. Davis, give it a try."

Oh shit, I thought. *I've never had great upper body strength. This looks like it takes a lot of that.* "Yes, Sir," I said.

"When you mount, you have to swing your right leg up and grasp the handle underneath with your right hand putting you in a straddle position.

I grabbed the handle, swung my right leg out, caught the handle and came down fairly hard. "Oooof," I gasped. *Crap, if I do that very much, I'll come out a soprano.* I did a decent handstand, but couldn't dismount from there, fearing I'd land on the horse on the way down. Letting down to a straddle, I did a flare, swung my left leg over and staggered two steps to my right. With two more tries, I improved some.

"Well, that wasn't a 10 performance, Davis, but you should be able to get through the basic maneuvers. By the way, scoring is from 1 to 10; 10 being a perfect performance. You must get at least a five from your instructor on an event to pass.

The high bar came next. As we approached, Bill Gibbons, our squadron mate, was finishing a routine; completing two gigantic swings to a summersault dismount.

"Damn, Paul," I said. "He's good!"

"Yeah, Bill was the Ohio high school state champ on the high bar."

"How do you know so much about him?" I asked.

"Oh, we've had tryouts for the gymnastics team. Bill and I talked quite a bit. He spent a year in the Air Force before the Academy. We'll be on the team together."

"Gentlemen, I'm Lt. Forrest. High bar moves include: giants, releases, twists, handstands, and changes of direction. Lt Forrest grabbed a handful of chalk and demonstrated a simple routine consisting of several giants, two changes of direction, two releases and a twist. His dismount was a forward gainer.

Damn. I thought, *this looks like another way to kill yourself. The giants look okay, but those releases are scary. If you fall off the horse, you wouldn't do much damage, but this could break your neck.*

Sensing our apprehension, Lt. Forrest said, "There will be two spotters, one on each side of the apparatus. If one of you slips off the bar or fails to execute a release or twist properly, the spotters will ensure a soft landing."

First up, PR did a short, impressive routine. Following three giants, he did two releases in a row, putting a twist on the second one. He did a one and a half back salto as his dismount.

Hertz and Butch completed their maneuvers without falling. I chalked my hands, jumped up on the bar and began swinging. After one giant, I did a release; almost missing the bar. On the second swing, I felt my hands slipping. I left the bar almost horizontally. Hertz and Butch were poorly placed to cushion my fall. I slipped through their hands. Instinctively, I did a double arm judo slap. My arms stung, but my back did not crash into the ground

"Well, Davis, that was spectacular," said Lt. Forrest, chuckling. "Okay. It's like being thrown from a horse or crashing an airplane. You have to do it again right away. Get some more chalk and get back on the bar."

After two giants and a release (reasonably completed), I did another giant and a straight forward release. I had two forward steps but did not fall.

"See, Davis, no sweat!" said Lt. Forrest.

"Good morning, gentlemen. I'm Lt. Schultz. The parallel bars are a skill and strength apparatus." Lt. Schultz lithely rose to a starting position. "You begin by bringing your legs up parallel to the ground. You then do a back flip" (which he did) "and return to the legs parallel position. You can bring yourself to a handstand" (which he accomplished) "and then swing down to a dismount. The objective is to do the maneuvers smoothly and continuously."

Wow, this is actually fun, I thought as I concluded a second, consecutive flip. I tentatively pulled my feet up to perform a handstand. After a hesitant 10 seconds in the handstand, my feet flipped over my head, and I completed a backward swing. Not smooth and not continuous.

At the next station, midway up the 30-foot rope climb, I came to an awkward stop. *Damn, I'll never make it the next 15 feet. Crap, if my arms give out, I'm going to fall on my head. Oh, well, that's probably the easy way out of this place.*

"Come on, Davis," yelled Cadet Lt. Col. Roger Mason, a high school gymnastics star who won the Rocky Mountain AAU Regional Competition this year. "Use your feet, not just your arms. Clasp the rope with your feet, reach up with your arms, then pull your feet up and get another grip."

I made a series of inch worm push and pulls, slowly moving up the rope. My progress, I felt, was no better than an inch worm. Suddenly, my arm touched the ring at the top. *Damn, I made it. I actually made it. I guess the third time is the charm.*

"Okay, Davis, same technique with your feet coming down. If you just use your hands you'll come down too fast and get rope burn."

What's this; a second classman helping without the "Fourth Class Cadet" crap? Hope there are more like Mason.

Hertz and I were last on the rope climb. My hands and arms were tired. The parallel bars had chaffed my underarms, which were now beginning to sting.

"OK, guys, move over to the trampoline with the rest of your group. Good luck," said Cadet Lt. Col. Mason pleasantly. Later I found out the cadets assisting were Gymnastic Team Members taking part in an instructor training class. Cadets trained to be coaches and referees in their Second and First Class years.

As we approached the trampoline, PR was showing off again. Springing eight to ten feet in the air, he easily completed forward and backward summersaults.

For safety purposes, a harness was worn by the cadet on the trampoline, tramp for short. A rope extended from each side of the harness, manned by fellow classmates. Our instructions were: if a cadet is coming down awkwardly or in danger of landing outside the trampoline, we were to back off, tighten the ropes on the safety harness, and suspend the jumper in the air.

"Yahoo!" yelled Butch as he bounced six feet in the air. Having mastered the bounce, he attempted to duplicate one of P.R.s forward summersaults. Butch had the necessary height, but his trajectory was off; he was going over the side.

"**Pull, pull,**" shouted Lt. Biernaki. Jim Dickson and I pulled the ropes taunt, catching Butch in midair. He landed on the very edge of the tramp. Dickson and I yanked harder on our ropes, pulling Butch two feet in the air and causing him to swing toward the middle. Jim gave me a wink, and we unceremoniously dumped Butch.

"OK, Mister Riselman, nice try," said Lt. Biernaki. "Give it a rest."

Cadet Captain Smart took Butch aside and began instructing him on how to accomplish summersaults while remaining under control. We enjoyed the trampoline. It was like backyard equipment many of us had at home.

Arriving at the rings, we were treated to another spectacular exhibition by classmate Bill Gibbons. From giant swings, he went to a position with his legs extended in front of him. The rings remained absolutely motionless. We didn't appreciate his skill until we tried to emulate his trick. Bill did two more giant loops and a forward one and a half gainer dismount.

We all applauded. Bill did a mock bow, saluted loosely, and strode off like a circus performer after his act. We noted the PE instructor had a smile on his face.

Except for PR, the rest of us struggled with the rings, particularly attempting to keep the rings perfectly still in a "hold" position. For most of us, the rings gyrated in and out in the hold position. No one, however, was hurt or even fell off the rings.

As we approached the floor exercise, I thought, *I don't know about the rest of you, but I'm getting tired. My hands are sore, my legs are sore, and my arm pits are burning. I've had about all the fun I can stand. Can't we just finish with some good old PT exercises?*

"Gentlemen," Lt. Oscar Juno began. "In regular men's gymnastics competition, you do tumbling runs along with free dance and handstands. We're only going to teach tumbling and back springs. We will do two runs today, one forward with a turn at the end and a run back. On the second run we want to see a back flip." Lt. Juno and C2C Corky Jones demonstrated the exercises twice. Jones did the maneuvers while Lt. Juno narrated. "Okay. Who's first?"

PR stepped forward. He told us earlier floor exercise was his best venue. "Ah, Sir, I'll give it a try." Purposely a little hesitant on his first run, PR smirked, then proceeded to do a first-place run, including two tumbles into a back flip and finishing with a one and a half gainer. He pegged the dismount.

"OK, smart ass. You got me. Obviously, this is not your first exposure to gymnastics. Take the harness off and show us what you've got."

PR repeated his runs, adding twists and a backward one and a half flip to finish.

"Very impressive," said Lt Juno. "You're going out for the team, aren't you?"

"Yes, SIR," PR replied with a broad grin.

At the end of the period, Lt. Sullivan gathered the class. "Men that was your gymnastics introduction. You'll have two hours practice each day next week and the test on Friday. From what I saw today, none of you should have too much trouble passing the course, but you'll have to put some effort into it. A few of you are marginal in several of the events. If you feel you are struggling, take advantage of extra instruction. We want all of you to pass.

O.K, men, saddle up. We'll see you tomorrow, same time, same place."

Damn, I thought, *more chances to break your neck. This is not going to be a "gimme." I might even ask for some EI.*[80]

---

[80] EI – Extra Instruction was available in academics and other graded courses such as PE and Military Training. In the case of the Forth Class System, we had many opportunities for EI, most of a personal nature.

United States Air Force Academy

Friday, 20 September, 1957, 2030 Hours

Dear Folks,

With no game tomorrow, no pep rally tonight. Our first week grades will be out next week. All cadet grades are posted on a large bulletin board by Command Post. Everybody knows how everybody else is doing. Think I'm doing fine in academics.

English is fun. Major Galt knows his subject and is always telling us great war stories about WWII. Math is okay, but I failed a pop quiz yesterday.. I probably should get some extra instruction. If I bust another quiz, I'll go see Captain Marsh, my math instructor.

We started gymnastics this week. We did floor exercises, still rings, parallel bars, the high bar, the trampoline, and the rope climb. Floor exercise was tumbling only; not too hard. Rings are hard, especially in a sitting positon with your legs straight out in front of you. The rings aren't supposed to move, but it's tough to keep them at your side.

The parallel bars are fun, but chap you under the arms. The high bar is scary. You swing around and around the bar, then let go and catch the bar again. The secret is re-catching the bar. I only fell once.

The trampoline is fun. It's like Lucille's kids had, but bigger, and you can go higher. Jim Dickson and I saved a classmate from breaking his neck. He was about to come down on his head. We jerked on the safety harness and left him hanging in midair. We thought it was funny; he didn't.

The rope climb had me going. Didn't think I would ever make it the 30 feet to the top. They time you. If you miss the time limit, you start all over again. C2C Mason, an NCAA champ, showed me the proper technique for climbing the rope. I made it to the top, within the time limit.

We've had gymnastics Thursday and Friday and will have it all next week; with a test on Friday. I think I can pass, but I'm not going to shine. The high bar is for me like the wall was in the obstacle course. What the heck, I conquered the wall; I can do the high bar.

The classmates who are gymnasts make the rest of us look bad. But I think if you make a real effort and do half way decent exercises you will pass. They know we haven't all had 10 years of practice.

Well, it's Friday, that means room and in-ranks inspections and a parade tomorrow. I got two demerits yesterday from Cadet Garvey - I had my hat on in the dining hall. I was still a little shook from the Honor Code business and just wasn't thinking. I may not hack (do well) in academics, but at least at the moment, I won't get thrown out on military aptitude.

Give my love to Lucille and all her tribe. Tell Pa to go fishing for me and to take Gene to keep him out of trouble. I will write when I can. Hope the cake Lucille made gets here for my birthday. It will be a lot better at my new table. Oh yeah, forgot to tell you. I got moved to a new table. The table commandant is my Flight Commander, Cadet Second Class Thomas. He believes Fourth Class knowledge should be limited to the first ten minutes, so I am getting more to eat. Keep the boodle packages coming anyway. Write!!!

God Bless,
Your loving son,
Don

Chapter 27

*Cadets have no reputation for bashfulness, so take the initiative
and introduce yourself to the young ladies you wish to meet*
USAFA Decorum

Dance Lessons

Saturday 21 September 1957

We must be getting used to the system; in-room and in-ranks inspections were a piece of cake. Tom and I aced room inspection. I got a demerit for a crooked name tag.

Sixth took first place in the parade. First place and few upperclassmen made lunch tolerable. C3C Whiteman, Mr. Short's friend, was at my table. C2C Thomas, my Flight Commander, was Table Commandant. Dickson, Sanders, Hertz, were also at the table. Lunch was hamburgers and French Fries with the usual beverages.

"Mr. Davis," said Cadet Whiteman, "Give me provisions of the Honor Code and the eight squadron honor representatives. *You SOB, you're trying to get even for your washed-out friend. Oh, well . . .* "Sir, the Honor Code says I will not lie, steal, or cheat, nor allow among us those who do. Sixth Squadron Honor Representative is Cadet C2C Garvey. Ah . . ."

"Eat, Mister Davis," interjected Cadet Thomas. "Mister Whiteman, I'll see you in my room after lunch."

Wow, a guardian angel, I thought, taking a small bite of my hamburger.

***

"Say, Don," Tom asked, "what was that all about with Whiteman and Thomas?"

"Well, Whiteman was Short's buddy. I think he's trying to get to me; stack up some demerits. I heard Cadet Jay called the Squadron Second Classmen together and briefed them about Short. Cadet Thomas said the word is to treat me like all other Fourth Classmen, but there will be no retribution for what happened to Short."

"Must be nice to be the upperclassmen's' pet . . ."

"Oh, go to hell. You didn't have to put up with Short. Get your gloves. We have to be at the Fourth Class Club by 1300 hours."

"Can't wait. Up close and personal with real girls. Nice of them to let us walk over instead of marching. Marching would have impressed the young ladies."

***

Mrs. McComas and Peej were waiting. Each flight had an hour and a half on Saturday, Sunday, or Friday evening for dance lessons. Our flight was lucky to be first;

getting the pick of the young ladies. The ladies were Colorado girls, ranging (we learned) from high school seniors to College sophomores. We were excited about dance lessons with real live female partners.

We adapted quickly to the introduction routine. In the procedure, cadets lined up on one side of the room and ladies on the other. Each line moved toward the front of the room where you met your partner—sort of like at a square dance.

After three months of regimentation, we moved uniformly in line. Once in a while girls would switch positions. I thought it a little strange until I figured out the girls were sizing the cadets to ensure they did not get a cadet shorter than they were.

I also noticed one girl matching places with Terry Cloud as the lines moved. I guessed the petite, pert redhead was Terry's friend, Cindy. I could see why he was enamored of her; in addition, of course, to her being a fount of knowledge about classmates and Academy operations. I was a curious how she arranged to be here since I understood the girls were all in school. *Of course, she works in the head shed, she has ways.* I was hoping to meet Cindy.

As I reached the head of the line, I looked across and saw a cute-as-a-button petite blonde. I was delighted. "Hi," I said, "I'm Cadet Fourth Class Davis."

The little blonde giggled. "Hi, I'm Linda Jackson. Do you always introduce yourself that way? Do you have a first name?"

"Sorry, my name is Don." *Great, first chance to meet a girl and I'm Mister awkward.*

"Keep the line moving," Mrs. McComas called out. "We don't have all day."

Introductions took 20 minutes. Tables and chairs arranged on the edge of the room allowed you to sit with your "date" and become acquainted.

"Where're you from?" Linda asked.

"Sacramento, California," I replied.

"Oh, I have an aunt who lives in San Francisco. I've never been to California. Is Sacramento close to San Francisco?"

"Yeah, uh, yes," I said, remembering the polite conversation form in *Decorum.* "Do you go to college here?"

"No," she said smiling sweetly. "I'm a senior at Aurora High School."

Great, I thought, must be nearly my age. What a cute thing. Wish she hadn't worn that perfume. I'll have trouble sleeping tonight. "Is your father military?"

"No, he was a fighter pilot in Korea but has a Chevy and Ford car dealership in downtown Denver. He gave me a Bel Air Convertible as an early graduation present."

Wow, again. That has to be good news. "What brought you . . ."

"O.K., ladies and gentlemen," Mrs. McComas announced. "Today, we are going to learn the waltz. Please pay attention to Mrs. Turner and Cadet Foreman as they do the steps. Notice the steps are done to three quarter time. Music, please."

Larry Foreman and Peej demonstrated the dance. "All right, Gentlemen, escort your ladies onto the dance floor." Mrs. McComas passed around the floor giving individual instruction to couples. Linda and I had no trouble with the dance.

***

As we waltzed into the room, Tom said, "Nice to hold and smell a girl again."

"Nice," I said. "Linda is a cute, charming little girl."

"Ah, she didn't look so little to me. Nice accessories."

"I'm not sure what you mean by accessories, but she has a nice figure and you have a dirty mind. She's a high school senior, lives right off the base, and her father is a car dealer."

"Wow, did you get her number?"

"Better than that. I asked her to come for a coke and the show tonight. I told her we don't have much free time, but we can go to the Fourth Class Club. She agreed to come back."

"Oh, so you swept her off her feet."

"No, but I didn't step on them either. She said she knows the stroll and the chicken, but never had a chance to learn ballroom dancing.

"You'd better be careful, Don. If there had been an AOC or upperclassman there, they'd have nailed you for PDA.[81] You looked like you were getting preeety close to Linda"

"Well, it was hard. With her perfume and nice, soft body, it was difficult to remain a gentleman and not revert to being a Rio Linda stud."

"How was your meeting with the Chaplin?"

"Oh, I've changed my mind. I need to write a letter to my folks. Get lost. Write to your sister or shine your shoes or something."

***

I could hardly wait to finish dinner. I was nervous about meeting Linda. It was hard to get out of the "Yes, Sir, No Sir, No Excuse, Sir" mode. I didn't eat much,

---

[81] PDA – Public Display of Affection: *Decorum*, the cadet etiquette bible: ". . . keep in mind any ostentatious display of affection is taboo . . . Holding hands or walking arm in arm, by the way, are for teenagers, not for the man in uniform." A most notable PDA was the case of an upperclassman who dated "Little Moose," the Commandant's daughter. The upperclassman earned four tours for his efforts.

anticipating a Club hamburger. A Third Classman, Shriver from Fifth Squadron, had me recite the football schedule. Otherwise the meal was quiet. We only had Cadets Thomas and Shriver at the table.

***

Linda was wearing a light blue dress and blouse with a white button-down sweater that highlighted her exciting (hell, anything she wore would be exciting) figure.

"Hi," I said.

"Hi," she responded.

"I'm glad you came. Let's get a table. Would you like a hamburger or pizza?"

"Well, I had supper, so a coke would be great. Cherry coke, if they have it."

"Yes, Ma'am," I said playfully. "Coming right up." *Damn, wished I'd eaten a little more at dinner. Can't get anything if she isn't eating. Oh, well. It's worth it. Linda sure is cute.*

Setting the coke on the table, I asked, "What kind of things do you do in school?"

"Oh, I'm on the volleyball team and a cheerleader during football season. I have a pre-college program but also take home economics. I've been in a couple of plays, and I'm the president of our National Honor Society Chapter."

"Wow, sounds like you are doing well. Where're you going to college?"

"I'm going to apply to Denver University and maybe CSU."

"What's CSU?"

"Oh, yeah. Forgot you're new to Colorado. CSU is Colorado State University. I'm going to major in English."

"I like English. I was the Sports Editor on my high school paper. I have a great English teacher here. Not only does he teach us English, he tells great war stories. He was a bomber pilot in World War II. You told me your father gave you a red Bel Air Convertible to drive. That's cool. I have a 49 Chevy coup at home."

"Yes, it's a little big; I wanted a Corvette, but he said I'd be safer in a larger car."

Great . . . wheels. "We can't have a car until our First Class . . . ah, senior year. And right now, we don't have much free time. That's hard."

"I heard that, but it's nice you have some free time. It's kind of cool you have a club where you can meet dates. I think it's exciting having cadets here."

***

The movie, *Gunfight at the O.K. Corral*, starred Burt Lancaster, Kirk Douglas, and Rhonda Fleming. Linda and I sat in the back row. Linda wanted popcorn, so I got a big bag to make up for my skimpy dinner. When the show got tense just before the gunfight, Linda reached over and put her hand on mine. I looked around to make sure there were no upperclassmen nearby and took her hand. My pulse must have doubled.

After the show, we got another coke. As taps neared, I told her what a good time I had. "Unfortunately," I said, "I have to go back to my room."

Linda said she understood and accepted my offer to take her to see *Around the World in Eighty Days* the next day in Denver. I explained I had to ride in on the bus, but I could meet her in front of the Taber Theater at 1345.

"Ah, what is that in real time?" Linda asked coyly.

"Oh, sorry, that would be 1:45 . . . **PM,**" I added, smirking.

Linda smiled, "Okay, see your there."

As I suspected, the lingering aroma of Linda's perfume kept me awake.

***

Sunday morning was full of anticipation. I had a hard time concentrating on the music for the service. I barely heard Chaplin Bennett's sermon. I don't remember going back to the room. Lunch seemed to take forever. At Cadet Thomas' table, I recited the major commands and their commanders. I ate lightly; having only two pancakes, a portion of scrambled eggs, a medium serving of hash browns, two sausages, a muffin, orange juice, and a glass of milk.

***

The Blue Beetle ride downtown brought flashbacks of the first ride to the base. The feeling today was much different. I felt more mature, with a pride in being a Fourth Classman. The bus was filled with Squadron members of all classes.

Upperclassmen were cordial, engaging in reasonable conversations and suspending the "System." Protestant Choir was the same: treatment as a fellow cadet rather than as a Doolie. *Only 254 days of the Mickey Mouse left. Like the Little Engine . . . I think I can, I think I can.*

Waiting by the box office, her page boy blowing gently in the wind, Linda was wearing a bright red skirt, a red and white striped blouse with a Peter Pan collar, and a white unzipped leather jacket (to counter the cool, 50 degree dry sun-lit weather). Other than the ballerina flats, she looked like a model cheerleader. Her cheeks were slightly pink from the cool weather, contrasting with her bright skirt-matching red lipstick.

***

"Hi, Linda," I said, feeling a slight flutter at the sight of her.

"Hi," she said with the coyest of smiles.

I paid the $3.00 for the tickets and let her take my arm (allowed according to Decorum) to escort her inside. I bought two 25-cent bags of popcorn. *Hmmm, I thought, all together that's a third of my 12-dollar monthly allowance. Dating is going to be tricky.*

"Isn't this a great theater?" Linda asked.

"Yes," I replied. "It has the feel of a Southern California Spanish motif."

"It was built by Horace Tabor, who made a fortune in the Leadville silver mines. Originally, it was a grand opera house for 1500 people. In the 1920's it was remodeled to run movies, although they still had live shows. Judy Garland, Donald O'Conner, and the Andrew Sisters all performed here early in their careers."

"How do you know so much about this place?"

"Oh, my Dad is a movie and architect buff. He says you should know something about the history and buildings where you live."

Wow, she's not only cute; she's smart. "I think I'd like your Dad."

"Well, maybe if they ever loosen the reins on you, you can meet him."

The theater's darkness caused Linda to take my hand for guidance. We slipped into the third row from the back of the theater. The two rows behind me were filled with classmates with dates. The upperclassmen had moved to seats toward the front, even those with dates.

Linda and I held hands during the movie. We laughed at Cantiflas; applauded David Niven's role as Phileas Fogg as he went by train, elephant, balloon, and steamers to get around the world in 80 days to win a wager of 20,000 English Pounds. .I told Linda I couldn't hold her hand going out. "But, I'd like to see you again."

"That would be nice," she said.

***

The ride back to the base was depressing. Most cadets were discussing the movie, the imaginative plot and improbable Philias Fogg accomplishments. I was thinking how charming Linda was and sadly aware I wouldn't get to see much of her.

I was even more upset, when Val Bourque, a Third Classman said, "Say, Davis, cute date. What's her name?"

I had heard upperclassman were always a threat to Fourth Class relationships. They have more off base free time, greater phone access, and power of the demerit. There is, however; a code of ethics among cadets. Unwarranted use of the system was frowned upon and was known to get one in hot water with other upperclassmen.

"Sir, her name is Linda."

"Okay, but tell me more. Do you have her telephone number?"

"Sir, I believe that is an improper question," I said, hoping to ward off the attack. Besides, she asked me not to give out her phone number. *Thank goodness that's true. She has heard about upperclassmen "poaching" on Fourth Class dates. She is uncomfortable with the older ages of the upperclassmen.*

"Okay, Davis. Nice Defense," Bourque said, with a slight smirk on his face.

United States Air Force Academy
Sunday, 22 September 1957 2130 Hours

Dear Folks,

I don't have much time for a letter. I have to study math. Today I saw *Around the World in Eighty Days* with David Niven at the Tabor Theater in Denver. Had a date with a cute blond named Linda. I met her in dance class. She's a high school senior and my age - at least until Thursday. Linda is active in school and very bright. Too bad I won't have much time to see her.

Intramurals (inter-murder as it is known here) starts next week. I'd like to play football, but upperclassmen have first choice of teams. We also play soccer, gymnastics, boxing, and water polo. Boxing isn't my thing and water polo would be horrific. Hate to close, but I have to go. Send boodle, stamps, and a couple of bucks if you can spare it. Dating on our "salary" is going to be challenging.

God Bless,
Your Loving Son,
Don

Chapter 28

The Department of Mathematics prepares the cadet for advanced study with instruction in algebra, trigonometry and analytical geometry
Contrails

Academic Trials

September 28, 1957

"How'd you do on the Algebra GR[82], Tom?" I asked.

"Ah, I missed a couple of problems, but should be a 90 at least. How about you?"

"Damn, don't think I did well. It's sure not like high school algebra. I think I'll have to see Captain Marsh for some EI. I'm just not good at digging it out of the book. If someone explains a problem and I see it a couple of times, I do okay, but . . ."

"Hell, Davis, after dinner tonight, we'll go over problems and get you on track."

"Great, let's see if we can get permission for a study group in our room. Hertz was screaming like a stuck pig. He's really struggling. Maybe you can help him too?"

"Sure, no sweat."

***

Academics were heating up. At dinner, the Third Classmen discussed a GR in Trigonometry and asked no Fourth Class poop. The three Second Classmen, Cadets Thomas, Low, and DeSantis talked about the Squadron intramural teams.

"Mister Davis," Cadet DeSantis put down his fork and looked at me.

"Yes, Sir," I said.

"Understand you will be on my water polo team. You ever played before?"

"Ah, no, sir. I want to go out for football. I was on the varsity in high school"

"Football has enough players. You a good swimmer?"

"NO, sir. I barely passed the swimming test." *Damn, I thought telling him I didn't do well on the swim test would make him reconsider putting me on the team.*

"No sweat, Davis, we'll play you in the shallow end."

***

[82] GR – Graded Review. Cadets had pop quizzes (daily recitations --truly daily in some courses), graded reviews (progress tests), and finals. In social sciences, periodic papers and, often, a term paper were required. It was important to be "proficient," a 70 average or better in order to retain privileges.

"Okay, my Pythagorean geniuses. Let's start at the beginning. Do you know what integers, rational numbers, and irrational numbers are?" Tom asked, pulling his chair over by my desk. I gave Bob my chair and sat on the bed.

"You've got to be kidding," Bob said. "I didn't understand when Captain Marsh explained them, I still don't."

"Here's the deal: and integer is a number used in counting – you know 1, 2, 3, etc. A rational number is one that can be expressed as the quotient of two integers. That is, numbers that can make up fractions are rational numbers: one divided by four; two divided by six, etc.

An irrational number is a real number that cannot be expressed as the quotient of two integers: the square root of two or the symbol 'pi'."

"Damn," Bob said. "Do we have to know those to do the problems?"

"No, but you might get a few points for knowing the definitions. Okay, we can go on from there; do you know the concept of positive and negative numbers?"

"Yeah," I said, "I got that. You draw a vertical line at zero. Anything to left is minus and any number to the right is positive."

"And if you add positive and negative numbers, what happens?"

"You take the difference and use the sign of the larger integer. If you have a negative seven and add a positive three, you get a negative four," Bob said smiling.

"That's right. And if you subtract a negative number from a positive number?'

"That's a little trickier," I said, "if you have a positive four and you subtract a minus seven, you change the sign of the minus and end up with a positive eleven. That's because you are adding the distance of the numbers on either side of zero."

"Incredible," said Tom. "What bright fellows."

The tutoring session went for an hour and a half; interrupted only by the CCQ[83] asking for an "all right." Tom and I looked at each other. We didn't know what to say. Bob was authorized to be in the room for study, but we weren't sure how to respond.

With a loud rap, C3C Bourque bounded into the room. "Well?"

Since I initiated the study session, I answered. "Sir, Cadet Jay authorized us to study Algebra together. I handed Cadet Bourque the memo which read: "C4C Bob Hertz is authorized to visit C4C Davis's quarters during Call to Quarters for a math study

[83] CCQ – Cadet in Charge of Quarters The CCQ stays in the orderly room, answers the telephone, and makes dormitory rounds during call to quarters to ensure cadets are in their rooms or on an authorized absence. The CCQ raps on the door and asks: "All right, Sir." The answer is: "All right, Sir," if everyone is in the room is authorized to be there.

session. The memo was dated and signed "Cadet Lt. Col, Jimmy L. Jay, Commander, 6th Squadron."

"Well, Dumbsquat Davis, why didn't you just say 'all right,' since everyone in the room is authorized to be here?" Bourque said with his familiar smirk.

I stood stiffly at attention and said, "NO EXCUSE, SIR."

Bourque smiled slightly, turned smartly, and left.

"Man, I've had it," Bob said. "I've got to go home and get some rest. My head is about to bust. But, thanks, Tom, I feel more confident I can squeak by.

***

Thursday was a great. After Algebra, I polished off my essay, "Why I choose the Air Force Academy," for Major Galt's class. I slept so soundly Tom had to wake me at reveille. The air was full of fall scents.

"Why is today important?" Cadet Major Thomas asked as soon as we sat down.

Feeling adventurous, I said, "Sir, today is important because it is my birthday."

"Ah, finally sweet 16, Davis. Well, you can't sit at ease because I haven't seen a cake, but I have a headache, so do your duties quietly; no unnecessary jabber. Understood? By the way, today is important because it is my fiancée's birthday."

Given Cadet Thomas' relaxed attitude, I had my fill of two pancakes, sausage, scrambled eggs, wheat toast with butter and strawberry jam, grapefruit slices, ti-ger-pis, and even a cup of coffee with half and half.

***

Major Galt was in rare form. After he collected our essays and we finished a review of subjunctive verbs, he launched into a story about his squadron's raid on Ploesti, Romania.

"Ploesti," he began, "was an oil refining area producing a third of Nazi Germany's petroleum requirements. Allied forces conducted 25 bomber raids on Ploesti facilities from April 1943 to August 1944 using B-17 and B-24 aircraft.

The first large raid, with 177 B-24s, flew a low-level mission; one of the first and last low-level raids flown by the Army Air Forces. Ploesti's 3d strongest European defense position, including anti-aircraft artillery and fighter aircraft, downed 54 airplanes and crews. My Fifteenth Air Force B-17 was part of the 520 April 24, 1944, bomber force. One hundred and fifty P-51 and P-38 fighters accompanied us and engaged the swarming German fighters.

We left the African Coast at Bengasi, Libya, preceded across the Mediterranean over Italy and into Romania. We had to climb over some mountains and ended up between 21and 24 thousand feet for our run in. Flack was so thick you could walk on it.

At one point, my left gunner, Sergeant Patterson, called out: 'Pilot, there are four Fokkers coming right at me.' Looking out of my side window, I replied: 'Son, those Fokkers are Messerschmitts, keep firing.'

Fortunately, Three P-51s dove out of the sun and drove off the Messerschmitts. We took several hits from the fighters, but no critical damage. None of my crew was hurt and we made it back the 600 miles to Libya."

Art Kerr put up his hand. "Sir, did your crews get any recognition for the raids?"

"Yes, Kerr, we did. Crew members received an Air Medal for each Ploesti run. Our lead crew took significant ground fire, dropped their bombs early, but proceeded to the target so the rest of the bombers would follow and hit the target.

Major Hanson's aircraft caught fire, the wing collapsed, and the entire crew perished. The Major was awarded the Medal of Honor. The crew all received the Air Force Cross."

"Wow," said Art. "What incredible heroism."

Just then the bell rang. "Okay, that's it for today. I'll have your essays graded and the results posted tomorrow."

***

As I coasted into my hot pilot position, I noticed the cake at the end of the table; a double decker carrot cake—my favorite. Taking an unauthorized gaze, I saw the words "Happy Birthday, Don" in large letters on the top of the cake.

"Take seats," said Cadet Thomas. "Davis, let's have the President's cabinet."

Oh, crap, I thought. *What is this? It's my birthday, and Thomas is going to grill me on Fourth Class knowledge.* With a lightly disguised sigh and a shrug, I began: "Sir, the Vice President of the United States is the Honorable Richard M. Nixon; the Secretary of State is the Honorable John Foster Dulles; the Secretary of Defense is . . .'"

"Okay, Davis, ditch the scowl. Nice cake. Who made it?"

"Sir, my sister Lucille made it. She does cakes for parties and birthdays."

"Nice. You lucked out. Dinner tonight is lobster casserole. Fourth Classmen, at ease, courtesy of Mister Davis."

Testing my summer experience, I sat back in my chair. My classmates immediately picked up on the maneuver. Cadet Thomas smirked but said nothing.

Lt. Col. Echelberger supplied a variety of ice cream to go with the cake. Two cake boxes appeared; one for the remnants of my cake and one for the chocolate one provided by the mess hall. Cadet Thomas escorted me safely back to the dorm, at the price of an extra piece of cake.

Before Call to Quarters, Tom and I invited Cadets Third Class Bourque and Bush from across the hall in for cake. Might as well make a few brownie, ah, cake points with the enemy. The mess hall provided a knife, forks, paper plates, and napkins. Ice cream would have been nice, but, of course, there was no way to transport it to the room.

***

For some reason, Friday was a light day. The upperclassmen were engaged in academic discussions at breakfast and lunch. At dinner, the talk was about the game tomorrow and the chances of beating Occidental.

"Davis," queried Cadet Bourque, "would you like to bet a dessert on the game?"

"Yes, Sir," I said. "I'll take Air Force."

"Oh, no, Davis, **nobody** here bets against the team. We have to do it on scores. Tell me how many touchdowns you'll give me."

"Sir, I don't understand."-

"Okay, here it is. You say the team wins by three touchdowns. If they score more than three touchdowns over Occidental, you win; otherwise I win."

"Yes, Sir. How about two touchdowns? We didn't do well against UCLA."

"What a weaseler," said Bourque, "two it is."

***

As promised, Major Galt had the papers graded. I got a 92, edging out Sutter's 91; bringing my average to 86 overall. Major Galt was tough, but a fair grader. Considering the competition in my section, I felt good about my grade.

"I liked the papers," said Major Galt. "But most of you have the fault of beginning writers. Your stories are more tell than show. They are narratives. You will find good writers show the reader their story through dynamic actions rather than simply narrating the tale."

Pausing, Major Galt looked at me. "Mister Davis, why did you choose the Air Force Academy over the Coast Guard Academy? After all, the Coast Guard Academy is established and USAFA is new."

"Yes, Sir," I replied. "That was one of the attractions. When I started at my junior high school it was brand new. It was exciting and interesting to establish new traditions. Besides, I have been interested in the Air Force ever since elementary school. Airplanes on their way to Korea from McClellan Air Force Base were towed on the road by the school on their way to the port of Sacramento for shipment. The sight of the airplanes and the thought of flying intrigued me; made me want to join the Air Force.

In high school, my advisor made a case for the Air Force Academy's educational opportunities. My prospects, besides the Coast Guard Academy, were slim. I would have to attend a junior college. That didn't compare with the Academy opportunity."

"How many cadets are there in your class from California?"

"Sir, there are 20 from California."

The bell rang. We formed up to return to the dorms. In the corridor, Art said, "Hey Tom, drive the section by the outside bulletin board to check grades."

Grades were posted on the bulletin boards on the west side of the quadrangle. We were allowed to "fall out" to scan our grades.

My academic grades ranged from a 94 in Military Studies (Air Power and National Security) to an 81.2 in Engineering Drawing. I had a drafting course in high school and didn't like it then. My worst grade was a 75.9 in physical education, reflecting my "gymnasty" struggles. The Air Power grade put me in the top seventh percentile of the class.

If I can bring my PE grade up, I could make the Dean's list, worth a couple of extra privileges. The PE grade was passing, but put me in the lower fiftieth percentile. Since these were initial grades, there were no real consequences for failing. With mid-term grades averages below 70 meant loss of our meager privileges. You could not regain privileges until you achieved a 70 average in the deficient course. I noted Bob's Algebra grade was a 69.8. *Of course,* I thought, *that was before Tom's tutoring. If we keep it up, I'll bet Bob is above the line after the next GR.*

***

Evening meal started out with the usual. Cadet Lowe was on a tear. "Davis, let's have the Code of Conduct." Rumor was Cadet Lowe received a Dear John.

"I am an American fighting man. I serve in the forces which guard my country …

From the far side of the dining hall a loud, off-key band of Fourth Class voices rang out with the Air Force Fight Song:

> *Gear up and go Falcons to the fight,*
> *For our spirit is high.*

The volume increased as more and more cadets joined in.

> **Gear up and Go Falcons, surge ahead,**
> **On the field as in the sky.**
> **For you will see sil-ver and the blue,**
> **Reign supreme u-pon the field.**
> **We will prove that we can't be beat-en,**
> **For the Falcons nev eer yield.**

"Well, Hertz, you going to let dumbsquats from Second Squadron outshine us?"

"**NO SIR,**" shouted Bob jumping up. "**Everybody, Slash'm with a beak!**

> **SLASH'M WITH A BEAK!**
> **RIP'M WITH A CLAW,**
> **KICK'M IN THE ASS,**
> **RAH! RAH! RAH!**"

"**Mister Hertz**, I believe the term is: 'Bring on the meat wagon!' **Do it again.**"

"**YES, SIR!**

SLASH'M WITH A BEAK!
RIP'M WITH A CLAW,
BRING ON THE MEAT WAGON,
RAH! RAH! RAH!"

Pandemonium broke out as each squadron tried to outdo the others. Twice the adjutant yelled into the microphone, "**DISMISSED, THE WING IS DISMISSED.**"

Suddenly, Kerr began the Air Force song, picked up by our table and tables on either side. Finally, the entire mess hall rang out with "**Here's a toast to the host . . .**"

When the last words of the song trailed off, the Adjutant said, "**Wing, Dismissed!**"

***

Surrounded by the Academy's entire contingent of Air Police and a cordon of AOCs, the quadrangle pep rally was more subdued than the previous one. Nonetheless, a bonfire and enthusiastic cheering went on well past midnight. The DO's announcement that SAMIs would begin as scheduled at 0730 sent cadets off toward their barracks. At 0045, the quad was silent.

***

Morning broke with a chill in the air, grey low-hanging clouds, and a 10-knot north wind. The weather forecast was for light snow flurries around ten o'clock.

"Sir, does that mean they will cancel the parade?" Bob asked.

Cadet Thomas smirked. "No, Hertz, you might get to wear your rubbers and overcoat, but don't count on not marching."

A crazy event happened during the breakfast formation. One of the squadrons had "kidnapped" Colonel Cassidy's sports car and put it on the Headquarters Building roof during the night. Rumor was Fifth Squadron had a friend in Civil Engineering who provided a forklift to hoist the car onto the roof.

Another squadron stole the Officer-of-the-Day's pants and ran them up the Headquarters' flag pole. As we stood ready to go to breakfast, Captain Sherman Brown, the OD, stood in front of the Wing formation in a bathrobe. He shouted: "**You men think you're smart. Well, you're not going to breakfast until those who ran my pants up the flagpole come forward.**"

Damn, I thought, *that's a giant improper question.*

We were standing in formation for 10 minutes. No one moved. Out of the corner of my eye I saw a uniformed figure approach Captain Brown. A few words were exchanged. Captain Brown, with a very red face, turned toward the formation and said loudly, "**Carry On.**"

Later, Cadet Jay, who was close enough to Captain Brown to see what went on, relayed what happened. Colonel Cassidy, seeing the Wing standing in formation and not proceeding to breakfast, approached Captain Brown. "What the hell is going on," Cassidy is said to have said. After a heated exchange, Cassidy said to Brown, "Captain, you're an idiot. You can't enforce rules that way. Dismiss the Wing. I'll see you in my office after the parade."

***

Tom and I each got a demerit for room inspection. Mine was a demerit for picture not properly displayed—the picture of Rex the dog was still on the shelf. Captain Braswell didn't bother saying the picture wasn't properly centered, simply improperly displayed. *Damn, I'll have to get a nice picture of Linda. I understand if you have a good-looking girl displayed, Captain Braswell looks at the picture while inspecting and overlooks little discrepancies.*

"Waste basket improperly displayed," Captain Braswell called out to Cadet Jay who was following him with a notepad. *Hah! Braswell got Tom again. That will teach him not to put the basket exactly in the middle. I always put it on my side when it's my turn.*

As we turned on line in the parade, the temperature dropped 15 degrees. At "Officers, Front," snowflakes began to fall, lightly at first, then in a flurry as the wind picked up. The reviewing stands were bare except for the required AOCs and staff.

"Damn, Tom, it was cold out there. Not good weather for a California boy."

"Ah, quit gripping. Back home we got three and four feet of snow and the temperature stayed around freezing for days. You'd better get used to it fast. Standing in Denver Stadium for three hours is going to freeze your butt off."

***

The crowd greeted us warmly during march-on. As each group and squadron came online, the PA system announced Commanders and staffs, drawing applause. The weather warmed for the game; the temperature rising into the 40s. DU Stadium seats weren't comfortable, but it didn't matter because the Wing stood the entire game.

The team was playing good ball. The last two scores were by classmates. Rich Marble took the team from the 20-yard line for a touchdown. He threw the ball on a crossing pattern to end, Bob Brickey, for the score. The other touchdown was a 40 yard run-back of a punt by Monte Moorberg. Monte had a 30 yard run in the previous drive. We were jubilant since the final score was AFA 40, Occidental 6.

***

Although Linda said she was coming to the game, I couldn't spot her in the crowd. I looked for her after the game, but Doolies only had 20 minutes after the game to get on assigned busses. *Oh, well, Linda said she'd meet me at Arnold Hall after dinner.*

***

Dinner was great. Hamburgers, hot dogs, and French fries; with the usual drinks and make-your-own sundaes for dessert. I had two hamburgers and a hot dog. I wouldn't need popcorn to fill me up this time. Only upperclassmen on restrictions were in the mess hall. There were just enough to have upper-class table commandants. "At ease' was given before the official announcement from the command tower.

***

Linda was waiting at Arnold Hall, wearing a cheerleader dark blue skirt and a gold sweater with blue letters "AHS" on it. "These are my school colors", she said. "I already put my coat in the cloak room."

I recognized the letter sweater and asked, "What is the letter for?"

"It's for volleyball and the little bulldog is for cheerleading."

AHS, Aroura High School; of course, they couldn't use just a large "A" for the girls.

We had the run of Arnold Hall with the upperclassmen out on the town. It was 1900, just in time to make the movie, *Pal Joey,* starring Rita Hayworth, Frank Sinatra, and Kim Novak. Linda took my hand as the lights went down.

As I sat the cherry coke and strawberry shake down, I said," do you suppose you could get me a nice framed 8X10 picture of you for my room?"

"I'm sure I can manage that. What did you think of the movie?"

"I thought Sinatra was good as a second-rate singer. And Rita Hayworth was pretty convincing as an ex-stripper, gold digger and now wealthy widow."

"What about Kim Novak?"

"Oh, she was bitchin'." From her look, I didn't think Linda understood or approved of my California slang.

"I guess, if you like blonde floozies," Linda said with a smirk.

Wow, that's interesting, since Linda's a blonde. Ironic Kim was a Linda. I don't know if Linda is being critical or enticing. "Hmmm, I thought she played the innocent part well."

"Well, I'm not sure being seductive is innocent, but I guess that's good acting."

I sensed Linda was being a tease. *Wow, again. I can't wait to be alone with you.* "Would you like to practice some dance steps?" I said, reaching for Linda's hand. A small band was playing smooth, danceable music. We spent the evening enjoying slow dances. Great that there were no upperclassmen around to give out Form 10s for PDA.

As we sat down, I saw Terry and Cindy come in. "Hey, Terry, come join us."

Cindy was stunning in a red dress, a string of pearls, and very nice cleavage. "Hi, Cindy, I've heard a lot about you. Cindy, this is Linda. Linda this is Terry Cloud and Cindy." *I couldn't believe how comfortable I was with the introductions—Thank you Decorum.*

"Hi," said Cindy and Terry simultaneously. "Cindy, this is Don Davis. We have had a few adventures together, especially during FASE."

Noticing the puzzled look on Linda's face, Terry said, "Oh sorry, Linda, that's the Forward Air Strip Encampment. That's when we got our Boy Scout badges for playing war. Cindy works in the Commandant's Office and keeps us informed about things that are going to happen and the fates of our classmates who leave."

"Yes," said Cindy. "I knew about the encampment but not the acronym. Anyway, Dean McDermott has been throwing the books at cadets; four more Fourth Classmen left this week."

I groaned at Cindy's pun and asked, "Who were they, Cindy?"

"They were David Mitchell, Randy Monroe, Denny Pogue, and Steve Wilson. They all had at least two deficient classes on the first grading sheet. And they weren't 69s, they were much lower scores. They probably could have survived with extra instruction, but I don't think they were motivated to stay. They just quit."

"They were from 2nd and 7th Squadrons," added Terry. "Interestingly, none were varsity sports players. I met Mitchell and Wilson during summer training. They seemed like pretty good guys, but who knows."

"How many are left in the Class?" I asked.

"The latest count is 280, which means 41 have gone since we have 7 turn backs."

"Would anyone like to dance before the music goes away and you charming gentlemen turn into pumpkins?" Linda asked.

Damn, that was bad. I'm sure Linda doesn't give a twit about the class and academics. That was really boorish. I want to continue seeing Linda. I'd better try to recover. "Of course, who can resist dancing with a beautiful and graceful partner?"

"Nice try, Davis," Linda said, giving me her precocious little smile.

Call to Quarters came too soon. I escorted Linda to the door of Arnold Hall and helped put on her mid-length jacket. "Can I see you next week?" I said.

"Well, Don, our Senior Prom is next week and I'd really like to go—with a good friend of mine. You don't mind, do you?"

"Of course not. I'll just suffer studying in my room. Seriously, that's fine. You shouldn't miss your Senior Prom. We can get together later, right?"

"I like you, Don, and enjoy being with you. Of course, we *will* get together later."

Chapter 29

. . . there are three flight surgeons . . . responsible for keeping
the cadets in the best of health.
The Story of the US Air Force Academy

Sunday, October 13, 1957—Flu Epidemic

My stay in the hospital was good for "limited duty" until Monday. I didn't have to march in the parade on Saturday or stand in-ranks inspection. That, of course, brought derisive comments from Tom.

Worse, however, was the reaction of the upperclassmen at the Saturday noon meal. I had to go through my favorite: all four versus of the Air Force Song, Washington's treatise on vulgarity, and MacArthur's statement on "Victory." Fortunately, I wasn't hungry anyway.

"Okay, Davis," said Cadet Bourque, "I'll give you two touchdowns and, let's make it interesting; a week's worth of deserts."

"Sir, so, George Washington has to beat us by more than two touchdowns?"

"You're pretty smart for a Doolie, Davis. Are we on?"

"Yes, Sir."

"Great. I like desserts. EAT."

***

All right, tenors, you're flat." Mr. Boyd, the Protestant Choir Director, was being very picky. He had called the Saturday practice because he was worried about our Washington DC appearances. The schedule was not completely set, but we knew we were going to sing in the National Cathedral, The Arlington Cemetery Bowl, and possibly on a television show or two.

A Second Classman, wanting to start early on the Open Post, asked Mr. Boyd at as the session began, "Sir, do the Second Classmen have to be here for this rehearsal?"

"No, Mr. Franklin, you don't have to stay . . . unless you want to go to DC with the rest of the choir." Knowing Mr. Boyd meant business, everyone settled down to work on the music.

We were rehearsing three major pieces: Handel's *Alleluia Chorus* from *The Messiah*; *The Battle Hymn of the Republic*; and *the Air Force Song* Mr. Boyd started the rehearsal by explaining each piece. He believes you sing better if you know the background of the music.

"*The Alleluia Chorus*, of course, comes from the *Messiah*, the masterful religious work by George Frederic Handel. He was German and wrote the song in 1741. It is a great piece for us because there is such a range and depth to explore.

The *Battle Hymn of the Republic* was composed in the beginning of the US Civil War. The words were from Julia Ward Howe and the music came from a tune called John Brown's Body. The Hymn became the rallying song of the Union Forces.

You all know the Air Force Song. You probably don't know it came from a push by General Hap Arnold. In a thousand dollar contest, Robert MacArthur Crawford won the prize. The song was originally written for the Army Air Corps, but was adapted when the Air Force became a separate service in . . . what year Mister Davis?

"It was 1947, Sir."

"Right. I don't think we'll have trouble with the words since you've had to learn the song by heart. We will work on the music so that it becomes melodious, rather than the version sung in the mess hall for rallies. All right, men, let's get to work!"

Chapel on Sunday was enjoyable because the upperclassmen acted like human beings in choir practice and during the service. Mr. Boyd was over his grumpy spell; things went smoothly on Sunday. I was beginning to regain my strength, but still didn't feel a hundred percent, so I appreciated the quiet practice and service. Attendance was down, reflecting, obviously, the consequences of the Great Flu Epidemic of 1957.

***

I was anxiously awaiting Linda's arrival at the scheduled Sunday dance lesson. The chilling north wind was pushing on the door as I held it open for Linda. "Thank you," she said as she stepped inside and unzipped her white leather jacket. "Hi."

"Hi," I said. took her jacket and put it in the cloak room.

Walking back, I realized how cute Linda was. She was wearing a rust and ochre plaid skirt, a white blouse, and a pumpkin colored pullover sweater.

"I'm glad to see you; it seems like a long time."

"It's only been two weeks . . ."

"Yeah, but when you live in a monastery, time goes slowly sometimes. Although I actually missed classes most of last week. I was in the hospital with the flu and strep throat."

"Oh, Don, I'm sorry. If I'd known, I'd have come visit you."

"No, it was better you didn't. We have had an epidemic of the flu in the Wing. I wouldn't want you to get it . . . I missed you."

"I missed you, too, but the time was easier for me. The prom was nice. Four of us went to *La Cueva*, a Mexican restaurant down on Colfax Street. They have great food. I had a shredded beef burrito and refried beans. The five-piece band was great. I even got to use some of our dance steps, although I had to show my date how to do them.

Then we had extra cheer leading practice. We even learned some new routines for our game Friday when we played our rivals, East High School."

"How'd the game go?"

"It was great. We won 21 to 14. Bill, Sue, John, and I went to Shakey's Pizza after the game and shared a large pizza. Bill's a halfback on the team. He scored one of the touchdowns. He's the one who took me to the prom."

Wonderful, a football hero and all the time in the world to woo Linda. "Great, we had a Shakey's in Sacramento. We went there with dates after our games and plays sometimes." *Might as well let Linda know that I'm only a recluse here . . . and now.* "Glad you like pizza. We have a lot in common."

As we went into the dining room, aka the "ballroom," the last cadets in the matchup line were meeting their dancing partners. Those already with partners, like Terry and I, were excused from the Congo Line introductions. I noticed Tom had wormed his way toward the back of the line so that he was now aligned with a very pert and pretty redhead.

Spying Terry and Chris at a table at the side of the room, I maneuvered Linda toward their table. "Hi, Terry, Chris, how's it going?"

"Hi, Linda, Hi Don," they both responded. "It's all good" said Terry. "Heard you were in the hospital. What was that all about? We missed you in class."

"Yeah, had the flu and strep throat. The instructors came over and gave us EI in the hospital, but I still feel behind. I'll find out tomorrow how much I'm behind. There were some 30 cadets in the hospital. It's a real epidemic."

"Stay away," Chris said, making the sign of the cross as if warding off Dracula.

"Nah, Flight Surgeon says he won't let us out if we're still contagious. You don't think I'd ask Linda out if I were still contagious, do you?"

"Thanks," said Linda, just as Mrs. Mac announced the lesson was the "jitterbug."

"Gentlemen, escort your ladies to the dance floor. Watch Mrs. Turner and Cadet Foreman. *Wow, Larry certainly is teacher's pet. Bet he's trying to get good phone numbers from Peej.* "Now," Mrs. Mac continued, "you may see wild jitterbug maneuvers in movies—people throwing each other up in the air. We're going to teach more refined steps so no one gets hurt." There was a polite chuckle from the cadets and their partners.

The lesson was entirely too short. We were getting close to Call to Quarters before the session ended. However, this was an official function and we were allowed 20 minutes after the lessons ended to get to our rooms. I was excited to see Linda, but the jitterbug didn't give me much opportunity to get close to her. Nonetheless, the soft, enticing scent of her perfume began arousing my latent hormones. Her sweet smile gave me a feeling I hadn't had since going steady with Sandy in high school.

I escorted Linda to the door. "Can I see you again next Saturday evening?"

"I don't know, Don, we have an away game in Colorado Springs next Friday. My folks are taking me and a couple other girls down. We're staying at the Broadmoor. Oh, I forgot you haven't been to the Springs. The Broadmoor is the fanciest hotel in Colorado Springs. The US Olympic skating team practices there. I think the girls are going to a movie Saturday night and ice skating at the Broadmoor Sunday. I've had some lessons, but haven't had much chance to skate because of the cheerleading."

"Oh, okay," I said, hoping the disappointment wasn't too evident. *At least she didn't mention Bill. That's positive.* "Actually that's probably good for me. I'm sure I have a lot of classwork to catch up on. Oh, and Mister Boyd, the choir director, says we are going to have a couple of extra practices authorized for the Washington, DC, trip."

"The DC trip?"

"Oh, didn't I tell you? The Protestant Choir is going to Washington next month. We're going to sing in the Arlington Amphitheater and in the National Cathedral."

"NO, you didn't tell me!" Linda said with a pouty face.

"I'm sorry. We just learned about it the week before last and I was so bummed out last week and I didn't see you and . . ."

"Okay, it's all right. I forgive you," she said with her precocious smile. "Call me when you can this week. We can work something out for later. I like hearing your voice; even if I can't see you."

The wind was biting cold as I double-timed to my room.

***

214

United States Air Force Academy
Sunday, 13 October 1957, 2200 Hours

Dear Folks,

   Sorry I haven't written. It's been a terrible two weeks. This week I spent five days in the hospital. The Cadet Wing is suffering a flu epidemic. I felt fine until Sunday night. I had a fever, chills, and began throwing up. Tom saw me in the head (bathroom); got the CCQ who woke up the Squadron Commander. Cadet Jay called the Security Police to take me to the hospital.

   The corpsman said I had flu, strep throat, and severe dehydration. He said 160 cadets, almost a fifth of the Wing, were on sick call Monday, with 30 of us in the hospital. When I woke Monday morning, my head hurt, my throat was sore, and every bone in my body ached. I slept 12 to 14 hours a day.

   The instructors made rounds and gave us assignments. No daily recitations. Well, that's not exactly true; they gave us the pop quizzes, but also the answers. I'd like to take the rest of the courses that way.

   Hertz came to see me in the hospital. He was in for four days the week before. He was griping about grades; said he received a 72 in Judo, but took the test when he was feeling crummy. I lucked out. I took the test before I started to get sick; got an 82 which will bring my PE grade up some.

   I got out of the hospital Friday afternoon after lunch. That was good because I really didn't feel like facing the "system."

   Friday evening's pep rally was great; almost as big as our first one. We didn't go outside the gate. The Supe wasn't happy after the first rally; said if we went into Aurora again, he'd definitely cancel the upper-class Open Post.

   Friday night we went on a spirit raid. Ten of us, including four upperclassmen, went to Arnold Hall and loosened the cables on the X-4 (the X-4 is a small experimental airplane. Sixth Squadron got the spirit award when everyone saw the X-4 sitting in front of our dorm Saturday morning.

We almost got caught halfway through the operation. The Air Police came and flashed their searchlight around. If they spotted us, they didn't let on. I think they like cadet pranks and wish they could take part. Since they didn't "apprehend" us, however, the head shed couldn't ask everyone "who done it." A "squad" from Dorm 914 hung a sign between the chimneys on the mess hall saying: "Cream George Washington."

It was cool pulling off the tricks with the upperclassmen. I might survive after all if things keep getting better. I like Cadet Bourke, he's funny. George Washington, like UCLA, didn't get the word about our rally. We lost 20 to 0.

Well, I'm going to close and hit the sack. I'm still a little tired. The dance lesson tonight was the jitterbug. Linda came out. It was good to see her. She's going to Colorado Springs next week. She was a miffed at me because I hadn't told her about the choir trip to D.C. . . . come to think of it, I haven't told you about it. The whole Protestant choir is going to Washington. We are going to sing in the National Cathedral and in the Arlington Bowl. It should be a great trip. I've always wanted to see D.C.

Gosh, I think the jitterbugging did me in. I just have to go to bed.

God Bless,
Your loving son,
Don

Chapter 30

The various sports taught in the physical training program are designed to build courage, stamina, and a respect for the other man's abilities . . .
Contrails

Sunday, October 20, 1957

"Jab, Davis, left jab . . . jab!" Lt. Robert McNamara called out as the second round of my match with Ken Seymour began. An inch taller and five pounds heavier, Ken had a reach and weight advantage.

Boxing classes began the first of the week. I was still weak from my hospital time. Fortunately, we only learned fundamentals the first three days. Fundamentals focused on footwork (left foot forward, feet apart), movement, body position (elbows up, close to the body – hands up, protect the head), and basic punches (jab, right cross, left hook, right hook, and uppercut). Friday brought actual matches. I felt overmatched with Ken. I kept weaving and bobbing to keep away from his jabs. **"Come on, Davis, box!"** yelled McNamara.

"Jab, jab, cross," came from Lt. George Brown, Ken's instructor. **"Use your right! Move in, move in. Jab, jab, right cross,"** Brown continued.

I was fatigued even before the bell rang. "Not bad, Davis," said Lt. McNamara, "Be more aggressive. Go after him. When he jabs, parry with a left and counter to the body."

I improved in the second round. Despite Ken's reach, I parried his jabs and ducked under his right to deliver a body blow. That worked twice. When I ducked under the third time, Ken met me with a left to the head. Fortunately, he hit my head guard, not my nose. The second bell, ending my first-ever boxing match, came none too soon.

***

"All right, Mister Davis, what do we know about Sputnik?" asked Cadet 3C Long.

"Sir, the Soviet Union launched Sputnik, the world's first artificial satellite, on October 4th from their facility in the Kazakh Republic. Sputnik is 22 inches in diameter, weighs 184 pounds and circles earth every hour and 36 minutes. Its elliptical orbit has an apogee[84] of 584 miles and a perigee[85] of 143 miles. It emits a constant 'beeping' signal."

---

[84] The farthest point of the orbit from the Earth.
[85] The nearest point of the orbit to the Earth.

"Okay, why do we care about Sputnik?"

"Sir, it demonstrates Soviet ability to reach the United States with a nuclear warhead. The Sputnik payload is 10 times the weight of any US . . . ah, United States throw-weight."

"Okay, Davis, where did you get your information?"

"Sir, the information came from Popular Science Magazine."

"Eat!"

***

After dinner Thursday night, I called Linda on the pay phone outside our barracks. I'd been thinking about her all week—in between battling academics and preparing for my Friday Boxing Graded Review by running extra laps in the gym.

"Hi, Linda, what's going on?"

"Well, we have a game tomorrow against Longwood. If we win, we'll go to District."

"Great, wish I could take you out after the game. Can you come out Saturday?"

"Oh, dinner with you would be fun. Anyway, I'm going to the dance with Bill, and we'll probably go for hamburgers after. Oh sure, I'd like to come out Saturday. What's the show?"

Damn, Bill again. Well, I can't blame her. "What's the show ?" Nice dig. "Hmm, the show is Funny Face with Fred Astaire, Audrey Hepburn, and Kay Thomas. Do you like musicals?"

"Yes, actually I do. Do you like musicals and are you buying me a pizza?"

"Not my favorite and yes, of course. You have a choice of our famous pizza, hot dogs, or hamburgers. Thanks for coming. I really want to see you."

"Okay, see you Saturday."

I stared at the phone as the dial tone buzzed in my ear.

I was pumped Friday after receiving a 97 for my essay "Why I choose the Air Force Academy." Major Galt joked I should write public relations material for USAFA. Friday afternoon caused a little more anxiety. The boxing Graded Reviews were scheduled from 1400 until 1700. The GR consisted of two matches of two rounds each with different opponents.

"O.K, Davis, your first match is with Bob Hertz," said Lt. McNamara. "Let's see if we taught you anything other than ballet steps."

Halfway through the first round, Hertz landed a right cross to my left eye. I staggered back and covered up. Bob came at me with a series of jabs and right hooks. I took the blows and countered with a right cross when Bob dropped his left to throw another hook. My blow caught him entirely off guard, and he went down with a thud.

The round ended as Bob took a five count. "Nice shot," said McNamara, tending to my now swelling left eye. "You're doing O.K., but you're behind. If you want to win, you'd better show a little more action."

Motivated by McNamara, I came out strong, landing a series of jabs and throwing a right hook followed by a left hook. Bob covered well, and while he fell back, he wasn't hurt. I kept the pressure on the rest of the round. Neither of us landed a telling blow.

Instructors served as judges. Second Classman, Cadet Staff Sergeant (C/SSgt) Simons, taking the Coaching Course, was the referee. The two instructor judges split; one for Hertz and the other for me. Simons called the bout even, resulting in a tie. Bob and I got equal credit.

My second opponent was Tom Bronson. Tom was my height but about seven pounds heavier. My eye was puffy, but I could see all right. "You okay to go on?" asked McNamara.

"Yes, Sir," I replied. *I don't want this hanging over me for the weekend. I have a lot to do rather than a make-up boxing match.*

For the first 30 seconds, Tom and I danced around the ring, testing each other with light jabs. I noticed Tom had a bad habit of dropping his right hand as he jabbed. , He became aggressive and backed me up with his jab. As I backed toward my corner, I waited for him to drop his right. He did. I parried his jab and hit him with a solid right hook to the body and a left hook to the head. The left hook hit Tom square on the jaw. Tom collapsed on the mat and took a 10 count. The match was over. *Sorry, Tom, but you really helped my grade.*

"How'd you do, Ace?" Tom asked as I came into the room.

"Are you talking about academics or boxing?"

"Well, I saw your second bout when you coldcocked Bronson, but I was in the other ring during the first match."

"Well, Bob and I got 89's for the first go around. I got a 93 for knocking Tom out. The 91 average should bring my PE grade up. As far as academics, I got a 97 on my English essay and an 84 on the math GR thanks to you. How about you?"

"Not bad. Got an 83 on my Philosophy GR and a 94 on the math GR. I won both boxing matches on points. Wrestling taught me a lot about movement. I had easy opponents. Jim Deming had me by about 10 pounds, but he was slow. I got a lot of points on jabs and landed an uppercut that put him on his butt. He had pretty good stamina though.

Twy was harder, but I outweighed him and had a good inch reach on him. He kept backpedaling for both rounds. Don't think the instructors like that. Anyway, I got 94 and a 91. Good days work. How's it going with Linda?"

"Okay, but she's going out with this Bill character. He's a football stud at school. She's coming out tomorrow. How'd you do with that redhead I saw you pick up at dance lessons?"

"Oh, Sue. Yeah, she's a good looker and can carry on a conversation. She's a sophomore at Denver, but she's dating a Second Classman. Says she's coming to the lessons just to learn steps. I don't need grief from some Second Classman, so I guess I'll just keep looking. By the way, did you see what happened to Paul Dutch?"

"The Second Classman?"

"Yeah, seems he missed chapel last week?"

"What did they do to him? Not that I mind. He's been on my case a couple of times."

"It's on the Squadron Bulletin Board. Go read it."

Leaving my room, I went down the hall to the Bulletin Board to read the special orders.

SO429, TAFCW USAFA, Colorado   *18 October 1957*
3. C/SSGT Paul Dutch, 241K, 6th Squadron, 2nd Group, this station, having appeared before the Commandant's Board for Class III Offenses and the proceedings of such Board having been approved by the Commandant and the Superintendent, is reduced to the grade of Cadet Second Class and awarded the following punishments, effective this date, for the offense, "Absence from Chapel Formation 0830, 13 October 1957."

    15 Demerits
    15 Punishments (Tours)
    1 Month's restriction to specified disciplinary limits
               Signed: Joseph G. Michaloski
               CWO, WD-3, USAF,
               Administrative Officer

"As I came back into the room, I said, "Wow I guess you don't want to miss chapel."

***

Friday brought a pleasant surprise. The new Cecile B. De Mille Class A Blues and Blue (Winter) Parade Uniforms came. Two Class A blouses and three pair of trousers and the Winter Parade Uniform were delivered to the Squadron Day rooms. The overcoat, a thick wool coat, was quickly nicknamed the horse blanket.

"Damn, Tom, are these uniforms sharp or what?"

"Yeah, it's a good thing they came. The mornings and evenings have been getting colder by the day. I bet we have snow before the month is out. Did you see the cadet officers' outfits; with a white crossing belt that holds the saber scabbard and a gold sash?"

"Now, of course, the upperclassmen will be all over us for in-ranks and the parade tomorrow. Terry told me the Denver Post ran a big story on the uniforms. The reporter touted the fact that we would be in the new parade uniforms tomorrow. I bet we get a crowd."

"You know, I think I'll call Linda again and tell her to come to the parade to see the new uniforms. I can wear the blues on my date with her tomorrow night."

"Yeah, that'll be hard for her football stud to match."

"Go pound rocks, you Romeo loser."

***

Captain Braswell and the upperclassmen were all over us for the in-ranks inspection. Surprisingly, they were intent on making positive uniform corrections rather than awarding demerits. With no football game, this was the first parade in several weeks.

"Davis, I don't know how you'll manage anything as complex as flying an airplane, you can't even get your parade uniform collar right," said C3C Bourke, attaching the white collar insert to the stud on the of uniform Collar. "Don't think you'll make it as a priest either."

Under thickening clouds and dropping temperatures, the Wing performed with precision and pride modeling the new uniforms. The crowd applauded as the Wing marched on in the new blues. The Superintendent, the Commandant, and the Dean were all part of the reviewing party. Cadet Jay's saber training sessions paid off: Sixth Squadron's "officers front and center" went flawlessly.

Tom and I skated through SAMI again with only Captain Braswell's token one demerit. Tom hadn't put away his ashtray. I still didn't have a decent picture displayed, despite the fact that I had asked Linda for one – one demerit.

***

With dinner a couple of hours away, Tom and I decided to go to the Club for a hot dog to tide us over. When we got there Hertz, Carr, Cloud, and Tom Bronson were sitting at a large table drinking cokes and milk shakes. "Hello Fellow Doolies." I said as Tom and I pulled up chairs from an adjacent table.

"How's it going, guys?" I asked as we joined the circle.

"We were just discussing life in the Blue Zoo," said Kerr.

"Bemoaning the lack of freedom, but sort of counting blessings too," added Hertz.

"Everybody is leery of the horrible 70 or below ogre, but Kerr was comparing our digs with what he had at Columbia," offered Cloud.

"Yeah, I wrote my folks that our classrooms are the best I've ever seen or been in. In addition to the first class equipment and training aids, our classes have no more than 13 or 14 people. That means that everyone gets individual attention . . ."

"Right," interjected Hertz, "whether you want it or not."

"As I was saying before I was so rudely interrupted," Kerr continued, "the instructors are sharp too. For instance, my chemistry prof, Major Robinson, is a WooPooer[86] and a pilot. Although we hear a lot about the long, grey line and his Korean combat exploits, we still learn a lot about molecules and reactions—enough for me to carry an 85 average in there.

And the equipment beats any civilian college I know of. The six Christian Brothers balances are worth about eight hundred bucks—for a lab of 12. At Columbia, we had one or two balances for 50 or 60 students. Man, what a hassle."

"Come on, Kerr. Nothings too good for the cream of the crop," said Tom.

"Right, and I thanked my parents and the rest of the Great American Public in the neighborhood for supporting our government largess."

Hoping to change the subject, I looked at Bronson and said, "Thanks, Tom."

"What for?" Tom replied.

"For the 93 I got in boxing, couldn't have done it without you."

"Yeah, you owe me. My jaw still hurts."

"Hey, how about we all splurge for a couple of mushroom and pepperoni pizzas. I'll even go get them, "offered Hertz.

"Hertz, you're always hungry," I said.

"Well, hell, fellas, my boodle supply network is on the fritz."

***

Linda looked fabulous in a blue plaid skirt, a bright yellow sweater and an open blue suede jacket that matched the blue of her skirt. I marveled at her taste in clothes that always accented her trim figure. She was carrying a small brown paper wrapped package.

"Hi," I said. "Who won the game?"

---

[86] "West Pointer"

"Oh, that damn Longwood did. With a minute to go, we drove 60 yards to the eight yard line. Bill fumbled the ball and Longwood recovered. The final score was 20 to 14."

Oh, poor Bill, I thought to myself. *Hail the fallen hero.* "That's too bad. I'm sure you were the better team. Sometimes bad luck happens."

"Wow," said Linda. "I really like the new blues. You all looked sharp in the parade. Three of my girlfriends went with me and ooohed and ahhed over the uniforms. Mom and Dad were impressed too. By the way, do you think you could get dates for my girlfriends?"

"Oh, I'm sure I can. Somebody is always looking for a date. Did you tell them how boring it is; going to a movie and having hamburgers every date?"

"Well . . . NO! Besides it's good seeing you. I know it will get better."

"Yeah, I can't wait for the Open Post after the Colorado game. You're going to be available, aren't you?"

"Of course, Don. I'm looking forward to it as much as you are."

Funny Face was entertaining. Linda and I laughed as we held hands in the back row of the theater. As we exited and started toward the Fourth Class Club, I picked up the pace.

"What's the hurry?" Linda inquired.

Not wanting to admit I had seen Cadet Bourque coming out of the theater and didn't want him talking to Linda, I said, "Oh, I just wanted to get in line first to get our burgers."

After she finished her hamburger, Linda noticed the recently installed Wurlitzer Jukebox. "Let's play some music and dance," she said. Her package sat on a corner of the table.

I fished out a quarter for the Jukebox. "Okay, you pick two and I'll pick one."

Linda mulled over the list. She selected A4, *Let Me Be Your Teddy Bear* by Elvis Presley, then C9, *Young Love* by Tab Hunter.

"Good choices," I said looking fondly at Linda. I searched the menu and chose G4, *Jailhouse Rock* by Elvis, a favorite of the cadets.

We danced the two slow songs and then jitterbugged to the last Elvis song. Feeling a little tired, I suggested we sit and have another coke.

When I brought the cokes back, Linda said, "I have something for you. I hope you like it." She handed the brown paper package to me.

I sensed immediately what the gift was—an 8x10 picture of Linda. Quickly unwrapping the package, I was delighted with Linda's picture. The photographer had captured Linda's coy smile, pert face, and pretty blond hair in a pose I would be proud to display (*sorry, Rex, you'll just have to go in the drawer*).

"Wow, that's a great picture. I'll have a hard time studying because I'll be looking at your picture and dreaming."

Linda blushed. "You know, I don't have a picture of you," she said, with a mock scowl.

"Oh, I can fix that." I said. "The bonus for me with your picture is I won't get demerits for having my dog's picture on my shelf. I'm sure when Captain Braswell sees your picture, he'll forget all about demerits."

Someone else had invested in the Wurlitzer. Linda and I slow danced to *Young Love*. As Linda pressed closely against me, I knew I was going to have a hard time sleeping.

***

"This is going to be a tough week for all of us," began Cadet Jay. Mid-term exams begin Monday. You Doolies, who have not experienced this before, are going to be numb at the end of the week. Upperclassmen, you are charged with assisting the Fourth Classmen. That means no extra table exercises and absolutely no special inspections.

Fourth Classmen, you will perform your normal table and Squadron duties. You should form study groups. Those who excel should share your knowledge with classmates. You are all granted late nights; however, experience has shown that adequate sleep is also key. Do your boning up this week. Get at least eight hours sleep next week before your exams.

Are there any questions? No . . . good. It's almost call to quarters. Start tonight on your weakest subjects. Dismissed."

Chapter 31

Cadets are graded frequently so that their progress may be carefully evaluated . . .
US Air Force Academy Catalog

United States Air Force Academy
Sunday, November 3, 1957

Dear Folks,

What a couple of weeks. Haven't had time to catch my breath. The Wing went to the Wyoming game. We'll get mid-term grades Monday. If I fail a mid-term I might not get to go on the D.C. choir trip. That would be terrible.

I haven't seen Linda for two weeks. However, she did give me a cute 8X10 picture. We had a big parade a week ago Saturday. The Denver Post ran a story on the new uniforms and the parade so we had a big turnout.

I did well in boxing classes. Had two bouts; tied one and ko'd a classmate in the other. Not sure it was a good idea to do well. The second match referee was C2C Simons our Squadron boxing coach. After he saw me box, he put me on the intramural boxing team. I'm not thrilled about boxing; but better than water polo.

We had two extra choir practices last week. Mr. Boyd is really driving us. The music, however, is sounding good. Handel's *Alleluia Chorus* from *The Messiah* is really stirring. Mr. Boyd says it will sound even better at the Arlington Bowl and National Cathedral. We are also supposed to do two television programs. We leave on the 9th of November right after the football game. We will have some free time in D.C. There are upsides to being here.

Art Kerr had a "Brownie Party" in his room last Sunday. He always gets <u>BIG</u> boodle boxes (Hint! Hint!). We devoured the brownies in 20 minutes and spent an hour shooting the breeze. Art bragged he had a Supe's letter that allows him to go to

Stapleton Field or Sky-Ranch Air Park for "flying privileges." I think he may have his private license. Anyway, Kerr says he can get off on Saturdays, Sundays, and holidays if he doesn't have any duties.

He says now he can meet the East High School girl who showed up at the Club in a 1957 purple and white Cadillac sedan -- away from the prying eyes of the upperclassmen and AOCs. It's a good thing he threw the brownie party or we would have all pounced on him. The good news is on our salary, he won't be able to use the privilege too often.

We had a pep rally the Friday before we played Tulsa University at Tulsa. The rally wasn't much and we lost 12 to 7. I've heard a couple of classmate football players grumble that Buck Shaw may know a lot about professional football but doesn't understand college ball, especially cadet life. He's all business in practice and doesn't understand the cadet system. Doolies live for home games, especially if we win, because the upperclassmen are happy and therefore our lives are a lot easier.

Have you received copies of the *Talon*, the Cadet Magazine? I got you a subscription. The humor tends to be "jail house humor," funny only to the inmates. This month's mag has a story by my classmate, Lee Butler, titled "What I Wish I'd Known." It and Upper Classman, Joe DeSantis' "As Fate Would Have It" are satires on cadet life, while Joe Higgens' article, "Cadets Abroad," outlines the foreign trips we get to take.

The trip to the Wyoming game was fun. And no parade and no Saturday morning inspection. The game was good, we tied 7 to 7; should have won, but made mistakes. They were 2 touchdown favorites. I also won a week's worth of desserts. Of course, I may not get to eat them. The sororities had open houses. I met a cute little blond, Susie, who may visit for Christmas.

If you want to do something for me, you and Lucille can send boodle boxes to sustain Tom and me until the Christmas break. Cookies and brownies are always good and go fast. The cookies weren't just crumbs when you packed the boxes with

> *popcorn. Not that there is anything wrong with cookie crumbs. The popcorn was a little stale though.*
>
> *We have extra choir practices this week. The instructors have promised to get us ahead in class so we can enjoy Washington.*
>
> *Call Walt and Jim LeDoux and tell them to write. The letter supply has really dwindled. I try to answer letters as soon as I can so people will write back. Be sure you write, it helps me to put up with the system.*
>
>
>
> *God Bless,*
> *Your loving son,*
> *Don*
>
>

The Friday night pep rally was spirited, but short. The cadets circled a small bonfire while the cheerleaders went through the cheers. Linda, along with several other local girls, joined us for the rally. The Air Force Song ended events at 2330. Saying goodnight to Linda, I snuck a quick kiss, and said I wished she could be with me in Washington.

***

Breakfast was boisterous, with cheers ringing throughout the dining hall. The upperclassmen were obviously pumped up; the atmosphere was dynamic, but congenial.

"O.K., Davis, I'll take two touchdowns for a week of desserts," said Cadet Bourque.

"Sir, do you mean Air Force has to win by two touchdowns?"

"That's what 'I'll take two touchdowns' means."

"No, Sir," I said. "Wyoming is a two touchdown favorite. I would be giving you a four touchdown spread. That is not fair"

"O.K. Done your homework, I see," Cadet Bourke said smirking. "Here's what we'll do. I'll give you one touchdown; that is Wyoming has to win by one touchdown. How's that?"

"Yes, Sir. That is a good bet."

***

Loaded in Academy and rented buses, 600 blue suited cadets started the four hour, 150 mile trek to Laramie at 0930. Upperclassmen were talking and joking amongst themselves, leaving the Doolies in the back of the bus to their own means. The weather was threatening, with cold temperatures and low lying grey clouds. The game uniform was Class A Blues with the horse blanket overcoats and gloves as a precaution against the forecast bitter weather.

Arriving outside Cowboy stadium, we put on blouses and overcoats. The Academy Band greeted us with a rousing rendition of the Air Force Song. The squadrons formed, lined up, and in less than 20 minutes marched into the stadium. The notes of my favorite march, *The National Emblem,* hung in the air like ice crystals. The small, gathering crowd applauded vigorously at their first sight of the Air Force Academy Cadet Wing.

***

A Marble to Brickey pass from the 20-yard line put the Academy ahead 7 to 0. The rest of the game was a defensive struggle, punctuated by several fumbles on both sides, attributable to the declining temperature and the increasing snow flurries.

In the second half, the Cowboys took the opening kickoff and marched 80 yards to the three yard line. Their 220-pound senior fullback smashed the ball into the end zone. The game went back and forth throughout the second half; neither team able to score. With two minutes left, Monte Moorberg broke away at the Academy 10 and went to the Cowboy 40. Two plays didn't go anywhere. On the next play, however, the ball came loose on a handoff and Wyoming took over with 11 seconds left on the clock. On the next play, Roundtree sacked the Wyoming quarterback. The score stood at 7 to 7.

***

After the game, Tom and I followed Cadet Bourque to the Gamma Phi Beta Sorority House. They, like the other sororities on campus, were holding open houses for cadets. An attractive, curly-haired blond met us at the door and asked me if I would like to dance. We danced and sang and enjoyed the girls' home-made refreshments. My date's name was Susie. She was a Laramie native and a freshman majoring in English.

Four or five of the upperclassmen tried to shoot me down (cutting in on dances), but Susie stayed with me for the three free hours we had until bus time. "Do you ever get to Denver?" I asked as we neared bus time.

"Sometimes, why?"

"I had a great time; I thought you might give me a call. I could show you the Academy. Doolies . . . ah . . . Fourth Classmen . . . ah . . . Freshmen don't get off base, but if you came on Sunday, we could meet in the Fourth Class Club after church. I could show you around."

"That would be nice, Don. I might be there over the Christmas holidays."

"That'd be great. Here's my Squadron number. If you call, they will get a message to me." *Linda probably wouldn't be happy if I escort Susie around, but what the hell, Bill seems to be Linda's fairly steady companion. Never hurts to have a few options. Besides I really should reciprocate for Sue's wonderful hospitality.* "Hope to see you in December."

"Yes, good night, Don." Sue held out her hand. "It's been fun." I gave her hand a small squeeze. Apparently the girls had been briefed on our "no public display of affection" clause.

***

The roads had iced in places. The wind, intermittently gusting to 30 miles an hour, made our trip home an adventure. Two buses slid off the road, but no one was hurt. The head shed, planning ahead, had a military ton and half truck, with winch, accompanying the convoy. The buses didn't sustain any damage and were back on the road in short order. The ugly weather caused a six hour, uncomfortable journey back to Lowry.

The warm buses, the outcome of the game, and the festive sorority activities stoked the jovial mood of the cadets. The bus buzzed with conversations—mostly about the girls.

"How'd you make out, Terry?" I asked, as he, Hertz, Kerr, and I sat in the back.

"Great, I found a cute little redhead. We danced most of the night. We went out back of the sorority and talked for a while. I thought the Gamma Phi's were all hot. The only problem was keeping the upperclassmen at bay."

"I know what you mean. A pretty, petite blond picked me up as we went in. She got hit on a lot; but stuck with me. he might come to Denver for the Christmas holiday."

"Hey, I thought you were all wrapped up with Linda," Hertz snorted.

"Didn't you learn anything in military studies? It's a good plan to have a reserve."

After a couple of hours of slipping and sliding and devouring box lunches, the conversations died off and everyone flew off to Cadet Dreamland. Occasionally, I was startled awake by the howling wind and the unnerving slide toward the shoulders of the road. The welcoming blue comforter swept me away five minutes after I hit the room.

***

During the two choir practices today, we focused on *The Messiah*. Frequent interruptions found Mr. Boyd waving his baton and pointing at sections: "**NO, NO, NO!**" he would exclaim. "You have to hit the notes, you can't be flat," he said, aiming his remarks at the altos. "You'll throw off the rest of the voices. It'll sound like a New York traffic jam, not sacred music."

Excerpts from the *Halleluiah Chorus* got a marvelous reaction Sunday morning. The theater overflowed, not only with the mandatory cadet audience, but with staff families, and visitors from the local area. The minute of silence following the end of the piece was inspirational. *I think we are ready for Washington, even if Mr. Boyd is about to have puppies.*

***

"How was the trip to Wyoming?" Linda asked as we shared French Fries and shakes.

"Oh, it was great. You know we tied the football game even though we were two touchdown underdogs. Several classmates played super games. Brickey caught a pass for our only touchdown. We should have won, but the weather caused too many fumbles."

"What did you do after the game? I hear you didn't get back until late."

"Well, some sororities had open houses. And, of course, the miserable weather made the trip back really long."

"Oh, and what were the sororities serving?"

"Ah, well, they had refreshments and music . . ."

"And dancing?"

"Yeah."

"And you danced?"

"Sure, can't let those dance lessons go to waste."

"Who'd you dance with?"

"Mostly with a freshman. She's from Laramie."

"Was she CUTE?" Linda was wearing her little pout.

"Well, ah . . . she was all right. Nice personality," I said, being truthful if not completely forthcoming. "Look, I'll probably never see her again. Let's not discuss her… or Bill."

Linda was quiet for a moment, then said, "Are you visiting colleges in Washington?"

"No, we have a military dinner and some free time to see the city." *Maybe I can get back on track with Linda.* "I wish you were going to be there. That would be fun."

"Yes. Me too."

I escorted Linda to the door. "Look, I'll call as soon as I get back."

Chapter 32

USAFA Entry Exam: "What is a tutu? [a ballet skirt]"
"If a boy answers to too many such questions, The Air Force figures
he spends too much time on culture and not enough on doing."
[Boxers are doers.[87]]
Newsweek Article, September, 1958

Washington, D.C., Saturday, November 9, 1957

Mid-term grades appeared on the bulletin board Monday. Sixth Squadron had the best overall Doolie average in the Wing. The only one in our 'gang' who had any trouble was Hertz. He scraped by with a 72 in math and a 74 in chemistry. Because our squadron had the top average for Doolies, Cadet Lt. Col. Jay congratulated us and told the upperclassmen we would have a "relaxed" week at the ramp. It wasn't at ease, but there were few questions, mostly on current events; almost none on Fourth Class Knowledge. Normal duties were observed.

***

"O.K., Davis," said C2C Simons, the intramural boxing coach, "I need you to box in the 168 weight class on Thursday."

"But, coach," I said. I am at 171 pounds because you said I was going to box at 175 pounds. I don't know if I can lose three pounds in two days."

"Sure you can, Davis. Just pretend you're back in Summer Training. Tell you what I'll do, I'll sit you at my table and help you along." *The SOB is going to starve me for two days.*

"Coach, how about Kerr, he is under 168 pounds."

"Nah, he's had a relapse of the flu and is on limited duty. You're it."

***

Mr. Boyd received permission to have choir rehearsals for two hours every night. Since we'd just finished mid-terms, the academic load was light. The Faculty was redoing lesson plans and tending to marginal cadets. Up to 20 cadets from each class failed mid-terms. Additionally, word was the Supe was keen on a good showing by the choir in Washington.

---

[87] Author's opinion.

"Damn, Davis, it's almost taps. I thought you had to quit at 2030. Who do you think you are, the Mormon Tabernacle Choir?"

"Nah, we're going to be better."

"Have to admit I heard you were pretty good Sunday. However, I still think it's more like the Vienna Boys Choir!"

"Very funny. Everyone except the tenors shave every day. You're just sore because you're Catholic and don't get to go to DC."

***

At the gym, I was spitting and urinating desperately trying to make the 168 pound weight limit. As I came out of the latrine, Coach Simons looked at me and said, "Okay, Davis, don't worry about the weight. Second Squadron forfeited the middle weight class, so I need you to box light heavy weight. You can go up to 175 pounds."

Why you son-of-a-bitch I thought. *You starved me for two days and now you are going to throw me in the lions' den with the big lions.* I felt light-headed as I put on my gloves.

Jack Lite, a classmate, weighed in at 174 and a half pounds. At six foot, two inches, he had a three inch reach on me. Jack looked menacing as we touched gloves in the center of the ring. As the bell rang. I moved toward Jack, feeling slightly faint. Jack threw three or four jabs that set me back on my heels. I covered well, but could feel the force of Jack's blows. I moved forward with two jabs. Jack feigned a jab and threw a right cross. Fortunately, the blow landed on the head gear. Nonetheless, I was momentarily stunned, lost my balance, and fell.

"Take an eight count," Cadet Simons yelled from my corner. **"Stay down!!"**

I took Simons advice and an eight count. When I got up Jack was waiting anxiously. He stepped forward and threw a jab. I parried the jab and landed a solid right to the midsection. Jack looked surprised, stepped back, and then came after me. For the remaining 40 seconds, I covered up, but took multiple hits on my arms. *Damn, won't this round ever end?* Jack feigned a jab, threw a right cross -- which I blocked – then he came around with a left hook. The bell rang as I staggered toward my corner.

"All right, Davis, probably shouldn't have moved you up. Still, you're doing a respectable job. Keep away from him this round." The bell sounded all too soon.

I circled to Jack's left, warding off jabs; staying away from his right. My legs felt heavy and my arms were getting tired. Jack hit me with three jabs, driving me backward. I never saw his right. Again, he hit the headgear. And again, I staggered, but did not fall. Just then the referee stepped between us. "Fight's over," said Cadet James, the referee, holding up Jack's right hand. Cadet Simons had literally thrown in the towel from the corner, ending the fight.

***

Still bruised and sore, I groused as C3C Bourque and C3C Miller charged into our room at 2300 on Friday night. "O.K. Combat Doolies", said Cadet Bourque, "we're going on an expedition. Get in your sweats and tennis shoes. Be in the hall in five minutes." Thus began the operation that created an intense rivalry between the Academy and Denver University.

Six station wagons, two Fords and two Chevys, joined two Dodge pickups, all driven by young ladies. The caravan proceeded to the parking lot just outside Denver University stadium. The midnight raiders gathered their materials, set up sentinels, and began to transform Pioneer Stadium into Falcon Land.

The 22 cadet squad went to work. Five upperclassmen directed the five Fourth Class groups according to preset plans. Two upperclassmen were lookouts. The girls waited in the cars with instructions to drive off if anything went awry. Goalposts turned blue and silver with the Academy colors. "Go Falcons," in giant white letters trimmed in blue, appeared on the press box over the "Denver Pioneers" logo. Another team infiltrated the DU football locker room and painted all of the locker doors Air Force blue. The squads worked feverously, interrupted only by the shrill whistle that warned of a roaming security guard.

A large white "AFA" was stenciled on an outside wall, 30 feet from the ground and 20 feet below the top was the piece de resistance. The Denver Post Saturday front-page morning story marveled at the placement of the AFA symbol. Cadets speculated that Second Classmen who received repel training during paratroop qualifications had accomplished the feat.

The Wing marched into Denver Stadium accompanied by the Academy Band. Inspired by the work of their fellow cadets, each of the eight squadrons shouted a boisterous "Air Force" as they broke ranks and rushed toward the assigned seats.

In spite of the Friday pep rally, the spirit mission on the Denver campus, and good plays by the Academy football team, Denver won 26 to 14.

Protestant Choir members had little time to lament the loss. Three buses waited to take the 120-choir contingent back to the Academy. We had 45 minutes to change into flight suits and pick up our B-4[88] bags for the bus ride to the Naval Air Station.

***

Three Military Air Transport Service C-124 "Globemaster" aircraft sat on the ramp at Stapleton Naval Air Station to transport the choir to Washington, D.C. Two aircraft were assigned the mission; the third served as a reserve. The sun edged toward the Rocky Mountains as we received the emergency briefing and prepared to board.

---

[88] B-4 bags were canvass fold-over bags that were military personnel suitcases.

During the ride from the Academy, Captain Braswell briefed us on aircraft protocol. Seat belts are mandatory for takeoff, landing, and turbulence. Use of "honey buckets[89]" was explained. We were handed two box lunches; one for after takeoff and one for later enroute.

In addition to Mr. Boyd and Chaplin Bennett; the Deputy Commandant, Colonel Cassidy, Major Tallman, and Captain Braswell, AOCs, were escorts. We had supervision, but it wasn't overwhelming. Upperclassmen demonstrated a different attitude as soon as we left the Academy. Comradery was promoted over the class system.

"Man, they look like grounded whales with their mouths open," observed Terry as we approached the open clamshell doors of the huge C-124s. Two parallel three-foot wide ramps angled from the ground to the cargo deck.

"Yeah, but I don't know how we'll ever get off the ground with those tiny fins on the side," I said looking at the stubby aircraft wings.

"Gentlemen, I'm Captain Parker, the aircraft commander. Gather around in a circle. When I finish briefing, you will take your bags to the back of the aircraft where Staff Sergeant Johnsten, our loadmaster, will secure the baggage.

Safety is paramount. Old Shakey is a reliable aircraft, but in case of emergency, announced by three short rings on the alarm bell and accompanied by a public address system announcement, you will sit in your seats with the seat belt snugly fastened.

We don't have pressurization, so oxygen isn't a factor. You may feel a little light headed, but it's nothing serious, sort of like hiking in the mountains. We will be cruising at an altitude of seven thousand, five hundred feet. The forecast is for us to pass through a front approaching Ohio. If you feel like you're going to lose your cookies[90], be sure to use a barf bag. The loadmaster will give every individual a bag. Put the leftovers from you lunches in the trash cans located on the forward bulkhead.

---

[89] "Honey buckets" were oversized port-a-potties installed in the rear of the aircraft. For troop missions a detail was required to empty the honey buckets, usually those who had used it.
[90] A polite term for throwing up.

We have room for all of you on the upper deck. We have aircraft heat, but it will probably still be cold. Make sure you have jackets out. It will also be noisy. Ear plugs will be passed out—use them. If there is no turbulence, you may come up to the cockpit in twos or threes. Remember there are 40 of you on this plane, so share the time. Are there any questions? Ah, yes, Cadet . . . Kerr."

"Sir, how long is the flight and where are we going to land?"

"With a good tailwind, the flight plan shows five hours to Bolling Air Force Base. We fly at 265 knots, about 300 miles per hour. With the D.C. area traffic, we'll have 30 minutes for an approach. Losing two hours' time change and a 1730 takeoff, we should have at your quarters by 0100, Okay, grab your bags and get them on board."

"Man, this sure is an ugly airplane," said Terry Koonce. Terry was sitting between Kerr and me. Cloud was on the other side of Kerr. He was already grumbling about the comfort of the combat sling seats attached to the sides of the aircraft.

"Yeah, but it's a workhorse of the Military Air Transport Command or MATS," offered Kerr. "It's the only outsize cargo plane in the inventory besides a C-133, which is like a bigger C-130. The C-124 can carry 68,500 pounds of cargo, including tanks, trucks, and heavy artillery. It'll hold 200 fully equipped troops in the upper and lower decks."

"How do you know so damn much about the C-124, Kerr?"

"Ah, Cadet Third Class Miller was on my case and made me look up the information. Seems his old man was a major and flew C-124s in the Korean War. After Miller's Dad finished an active duty tour, he went to the Georgia Air National Guard and flew C-124s for them."

"Yeah," I said, "I wouldn't want to fly one of these clunkers. Wouldn't mind the mission though; flying around the world supporting the troops."

"Ah, give me a fighter, that's the real Air Force," said Koonce.

Just then one of the engines gave a whine, a chug, and rumbled into action. All four Pratt and Whitney R-4360 engines were turning within five minutes. We taxied five minutes after engine start. At 1730, the engineer[91] applied takeoff power and we started the roll, the aircraft shook from side to side living up to its moniker of "Old Shakey."

Compared to my earlier ride in the T-33, the C-124 felt like riding on an elephant lumbering down a jungle trail. When Old Shakey broke ground, you heard the spinning

[91] The C-124 is unique among transport aircraft because the Flight Engineer has a set of throttles and is often given the responsibilities of managing the aircraft power. A major accident happened in the Azores – an island chain in the Atlantic where the Air Force has a base – when the pilot, trying to recover from a bad landing, called for "take off power." The flight engineer took off power; i.e., reduced the power, inducing a crash.

wheels come to an abrupt stop as the gear swung into the undercarriage of the aircraft. Minutes later, the hydraulic pumps squealed as the copilot raised the flaps.

The cargo giant climbed slowly, reaching cruising altitude in a short time. With our takeoff at 5,000 feet, we only had to climb two thousand, five hundred feet.

When the "seat belts" sign went off, cadets loosened their seat belts and crowded along the sides of the aircraft, peering out the small porthole windows. After all the upperclassmen had visited the cockpit, I ventured up the steps to stand behind the pilots' console. Both pilots were checking the route against the filed flight plan using low altitude airway maps.

"Copilot, how about dialing in the Kansas City VOR and checking the signal," instructed the pilot."

"Roger, it's on the number two VOR. Good ID."

The rows of engine and navigation instruments on the front panel amazed me. Engine instruments in the center row indicated engine temperatures, oil pressure, and fuel flow for each of the four engines. I recognized the VOR and ADF instruments from our navigation orientation flight. The attitude indicator, air speed, and altitude instruments in front of the pilots all looked familiar from my T-Bird ride. With the aircraft on autopilot, the pilots busied themselves following the route and communicating with the ground air traffic controllers.

After a couple of hours, I joined the other cadets in our favorite pastime – napping. Sleep was hampered by the constant noise and aircraft vibration. The chilling cabin temperature added to our discomfort.

Approaching Ohio, the promised weather front appeared. The PA came to life: "Gentlemen, you need to wake up and fasten your seat belts. Looks like we can navigate between the thunderstorm cells, but it's going to be bumpy. If you feel ill, use the barf bags. Cleaning the deck after landing if you don't use the bags will not be fun."

A series of strong jolts, accompanied by lightning flashes outside the portals, made for an uncomfortable ride. Several cadets reached for barf bags, but fortunately did not use them. Nonetheless, many cadets wore pale, stressed looks.

The tumultuous flight lasted 30 minutes. "Okay, Gentlemen, should be smooth from here on in," advised Captain Parker. "You may get up and walk around until I call for the descent. At that time, return to your seats and keep your seat belts on until we are parked."

"Damn, that was bumpy," said Kerr, "like some flights with my Dad in Alaska."

"Yeah," offered Koonce," glad somebody didn't puke. That would've got us all. Sure be glad to get on the ground."

"We're not going to get much sleep. By the time we get our bags, get on the bus, go to Bolling Billeting and check in, it's going to be midnight. Understand we have to sing at the National Cathedral at 1000 hours. Hope they have good beds."

"Stop whining, Davis, You've gone on less sleep before. Besides, with all the oxygen down here, you should really be pepped up."

The pilot made a smooth approach and landing. Buses took us directly to the Visiting Officers Quarters at Bolling Air Force Base. We were checked in and assigned roommates. An airman contingent put our bags in rooms. Terry Koonce dragged into the room with me. I was excited about tomorrow, but very tired. It was 0100; I slipped into bed and fell fast asleep.

Chapter 33

A wide variety of religious opportunities is afforded, including daily worship services
. . . choir participation, and religious instruction classes.
US Air Force Academy Catalog

Washington, D.C., Wednesday, November 13, 1957

"Hey, Davis, get up. We just got a wakeup call."

"Damn, Koonce, what time is it? Must be the middle of the night."

"Nah, its 0600. Anyway, get your butt out of bed. The mess hall is a 10-minute walk and we only have 40 minutes for breakfast. Not to mention we have to get into parade uniform. Take your coat and gloves." I stuck my head out. "It's cold out there."

"Yeah, we'd better shave too. Did you find the latrine?"

"Wake up, Davis, it's between our room and Kerr's. Hurry, we have to beat them to it."

***

"Gentlemen, I'm Major Thomas Woodson, Commander of the Arlington Ceremonial Detachment. My men guard the tomb of the Unknown Soldier. You are currently in the Memorial Display Room situated between the Unknowns' Tomb and the Amphitheater.

About 2,000 people will attend the ceremonies, although the amphitheater only seats 1500. Your performance will be standing room only. Congress authorized this structure on March 4, 1913. President Woodrow Wilson laid the cornerstone on October 15, 1915. Imbedded in the cornerstone are a Bible and a copy of the Constitution.

Mr. Ivory Kimball, a D.C. judge, to honor America's servicemen and women, led the drive for the Amphitheater. The main section consists mostly of Imperial Danby marble from Vermont; this section features Botticino stone, imported from Italy. The marble dais, "the Rostrum," is inscribed with the National Motto: E Pluribus Unum."

"Wow," said Terry marveling at the semicircular row of columns stretched out on either side of the stage. "This looks like a Greek Temple, the Parthenon or something. They could have put in heaters though. It's colder than hell," Terry said exhaling a small misty cloud.

"Quit griping, Terry. They issued you an overcoat and gloves. Just get ready to sing."

***

"All right, men," Mr. Boyd said, clapping his hands together. "I know it's cold, but we need to practice for tomorrow. There will be admirals, generals, and other dignitaries and a large crowd. This is the first chance many will have to see and hear you. So let's give them a show. We will start with *Worthy is the Lamb*; follow with the *Halleluiah Chorus*, run through the *Battle Hymn of the Republic* and end with the *Air Force Song*.

It's the same program we did this morning for the 'Chapel of the Air' Television show. AFRTS[92] filmed the program for our overseas troops. Since you've had that warmup, I expect nothing but beautiful rehearsal music. "

***

"Damn Terry, it's only 1300. We have until 2300 before we check in at Bolling. Want to go downtown?" I'd met Terry Cloud after rehearsal and decided to hang out with him.

"No, I have a friend at Annapolis," Terry said. "I called him, and he's going to meet me and give me a tour of Canoe U. Want to come along?"

"Sure, that sounds like fun. How do we get there?"

"Catch a local bus out front and then grab a Greyhound Bus to Annapolis. Costs about four bucks, can you handle that?"

"Sure, with all the per diem they gave us, I think I can manage four dollars. Let's go."

***

East of the Potomac River, dense woods lined US 50 East going toward Annapolis. Terry was napping. *Hmm, isn't what I imagined. I thought the East Coast was wall to wall with people. Didn't know it was this pretty.* The bus ride ended at the front gate of the US Naval Academy.

The 388-acre campus sprawled along the banks of the Severn River. The massive multi-columned buildings stood majestic in the mid-November sun. Midshipmen were everywhere.

Terry's friend George, in his Class A uniform, greeted us as we stepped off the bus. George looked trim in the Navy blue suit. Two rows of brass buttons ran down the front of the jacket. On the lapel were twin anchor emblems. His white hat had a black rim and brim with a high gloss shine, as did his black shoes. The sleeves of the jacket were plain, reflecting George's plebe[93] status, rather than with the thin gold stripes worn by upperclassmen.

---

[92] Armed Forces Radio & Television Service
[93] Nickname for Annapolis freshmen/fourth classmen is "plebes"

"Hi, Terry," George said, saluting, offering his hand, and then embracing Terry. "Damn, it's good to see you."

"Likewise. Is that your normal Sunday uniform?"

"Yeah, we wear it for chapel formation, escorting, or meeting a date. Those must be your new uniforms. They are pretty spiffy. When did you get them?"

"Oh, just a couple of weeks ago. When we changed over from summer khakis, we got the new blues and parade uniforms." Noticing that several college-aged girls, who had just stepped down from their tourist bus, were looking and pointing our way, Terry added, "And the girls really like them!"

"Yeah, yeah," said George, "who's your friend?"

"Oh, I'm sorry. George, this is Don Davis, a classmate. Don, this is George Lawrence, a classmate from high school. We played together on the varsity baseball team."

"Hi, Don," George said, extending his hand.

"Hi, George, my pleasure." *Hmm, Mrs. Mac would be proud of our manners.*

"Let's get going. Dinner is at 1800, and it's already 1630 ."

***

George led us on a quick-step tour of the facilities to include the chapel, a pass by of Bancroft Hall, the dormitory that houses the entire Midshipmen Brigade, the Nimitz Library, and finally the Armel Leftwich Visitors' Center.

We were pleasantly slowed in the tour by college girls from Penn State. They wanted to know where we were from, gushed over our uniforms (thank you Cecil B. DeMille), and took dozens of pictures. Looking at his watch, George said," Damn, it's only 10 minutes to dinner formation. You guys can watch the formation, and then I suppose catch the 1830 bus back to D.C. It's been great seeing you, Terry. Keep writing."

***

We watched the dinner formation and lingered while the Brigade started to enter Bancroft Hall. Suddenly, one of the midshipmen broke out of the crowd and ran toward us.

"Hey Terry, Don, I talked with Captain Snow, the Battalion Officer in Charge, and he said he didn't see why you couldn't eat with us. You're going to be the first Air Force Academy cadets to eat in Bancroft."

We stood at attention at George's table as the adjutant announced that "in honor of the first Air Force Academy cadets to eat in Bancroft Hall," plebes may sit "at ease." There was a resounding roar, followed by three rounds of the song, "Into the Air Junior Birdmen."

I don't think I was ever so conscious of eating and using good manners—even when prompted by the ATOs—because we certainly felt everyone in the place was watching us.

***

When we got back in town around 2130, I asked Terry if he was going to call their Congressman, Representative Wilson, like Gorge suggested. George understood the Wilsons had a good -ooking daughter; maybe Terry could get a date with her.

"Oh, I don't know. I went to the Congressman's house for dinner a couple of times, and my folks know them, but . . . I don't know."

"Come on, Terry, I dare you. Maybe you can get us dates for tomorrow night and they might even show us around town after the performance."

***

"Mrs. Wilson, this is Terry Cloud. Your husband appointed me to the Air Force Academy. I'm here with the Cadet Protestant Choir. I understand your daughter Sally is here also. I was wondering if she might like to show me and a friend around town tomorrow, since it's Veterans' Day and I guess she isn't in school."

Only able to hear Terry's end of the conversation, I wasn't sure if he was getting anywhere with Mrs. Wilson. I was hoping he would get us dates for tomorrow.

"Ah, sure Mrs. Wilson, that would be great. I'd love to see you and Sally again. And you say Sally has a friend from school who will join us. Meet you and the girls at the House of Representatives Building at 1500, ah, 3:00 p.m. That's great. Thank you. Yes, Ma'am, Goodbye."

"Good work, Terry. Dates for both of us. I hope they're good looking. I'm excited about seeing Washington. I've never been east of Colorado. Did she mention my date's name? Hope they don't choose some expensive place to eat tomorrow. I was kind of counting on part of the per diem to get some Christmas presents for my folks."

"Stop being a Scrooge. The per diem is like 25 dollars a day. And your dates name is Jenifer—think Mrs. Wilson said she goes by Jen."

***

"Davis, you could sleep through a hurricane. Get up. Breakfast starts in 10 minutes."

"What time is it? No wonder; it's pitch black out, it's 0415. Hurricanes, how would you know about hurricanes, you're from Colorado," I retorted, dragging myself from the bed.

"Well, my folks used to vacation in Florida, One year we got caught in a hurricane and had to stray in the hotel. On the 7th floor we weren't going to get flooded out, but the wind howled like a banshee. It was scary. Anyway, get in the latrine and get out. We have to go."

"Don't forget to get everything for your Class A's and put them in your hang-up bag," advised Terry. "After the performances, they'll let us change so we can go out on the town."

"That's great. Hope they don't lose our parade uniforms."

"They're putting them on the buses, and airmen will put them in our rooms. Come on. We only have five minutes to get down to the bus."

***

Dave Garraway swooped into the recording studio just after we finished *The Air Force Song*. "Boys, that was fantastic. I've had other choirs on—West Point and Annapolis—but no one topped your performance. Just superb. Good luck with Arlington. There'll be a lot of brass there, so 'give'em hell' as Harry Truman would say. Break a leg. Thanks a lot."

We, in fact, did two shows, one especially for the West Coast. The sound in the studio was good but didn't compare with the acoustics in the Amphitheater in Arlington, pictured below.

***

Despite the bone chilling weather, the amphitheater was full. Uniformed personnel from all services sat with their families. Further back, an overflow crowd several rows deep circled the rim of the amphitheater. I marveled at the dedication of those who came to see us and participate in the Veterans Day ceremonies. Occasionally, a snow flake drifted down from the dark clouds, now tinged with a halo from the rising sun.

Singing the Hallelujah Chorus, I felt chills, not from the weather, but from the stirring music reverberating from the marble walls of the amphitheater. I had never participated in such a stirring program. As we finished the concert, we received a standing ovation.

The wreath laying ceremony at the Tomb of the Unknown Soldier was scheduled 45 minutes after the performance. As President Eisenhower laid the wreath, we sang the

Battle Hymn of the Republic. Vice President Richard Nixon, Chief Justice Earl Warren, and numerous Generals and Admirals populated the large crowd viewing the ceremony.

An unexpected ceremony involved President Eisenhower awarding the two on-duty Tomb sentinels the first ever Tomb Guard Identification Badges. Each guard received the badge individually, so the other could remain at his post.

***

"Wow, some spread," I whispered to Terry Cloud.

"Yeah, I heard the Veterans of Foreign Wars (VFW) was providing lunch, but I expected sandwiches not a banquet. Oh, well, we can treat the girls to hamburgers tonight, pleading overeating at lunch."

"Fat chance, I'll bet Sally has some nice, real expensive restaurant picked out. Oh well, it's worth it for the transportation and tour. Problem is I won't have enough to buy Linda a pizza when we get back. *Geez, haven't thought about Linda since we got here. I know, I'll give her that anchor charm I got at Canoe U. and tell her I was out with the boys.*

The VFW Commander profusely praised our performance at Arlington, saying it added immensely to the Veterans Day Ceremony. He presented Mr. Boyd and Colonel Cassidy with plaques reading: "In Appreciation to the Protestant Choir of the United States Air Force Academy, Veterans Day, November 22, 1957. General William S. Sanders, Post Commander."

In addition, each cadet received a "Certificate of Appreciation" and a 20 dollar gift certificate for one of the premier restaurants in D.C. "Colonel James Reston, a VFW member and owner of the restaurant donated the certificates," Concluded General Sanders.

***

"Wow, this place is impressive, Terry," I said as we entered the Capitol and began searching for Representative Wilson's Office.

"Yeah, but his office isn't here. We have to take an escalator to the floor below and the corridor leading to the Cannon Office Building. There's the escalator. Let's go."

***

"Hello, Mrs. Wilson. It's been awhile. I'm Terry, and this is my classmate, Don Davis."

Two beautiful young girls stood next to Mrs. Wilson. *Hmm, I wonder if I get the blonde. If not, the redhead is really cute too*

"Boys, welcome to Washington. This is my daughter, Sally," she said indicating the blond. "And this is her friend, Jen."

We'll go back to the Capitol Building, and I'll give you a quick tour. Then the girls can take you downtown and show you around. Have either of you been to Washington before?"

"No Ma'am," Terry and I answered simultaneously.

"Great, then I think you will find the tour interesting."

Indeed, the 45 minute tour of the Capitol was fascinating; making me wish we had more time. On the other hand, I couldn't wait to know Jen better. I could see Terry was enthralled with petite, blond-haired, blue-eyed Sally. At 5'6", Sally had a dynamite figure with beautiful legs and a creamy complexion that put vanilla ice cream to shame.

Jen also carried a nice figure on her 5'3" frame. *Must be 33-22-32*, I thought.

"I know Terry's from Alaska, because I went to school with him," Sally said. "Where are you from, Don?"

"I'm from Sacramento, California; actually an area called Del Paso Heights."

We left the Capitol and headed for a public parking lot. "Wow," I said as Sally put the key in a 1956 Pontiac convertible with a white top and upholstery and a mirror finish black body. "That's some transportation."

"Thanks, I tried to talk Dad out of his Chrysler, which is newer than mine, but he said 'No deal, use yours.' Convertibles are more fun anyway. Where'd you guys like to go?"

"Gee, Sally, we haven't been here before. How about showing us the White House and the Monuments?" Terry said.

We drove by the White House. We parked and took a walking tour of the Mall and the Lincoln and Washington Monuments. As we walked along the Mall between the Washington and Lincoln Monuments, Jen reached over and took my hand.

"My hands are cold. It must be 40 degrees out," she said.

I checked the area for upperclassmen. The Mall was full of people, but I only saw regular military uniforms. *What the hell*, I thought; *I can't be a prude; Jen has no idea about public display of affection rules. Besides it may make the evening more interesting*. "Yeah, it is cold. Would you like to borrow my gloves?"

"No," Jen said. "I'll just hold your hand for a while".

A small 8 by 10 foot kiosk sat in the middle of the Mall, advertising hot coffee and chocolate and donuts for sale. "Hey, guys," I said, wandering in front of the kiosk. "Let's get some hot chocolate and donuts."

After our 1530 snack, Sally took Ohio Drive to the East Basin and the Thomas Jefferson Memorial. The temperature had risen to 55 degrees, but dark clouds still covered the sky.

Just as we stepped out of the Jefferson Memorial, Jen said, "I hate to be a party pooper, gang; but I'm feeling a little dizzy and my stomach hurts."

"Goodness," Terry said. "Do you suppose it was the donuts? They were fried; might have been the grease."

"No, I think it might be a touch of the flu. Half of my English class was out sick last week. I'm sorry, Don. But the last thing I want to do is give you the flu."

"That's really considerate," I said. "I just spent about a week in the hospital. Half of the Wing was down with the flu. We'd better get you home."

Sally jumped on US 1 South, crossed the Rochambeau Memorial Bridge across the Potomac, then sped down the George Washington Memorial Parkway south. As we swung around a wide curve in the road, Sally pointed left and said: "That's George Washington's Home, Mount Vernon. Shame you guys don't have more time. We could hit Mount Vernon and . . . oh, the Smithsonian. That's fabulous."

After Jen left, I didn't want to be a third wheel, so I said, "Sally, why don't you drop me off back in town. I'll get something to eat and wander around town seeing the sights." *Damn, Terry, you owe me. Sally sure is fine.*

***

Sally let me out by the White House on Pennsylvania Avenue. I looked at my watch which read 1830. I realized the approaching darkness was earlier than back home—*back home, man am I getting brainwashed*—in Colorado. I walked up 15th street and crossed in front of the White House on Pennsylvania Avenue.

A bright glow lit up the White House as the inside and yard lights came on sequentially. I wandered past the cast iron picket fence that fronted the White House. *Wonder what President Eisenhower and Mamie are doing. They're sure not looking for a place to eat.*

I turned and retraced my steps toward 15th Street. I was aware of people staring at me as I passed them. *Probably think I'm some Latin American officer with this spiffy uniform.*

As I came up 15th Street, I had noticed the Willard Hotel. The huge, white square building looked interesting, but not impressive. My brother-in-law, Elmer, stayed at the Willard while on California Department of Motor Vehicle business. He said if I ever get to Washington, I should see the Willard.

An older gentleman in a Phillip Morris-like uniform greeted me as I entered. Do you have a reservation, Sir?" he inquired.

"No, I replied. "I'm a cadet at the Air Force Academy and we are in town for the program at the Arlington Cemetery for Veterans' Day. I just wanted to look around."

"Great," he said and began asking me questions about the Academy and the life of a cadet. He offered that he had been a gunner in B-17s during WWII. We talked for about 15 minutes, then he said, "Well, Cadet Davis, The Willard is pleased to have you here. Feel free to take a tour of the hotel at your leisure."

A magnificent entrance with plush red square patterned carpet welcomes the visitor. Four grand marble columns provide the atmosphere of a Greek palace. I quietly peeked into the Crystal Room, which contained an oblong table in a back corner set with fine china and silverware. A dozen more circular tables seating eight, also with fine layered china and glistening silverware, filled the rest of the room.

A plaque on the wall provided some interesting facts about the hotel. The Willard had hosted the President in the 1800's. An impressive array of distinguished guests who have visited the Willard over the years was on the plaque. The list included Mark Twain, Charles Dickens, Buffalo Bill, and P.T. Barnum.

As I was leaving, a fortyish, powerful looking man about six feet two in a tuxedo was escorting an elegantly dressed red-headed woman. In a straight line black dress with a large string of pearls that highlighted her portrait-like face, the lady was a step and a half in front. Instinctively, I held the door open for the couple.

"Thanks, son," the man said and pressed a 20 dollar bill into my hand.

"Sir, sir, I can't take this money," I called after the man. He, however, never looked back and swept into the Crystal room with the lady on his arm. I didn't know what to do. I couldn't chase after the two and make a scene in the dining room. So I put the bill in my pocket and began my search for the restaurant on our coupon. *Damn,* I thought, *I don't think our uniform looks like a doorman's. Anyway, with a free meal and an extra 20 dollars, I'll be able to get some Christmas presents at the C Store.*

***

The C-124 lumbered into the air through a falling snow. We lifted off at 0700 as scheduled and climbed through heavy clouds. Fortunately, turbulence was minimal, and we broke through the clouds at 6,000 feet. The sun reflected brightly off of the layered clouds that stretched from horizon to horizon under the aircraft.

"So, how was Sally?" I asked Terry.

"Man, what a doll. After we dropped you off, we drove to the Officer's Club at Bolling. With Veteran's Day and the holiday, the Club had a combo playing sweet music. We got there at 1930 and had dinner. I gave Sally my dinner coupon and told her to take Jen there.

There were only officers and their wives and families in the club. We had the dance floor to ourselves for a half hour. The only problem I had was Bourque and his classmate Miller showed up and kept trying to cut in on me. Sally said she preferred dancing with me."

"Hmm, sounds like you're a little smitten. Is she going to come out for Christmas?"

"She says she wants to but has to talk her father into it. She can convince her Mom, but her Dad's another issue. How about you, what'd you do after we dumped you?"

"Yeah, thanks. Some buddy. But thanks for the date with Jen, even if it didn't work out. Just as well, I could probably alibi the tour, but I'd have a tough time explaining dancing away the night with Jen. So after eating at the Italian place, I caught a cab and went back to Bolling. By the way, what're you going to do about Cindy if Sally comes out?"

"Oh, I don't know. I'll work something out. Maybe say Sally's a cousin or something."

I told Terry about the "doorman" incident. He joked I might have to turn myself in for an honor violation. But we agreed it wasn't stealing; I really couldn't give the money back.

The airplane became very quiet as everyone began napping. It must have been hypoxia.

Chapter 34

Now that Christmas is approaching, you can be sure every cadet
is eager for the holidays to begin.
Air Officer Commanding Letter to Parents

Sunday, November 17, 1957

"Davis, why do you think Captain Braswell was so hard ass today? You and I haven't picked up hardly any demerits recently. Today, he gave me two in ranks for shoe shine and three more for the room. And he gave you three, too. I thought the beds were good. And your hit for Linda's picture being out of place was wrong. I thought he liked pictures of cute girls."

"Ah, they're just trying to tighten up for Christmas break. Cadet Bourque says they've done that the last two years. Everybody looks forward to the break, so stuff starts getting lax. Bourque jumped me this morning, but I think partly because he didn't do well in DC."

"Oh, yeah, what'd he say?"

"Well, he said, 'Where were you hiding in DC, Davis? I saw your buddy, Cloud, with a hot number at the club, but I didn't see you?'"

"Ah, Sir, I had a date with a friend of Cadet Cloud's date; but after we toured the town, she got sick and had to go home."

"Was it your driving or just your ugly face that made her sick?"

"Sir, I think that is an improper question," I said with a smirk. "Besides the car was Sally's, so it would have been Cadet Cloud driving . . . If either one of us were driving."

"Okay, smart ass, how about all four verses of the Star Spangled Banner—since you enjoyed such a patriotic trip to our nation's capital."

***

"Boy, I didn't get a lot to eat at breakfast. Sure glad your folks sent brownies and chocolate chip cookies."

"We really haven't talked much since you got back. Did you score in Washington?"

"Is that all you think about, Tom?"

"No, Davis, that comes right after food. You didn't answer the question."

"You weren't listening. I wouldn't tell Cadet Bourque something that wasn't true, would I? Jennie was cute and somewhat affectionate, but I really didn't get a chance to know her. Besides, it was a first date. I know you are a New York Romeo, but some of us have class."

"Yeah, very little class. Well, too bad, Davis. I'll have to introduce you to some 'nice' New York girls. Even you can make out with them. By the way, speaking of making out, didn't you have a date with Linda today?"

"No, her folks took her on a trip to visit an aunt in New Mexico. She'll be back tomorrow, but I have Security Flight, so I still won't get to see her. Enough, Sanders, let's go down to the day room and shoot some pool."

***

United States Air Force Academy
Sunday, November 17, 1957 1400 Hours

Dear Folks,

What an incredible trip to Washington, D.C. I'm sorry you took off work and didn't get to see the Dave Garraway Show. Must have been a SNAFU (situation normal, all fouled up) at the network.

Singing in the Arlington Amphitheater sent shivers up and down my spine. The Washington Post reported we were the first all-male chorus to perform the Messiah in Washington. A local critic said "The Air Force Academy Protestant Men's Chorale is World Class."

I never saw so many Generals, Admirals, and government high rollers in my life. We even got to see President Eisenhower place the ceremonial wreath. At the Unknown Soldiers ceremony, After the performance, Terry Cloud and I went to Annapolis, the Naval Academy, to see his friend George Lawrence. Being an Air Force Cadet is great in public. But, you feel you are under a microscope, especially at Annapolis. At the DC Italian restaurant where I ate, I felt everyone was staring at me.

The second day, Cloud and I had dates. Cloud's date, the daughter of the his Congressman, is a beautiful blonde. My date, Jennifer, was also cute Unfortunately, Jen got sick and had to go home.

Cloud and his date dropped me off downtown. I walked past the White House. Then I went to the Willard Hotel. Elmer told me if I got to Washington I should visit the Willard. Outside it's like a big box, but inside it's spectacular.

Elmer stayed at the Willard, but I don't think I could afford a room. The menu prices for things I can't even pronounce were sixty or seventy dollars.

One good thing about Jenifer getting sick was I didn't have to buy her an expensive meal. Also, I didn't have to tell Linda about my date. Anyway, Linda dates and we aren't pinned. "Pinned" is like going steady, but instead of a high school ring, we give the girl an Academy pin.

How is everyone at home? Write and tell me everything. Are you still looking at that fish camp at Clear Lake? I certainly would like to see you at Christmas, but I understand some things are not doable. I'll do the next best thing and call home Christmas Eve. Have you been getting the things I've been sending; you know decals and calendars? Please write. My mail has dwindled to almost nothing. Not my fault. The week we left for Washington, I wrote 15 letters and 10 the week before. Letters really help get through the week.

My grade point average is 83.6. I had a 91 on an English speech last week. I have to finish a Philosophy research paper this week. Don't worry about the PE grade. I didn't do well in gymnastics. But I got an 89 and 93 in boxing, so my PE average is now about 80. I got the 93 in boxing because I knocked out a classmate in 20 seconds of the first round.

The upperclassmen are all over us about studying. They say we haven't seen anything like mid-term week. And the word is we will lose several classmates to academics. Hope it's not any of my buddies. My friend, Hertz, is probably in the most danger of failing a course or two.

Had an interesting experience last night. I was on sentry flight duty. We wear fatigues and a parka (man, was it cold) around our squadron barracks. The toughest part is staying awake. It is so quiet from 0200 to 0400. As cold as it was, I didn't have any trouble staying awake. It's a good thing because an upperclassmen from Security Flight came around checking. It was like what we did in the field exercise. If they catch you sleeping, you get a class III, which is bad.

Anyway, looking forward to Christmas. You can tell the upperclassmen are getting antsy to leave. My classmates and I, are waiting with bated breath.

Tell everyone I could use money instead of presents. And if you are strapped, don't worry about sending any money. I saved a little of my per diem from the trip, so I will have some to spend on the Christmas break. Oh, yeah, and I have the 20 dollar "tip." But, of course, brownies, fudge, cookies, etc. are always welcome and don't have to wait for Christmas.

Well, will close now. Have to do some work on my research project.

> God Bless
> Your loving son,
> Don

P.S. After the football game against Colorado State, we, the Doolies, get an Open Post. That means we can go down town with our dates and don't' have to be in until midnight. I'll finally have a real date with Linda.

Chapter 35

One of the established mores of our society is that members of the fairer sex deserve special courtesy and consideration from gentlemen . . .
USAF Academy Decorum

Sunday, December 1, 1957

The march-on went well Saturday. The crowd in the nearly full stadium cheered and applauded as we broke for the stands. In the opening quarter of the game, the team marched down the field and scored in 12 plays to put us ahead. Our triple option offense kept the Colorado State defense off balance. The Rams drove back and scored on four plays, with two 30 yard passes. Randy Rico came from outside the end and blocked the attempted point after, leaving the score at 7 to 6. We stopped the Rams on their next drive on our 40 yard line. Colorado State; however, scored two touchdowns in the second half to take the game 20 to 7.

***

Despite the loss, I was excited. Linda was waiting for me by the front stadium entrance.

"Are you upset about the game?" Linda asked. I hadn't seen Linda the two weeks since our return from Washington. She'd gone to New Mexico with her folks one weekend, and I was the Security Flight runner the other weekend.

"Nah, like my roommate Tom says, we don't have seniors yet so we just have to grow. We've played some top level teams and did all right. Besides, seeing you, how could I be upset? I missed you." Linda was stunning in her plaid skirt, white sweater, and light blue jacket that matched her eyes. Her open jacket revealed her firm, well-proportioned breasts.

"I missed you too. What do you want to do?"

"That's a loaded question, but I think I'll settle for a hamburger and going to a matinee show. Then we can go for dinner somewhere."

"Okay, there is a good burger place out on West Colfax called Red Top. But we'll have to split a cheeseburger because they are huge."

***

"Why do you suppose Lady Ashley kept chasing Jake Harris after she found out he was impotent? She was such a nymph; it couldn't have been a satisfactory relationship. Besides, Errol Flynn is a lot sexier than Tyron Power."

Linda and I were walking down Colfax Avenue toward the public parking lot. We had just seen *The Sun Also Rises* at the Tabor Theater. I fished out a dollar to pay for parking.

"I don't know. That's the way Hemmingway wrote it. The driving force was having a good time after the war. I guess Paris and Spain were pretty wild during those times."

"Yeah, I guess you're right. They weren't very conventional characters. I would much prefer a romantic relationship if sex were involved. Do you want to drive?"

Wow I'm glad she got off that topic. She's so cute. I just don't see her as a sex bomb, although the thought is intriguing. "That would be great. You don't see any upperclassmen around, do you?"

"No, it should be all right. It's pretty dark," she said handing me the keys. She held my hand a little longer and smiled.

Damn, it's going to be hard behaving. "Where are we going by the way?"

"I thought we'd drive up Lookup Mountain. The view of Denver from there is incredible. There's also a tavern with good food and reasonable prices. On Saturday nights they have entertainment. Tonight, I think it's a Blue Grass band."

Lookout Mountain. Bourque was talking about taking his date up there to make out. Wonder if Linda has been up there with Bill. Oh, hell what does that matter? She's up here with me tonight. "You'll have to be my navigator. Think you can get us to our destination?"

"Oh, I'm sure of it, Don. I'm very talented."

***

As advertised, Sam's had a great menu at a price that a Doolie could afford. Linda had raviolis. I had the spaghetti and meat balls. Dinner included salad, the entrée, and Italian Ices. We both drank cokes. The bill was $5.00. We lingered over dinner talking about our high school experiences and laughing about our first meeting.

The Blue Grass Band turned out to be a folk song trio named the Mountain Boys. Their opening song, stolen from the Kingston Trio, was *Tom Dooley*. Linda liked the music so we stayed for the whole show.

After the trio finished, a disc jockey played danceable music. We were only one of six couples in the restaurant. There were no other cadets. Linda began dancing very close to me. I could feel the tension rising in me. About 10:30, Linda suggested we go see the view of Denver from the bluff at Look Out Mountain.

Colfax Avenue ran like a brilliant milky way through the heart of the City. Lights twinkled everywhere. The scene, as promised, was "incredible." I put my arm around Linda and moved her toward me. She met my proffered kiss willingly. Her kiss was as sweet as her personality. We kissed again passionately several times. I put my hand in

Linda's lap. She moved my hand up to her breasts. I could feel her responsiveness as we kissed again.

I dropped my hand to her lap and moved it up her leg under her dress.

"Don, don't," Linda said breathlessly, taking my hand in hers.

I stopped and sat up in the seat. *Damn, Davis, what are you thinking? You can't get that involved. You don't want to quit or get thrown out and that's what could happen. Bu, she is so tempting.* "I'm sorry, Linda. I really find you exciting."

"It's okay, Don. I've had some fantasies too. But I don't think it's right just now. I hope I haven't turned you off."

"No. I think you're sweet. I really enjoy being with you. You know what? It's almost 2300. We need to start back. It's about 30 minutes back. You'll have to drive on the base."

"You're not mad?"

"No, frustrated, but not mad. Good thing I have a curfew. Saved by the clock."

Linda reached over and kissed me then she got out to come around to the driver's side.

We got on the drive by the quadrangle at quarter of twelve. I walked around to say good night. Linda discretely put her hand on top of mine. "Will I see you next weekend?" I asked.

"I certainly hope so," she said, giving me her sweetest smile.

***

"So, how'd you make out last night?" Tom asked.

"Linda and I had a great time. It was good to feel like a real human being again. They could have given us an Open Post earlier. Rotten we lost 20 to 7 to Colorado State. A 3-6-1 record isn't much to write home about."

"Yeah, Davis, but we beat New Mexico last week 31 to zip, and they were supposed to be pretty good. We'll get better. What's important is beating West Point and Annapolis."

"How about you, what'd you do yesterday?"

"Had a great time. Bill Gibbons and I met our girls after the game. My date was Karen West, a little blonde, a freshman at DU . . . ah, Denver University. I met her at dance class. Her black 56 Oldsmobile had a full tank of gas, and she and Dorothy—Dot for short—Bill's date, were looking forward to an evening on the town. Dorothy is also a Denver Freshman.

Anyway, we went to Karen's girlfriend's house for a party. Sharon had pizza and beer and music for dancing. It was still light so it wasn't too romantic. A couple of Denver

SAE Fraternity guys got the beer. They were pretty friendly. They thanked us for doing up Denver stadium before the game. They think that's why they beat us.

After an hour, we got into the Olds and headed for the mountains. We stopped at a vista spot on Lookout Mountain. We could see downtown Denver lit up like a Christmas tree.

We had a little bit of a fright. Bill locked the car doors when we got out. Unfortunately, I left the keys in the ignition. It looked like the evening was going to end early. I recalled my good old New York training, found a coat hanger on a dump pile, and had the door open in five minutes—without damage."

"I'm impressed."

"Karen suggested we go to Central City, a ghost town on the Continental Divide. The road was one of the trickiest I've ever driven. One side was sheer cliff. The other side was a rock wall. Dot said it was an old stage coach road. The ruts were still in it. Three tunnels, four heart attacks, and 20 miles later, we arrived at Central City.

The dive was named "Toll Gate," probably because of the prices. We ordered Coors beers. I ordered cherry pie. Don't know what gagged me more, the price or the rancid pie."

"Didn't they ID you," I asked.

"Nah, guess they figured we wouldn't do anything illegal in uniform. The saloon looked like a scene in an old west movie, complete with a skinny old gentleman in a cowboy hat playing an old-fashioned piano. Wax on the candles, stuck in beer bottles, looked 20 years old."

"Weren't you worried about getting back by sign-in?

"Right, we had two beers, then decided to head back. I almost messed my pants when we met another car as we were climbing a hill. It got worse when Karen told me I had to back down. We finally made it to a wide spot in the road and let the other car pass.

Down off the mountain, we still had an hour and a half to sign-in. Dot knew another party we could crash; so we did. Bill and I drank cokes. We started back with an hour to go.

Of course, our good buddy, C3C Whitman was CCQ and waiting for us as we signed in. 'Okay, Dumbsquats,' he said, 'Run your chins, in . . . in . . . in.'"

"Well, Tom, sounds like you had an exciting Open Post."

"Right. By the way, did you hear about Kenny Myers? He wasn't so lucky."

"No, what happened?"

"The 2nd Squadron CCQ smelled booze on Ken's breath and asked him if he'd been drinking. Ken was still a little woozy but answered 'Yes.[94]' The CCQ wrote Ken up. That's a Class III offense. Bourque says he'll get 50 demerits, 70 to 100 tours, and 3-6 months restriction. Punishments aren't waived for Christmas, so he's going to be miserable."

"That's really tough. I wonder if he'll stay."

---

[94] This was a proper question by the CCQ. Had Ken answered "no" it would have been an honor violation.

Chapter 36

*An annual review of the Air Force Academy objective is only one
of the many examples of Air Force abhorrence of compliancy . . .*
Major General James E. Briggs, Superintendent, USAFA

Sunday, December 15, 1957

Breakfast began ominously. As soon as the food was served, Cadet Thomas jumped on Jim Dickson. We had a group of visiting generals on campus all week. General White, the Air Force Chief of Staff, was scheduled to give an after-diner address this evening.

"Okay, Mister Dickson, who's the Chief of Staff of the Air Force," asked Cadet Thomas.

"Sir," said Jim, "The Air Force Chief of the Staff is General Nathan F. Twinning."

"Nice try, Mr. Dickson. You're five months behind. You pulling a Rip Van Winkle?"

"Ah, no sir, I . . ."

"Hertz, who is the Chief of Staff . . . and it better be right or we'll have an Air Force history lesson in my room after breakfast."

"Sir, the Chief of the Staff of the Air Force is General Thomas D. White."

"Bingo, Mister Hertz, now tell me a little about him. Make it short."

"Yes Sir, Born in Minnesota in 1901, General White graduated from West Point in July, 1920. He was immediately promoted to 1st Lieutenant. After an assignment at Fort Davis in the Panama Canal Zone, he returned to the United States for pilot training at Kelly Field in Texas. In 1927, General White became a four-year student in Peking, China. Putting his Chinese language to use, he was assigned as Assistant Military Attaché in Russia.

In 1944, the General joined the Air Staff in the Intelligence Division. He then became the Deputy Commander of the 13th Air Force in the Pacific; taking part in campaigns in New Guinea, the Southern Philippines, and Borneo.

General White was Vice Chief before becoming Chief of Staff in July."

"What's our interest in General White at the moment, Hertz?"

"Sir, General White is heading the group of generals evaluating the Academy.

"Good poop, Hertz, eat."

"Suh, cud ya pleeese pass tha gellee?" asked classmate Pat Grey. A stocky, jovial Georgian, Pat spoke with a southern accent which made him a favorite for upper-class taunting, **"What'd you say, Mister Grey**?" C3C Connors asked in a raised voice. A Californian, Cadet Clair Connors had little accent when he spoke.

"Suh," I said, "cud ya pleeese pass tha gellee?"

"Grayson, I'm not sure what language you're speaking, but in this man's Air Force, you'll have to speak English. If you are on final with an engine fire and call 'Reese Towah, this is Beah Can 23 with an ingin fiah?' the tower won't know you have an emergency. They'll think you have an Indian in the cockpit. Now, let's have your request in English."

Obviously struggling, Pat began, "Sira, pleese pass the JAM!'

Everyone snickered. "You're hopeless, Grey," Connors said, passing the jelly.

***

"Cripes, Tom, did you ever see so many stars in your life? Other than on top of Lookout Mountain, of course. Knowing you, I'll bet you weren't really stargazing."

"Yeah, and thanks to your friend, Bourque, I had to name them all at dinner, including their commands. Let's see, there was, of course, the Chief, General White; General Curtiss Lemay, Vice Chief . . . and Major General Bernard Schriever, Commander of the USAF Ballistic Missile Program."

"Wow, I'm impressed. But you know what impressed me most?"

"No, what?"

"That General White gave everybody on Class II or Class III total amnesty."

"Yeah, I'll bet Kenny Myers is really happy."

"Who is Kenny Myers?"

"He's our classmate who got hammered for drinking on the open post? He was going to have a lousy Christmas. Heard he was quitting. Guess he'll stay now.

***

"General Briggs, General Stillman, Colonel McDermott[95], Members of the Wing of Cadets," began General White, "as you know I and the other officers of the Academy General Officer Advisory Committee have been visiting the past several days. Generally speaking . . ." a slight groan went through the audience as cadets reacted to the General's unintended pun, "the Committee is impressed with the entire academic program and

---

[95] Colonel McDermott became the permanent Dean and was promoted to General Officer. There was resistance to the promotion because McDermott was so young and outranked by many officers. When he became Dean and no longer competing with regular line officers, he was promoted to general. McDermott is credited with establishing an extremely progressive, quality academic program at the Air Force Academy; an action that caused West Point and the Naval Academy to reluctantly follow suite.

particularly with the enrichment program. We like the idea that your instructors, being military, can imbue you with the history and the operational nature of the Air Force.

We support the concept of flying training at the Academy but have reservations about continuing navigator training. We plan to begin light plane flying at the new site.

"Speaking of the new site; we believe we're far enough along that you'll move next year.

The Soviet October Sputnik launch drives us to focus on new and different technologies. You'll see a growing emphasis on missiles and space. However, you will continue to be trained in problem solving and leadership development. After graduation, pilot training, maintenance officer courses, and post graduate work will prepare you for your first assignments.

Your Dean, Colonel McDermott, has changed the outlook of all service academies. He has ensured academic excellence that, combined with the rigorous military program, has earned the Academy the title of the 'Toughest School in America.'

The one area where we have some concern is the football team's record. You have time to grow but must be up to the challenge when we meet West Point and Annapolis on the fields of friendly strife; for 'There is no substitute for victory.'

The Committee applauds the Superintendent, General Briggs; the Commandant, General Stillman, and the Dean, Colonel McDermott. They are giving you a solid foundation in academics, military training, and leadership experiences that will serve you well in the Air Force. I congratulate you, the members of the Cadet Wing. Your achievements to date are excellent. We expect even greater things from you in the future. God's speed and good luck.[96]"

"Wing Attention!" rang the familiar baritone voice: "**DISMISSED!**"

***

"Wow, that was impressive; being in the auditorium with all that brass. The Chief was certainly complimentary. It's hard to be humble and not get a swelled head."

"Yeah," Tom said, "but being a Fourth Classman takes care of that. It's hard to smell the roses when you are at the bottom of a manure pile."

"Cheer up, Tom, another week and we'll be free of the Gestapo. And you'll have your folks here. Wish mine could come, but they can't squeeze out the money. Thaine, my step-dad, had the flu. He's a carpenter and was out of work for a week."

"No sweat, I'll share my parents. My sister's coming. She's good looking and a charmer. Maybe I'll let you date her . . . if you promise to keep your hands off her! If

---

[96] This is not a transcript of General White's talk; rather it is a synopsis of Academy issues at the time.

Linda's not here, you could take Sarah to the dance on Christmas eve. I've got a date with Karen, the little blond from DU, so I can keep my eye on you."

"Right, I'm not afraid of you. Hey, we'd better hit the books. I heard the Academic Department is going to use pop quizzes and GRs to remind us of finals after Christmas."

"Yeah, wish they'd end the semester before Christmas break. It would be a lot easier on us. That and it wouldn't give Third Classmen time to harass us with their 'buck up program.'"

"Right! Cadet Whiteman told me, 'Davis, we're doing this for the Academy. We don't want you to embarrass us while we're gone.' Like he's a Steve Canyon image. By the way, remind me what your folks do."

"Dad flies with Pan Am. Mom's a stay-at-home mom. You'll have to visit next summer. If you behave during Christmas, you might get to date Sarah again."

***

 # United States Air Force Academy
Sunday, December 15, 1957 2000 Hours.

Dear Folks,

Sorry I haven't written. We've been really busy; besides I haven't received a letter since the 5th. We just had an inspection visit from the top Air Force generals. The Chief of Staff, General White, was very complimentary of the Wing. He said while this is the toughest school in America, we are doing well. But, like Tom said, it's hard to get a swelled head when you're at the bottom of the barrel and the upperclassmen are pouring water in on you.

We had an Open Post after the last football game. (We lost, but oh well.) Linda and I went to see The Sun Also Rises. After, we went to Sam's Italian restaurant on Lookout Mountain, west of Denver at the base of the Rockies. Parking by the restaurant, you get an incredible view of downtown. A folk song trio called "The Mountain Boys" played for a couple of hours. Then a DJ played dance music. It was a great evening.

You may not hear from me for a couple of weeks. It's getting close to Christmas leave and the upperclassmen are on a "buck up," - requiring a lot of Fourth Class nonsense again. They say they don't want us to forget them over Christmas vacation. Fat chance.

Actually, our Squadron upper-classmen are pretty reasonable. Classmates in other squadrons say they have even have the infamous shower formations again. What's bad is the jerk upperclassmen we run into on the quadrangle on the way to and from class. They give us a hard time. It's interesting, our upperclassmen sometimes protect us; they run their classmates off. I think it's the philosophy: "Leave him alone, he's mine."

Well, I'd better work on my shoes, hats, and belt buckles.

God Bless,
Your loving son,
Don

Chapter 37

With Christmas approaching, you can be sure that every cadet is eager
for the holidays to begin.
Air Officer Commanding Letter to Parents

Saturday, December 21, 1957

 United States Air Force Academy
Saturday, December 21, 1957 1600 Hours

Dear Folks,

What a wonderful feeling. Like I just got out of prison, or more appropriately, a prisoner of war camp. After the parade, upperclassmen began leaving. They will be all gone by dinner time. Hooray!

We're in charge of the Wing until Sunday, January 5th. Tom is the 6th Squadron Commander. I'm an element leader. We have three elements, not three flights since we have only 33 Fourth Classmen.

My last grades were all 80s except PE. Gymnastics pulled me down, but the boxing grades are not included. I had 84 in chemistry, 84 in English, 80 in geography, 90 in philosophy, 82 in algebra, and 94 in air power studies. PE was 76. My military standing was 85 of 283.

I'm going to see Linda tonight. There's an informal dance in Arnold Hall, the cadet social center. Linda is going away with her folks for the Christmas vacation. I'm going to do Tom a favor and take his sister, Sarah, to some of the events, like the Christmas Eve formal..

I spent the $25 you sent me for Christmas. The colored pictures of Tom and me are my Christmas present to you. I bought Gene an AFA sweatshirt. I got Lucille and Elmer an Academy calendar book.

Tell Pa thanks for fixing my Chevy. Sell the car and keep the money. The Chevy has a lot of miles on it, and I don't mean the odometer. Ha!

Aunt Jean sent Louisiana "turtles," and cookies. Aunt Elsie sent brownies, cookies, and dates. There were also some little cakes made with rum. Man, are they good. Tom and I hid those and didn't share.

I just found Mrs. McComas' Christmas Letter. Sounds like a cadet regulation. It has everything from dress codes to a caution that "Young Ladies should be prepared to pay their own expenses." It's been a long time since I went on a "Dutch-Treat" date. Good old Mrs. McComas - always looking out for the cadets.

She has useful information as well: Motels are $5.00 to $6.00 for singles and $6.00 to $12.00 for doubles .Her office will make reservations. Average taxi fares from the local motels are $.75. She says families may use the Cadet Dining Hall and lists times and cost of meals: $.90 for lunch and dinner, except the Christmas meal, which will be $1.50 per person.

We will have unlimited off-base dining privileges and even two Open Posts; one on New Year's Eve which is an overnighter. Tom, Hertz, Cloud, Kerr, and I are getting a motel room together for New Year's Eve.

Kerr's and Cloud's girls have offered transportation for the night. Cindy, Cloud's girl, is throwing a New Year's party for our gang and dates. Cindy's apartment is close to the motel. We're going to dance and party until midnight; then get a taxi to the motel. Can't believe the Academy is going to let us pretend we are adults for a night.

Tom and I are going skiing tomorrow. The Academy pays for everything - skis, boots, and lift tickets. They take us up on buses. They even pay for lessons. Guess they don't want us to hurt ourselves. I invited Linda, but she says they're leaving for New Mexico tomorrow. Tom says, "No sweat, there will be lots of college girls on the slopes. They come from all over for Christmas break because the skiing is so good at Winter Park."

I'll call you Christmas Eve. It'll be early, like four o'clock your time. We have a formal that night and dinner is early. The powers that be must think we need the extra time to get into our new formal uniforms. They're probably right. The formal "mess dress," as it's called, is really sharp, with an Academy blue tie and cummerbund. The ties strap on—fortunately, as much trouble as I have with ties.

Anyway, the Merriest of Christmases and a Happy New Year.

God Bless
Your loving son,
Don

"Hey, Tom, I'm going over to Cloud's room. I think he's taking Cindy to the dance, but I'm not sure. I want to sit with them. Who are you taking?"

"Whoa, Davis, you're not going out like that, are you?"

Wearing my gym sweats and USAFA tee shirt, I had no shoes or socks. "Okay, Mister Squadron Commander, I'll put on slippers, but just because it's cold, not because you're playing upperclassman. Anyway, who are you taking?"

"I told you, I'm taking that cute little redhead I met in Wyoming, Janet. She's only here for the weekend though; has to go back to Laramie for Christmas with her folks. By the way, she said her sorority sister, Susie, couldn't make it. But, she still would like to take you up on your offer to show her around the Academy. You must have made some kind of impression, can't figure what it would be. Anyway, Karen said Susie's folks wouldn't let her come with a bunch of girls to meet a bunch of guys.

I might invite Janet to go skiing tomorrow. She's staying with an aunt and has wheels. Her dad has a small construction company that did some of the missile silos up north, so she has plenty of money. I may have to buy her lunch, but I told her I couldn't do all the ski stuff. She's all right with that. My folks won't be here until Monday, so you don't have to worry about Sarah until then. You said Linda was leaving, right?"

"Yeah, but not sure when. I'll invite her to go skiing, if she's still here. I don't think she'll be here for Christmas Eve, so I'll take Sarah off your hands. Who're you taking to the Christmas Eve dance?"

"Don't know yet, but Bourque gave me a couple of names. He has a whole harem but doesn't want to get serious about any of them. Thinks it would interfere with his studies. You know he washed back from 59. Shame, he is a great guy. Says he won't make the same mistake again. It's all about studies."

***

"Is Cindy going to the dance tonight?" I asked Cloud. He was sitting on his bed eating cookies out of a huge box marked "Do not open until Christmas."

"Yeah, she's going and confirmed the party on New Year's Eve. You still on for the motel, even without Linda? Oh, want a cookie? My aunt makes the best cookies."

"Sure, you think I'd miss getting away from the blue zoo overnight. Besides, we all agreed, no girls in the motel, too much room for a disaster. Linda probably wouldn't have been able to go anyway. Her father's pretty strict about late hours. He feels safe when she comes out here. And, of course, he's right. Even with the upper class gone, there are still plenty of AOC and Dean Christmas help hall monitors."

"Hear you and Tom are going skiing tomorrow. What are you doing tomorrow evening? Understand we can get dining privileges, even with staff officers. Major Galt invited Cindy and me out to the Cattleman's Restaurant with him. Want to go?"

"Love to, but the choir's doing a Christmas program tomorrow night. Hope I don't break a leg skiing. We have to get into parade uniforms right after we get back from skiing. Normally we'd be in mess dress, but because of the formals and lack of formal shirts, the head shed decided to put us in parade uniforms. The program's early, like 1700. Mr. Boyd said a local TV station is going to film the program. TV stars no less.

Colonel Ike has a great steak dinner laid on after the concert. We're doing excerpts from the Messiah and then sing-along Christmas carols. I invited Linda and her folks. I'll get a chance to meet her father and maybe convince dad I'm not a monster looking to carry off the princess."

"Fat chance. You told me he was in the service, the Air Force even. Wasn't he a fighter pilot? He knows what you're after."

"Hey, Cloud, not all of us are like you. Thanks for the cookies, I've got to get back and get ready. See ya tonight."

***

I could feel the cold as I walked smartly toward Arnold Hall. Most classmates were macho like me and didn't wear horse blankets. Nonetheless, the Colorado nighttime 30 degree chill seeped through my blues and encouraged me to hurry to Arnold Hall. The bright stars looked like so many sparkling fireflies against the dark curtain of the night.

I saw Linda park her red Bel Air and walk briskly across the parking lot. I hurried out to meet her. "Hi, Linda. Bit nippy isn't it? Let's get inside."

"You're not wearing your overcoat, you'll freeze or catch pneumonia."

"It's not that cold; besides you can warm me up once we get on the dance floor."

"Oh, that's right; the nasty upperclassmen are gone, aren't they?"

As I returned from hanging up Linda's grey, full-length coat, I couldn't help but admire how pretty she was and her sense of fashion. Her cranberry-colored velveteen dress accented her well-proportioned body. The clothes fit Mrs. McComas' prescribed afternoon dress, but the pearl necklace and single pearl earrings added a touch of elegance. The boat neckline and mid-calf skirt line spoke of modesty, but Linda definitely pulsed my nervous system.

"Well, you know the officers can still write us up for PDA. Of course, there aren't as many of them and most are professors; good guys really. And they're with their wives, who usually take the cadets' side. Look, there's Cindy and Cloud."

"Hi, Cindy, hi, Terry," Linda and I said as we settled into the table with them.

"How are you all, tonight," I said, being polite.

"Fine," said Cindy. "Good to see the both of you."

"Hi," said Cloud. "Hey, Doolie, how about getting us some desserts and punch?"

"What, you have a broken leg? Come with me."

When we returned to the table, the girls were talking and pointing at various couples on the dance floor. "We've decided we like your new formals," said Linda. "Some of your classmates look more elegant than usual."

"Well, Cecil B. DeMille certainly knows how to dress stars," I said.

"Posh," said Cindy. "Be careful, you are beginning to believe the propaganda about being the cream of the crop. But, Linda and I know better . . ."

"Let's dance," I said to Linda. "It's getting chilly in here."

The hired combo played music for most of the steps we had learned. I think Mrs. McComas prepped them, probably threatening not to pay if they didn't play her music.

The first number was a slow dance. I enjoyed holding Linda in my arms. She was pressing warmly against my body. "So when are you and your folks leaving?" I asked.

"We're leaving early tomorrow morning for New Mexico."

I'm sure Linda noticed the disappointment in my face. "Oh, that's too bad. I was going to invite you to go skiing with Tom and me tomorrow and you and your parents to our Christmas concert tomorrow night."

"I'm sorry, Don. This is a family tradition. I'd like to be able to invite you."

"Yeah, of course we're stuck on the base, although we do get a couple of Open Posts and even an overnighter. When are you coming back?"

"Gee, after New Mexico, we're driving to California to visit an aunt and uncle. We won't be back until the evening of the 5th of January according to Dad."

"Bummer," I said, savoring Linda's perfume and pressing a little closer.

Linda and I danced almost every dance, occasionally returning to the table to join Terry and Cindy. They also spent most of the time dancing. I was enjoying myself, but I had an inner feeling of disappointment since I would not be with Linda during the Christmas break.

The band played until 2300. Call to quarters was at 2330 and taps at midnight. I walked Linda to her car. As she started to get into her car, she turned. I immediately hugged her and kissed her passionately. She responded, pressing herself to me.

"Damn," I said.

"Yes, damn," she replied, got into her car, started the engine, and drove off.

Chapter 38

Anticipation of the holiday respite from duty and study
makes December a welcome month of the cadet's first year . . .
Superintendent's Letter to Parents

Sunday, December 22, 1957

"Tom, get up. It's 0530. We only have 10 minutes to get to the dining hall and 25 to catch the bus to Winter Park."

"Crap, Davis, I thought Christmas holiday was supposed to be restful. And where the hell was the minute caller?"

"Ah, fine Squadron Commander, they ain't one, unless you appoint one."

"Right. I'll be ready in five minutes. Meet you in Mitchell Hall. Save me some pancakes. And, Davis . . ."

"Yeah?"

"Knock off the 'Squadron Commander' jazz. You're just jealous."

***

The bus was warm, so we were comfortable. "Anybody meeting you, Cloud?" I asked.

"Cindy's coming. I'm not sure how this's going to go. Cindy was on her high school ski team. She's threatened to race me down a black diamond course."

"They have high school ski teams?"

"Come on, Davis, this is Colorado! How about you, you got a date?"

"Nah, Linda's out of town, so I'll probably ski the kiddy slopes by myself. Of course, there's always the lodge. Too bad we have officers with us; we could sneak a draft or two."

"Yeah, but you know what's great?" Tom asked to no one in particular. "The Academy issued us everything: ski pants, parkas, mitts, skis with bear trap bindings, and leather boots. Other than the $3.50 ski lift tickets, it's all free. Almost compensates for the last six months."

"Yeah, right, remind me how lucky we are when big brothers return," Cloud said.

***

Skiing at Winter Park was exciting and tiring. Hertz and I met at the ticket line and decided to ski together. We made three runs before lunch and three after hamburgers and hot chocolate in the lodge. The bill was $2.50. At lunch, I spied a cute, petite blonde sitting with her friend, also a blonde. Both wore Denver University sweat shirts. Hertz and I asked to sit with the girls. Sally and Joanne were impressed we were cadets and suggested we ski together. Hertz hit it off immediately with Joanne as we attacked the slopes together.

I enjoyed skiing with Sally except at the top of the lift, she came off the chair and shoved me to keep her balance. I went down and had to scramble to avoid the next pair coming off the lift.

Everyone had a good laugh at Cloud's expense. After a morning lesson, Cindy took Cloud to an intermediate slope. On a rather steep part of the slope Cindy skied to the bottom of the hill, intending to coach Cloud on his way down. Using wide traverses, Hertz, Joanne, Sally, and I skied to the bottom of the hill next to Cindy.

Showing off, Cloud shouted "Geronimo" as he pushed off on a Kamikaze run down the hill. Realizing Cloud was getting out of control, Cindy shouted, "**Snow plow!!!**"

Having been introduced to the snow moving machine, Cloud thought he was being pursued by one. He turned his head abruptly, lost his balance, and tumbled down the hill. After she determined he was not hurt and quit laughing, Cindy said, "Well, Terry, I'll give you an eight on degree of difficulty for the maneuver, but only a two for execution."

***

As the sun crept over the western-most peaks and the chill began to set in; we got the girls' phone numbers, said goodbye, and helped them on their bus. There were five Academy buses for cadets. Only three had officers on board. Our bus had none.

As we came down the mountain, the bus started to chug and cough. It finally ground to a halt on the side of the road. Shortly after we coasted to a stop, Captain Enoch, the OIC for the trip who was on the bus behind us jumped on board. He talked with the driver. Then said, "Well, Gentlemen, it appears like this bus is out of commission. There's no room on the other buses. I'll to send another bus to you. Eat your box lunches. Stay close to the bus." Captain Enoch jumped off and scurried to his own bus.

We piled out of our bus as soon as the Captain's bus was out of sight. We built a snow fort and started a snow ball fight. Snowballs flew in every direction. Finally, Tom, Hertz, Kerr, Cloud, Dickson, and I formed a small army and drove the rest of the group back onto the bus.

"Hey," said Hertz, "did you see what I saw about a half mile back?"

"What's that?" asked Tom.

"There was a tavern back there called the Hofbrauhaus."

"What are we waiting for?" offered Kerr. "We're not signed out, and they might have some survival brandy. Let's go."

***

The inn was a replica of a German Brauhaus. The house specialty was dark German beer. The owner, in lederhosen, introduced himself simply as Hans. It was empty and quiet when we came in, but Hans walked over to the jukebox and called up German drinking songs.

"Are you all cadets at the Academy?" he asked in a slight accent.

"Ja vole," said Kerr with a smirk on his face. His family had been stationed in Hamburg. "Ve vould like *sechs biers*," Kerr said in broken German.

"All right," said Hans, "and I will have Louisa bring some bratwurst."

We drank dark ale and sang lusty German songs for two hours. Hans and Louisa were having a marvelous time. When we tried to pay for the beers and food, Hans said "Nein. We're happy to have you cadets here and hope you will tell your friends to come and visit with us."

"Hey," I shouted over the din of my lubricated classmates, "we'd better head back. If we miss the bus, it will be the end of Christmas for us."

"Hell, Davis," said Kerr, "we're just having fun."

"Nah, he's right," said Tom. "Headum up and movum out."

We got back to our broken Greyhound five minutes before the rescue bus. Fortunately, there were no officers on board. Our classmates jeered when we got back on, especially when we told them what a good time we had. However, no one broke the unspoken trust between classmates; no one reported the event.[97]

Two hours travel back from the mountains helped dampen the buzz from the dark ales. I slowly put on my blue parade uniform for the concert in the theater. The combined Catholic and Protestant choirs, directed by Mr. Boyd, produced a marvelous sound. The crowd was in a festive mood. I, on the other hand, anxiously awaited the tranquility of *Silent Night* that ended our Christmas programs so I could get to the room to take two aspirins.

***

Monday morning broke crisp and clear. **"Sir, there are five minutes until breakfast formation. The uniform is Class B Blues[98] with Parkas,"** sang out Art Kerr

---

[97] Our status was like an open post; we didn't have to report ourselves for drinking. Classmates, not in a position of authority, were not obligated to report us.

[98] A version of the new uniform had a long sleeve blue shirt, shoulder boards, and did not require wear of the blouse. The parka was a dark blue, hooded, wool jacket with USAFA and our class number on it.

who had volunteered as minute caller.[99] **"Get your sorry butts out of bed. This is the last minute to be called,"** Kerr shouted as he wandered down the hall toward formation.

***

"What's on the schedule today, Tom?"

"My folks are coming into Stapleton. They'll rent a car and drive here. We can go to lunch with them. You can meet the folks and Sarah. Hopefully, you won't scare her too badly."

"You're lucky to have someone to palm her off on. She'd better be cute as her picture."

"Or what?"

"Or you'll owe me a quart of ice cream!"

***

"Mom, this is my roommate, Don Davis. Don, this is my mom, Janet."

Tom's mom was an attractive, dark haired woman in her late thirties Her warm smile instantly made me feel at ease. "Hello, Mrs. Sanders, it's a pleasure to meet you. Thank you for all the boodle boxes, er … cookies you have sent. Tom's been good to share them with me."

"Hello, Don. We're so glad you could join us."

The Sanders met Tom and me in front of Arnold Hall. As we stood by the car, Tom introduced me to his dad. "Dad, this is Don. Don, my dad, Bud."

At six -foot-two with a relaxed air of confidence, Tom's dad could be a poster for a Pan American pilot. "Mister Sanders, my pleasure."

"Hello, Don. We've heard a lot about you . . . mostly good," he said smiling.

"And this, Don, is my brat of a sister, Sarah."

"Oh, Tom, quit it."

Noticing Sarah's blush, her cute, round face, and her petite body, I extended my hand. "Hi, Sarah, Tom's told me a lot about you. I look forward to going to the dance with you."

Sarah said nothing but smiled coyly.

***

Cadet Bourque had suggested Tom take his parents to the Buckhorn Restaurant. Established in 1893, the Buckhorn Exchange retained its old west ambiance with over 500 stuffed pumas, buffaloes, elk, wolves, and others mounted on the walls of various rooms.

---

[99] Since breakfast was still mandatory, we set up voluntary minute callers in the morning. We would rotate the "duty" amongst ourselves to make sure no one missed formation.

Lifelike, the animals peer down at customers eating their relatives. The menu features bear, deer, and rattlesnake. Being on a dinning privilege, Tom and I couldn't drink[100].

"Eww," said Sarah as a waiter attired in western wear seated us. "I don't think I can eat with all of those poor animals staring down at me."

"Come on, Sis," said Tom, "they can't get you, they're stuffed. Try the rattlesnake."

"Ewww," said Sarah again.

Mustering up as much courage as possible, Mrs. Sanders and Sarah ordered buffalo burgers. Mr. Sanders, Tom, and I ordered the large, sampler platter; consisting of generous portions of elk, bear, bison, deer, rattlesnake, and Rocky Mountain Oysters.

Noticing the Rocky Mountain Oysters on the menu, Sarah said, "I thought oysters came from the ocean. Are they really oysters? Do they come from lakes or something?" Sarah asked.

Tom was about to tell his sister all about Rocky Mountain Oysters, but I interrupted

"Uh, you really don't want to know about the oysters," I said. "They're very distinctive and a certain part of animals . . ."

"Try one when they come," said Tom smirking. "I've had them before, they're good."

I shook my head no. Sarah said, "Thanks big brother. I'll stick with the burger."

We spent an enjoyable hour and a half savoring the food, exchanging family tales, and describing our home towns. Sarah subtly glanced in my direction, giving me the impression I was being sized up for our dating during her stay.

Tom and I detailed the hardships of Doolie life. Mrs. Sanders and Sarah were empathetic, but Mr. Sanders said, "Well, it doesn't sound too bad to me; especially when you have all the perks—trips to Washington, D.C.—and a free education."

***

When we arrived back at quarters, I pleaded work on a semester project to allow Tom to enjoy his family alone. He suggested a tour of the campus, indicating he might drop by the room later to show it off. His glance subtly warned me in case I had intended to take a nap. Parents, accompanied by their cadet, were allowed to visit the dormitories until call to quarters.

***

---

[100] Of course, legally, since Tom and I were not 21, we could not drink alcoholic beverages anyway; but most places in 1957 were not stringent in their enforcement of the law.

"Wow, said Sarah, "that's the neatest I've ever seen Tom's room. The upperclassmen must beat him with a whip. I really enjoyed the tour of the rest of the Academy." She and her parents had arrived after dinner. I had put the room in inspection order ,anticipating their visit.

"Nah, Sarah, it's just that Tom has a great roommate to keep him straight. Actually, we have one of the best rooms in the Squadron, with the least amount of inspection demerits. Of course, Tom contributes most of the demerits."

Sarah snickered.

"Right, Davis, Captain Braswell didn't write me up for displaying a picture of a dog."

"You're jealous. My picture is better than the dog of a picture you had displayed."

"Boys," said Tom's Mom, "be nice."

Tom's folks said goodnight and assured us they would have Sarah at Arnold Hall at seven o'clock for the scheduled informal dance.

***

One of Mrs. McComas' planned events, the informal dance tonight was well attended. It was a good opportunity to get to know Sarah better.

The band began playing Elvis Presley's *Hound Dog.* "Want to dance?" I asked Sarah.

"Sure," she answered with a demur smile. Sara was a good jitterbug dancer.

Tom, Karen, Sarah, and I danced almost every dance, switching partners occasionally. I was impressed with Sarah's dancing abilities and enjoying her company. About 10 minutes before Call to Quarters, we walked the girls to Karen's car and discreetly said goodnight with a light peck on the cheek. Karen had offered to return Sarah to the hotel.

"Well, stud, I noticed you were pretty gentlemanly with my sister. Guess I won't have to pummel you all the way back to the room."

"Yeah, well you lucked out."

"How's that?"

"You won't have to buy me a quart of ice cream."

***

Tom's folks brought the girls to Winter Park on Christmas Eve morning. Tom and I rode the bus, which would return us to the Academy at 1500 in time to have dinner and get ready for the Christmas Eve formal dance. Riding the bus insured issue and return of all the ski equipment on the bus; a box lunch, and the added advantage of not being "signed out."

273

Not being signed out, we could indulge in an "egg nog" or two if the occasion presented itself. Fortunately, there were only two officer escorts on the trip, both faculty members and both with their families. They deliberately made themselves scarce during the day.

***

The Winter Park slopes were magnificent. The bright morning sun warmed the cool, crisp Colorado air. Newly fallen powder made the skiing challenging but enjoyable. Being excellent skiers, Tom's folks left for the more challenging black diamond courses. Tom, Karen, Sarah, and I began on the beginners' slopes.

Bud and Janet, as we were requested to call Tom's folks, bought our lift tickets and instructed us to meet them at the lodge at 1230.

"Whew," Janet exclaimed as we sat down at one of the large wooden tables inside the lodge. "I'm out of shape. The altitude's getting to me a little bit."

"Yes," Bud agreed, "I'm a little pooped myself. How're you kids doing?"

'Great, but we're ready for a break and some chow," Tom offered.

We sat for an hour, eating and talking about everything from Karen's Denver University life to Bud's F-86 fighter pilot experiences in Korea. Bud ordered two large pitchers of Canadian Moose Milk[101], as he called it; for us to share while singing several Christmas carols.

***

"Wow, I'm glad the bus was quiet on the way back so we could grab a nap. Don't know if I could make it through the dance tonight without that," said Tom as we entered our room.

"Hmmm, some stud you are. I'll tell Karen to keep you upright tonight."

"Don't worry about me. And watch the slow dances with my sister. As Squadron Commander, I'll have to report you for PDA."

"I'm not worried. You seem pretty taken with Karen. I think she'll keep you occupied."

"Yeah, too bad she's leaving with her folks tomorrow. "

"Knowing you, I suspect not having an escort won't last too long."

"Right, Davis, just remember what I said about my sister."

"Well, again you're lucky. I'm like the sheep dog, keeping your wolf classmates away from your innocent sister."

***

---

[101] "Moose milk is the Canadian name for egg nog."

United States Air Force Academy
Tuesday, December 24, 1957 1500

Dear Folks,

Wow, what an incredible feeling to be "at ease." Tom and I went skiing Sunday. Linda left for New Mexico Sunday morning with her parents, so I went by myself. Hertz and I met a couple of cute girls from DU. I sang in a combined Protestant and Catholic choir concert on Sunday night.

Tom's folks came in yesterday (certainly wish you all were here.) Tom's sister, Sarah, is kind of cute. I'm taking her to our informal dance tonight. A sixteen piece orchestra will play. They have catered snacks and punch (unspiked, of course).

Tom's folks took us to a cool restaurant in Denver called the Buckhorn. They have over 500 animal heads on the wall. They have deer, bear, rattlesnake, and Rocky Mountain Oysters. Pa would love the last one, but I doubt you'd eat any—like cat fish and perch. I'll call tomorrow morning to wish you a Merry Christmas. Hate to close on such a short note, but have to get to dinner and then the dance.

God Bless
Your loving son,
Don

Chapter 39

To round out [the Fourth Classmen's] common experiences in the development
of a cadet class spirit . . . they will celebrate Christmas together.
Superintendent's Letter to Parents

Tuesday, December 24, 1957

The strings of colored lights, tinsel, and pine wreaths lining the walls transformed Arnold Hall into a winter wonderland. The large banner ont the north wall reading "Merry Christmas" reminded us of the reason for the season. The 12 foot Christmas tree, covered with multi-colored balls and lights dominated the west wall. Gaily wrapped packages under the tree brought back memories of Christmases past.

"General Stillman[102], may I present Sarah Sanders, my roommate's sister."

"Welcome, Sarah, we hope you're enjoying your stay with us." Turning to his right, General Stillman said, "Mrs. Stillman, this is Sarah who is a guest of Cadet Davis."

"Please to meet you," Sarah repeated, blushing slightly.

When we finished traipsing the receiving line, Sarah said softly, "Wow, do you have to go through that all the time?"

"When we have formal events like this, a civilian reception, or visit a foreign country, we normally have receiving lines."

"Do you ever forget your name or your date's?"

"This was my first receiving line. It's easy for us because we have name tags. I did hear of an upperclassman who introduced his date, Debbie, as 'Dorothy.' She was a good sport, though, and didn't embarrass him. That's the secret of protocol—not to embarrass anyone."

The evening was exquisite. The ambiance, the music, the sweet smell of Sarah's perfume; even the snacks and liquor-less punch contributed to a great escape from being a Doolie. When Sarah pressed closely during the slow dances, I had a hard time thinking Christmassy thoughts. The dance ended; however, with the singing of Christmas carols which brought back the sense of the season. I ended the evening by giving Sarah an Academy pin.

"Thanks for a lovely evening. Sorry I'll turn into a pumpkin in 10 minutes."

---

[102] Receiving lines were an integral part of a formal dance. Mrs. McComas' instruction and our *Decorum* booklet ensured we were comfortable in introducing guests. We, of course, had name tags which made it easy for the receiving officials, even if we forgot our names.

Sarah stood on her tip toes to kiss me on the cheek. Tom and I scurried back to the dorm.

***

I woke at 0600 thinking about when I was young and couldn't wait until Christmas morning to open presents. We opened one present Christmas Eve but had to wait until Christmas morning for the main treasure trove.

I remembered one morning Santa left me a Sears Super Model Six Bicycle. We were living in downtown Sacramento. I jumped on the Super Six, rode it around the block, and tried to climb a tree with it—with disastrous scratches and a bent handle bar.

***

Breakfast was not until 0700, a concession to the late taps and an administrative Christmas Present. Mitchell Hall was quiet, much like mornings after an upper class open post.

"Who was the good looking chick you had at the dance last night, Davis?" asked Kerr.

"That 'chick's' my sister," interjected Tom. "And you bozos lay off of her."

"Oow, bad choice of words," Kerr responded amidst snickers around the table.

"True, Kerr," I said, "she's unavailable. Tom appointed me her guardian for her stay."

"Wow, that's putting the fox in the hen house," Dickson said.

"Enough," said Tom. "Eat while you can, gentlemen. It'll have to last you four months."

***

"Damn, Tom, sounds like it's a good thing I'm guarding your sister's chastity."

"Yeah, but I'm not sure Dickson isn't right."

"Ah, come on, Tom, you know better than that. Sarah's safe; remember Linda? I do." I changed out of my blues and into my winter parade uniform and started for the door.

"Now where're you going?" Tom asked.

"The Chapel. The choir has to be there at 0830. We're expecting the theater to be full of cadets and their parents. Would your folks and Sarah like to go to the 0900 service?"

"Nah, actually they're coming to the ten hundred services. We're Catholic, you know.

***

Mitchell Hall was packed with cadets and their families anticipating the Christmas feast. Tom had arranged for his family and me to sit at a table. Art Kerr had asked Tom if his family could join us. Art's family arrived after we were seated. Art began the introductions.

"Mom, Dad, these are classmates, Tom Sanders and Don Davis," Art said.

"Good afternoon," Tom and I said in unison and shook hands with the Kerrs.

"And this is my Mom, Janet, and my Dad, Bud," said Tom as the parents shook hands.

"This is my younger brother, Sam," said Kerr, "and my little sister, Melisa. Sam is a junior in high school and Melisa is in fifth grade."

"Hi, Sam; hi Melisa," we said as we shook hands with the siblings.

Once again Colonel Ike had outdone himself. In addition to a turkey with oyster stuffing at every table, the meal included: mashed and sweet potatoes (with marshmallow), green beans, fresh cranberries, and two crystal bowls containing celery stuffed with cream cheese, black olives, and petite onions. The meal began with creamed, curry cauliflower soup and a California ambrosia salad. With great bravado, the waiters brought out the pièce de résistance, baked Alaskan, for desert. Dinner lasted three hours.

***

"Wasn't that cool," Tom sad. "Art's Dad and mine talking about flying. The Coast Guard mission, especially the rescue flying in helicopters, sounds challenging and stimulating."

"Yeah, but Bud's flying is a lot less hazardous and pays a helluva lot more money. What was with all the twenties your Dad laid on you?"

"Ah, I had to make the Christmas meal reservations. If your guests don't show, you're still on the hook. Seems they had trouble collecting from some sixty guys last year. Dad was reimbursing me. I have to go over to the dining hall by Friday and pay for everything."

"Can you believe Art told his little brother not to think about coming to the Academy?"

"Ah, he's just frustrated. He got a Dear John from a girl back home, is sweating math finals, and C3C Jon McCarthy was on his back about Art's private flying. I don't think the girl was a keeper, McCarthy is just jealous, and with our study groups Art will get through the math. Teddy is only a junior; by next year, Art will be a Third Classman and singing the praises of USAFA and telling his brother to apply."

"Good thing the folks went back to the hotel. The altitude and the activities are getting to them. Look, I have to study English. Do you mind a little *King and I*? I'll keep it low."

"That'd be great. I need to study the sample math problems Captain Marsh handed out. Glad I'm out of the Air Power final with a 90 average; gives me more time to study the others.

***

"Get up, Tom. It's 0630. We have to get to the dining hall. Your folks are going to pick us up at 0800 to go horseback riding in the mountains."

"Damn, Davis, who said they wanted to go horseback riding? I sure didn't."

"I saw your Mother reading a schedule at the lodge and discussing it with your Dad. 'Bud, look,' she said. 'They have a special on horseback riding at a place called Sombrero Ranch. You can get a two hour ride through the mountains.'"

'Oh, let's go," Sarah squealed.'

'Okay, I'll look into it,' your Dad said."

"Yeah, sounds like Sarah. She took horseback riding lessons. But, it was eastern tack; I don't know how comfortable she'll be on a western saddle. Frankly, I could have slept in."

"Stop bitching, Tom. At least you have your folks here. Get dressed."

***

"Oh, look, Bud, at all the snow on those mountains. I'm glad Mrs. McComas' letter said to bring winter gear, especially if you planned on skiing or going into the mountains."

"Right, Janet. Great, but I'll be glad to get back for lunch and hot chocolate. That buffalo steak and 'frijoles' is sounding mighty good right now. Glad we only took the two-hour ride."

Tom and I had dug out clothes suitable for the ride. I had Levis, while Tom had to settle for civilian khakis. Fortunately, we both had purchased long johns at the Cadet Store.

The owner of Sombrero Ranch, a retired Master Sergeant in his mid-fifties, picked out four horses from his stable. "Folks," he said, "you don't look like regular riders, so I've picked out four of my gentlest horses for you. Enjoy!"

We rode through a couple of stands of Aspen trees, crossed several streams crusted with ice, and saw deer, elk, and a small pack of coyotes. Even though we had gentle horses and the ride was spectacular, after two hours my legs felt chaffed and my rear and thighs began to ache.

The ride back in the car was quiet. Sarah discreetly slipped her hand into mine. Tom pretended not to notice. Her parents were busy admiring the scenery. I made a mental note to write a thank you letter to Tom's folks. I appreciated their "sponsorship."

The 25 dollars for the trail ride was more than twice my monthly allowance. Tom and I, still depressurizing from the tension of being Fourth Classmen, quickly fell asleep. With the altitude, Sarah soon joined us.

***

Mrs. McComas arranged a mandatory "tea" at 1600 as the background for the Commandant's Reception; scheduling it after Christmas to allow General Stillman to spend Christmas with his family. We had an open post until 2400.

Slipping into my blouse, I looked to see if Tom was ready. "What are we going to do after the reception?" I asked.

"Well, Cindy, Terry's girl, is having a party in her apartment and we're invited. Sandy, my date, is a party girl, and I can keep an eye on you, so Sarah can go. Anyway, it's the best offer we have. My folks are going back to the hotel. The party doesn't start until eight. We can get hamburgers before the party. Dad said he'd pick us up and drop us at the party."

"Great, but how are we going to get back?"

"Sandy has a car and is going to meet us there and drive us back here and take Sarah to the hotel; so we're all set."

"Who's Sandy, again? I have trouble keeping up with all of your paramours. "

"Sandy's the cute redhead I met that first day we went skiing. She's a sophomore and goes to DU. She knows the girls you and Hertz met. She said she likes to party."

***

The regular "Conga Line" to match unaccompanied cadets with dates was at the north end of Arnold Hall before the receiving line began. Tom, Sandy, Sarah, and I grabbed a table along the wall to watch the match making.

The line progressed normally except for my classmate, Pat Grey, who kept moving back in the line. "Catch that, Tom, Grey's working the line. Guess he wants a princess for tonight."

Truly a southern gentleman from Georgia, Pat had a great personality, which compensated for his less than Rock Hudson looks. We were surprised when the girl Pat eventually matched with was not the princess of the ball. In cadet vernacular, she probably was a great cook, made her own clothes, and was a potential winner in the ghoul pool[103].

---

[103] When we had an event that matched cadets with blind dates, there was a pool among the cadets that rewarded the cadet with the least attractive escort with a monetary compensation.

With the match making done, we lined up to greet General and Mrs. Briggs, hosts of the reception. After going through the receiving line, Tom, Sandy, Sarah, and I went through the line for tea and crumpets.

"Wow, isn't this hoity toity?" I said as we sat down.

"Yeah, I wonder how many more of these we will have to do in our careers," Tom said.

"I think it's kind of nice," Sarah said.

"Right, Come on, Sandy, let's dance," Tom said.

***

Cindy's party was great. She had little buns to make sandwiches, macaroni salad, potato chips, and egg nog laced with rum. Several girls chose to drink her cranberry-ginger ale punch.

Actually, the party was sedate. Besides Tom, Cloud, Hertz, and I and our dates, Cindy had invited Bill Gibbons and Terry Koonce and their dates. We talked, ate, drank egg nog, and danced to the slow music. Despite a glare from Tom, Sarah had several cups of egg nog.

Toward the end of the evening, most couples were involved in steamy dancing and making out in the overstuffed chairs and couch. Sarah and I engaged in some heavy necking on one of the chairs. Tom was occupied elsewhere with Sandy.

When the clock struck eleven, it was like a scene from Cinderella. While no one lost a slipper, we quickly gathered our things preparing to leave.

***

As we entered the dorm, we met Pat Grey, who had a big smile on his face.

"Pat, how're you doing?" Tom said.

"I'm doing great."

"How was your date? It looked like you should have won the ghoul pool." I said.

"Well, yeah, I did, but Dora and I had a great time. We went to see the King and I, to dinner at a little restaurant called Fruition, to a club where they had a jazz combo, and caught a taxi back to the base. Dora's girlfriend met her and took her home."

"Damn, Pat, that sounds great, but how'd you do all that? I know you won the ghoul pool, but there wasn't that much money in the pot."

"True," Pat said, "but Dora won her ghoul pool too!! We shared expenses."

***

United States Air Force Academy

Thursday, December 26, 1957 2330

Dear Folks,

It was wonderful to talk to you yesterday. Christmas was wonderful; well, not really, I missed being home and opening the presents. And of course, I missed you all.

Sounds like Pa got a great gift, a milking goat. Good thing you have a couple acres. Seems Pa has never gotten over growing up on a farm. I'll bet your new dress is pretty. You can wear the Academy pin with it.

Christmas dinner with all the relatives is always a treat. Reminds me of the times we traveled down to Nanner Larsen's for Thanksgiving or Christmas. When I see the Norman Rockwell picture of the *Freedom from Want*, it reminds me of our family gatherings with Nanner Larsen. I remember she set a beautiful table with all the trimmings. We always had turkey, mashed potatoes, sweet potatoes, cranberries. I can see us in the picture; especially Nanner and Grandpa John.

Christmas dinner was incredible. We had turkey and all the trimmings, including a spectacular, flaming Baked Alaskan for dessert. I am including a dinner menu. Art Kerr had his family, including his younger brother and sister at the table.

Tom's folks and Sarah joined us. Sarah is cute and fun to be with, but long distance romances are hard. Also, she is only a junior in high school. AND, I would have to put up with Tom chaperoning his little sister all of the time. Besides, I do miss Linda. Unfortunately, Linda won't be back until we turn into monks again. I could have used some time alone with her.

Merry Christmas, Happy New Year
God Bless
Your Loving Son,
Don

Chapter 40

Fourth Classmen are anticipating [Christmas and] . . . the chance to relax
and enjoy life after the strenuous months behind them.
Air Officer Commanding's Letter to Parents

Friday, December 27, 1957

"Come on, Davis; get dressed. My folks will be here in 15 minutes. We're going to Central City for lunch."

"Right, thanks, but I need some study time. Besides, you need time with your folks. I appreciate being adopted, but I also have choir practice this morning for a concert at the Tabor.

"Sarah is going to be upset."

"Ah, I doubt it. Tell her I'll make amends by taking her to the Bob Hope show."

***

"Damn, Davis, Mr. Boyd is on a tear. We've sung the Hallelujah Chorus three times."

"Yeah, I hear you, Kerr. But remember, we only have Doolies, not the full chorus."

"Right. And Mr. Boyd certainly remembers the incredible sounds in the Arlington Bowl and National Cathedral," whispered Don Box from the second row.

"All right, gentlemen," said Mr. Boyd. "Let's take it again from the top."

***

The Tabor was packed. The Denver Post and KOA TV, Channel 4, were covering the event. "US Air Force Academy Choir, Christmas Concert, 2 p.m., conducted by Mr. J. R. Boyd, Free Admission," was on the marquee. Families and children filled the theater.

Built as an opera house, the superb acoustics in the Tabor enhanced the sounds of the choir. When we finished rehearsal, Art commented, "Well, it's not quite the Arlington Bowl sound, but that was pretty damn good."

"Yeah," I said, "Let's hope the real performance goes as well."

***

The exquisite Tabor Dining Room setting complimented the luncheon spread. The menu consisted of a ham and cheese sandwich plate, potato chips, and a Caesar salad.

Mr. Boyd sat at the head table with Mr. William Hornby, Denver Post Editor; and the President, Vice President, and Operations Manager of Channel 4.

Mr. Don Searle, the KOA President, expressed the pleasure of the citizens of Denver in having the Air Force Academy located in Denver. He said the City would miss the Academy when it moved to the permanent site in Colorado Springs.

***

"So, Caruso, how'd the concert go?" Tom asked, reclining on the bed.

"Great, we had a large crowd; the acoustics made us sound good. The Tabor was once an opera house. Of course, our music was more crowd pleasing than an opera."

"Ah, you should have been with us. The barbeque at the Teller House was fantastic. We saw the face on the barroom floor. You'll love this: a fellow named Herndon Davis was commissioned to do paintings in the Opera House and Teller Bar. He got in a fight with the project director and was fired. He was in a real huff.

Then the bell boy, Joe Libby, suggested Davis leave a painting to remember him by. Davis was inspired by a poet named Hugh Antoine D'Arcy and his wife. Actually, D'Arcy's poem was about a drunk who was jilted by a beautiful woman. The sot keeps bumming drinks and eventually promises to do a painting on the barroom floor. Trouble is, he dies and sprawls himself across the painting before it's finished."

"So, how'd you learn all this?"

"Easy, it was written up on the back of the menu," Tom said, handing it to me.

***

Wearing a mid-length dark blue skirt, a white sweater, and a blue leather jacket, Sarah greeted me with a mock whine. "Where were you? We missed you."

"Well, I had choir practice and a Christmas program downtown. I knew your folks had plans to visit Central City. I thought it would be nice if the family were alone for a change."

"Hmmmph," Sarah protested, "you could have invited ME to your concert."

"I would have, but I didn't have a way to get you there. It was at 1400, er . . . 2 p.m. Besides, I'm sure Tom enjoyed little sister's company. Anyway, doesn't the Bob Hope Show make up for it?"

***

The Sanders arrived early, about 1830, as Tom advised them. Since the theater was still relatively empty, we grabbed a quick coke before making our way to third row center seats. Quickly filling the theater cadets, guests, faculty, and staff occupied all the available seats.

***

"What a pleasure to be here at the nation's newest Academy," began Bob Hope. "It's nice to be in only freezing weather after giving a show in Elmendorf, Alaska, where the seals borrowed fur coats from the wives to keep warm. I've heard this is the toughest

284

school in America; I believe it. When my troupe arrived, General Stillman, the Commandant, gave us an in- ranks inspection. I had a button unbuttoned and lost my bathroom privileges."

Laughter greeted Hope's opening remarks. General Stillman, who introduced Hope, was still on stage.

"Thank you, General, you can go now, that is 'Post!'" The cadets snickered at the dismissal of the Commandant.

"You know, in Alaska, we saw all kinds of wild life; deer, bears, and meese, or is that mooses? Or better yet, just moose. Speaking of moose, I was surprised to find a Moose here on campus," Hope said, looking around to see if the General was backstage.

The cadets hooped at the play on General Stillman's nickname. "And, I understand," continued Hope, "that several second class cadets who set out on a little moose hunt ended up in bear traps." A groan went up from the Fourth Classmen at the reference to the Commandant's pretty daughter.[104]

The rest of the show featured skits, songs by Carol Morris—Miss Universe—and dancing with Hope and Ginger Rogers. One skit had Jerry Colona playing an upperclassman and Hope an unwitting Fourth Classman.

"Okay, Mister, what are you?" began Colona.

"Sir, I am a Doolie, SIR," said Hope.

"Doolie? Are you related to the famous General Doolittle?"

"No, sir!"

"And why not?" pressed Colona.

At Hope's answer: "No Excuse, SIR!" a groan went up from the cadets.

"Oh, so you aren't a do little?"

"No, SIR," said Hope, "I'm a do a lot!" eliciting another groan.

Despite the presence of parents and Academy staff, cadets hooped and hollered when Carol Morris came on stage and sang. The crowd applauded enthusiastically when Hope and Ginger Rogers did a duet, soft shoe dance.

At the close of the show, Carol Morris came out with Hope.

"Where are we going after the show?" Carol asked Hope.

"Well, I thought we'd go to this Arnold Hall, and I'd buy you a burger and a shake."

"Bob, I thought you didn't have any money."

---

[104] PDA is public display of affection. Even upperclassmen were subject to this military taboo. Upperclassmen were often "written up" by staff officers – Air Officers Commanding. Two second classmen who date the Commandant's daughter were written up for PDA by AOCs.

"Yeah, that's right, but seems the cadets' girlfriends got up a pool on the least attractive male on the show. It was a tossup between Colona and me, and I won. It was worth five bucks!"

"That's great," said Carol, "but before we go, we should sing the Air Force Song."

The show ended with a rousing audience participation rendition of the Air Force Song, followed by Hope's famous closing *Thanks for the Memory."*

***

"Wow that was great. Thank you, Don, for taking me. But I didn't understand that last bit between Hope and Morris," said Sarah.

"Well, ah . . . I think you'd better have Tom explain it to you. Would you like a milkshake before you go?" I said.

"Thanks a lot, Davis. I'll probably have to explain that to my folks too . . ."

***

A quintet from Les Brown's band played dancing music until 2330. Call to Quarters was 2345. Sarah and I danced. Tom went back to our room.

"So, are you going to write to me?" I asked.

"Sure, Don. I'll miss you. Maybe you can visit next summer."

"I'd like that. Tom has invited me. I'd like to see you again.

We spent what was left of the evening dancing without saying much. Sarah drove me crazy by pressing closely as we danced. *Damn, I'd really like to see Sarah again, but it certainly doesn't look too promising for that to happen very soon after she leaves."*

"Do you have to go, Don?" Sarah asked.

"I'm afraid so, Sarah. Besides your folks will be waiting. I'll walk you to the car."

When we got to the parking lot, Sarah's folks hadn't shown up yet. Sarah turned, embraced and French kissed me.

I returned her ardor, but just then a car swung into the parking lot and tooted its horn.

"Wow," I said, "much more of that and I wouldn't have made it back to my room in time and probably would have had to fight your brother. Saved by the horn."

"Oh, well," sighed Sarah.

"Yeah, see you tomorrow," I said, opening Sarah's door and waving to her folks.

The crisp, cold Colorado air, the glowing full moon, and a sky full of stars left me chilled. I hurried back to the room.

Chapter 41

The Christmas holidays provide Fourth Classmen with a respite from duty and studies, and they may enjoy all the privileges of an upperclassman at that time.
Superintendent's Letter to Parents

Saturday, December 28, 1957

The ringing alarm disrupted a dream; Linda and I were headed to Lookout Mountain on a warm, sunny, summer day. My thoughts were not entirely honorable and I couldn't wait to be alone with Linda. Just as Linda hit the starter on her car, the alarm sounded.

Damn, I thought, *why did I set that frapping alarm? Oh, yeah, we're going down to the new site and have to do breakfast at 0600.* "Tom, **Tom!** Get your butt out of bed; we only have 10 minutes until breakfast formation."

"I'm going to miss those breakfasts when the ogres come back," Tom said as we came into the room. He quickly changed into his grey pants and short sleeved white shirt "picnic" uniform. Given the cold winter air and the prospects of light snow in Colorado Springs, he also grabbed his parka from the closet. "And I don't see why we had to wear blues to breakfast and then change into picnic uniform for the trip."

"Stop griping, Tom, they don't want us to get too used to not being in the system. After all, we get a free trip to the new site, a box lunch, and you get time with your folks."

***

The five chartered buses rolled down the two lane road toward Colorado Springs. The pre-boarding weather briefing indicated there would be light snow at the new site, but most likely only in the mountains to the west.

"I don't know why they had to start at 0830. I'm sure your folks didn't appreciate driving to Lowry at oh dark hundred. It meant getting up at 0630 to have breakfast and get here by bus time. They and Sarah look tired."

"Yeah, but now they'll have a greater appreciation of what our lives are like: having to get up before the sun, eat fast, and get on with the day."

Despite the mix of cadets and families, the bus was quiet after the first few minutes. Most cadets and parents had been together for several days and were talked out. Tom's folks sat two rows up with Sarah on the opposite side. Cadets and guests soon were napping.

***

"Ladies and gentleman," began Lieutenant Will Thompson, an Academy Public Affairs Officer. "We're at the north entrance to the future home of the US Air Force Academy. The Wing is scheduled to matriculate—that is move—here after the Class of 1962 summer training. There are security gates at both the north and south entrances.

The Academy sits on 18,455 acres with a north to south orientation along the eastern slope of the Rocky Mountains. The Chamber of Commerce and other local citizens lobbied to have the Academy here as far back as 1949 when the first site selection committee was formed. The second site selection committee narrowed the choices to three locations: Lake Geneva, Wisconsin; Alton, Illinois; and Colorado Springs, Colorado. On June 24, 1954, the Air Force rewarded the Colorado Springs citizens' efforts by choosing this site."

"Damn, Tom, logistics with girls is going to be a real problem. Since we can't have cars until we're firsties[105], the girls will have to have wheels."

The bus passed over the roughshod road and parked at a future lookout point.

Lt. Simpson continued: "As you see by the snow on the mountains and the light dusting of the site, the 7,176 feet Academy elevation makes it subject to more weather than Denver.

The architectural firm of Skidmore, Owings, and Merrill, known as SOM, won the bid to design and build the Academy. Detractors of the preferred Air Force modernistic design included famed architect Frank Lloyd Wright, who declared the structures looked like 'glassified-boxes on stilts.' Mr. Wright, of course, was a losing bidder.

The campus consists of a dormitory area, Vandenberg Hall—which is behind the retaining wall running east and west; a dining area, Mitchell Hall—which is the 300 by 300 foot area with the 24 foot high steel columns beyond the dorm; a social hall, Arnold Hall, to the west of the dorm and north of the level area which will be the Honor Court; the academic area, Fairchild Hall—to the south of the dorm and east of the dining hall; and the admin building, Harmon Hall—just south of Arnold Hall.

The quarters are two blocks long and six stories high. The dining hall covers more than a city block. The academic building is also two blocks long.

In the foreground you can see the gymnasium, the tennis/basketball courts, and the athletic fields, General MacArthur's 'friendly fields which will sow the seeds that will later bear the fruits of (military) victory.'

---

[105] "Firsties"—Seniors

Eventually, four swimming pools, an indoor football field, eighteen soccer fields, 30 basketball courts, six baseball fields, and, of course, an Olympic track will condition our cadets and be available for competitions.

Interestingly, Mr. Walter Netsch, SOM lead designer, had a fascination with multiples of the number seven. Thus, Vandenberg Hall is 1,337 feet long, a 191 multiple of seven.

Between the cadet quarters and dining hall you see the air gardens. They will contain wading pools, pathways, and landscaping. A small firm, Site Landscaping, Inc., subcontracted to construct the air gardens and surrounding landscaping, including the parade grounds."

"Wow, Tom, you know Linda's Cousin, Judy. Her father, Mr. Willard Russell, and his partner, Bill Mathews, own that architectural landscaping company."

"So, they should make a killing. Maybe you should date Linda's cousin."

"Get out!"

"Are there any questions?" asked Lt. Thompson. "Ah, yes, ah, Mister Sanders," Lt. Thompson said.

"Lieutenant, I haven't heard you mention the chapel. I understand there is some controversy over the chapel."

"Yes Sir, the chapel, designed by Mr. Netsch, originally had 19 spires reaching 150 feet in the air. He reduced the spires to 17 for cost and design purposes. The chapel features aluminum, glass, and steel. On the inside, the large tetrahedrons shapes between the spires contain stain class windows. Basically two stories high; the upper portion will be reserved for Protestant services, the lower area chapels will support Catholic and Jewish services. The controversy centered on the design and three million dollar budget. But we believe all of the issues have been resolved and construction will go forward."

"Will cadets have an option of going downtown for services?"

"Ah, no sir. On base chapel will continue to be mandatory."

"Thank you, lieutenant," said Tom's Dad.

***

Looking at his watch, Lt. Thompson said, "Well, ladies and gentlemen, I know there isn't much to see yet at the site, but progress is steady and General Briggs believes the Class of 1962 will start the academic year here. Now, we're going to take the 40 minute ride to downtown Colorado Springs. You will have an hour and a half to find a restaurant for lunch. The buses will be parked on North Tejon Boulevard and will leave an hour and a half after we arrive. Please arrive on time." Everyone on the bus applauded Lt. Thompson.

***

Michelle's was crowded. The elongated dining room was chock full of booths, tables, and chairs to accommodate 60 people. The mirrored walls had shelves that supported a small scale railroad line. A small passenger train with Pullman cars and a freight train carrying army tanks and jeeps constantly circled the room, occasionally letting off sharp blasts of steam.

"Cadet Bourque told me the Monte Cristo sandwich is incredible. It has ham, turkey, provolone cheese, and raspberry jam grilled inside slices of bread like French Toast," I offered.

"I'm not sure I'm up to that," said Mrs. Sanders. "Think I'll try their grilled cheese."

The rest of us ordered the Monte Cristos. The table fell silent as we devoured the food.

"Wow, that was great," said Tom. "Good show, Davis." Looking at the menu he said, "Now, what should we take on for dessert? Here's one called the 'Volcano.' It serves 25—I heard the second classmen from Seventh came here for their Squadron Commander's birthday. They ordered the Volcano. All 28 came. It cost them fifty dollars. When they finished the dish, John Michopoulos, the owner, sounded the Claxton horn mounted on the front of the restaurant. That's probably a bit much for us."

"Here's one," said Tom's Dad. "Strawberry shortcake, three flavors of ice cream, a banana sliced into flower petal shapes, cinnamon strips and whipped cream, topped with a blazing sugar cube soaked in alcohol. It's called 'The Cadet.' And it's only six bucks."

***

The early morning rise, overindulgence at Michelle's, and altitude led to a silent bus on the ride back to Lowry. Everyone, cadets and parents, slipped into a two hour nap.

After being roused by the bus driver and dropped off in the parking lot by the Sander's car, Tom and I were ready to say goodbye for the day.

"Say, boys," said Mr. Sanders, "how about dinner downtown.

"Gee, Dad, thanks, but I think we'll skip dinner out tonight. We have to catch up on shoe shines and do a little academic reviewing. We have finals a couple of weeks after the break. And we'll have an early morning if we're going to Winter Park for skiing tomorrow."

Yeah, and I'll just be happy to kick back and listen to Tom's music. I'd also better get out and run a couple of miles. I'm sure the "Cadet" put on two more pounds, I thought.

"Okay, son, we will see you tomorrow."

Chapter 42

*This is the holiday period and most of your time will be spent
at a host of recreational activities.*
Contrails

Saturday, December 28, 1957

A light snow covered the road as the buses plodded toward the ski slopes of Winter Park. Tom and I chose to ride the bus so that we didn't have to mess with ski equipment in the car. The hour and 45 minute journey to the ski area and the clackity-clank of the snow tires induced the usual cadet trance. Most were asleep five minutes after the bus left Lowry.

I happened to sit across the aisle from Hertz, who seemed gloomy. "What's the matter Hertz; get another Dear John from home?"

"Nah, Just been thinking. The past seven days have been great. Loved having my folks here. I'm not sure I want to be an Air Force Officer. I discussed it with my folks; told them I'm going to do what they wanted me to do—go to a Catholic school; major in English."

"What was their response?"

"They were disappointed, saying how proud they were, and that their friends were impressed with my appointment. The hooker was they said they couldn't afford my tuition."

"And have you really thought this through? You know you'll have to face the people back home. They'll ask if you were sick or got thrown out. That's part of what keeps me here."

"Yeah, I know, but I'll probably flunk math and chemistry. I want to be a pilot, but I can do that through ROTC[106] at college. Another thing, religion is just another formation here."

"Gee, I don't think so. I was never very religious, but I find the program stimulating. In addition to Colonel Bennet's inspiration every Sunday, the choir activities have been great. The trip to DC was incredible. Maybe you should turn Protestant."

"That would go over great with my parents. I believe in the Honor Code, but it seems the Administration uses it to reinforce regulations. Remember when Captain Brown tried to find out who ran his pants up the flag pole by asking everyone who did it?"

---

[106] ROTC – Reserve Officer Training Corps

"Okay, but Colonel Cassidy stopped that and, I heard, chewed out Brown pretty severely. You ought to give finals your best shot and try to stay."

"I do enjoy classmate's friendships, and it is kind of neat to have people admire your uniform on the street. I'll think about it some more. How about a nap?"

"Right," I said and slipped into a cadet coma.

***

Sarah's red ski outfit highlighted her young, firm figure. In addition to being cute, she possessed a healthy complexion and body. Outfitted in a white ski ensemble, with pink trim and red gloves, Mrs. Sanders was a mature reflection of her daughter. Mr. Sanders, dressed in a black outfit could have passed for Bat Man.

"Let's get the tickets and hit the slopes," Mr. Sanders said. "I understand you have a dining permit tonight. I thought we would leave around three p.m. . . . . oh, that's right, 1500 military time. We'll go to the hotel, get some rest, and go to a nice place for dinner. Since we are leaving early in the morning, we'll get you boys back pretty early."

***

I had signed up for the free Academy ski lesson. Mr. Sanders signed up Sarah so she could be with me. I found out later that she could ski circles around me.

Erich Windisch, the instructor for the Willy Schaeffler Ski School, gave lessons in a broken German accent. However, he improved my skills significantly. By the third run down the beginner's slope I felt comfortable in joining Sarah on the intermediate slopes.

After the fifth run, Sarah took pity on me and said, "At the end of this run, let's go to the lodge and grab a cinnamon bun and hot chocolate."

"Sounds good to me," I said. Then foolishly said, "Come on, I'll race you."

Fortunately no classmates were around to jeer me when Sarah beat me down.

***

After polling Tom, Sarah and me, the Sanders agreed to dinner at the Red Top Hamburger Café. When they saw the size of the burgers on others' plates, Sarah and her Mother decided to split one. Tom, his Dad, and I had regular cheeseburgers.

After dinner, we went back to the Brown Palace Hotel so Tom and I could change into our uniforms. After the trip to the new site yesterday, we had given the Sanders civilian clothes and an extra set of uniforms. After the dinner, we had to get back in uniform.

Hmm, I thought, *the Brown Palace hasn't changed much in six months, but I sure have. I wonder if I would have just turned around and gone home if I knew what I was in for. Good grief, I'm passed the half-way point. Hell, I can make it.*

The antique clock on the mantle struck ten o'clock. "Okay, boys, let's go. We have to get you home safely and I have to get back to get some sleep."

Mrs. Sanders had a tear in her eye when she hugged Tom. Turning to me, she hugged me and said, "Don, it's been our pleasure to know you. You keep Tom out of trouble ,and we will see you again in May for Recognition."

"Yes, Ma'am," I said. "I'll do what I can with Tom, and I hope to see you again in May. I might even come to see you if I can manage it on leave," I said stealing a glance at Sarah who rewarded me with a slight smile. She also looked a little teary.

***

"Can I join you for the brunch tomorrow, Davis? I'm really missing my family already. You won't mind if I horn in on you and Linda and her family will you?" Tom asked.

Mrs. McComas and the staff had arranged for a pre-New Year's eve buffet so the families that had to return home would have a last chance to be with their sons.

"Hell, how could I refuse after all your family did for me? Just don't hit on Linda."

Linda had called the Squadron yesterday and left a message she and her family were back in town. I called Linda and invited her and her parents to the buffet.

I stopped by the dining hall office after breakfast and pleaded with the NCO in charge to let me make reservations for three. I explained the circumstance. Chief Otto said, "You know the last reservations were supposed to be made by the 27th . . ."

"Please," I said, "this is the first chance I've had to meet my girlfriend's parents. It would be a great way to make a good impression on them."

"Well, okay, Mister Davis. Do not tell anyone about this and bring the $4.50 to me as soon as you get back to your room. Bring the names of your guests, and I'll pencil them in."

"Yes, Sir," I said and hurried back to the room.

***

Tom and I spent Monday morning polishing shoes, grilling each other on Fourth Class Knowledge, and three hours hitting the books. I took time to write my folks and a long thank you letter to Tom's folks; mentioning all the wonderful experiences I had shared with them. I also ran six miles.

The combined Protestant and Catholic choirs had a fourteen hundred concert scheduled in the base theater. I invited Linda and her family to the concert, but they had another commitment. There was a Dean's Reception in the late afternoon, 1600, followed by another "tea." There was no open post.

***

I met Linda and her folks outside the dining hall. As I escorted Linda and her parents into the dining hall, we stopped to look at the menu. The International Buffet Menu took two pages to list. Colonel Ike and his staff had outdone themselves again.

"Wow, that looks like some feed," said Mr. Jackson, Linda's Dad. At 6 foot 2 inches, he had a muscular body that evidenced frequent visits to a gym. In his early forties, he wore a finely tailored dark grey suit. His dry humor startled me at first, but as we talked, he reminded me of Uncle Elmer, whose wry humor also took getting used to.

MENU
INTERNATIONAL BUFFET

Roast Tenderloin of Beef Bouquetiere *Tender cut of beef; delicately roasted.*	**Insalata Antipasta** *Fresh garden vegetables; tossed and garnished with Julienne cut cold meats; tuna filets, olives and cheese*
Chicken Breast Hawaiian *Tender strips of Chicken-breaded/sautéed to a golden brown; simmered in a delicate fruit sauce*	**California Ambrosia Salad** *Combination of fresh fruits; including oranges and grapefruits in a coconut sauce*
Homard Au Beurre *Select pieces of Lobster Tail; broiled and accompanied by clarified Lemon Butter*	**Le Plateau de Crudites** *Vegetarian delight with fresh vegetables, dill pickle wedges, colossal olives, and pickled vegies*
Trinidadian Rice Pilaf *Sautéed with Onions until brown; simmered with vegetable spices and poultry stock until tender*	**Seafood Table** *Smoked Clams, Smoked Oysters, Anchovy Filets, Marinated Herring, and Smoked King Salmon*
Fagiolini Verde Italiano *Italian Green Beans with Pimientos/Onions; sautéed and laced with clarified dairy butter*	**Adorno de Camarones** *Jumbo Cocktail Shrimp topped by spicy cocktail sauce and presented in a Falcon ice sculpture*
Broccoli Tipper Med Rort Smor *Norwegian dish steamed and served with fresh dairy butter, lemon juice and Worcestershire sauce*	**Petit Pains Au Beuree** *Hot Cloverleaf Rolls; Assortment of bite size Pastries*

Kalter Aufschnitt	*Fresh Hot Coffee*
Popular Cold Meats and Schinkenrollen surrounding a Chaud Froid Ham Centerpiece	*Blend of fresh roasted coffee beans*
International Cheese Tray	***Fruit Punch***
Assortment of foreign and domestic Cheeses with a fresh fruit centerpiece	*Combination of fruit juices for a delicious dinner drink*

Linda's Mom was a natural brunette. The resemblance of Linda to her mother easily explained Linda's good looks. Alice, more reserved than Jack, Linda's Dad, put one immediately at ease with her charm and slight Southern accent.

Linda's school activities, an outline of a Fourth Classman's life, and the marvelous spread provided by Colonel Ike sparked the conversation. Linda was quiet during most of the meal, and blushed when her parents extolled the wonders of her school work and activities.

"So, Don, you eat like this every day?" Jack (he said to call him Jack) asked.

"No, Sir," I said. "Well, the food is always good, but Fourth Class servings tend to be limited. I haven't eaten this well since July, well, except for the choir trip to Washington, DC."

"Linda told me you really enjoyed the trip. She said she was jealous; not only about the trip, but that you met some girls there."

"DAD!" Linda exclaimed.

It's nice to know Linda was jealous, but I'd better be careful what I say. "Well, we did meet some college girls at Annapolis. They were on buses touring Annapolis. What was impressive," I said, hoping to change the conversation, "was singing in the National Cathedral and in the Arlington Amphitheater."

"That must have been exciting." Changing the subject, Alice said, "Linda told me you are going on a date tonight. Are you going out on the town?"

"No, ma'am," I said. "One of my classmate's girlfriends, Cindy, has an apartment near the base. She's providing refreshments and records for dancing. She's also inviting the girls to sleep over so they don't have to be on the road at night. My classmates and I are getting a room at a motel near the Apartment. Cindy is going to drive Terry, Tom, Linda, and me to her apartment. We are going to take a taxi to the motel."

"A motel, hmmmm," said Alice, "I'm not sure about that. Can I get the girl's name and telephone number?"

"Yes, ma'am," I said.

"And is there going to be alcohol?"

"Well, ma'am, no one is 21, and we will be signed out on a special privilege, which means we can't drink." Looking at my watch, I said, "I'm sorry, but I must leave. Please stay and enjoy the rest of the desserts and coffee. I have to change into a formal uniform to attend the Superintendent's New Year's Reception at 1400 . . . ah, two o'clock. Mr. Jackson, could you drop Linda off at Arnold Hall after you finish brunch?"

"Sure, Don. Linda has an overnight case with her, and if Alice thinks it's all right for her to go with you tonight, you can leave from there."

"Thank you. Linda, I'll see you at Arnold Hall. We can dance for a while after the reception and tea. It was a pleasure meeting you, Mr. and Mrs. Jackson."

"Jack and Alice, please, Don, said Mr. Jackson."

"And we were glad to finally meet you, Don," Mrs. Jackson said.

***

"General Briggs, this is my date, Linda Jackson. Linda, this is General Briggs, the Academy Superintendent."

"Sir, I'm pleased to meet you," Linda said.

Turning to Mrs. Briggs, the General said, "Mrs. Briggs, this is Cadet Davis and his date, Linda."

"What a lovely ensemble, Linda. That light blue color compliments your beautiful complexion," Mrs. Briggs said.

Linda blushed slightly and demurely said, "Thank you."

Clearing the line, Linda and I headed toward a table where Terry and his girl, Cindy, sat engaged in conversation. "Hi, Cloud. Hello, Cindy."

"Hello, Don. Hello, Linda," Cindy and Terry said together. "I see you got through the line all right," Cindy said to Linda as we joined them. Cindy was wearing a blue cocktail dress that accented her eyes and striking red hair.

"Well, I was a little nervous, especially when Mrs. Briggs complimented my dress and jacket. Mom bought it at the Grey Rose in Colorado Springs. Thank goodness, Don told me what to expect going through the line."

***

United States Air Force Academy

December 27, 1957

Dear Folks

Wow, what a wonderful eight days. I'm exhausted. Friday, Tom took his folks to Central City, famous for a bar with a picture painted on the bar room floor. I didn't go. The choir had a show at the Tabor Theater. The local TV station provided lunch; then we did a half hour program. The audience loved the show. I ran six miles when we got back to the base. Despite all the "free living" and food, I've managed to stay in shape.

Friday night Bob Hope put on a show. Hope, Jerry Colona, Ginger Rogers, Miss Universe, Carol Morris, and others entertained us. Hope must have had a cadet spy; the jokes were very "insider." The cadets understood the skits, but some of the dates - especially the girls from back home - and the parents didn't.

We went to the new site Saturday. The setting and buildings are going to be fantastic. The modern design has critics, but I think it is going to be spectacular. And as Third Classmen, we will be able to enjoy it a lot more.

After the site visit, we went to a Colorado Springs ice cream parlor. The owner is a businessman who pushed to get the Academy here. His great sandwich, called the Monte Cristo, is scrumptious. His ice cream creations, the "Volcano" and "Cadet," have been featured in local newspapers.

Today we had another concert in the Theater. The Dean sponsored a reception at 1800 today after dinner. Mrs. McComas had another tea dance, but since Tom and I didn't have dates, we came back to the room to study. Finals and the upperclassmen are going to be a big headache after Christmas break.

I've written thank you letters to Tom's folks for the wonderful time I had with them. I also wrote to Lucille, Aunt Elsie, and Aunt Jean for all the marvelous goodies they sent. Aunt Jean's Louisiana pralines were a particular hit. And, of course I thank you for the Christmas boodle box.

God Bless
Your Loving Son,
Don

Chapter 43

At Christmas, all the facilities of Arnold Hall are open to [the Fourth Classmen]
Superintendent Message in "Cadet Life."

Wednesday, January 1, 1958

"Wow that was a great party. How'd you make out, Don?"

"Linda and I had a good time, but when it got really hot and heavy, we went outside for a walk. Didn't last long because we didn't have coats on. How'd it go with your latest?"

"Well, Susan and I did a lot of smooching, but with so many people around that's as far as it went. I would have liked to take her back to the motel—alone."

"Yeah, it would have been nice to have Linda alone too, but I wouldn't go that far."

"Right, Davis. What other tall tales do you know? I saw Linda sipping the Moose Milk."

"Knock it off. We'd better get into Blues. Formation is in fifteen minutes. I think marching to lunch is the Commandant's way of preparing us for when the gargoyles return."

At Arnold Hall, after lunch, the usual group was at the table. Kerr said, "Did you see the write up in the Tribune this morning? No? OKAY, then I'll read it to you:"

The Denver Tribune

December 31st 1957

DENVER DEBUTANTES DO DUTY AS DOOLIE DATES

Approximately 500 Denver girls, primarily from local colleges, were "screened" to provide dates for the nearly 300 Air Force Academy Fourth Class "Doolies" for a formal ball held December 24th at the Cadet Club.

"Doolie," derives from the term "Do-Willie," a derogatory term used by Air Training Officers during summer training to chastise new cadets (freshman). It is now an accepted term for Fourth Classman, much as "Plebe" is used for West Point freshmen.

Air Force Cadet Hostess, Mrs. Edward McComas, interviewed the young ladies. Academy spokesman, Captain Robert Gill, said the process was "not to exclude any girls, but to inform the ladies of the protocols cadets must observe, such as not showing affection in public and not being able to leave the base."

> Controversy arose when a rumor circulated that only area college girls were eligible to attend the ball. Several local working girls and high school girls' parents reportedly called the Academy and complained.
>
> Captain Gill further explained: "I think the confusion arose because our initial contacts were with the local colleges such as Colorado Women's College and Denver University. The intent was never to exclude any young lady desiring an opportunity to date a cadet."
>
> The formal dance is an opportunity for the Fourth Classmen, who must remain at the Academy during the Christmas holiday, to meet girls in a relaxed setting not overseen by upperclassmen.
>
> "Doolie," Cadet Fourth Class Ron Mueller said, "I have a girl back home, but this is a chance to socialize with local girls. Carla and I agreed that we each should do some dating until we can be together again."

"Leave it to Mueller to get his name in the paper," said Jim Dickson."

"Nice to know we are in such high demand," I said.

***

The Superintendent's Reception followed Air Force protocol. Commanders hold New Year's receptions that every officer on base is expected to attend and leave a personal calling card. Officers' Ladies attend; their attire including hats and gloves. Mrs. McComas advised cadet dates that cocktail dresses sans gloves and hats were appropriate.

We received cadet "calling cards" with raised printing indicating "Cadet Don Davis, Class of 1961." Each cadet was expected to leave his card in the tray at the Club entrance.

***

Wow, I thought, as Linda came through the door of Arnold Hall. *She looks ravishing.* I took her coat and admired her knee-length light coral cocktail dress. "Hi, you look gorgeous."

"Thank you, Mom bought this for me at the Grey Rose. She said it was very appropriate for a New Year's Reception. She also loaned me the string of pearls."

"Let me put your coat up, and then we can go through the line. I certainly had a wonderful time last night, even if we couldn't have any time to ourselves."

"I felt very romantic last night. It's probably better we couldn't be alone."

Yeah, and it's back into the monastery tomorrow; movies, hamburgers, and pizzas, blah. "Okay, let's do my duty, then we can get some snacks and watch the Rose Bowl Game."

***

Linda acted like the receiving line was old hat. She charmed the Superintendent with her smile and exchanged pleasantries with Mrs. Briggs. Exiting the receiving line, we headed for tables and chairs arranged for watching the football game. Terry and Cindy joined us.

"Cindy, that was a great party. Thanks for inviting Linda and me," I said. "Did my five dollars help cover the costs?"

"Not exactly, but that was my treat. After all, I am a working girl, not a college student."

"Obviously, you read the paper this morning," I said.

"Yes, but frankly, I thought it was lot of to-do about nothing. The girls I know are quite capable of getting a date with a cadet, but Mrs. McComas does a good job of match making. By the way, who's playing in the Rose Bowl? I haven't really been following the college games."

"It's Ohio State and Oregon," Terry said. "Coach Hayes has Ohio State at eight and one. Len Casenova has the Ducks at seven and three. They tied Oregon State for the conference championship. But since Oregon State was in the Rose Bowl last year, they couldn't repeat."

"Impressive," I said. "You should do sports for the Denver Post."

"Yeah, right. Hey, let's get some hamburgers and shakes before the game kicks off."

Ohio State scored first and looked like they might run away with the game. The Ducks, however, played tough. The game remained seven to nothing until the second quarter."

"Who you rooting for, Davis?" Terry asked.

"I'm from the West Coast, I like Oregon." The girls were talking about fashions.

"Okay I'll give you three TDs and take Ohio State for hamburgers at the Club."

"That's pretty generous, Terry. Deal," I said. We returned to watching the game, which ended at 35 to 19 in favor of Ohio State. My team lost the game, but I won hamburgers.

After the game, we were joined by Kerr, Tom, and Hertz. We ordered pizza. I told Terry I'd take a rain check on the hamburgers.

"So, Davis, what do you think the upperclassmen will be like when they get back?" asked Hertz.

"Oh, I think they will be their normal obnoxious selves. But I'll worry about that tomorrow. Come on, Linda, let's dance."

Terry and I danced with the girls the rest of the afternoon, knowing that it would be awhile before we could be alone with them again without the presence of upperclassmen.

***

"Hit the wall, chin in, Davis" growled C3C Whiteman as I entered the dorm. It was 2230;, 30 minutes until the holiday officially ended. *Damn, it's going to be a long five months until recognition. I don't know if I can take this crap for that long. Oh well, Junior College won't be so bad.*

"Give me the code of conduct!" Cadet Whiteman demanded.

Just then Cadet Lt. Col. Jay stepped out of the orderly room. Noticing I was pinned against the wall, Cadet Jay said, "Whiteman, what are you doing?"

"Well, Jimmie, I was just going to get this Doolie back in shape and I …"

"Whiteman, you can either address me as 'Sir' or "Cadet Jay." Seems you need a little refreshing on military bearing yourself. Christmas vacation isn't over until 2300. Why don't you just go to your room? I'll see you in the morning. Davis, I suggest you go to your room as well. It wouldn't hurt to study Contrails a bit. Good night."

"What the hell was that all about?" Tom asked as I came into the room.

"Ah, Whiteman wanted to start the buck up tonight, but Cadet Jay still had a little of the Christmas spirit left over. Damn, it's going to be hell next week getting back into the system."

***

United States Air Force Academy
Wednesday, 1 January, 1958

Dear Folks,

Happy New Year. I hope this year is healthy and prosperous for you. In five months, my year will be much better; after recognition day. I had a wonderful vacation; wish you all could have come. Tom's folks were a great surrogate. His little sister, cute and vivacious, added a lot.

We had a Superintendent's Reception today. Then we got to watch the Rose Bowl. They had a big "International "buffet lunch yesterday. Linda and her parents joined me for the fabulous food.

Thanks for sending the Sacramento Bee. I don't get to read it much, but I enjoy it. I saw a column by Stan Gilliam, my journalism teacher. He's doing local news interest. I'm sure he'll have a large following.

I bought a radio with the money folks sent me for Christmas. We're not supposed to listen to the radio during call to quarters, but mine has an ear phone and I can get the radio in the drawer in a heartbeat.

Christmas vacation was good to me. I weigh 175 pounds, We still have intramural boxing matches after vacation. I have to get down to 168 in two weeks. I'm sure the upperclassmen will help with my diet starting tomorrow.

Oh, I forgot to tell you. We got information on our trip to California after Recognition. We will be at Hamilton Air Force Base (San Rafael) by 4 June. Then we go to March AFB (Riverside). I can probably get weekends at both bases so I can see you and Nanner Larsen. I may try to bring Tom and Art to meet you if we can get off. I will let you know more later. Well, it's after lights out, so I'd better close. I love you and miss you.

God Bless,
Your Loving Son,
Don

Chapter 44

Time and many trials will discover the best of you.
Superintendent Message to the Class of 1961—Contrails

Thursday, January 2, 1958

The rasping sound of the PA system prior to the playing of reveille startled me out a deep uncomfortable sleep. I felt the damp pillow as I swung my feet over the edge of the bed. "Damn, Tom," I called across the room. "I hope the inquisition isn't as bad as that dream was!"

"Yeah," Tom replied, "it's great to be back in the system. Can't wait for breakfast."

We didn't have to wait for breakfast. C3C Whiteman was standing in the hallway when we left the room for reveille.

"Well, dumbsmacks, looks like you had a fine Christmas. How about you hit it for 10?"

Tom and I both did a quick 10 pushups. Anticipating today, we'd been running five or six miles a day and exercising in the gym. We were not back in top shape, but we were fit.

"Well, smacks, looks like you're smarter than you look. Obviously you did some conditioning while your mentors were gone. Post!"

***

My re-introduction to our Squadron Honor Representative, Cadet Major Jerry Garvey, was not pleasant. "Well, Mister Davis," Garvey said. "You always wear your hat in the dining hall or is this a special occasion?"

Oh crap, I thought, looking up at the brim of my hat. *Hell of a way to start. He didn't look at my name tag. He remembers me from the honor incident.* "No, Sir, ahh, I …"

"Well, Mister, what's the correct response?"

"Ah, no excuse, Sir." *Damn, they're back.*

"Give me a form 10. Nice start to the New Year, Davis. Post."

I found my table and slid into the hot pilot slot. Cadet Jay had mixed up table assignments again. My classmates: Pat Grey, A Flight; Terry Koonce, B Flight; and Bill Gibbons, B Flight, were at the table. Second Classmen were Joe DeSantis, B Flight; Charley Mays, A Flight; and Ken Thomas, C Flight Commander. Third Classmen Jon McCarthy, B Flight; Al Clark, A Flight; and (unfortunately) Ed Whiteman, C Flight, filled out the ramp.

Brief introductions preceded the food. Cadets Mays and Whiteman, known as "Fourth Class baiters" began as soon as the food was served. "Davis," Mays half-screeched, "tell me about your Christmas."

"Well, Sir, I had a good time. My roommate's parents were here, and we ate out several times. We went skiing and horseback riding. The choir had several performances, and we took a trip to the new site. I'm …

"Dumbsquat, do you animals use contractions?"

"Ah, no, Sir." Remembering my Cadet Garvey encounter, I added, "No, excuse, Sir."

"You're right about that, Doolie. Give me the four verses of the Air Force Song."

The rest of the breakfast followed a similar pattern with Cadets Mays and Whiteman alternating assaults on me and my classmates. My involuntary diet had begun.

***

Tom and I spent Friday evening shaping up the room, paying particular attention to the clothing shelves and the closets. We used Cadet Bourque's system; placing new shorts, tee-shirts, and socks on the top of the required stacks and used articles underneath.

Captain Braswell was in tune with the buck up. Tom got two demerits for records lying flat instead of being vertical on the book shelf. I got two demerits for dust on Linda's picture frame; although Captain Braswell commented: "Cute girl."

The in-ranks inspection was equally nit-picky. Tom got a demerit for "hat improperly aligned." I got a demerit because my overcoat top button was not buttoned. The heavy overcoat, appreciated in the 25 degree temperature, made rifle inspection difficult. In fact, Pat Grey dropped his rifle while trying to execute "inspection arms."

Cheers went up from everyone in the barracks as the public address system announced: "There will be no parade today because of the intensity of the storm."

***

The next week passed with more of the same. Toward the end of the week, the upperclassmen started to mellow. Table discussions turned to academics. Cadet Jay scheduled two periods of marching and close order drill on days we didn't have intramurals. He also scheduled five mile runs for all classes to "lose the Christmas fat," he said.

Instructors began a series of reviews. We were encouraged to form study groups. Tension began to rise among all cadets, but especially those who had marginal grades going into the finals. I joined study groups in math and chemistry. Tom and I used the library as a study hall. It provided a sanctuary from upperclassmen and allowed talking with classmates without special permission to visit other rooms during call to quarters.

I had one more intramural fight scheduled before finals. To get us in shape, Cadet Simons put the whole team through rigorous workouts including a three mile run at the beginning and end of practices. Between Cadet Simons regimen and the ramp diet, I went from 172 to 164 pounds before my match.

My opponent, Stanley Hammer, was 165 pounds, five-feet seven, giving me a good two inch reach on him. Cadet Hammer fought a defensive fight, backing and dodging. I kept hitting him with jabs; twice in the second round landing good left hooks followed by right uppercuts. Both times, the Second Classman staggered but did not go down. He was obviously out of condition. In the third round, Cadet Hammer practically ran backward. I only landed four or five jabs and one solid right cross.

"Great job," Cadet Simons said. "You outpointed him even without a knock down."

"Yeah," I said, "he was hard to catch."

The bell rang and the referee went to the center of the ring. "The bout is a draw. Cadet Hammer won the first round, Cadet Davis the second; and the final round was a tie."

"Hogwash," said Simons. "He didn't win a round." I was also disappointed. The small crowd, squadron partisans, booed. The only reason I could account for the decision was the referee and the two judges were Second Classman. The referee was from Hammer's squadron.

***

Toward the end of the second week after Christmas, the buck up stopped and we were allowed to eat our meals in relative peace. An occasional question was asked about current events or an academic subject. The SAMI and parade were cancelled on the weekend before finals. Anticipation and anxieties grew.

***

 # United States Air Force Academy
Sunday, 12 January 1958

Dear Folks,

Just a short note. Finals begin tomorrow. My Military Studies grades are high enough I don't have a final's test. I've been studying hard for two weeks, especially after the Mickey Mouse died down from the upperclassmen.

Everyone takes academics seriously. Upperclassmen gave us grief until Thursday. Then we were told to study, study, study. Upperclassmen are not immune from academic failure. Study cooperation is encouraged, but we can't share test information. That would be an honor violation. You can get extra instruction if you are weak in a subject.

Thank everyone for the Christmas money; spent most of it on Christmas. With Tom's folks help, I was able to do a lot. I loved the skiing. After two lessons, I got pretty good. Didn't run into trees or anything.

Gene's letter said he had a good time with Aunt Jean and Uncle Ed. He met a couple of nice girls at a dance and continues to enjoy being in Louisiana. Hope he stays there rather than going back to Sacramento and the crowd he runs around with there. The head shed has confirmed we will be going to Hamilton (San Rafael) Air Force Base near San Francisco. Things are a lot looser on field trips. They treat you more like junior officers than cadets. You have a normal duty day and the evening off - unless there is a reception or a dance. I'll probably be able to get a weekend - Friday evening to Sunday - off to come home. Tom would like to come with me. We'll be in the same squadron.

We'll also go to George and Norton Air Force Bases. Norton is by Riverside. I should be able to see Nanner Larsen. No, don't worry about money for the trip. We'll be paid Per Diem at the same rate as officers. It will be more than our cadet pay. The trip should be interesting. We will see Air Defense Command, the Military Air Transport Service , and Tactical Air Command operations. We'll travel by C-124 like we did when we went to D.C. Not all that comfortable, but free.

The weather here has been crazy since New Year's. We didn't have any rain or snow until last Saturday when we had a foot of snow. That was great because they cancelled the parade.

This will probably be the last letter for a while. Don't let that stop you from writing. And if you see Jim LeDoux, tell him and the gang (including the girls) to write. Well, must really close for now.

God Bless,
Your Loving Son,
Don

Chapter 45

Cadets are graded frequently so that their progress may be carefully evaluated . . .
US Air Force Academy Catalog

Monday, 14 January, 1958

Monday began what upperclassmen aptly describe as "Academic Hell Week." Major Galt was in fine form as he passed out his English final and the infamous "blue books.[107]" "I hope your study sessions had the right focus," he said. "You have three hours to provide in as much detail as possible: the history, the development of the plot, description and motivation of two characters, and the moral premise of Dostoyevsky in *Crime and Punishment.*

Thank you, Sutter, I thought. We had guessed right. Tom, Hertz, Gibbons, Koonce, Wilson, and I spent three hours Tuesday doing a complete analysis of *Crime and Punishment.* Even so, I struggled for the first hour and a half trying to organize my essay and address the history and development of Dostoyevsky's plot.

What made it difficult was that Dostoyevsky originally wrote the piece as a novella in September, 1865. In a letter to his friend, Alexander Wrangel, in February 1866, he admitted, "at the end of November much had been written and was ready; I burned it all; I can confess that now. I didn't like it myself. A new form . . . excited me, and I started all over again."

So the history was as complex as the plot and characters of the final Dostoyevsky novel. I characterized his protagonist, Rodion Raskolnikov and Rodion's prostitute friend, Sofia Semyonovna Marmeladova. I explained briefly their motivations and interrelationship. Sofia became a prostitute to provide for her family. She was compassionate and supported Rodion, even after he confessed his crimes of murder. A review by one critic who compared Sofia with Mary Magdalene made her character development easier.

Once I got rolling, my essay flowed quickly. Sutter gathered his papers and turned in his blue notebook about 0930, two hours into the class. I worked another half hour and felt I could not improve on what I had written.

---

[107] Blue books were 4"x6" booklets with blank, lined pages for entering your answers to essay questions.

Given the extra time by not having to take the Military Studies final and the fact we didn't have intramurals, a half hour nap seemed in order. Then I could hit the chemistry and math again before dinner. Chemistry's final was Tuesday; Math was on Wednesday.

Thursday morning was the graphics test with Philosophy on Thursday afternoon. Chemistry was a challenge, requiring the full four allotted hours. Fortunately, Jerry Leach's two years at Auburn in pre-med included a heavy dose of chemistry. Jerry covered the major elements and key formulas several times with the study group.

Tom was my savior in math. Math was a weaker area in the College Entrance Exams. In addition to the group sessions, Tom spent an extra two hours prepping me for the final. I used the allotted three hours.   solved all the problems completely except the final one which came directly out of *College Algebra — Third Edition.*

The Problem read: "A farmer can plow a piece of land in 4 days using his tractor. His hired hand can plow the same piece of land using a smaller tractor in 6 days. How many days will be required for the plowing if they work together?"

I wasn't sure how I was ever going to use this example as a pilot. I looked at the clock. *Oh, crap,* I thought, *I don't have enough time. Oh well, hell, here goes.*

If I let x be the number of days required to plow the field with both working, I can say 1/x is the part of the field plowed by the two in one day. And 1/4 is the part plowed by the farmer in a day and 1/6 is the part plowed by the hired hand.

Now, that means that $1/4 + 1/6 = 1/x$ . . .

"Time," called out Captain Marsh. "Pencils down. I'll be by to collect your blue books."

Crap, didn't finish. At least I got the formula set up. I should get at least 80 percent credit.

Graphics was a piece of cake compared to math and chemistry. I struggled a little, but completed the required drawing with a minimum of erasures. I recalled mechanical drawing was the one C I had in high school.

I loved Philosophy; playing with the mind seemed a good exercise. Philosophy was the last exam. Captain Stan Graham essentially taught us the final in the last two weeks of the course. He would read a statement and stamp his foot. Captain Graham said that his instruction was his belated Christmas present to us.

***

I was relieved, but exhausted when I finished the Philosophy exam at 1430. I headed for the Fourth Class Club where the gang had decided to go after the last final. The Club was open at 1500 and would be open until 2100. Call to Quarters had been moved back to 2130. Arnold Hall was open for upperclassmen. Those upperclassmen (both Third and Second Classmen) lucky enough to have Faculty sponsors could use a dining privilege.

Hertz, Kerr, Cloud, and Sutter were standing outside the Club waiting for the doors to open. I was surprised to see Sutter. Tom was considered somewhat of an academic nerd. He usually kept to himself. Yet, among all of us there was an unspoken and growing kindred ship.

***

Hi, guys," I said. as the doors opened. "What are we waiting for; let's go get a couple of pizzas." Hertz was up in an instant and began taking preferences. "Let's see: Two pepperoni and mushroom, two sausage and extra cheese, and two plain cheese."

"Where's Linda?" asked Cloud.

"School's not out yet. I didn't invite her. I'm too exhausted to talk. Where's Cindy?"

"She's working. Said she had some overtime things to do getting ready for military evaluation boards. Besides, I'm like you. Not sure I could carry on a decent conversation."

"Oh, too bad, your guys will just have to put up with male company," said Koonce.

"Ah, Koonce, just because you can't get a date with a girl, don't be a wise guy."

Since exams were over, we could discuss questions, answers, and grade prospects. Everyone, except Tom, bitched about the math test.

"I think I aced it," said Tom, causing hooting and expletives directed at him from the rest of the group.

"Did you hear what Ben Johnson did in Philosophy?" asked Kerr.

"No," said Twy in chorus with the rest of us, "but I heard he was quitting and taking the finals in hopes he could get some credit at a civilian college."

"Yeah, that's what I heard too. So on the Philosophy test where it asked 'What is a more?' he put 'When the moon hits your eye like a big pizza pie, that's a more.'"

Everyone groaned.

"Where'd you hear that?" asked Kerr.

"Ben told me himself. He said he was down two classes, math and chemistry, so he might as well have a little fun on the way out."

"How many do you think we'll lose?" asked Koonce?

"Well," said Cloud, "Cindy said the class of 1960 had 5% fail on their first finals. Since she said we have 280 right now that would be 14. Of course, there are still turn-outs and there might even be a turn back or two. I think some guys, like Johnson, are looking for a way out."

"Yeah, I've heard of classmates like that," I said, looking at Hertz.

He shrugged.

***

Friday was eerie. We expected a return of the inquisition at breakfast; however, conversations at virtually all squadron areas, except Second Squadron, were low key. Little was asked of Fourth Classmen except additional food requests. The upperclassmen bandied questions around about tests, gave their evaluations of how they did, and speculated about classmates who might have failed.

Shortly after the meal began, Cadet Thomas looked up and said, "Sit at ease. No talking and carry on with your regular duties" Pausing a minute, he asked, "Do any of you think you failed any courses?"

We all responded, "No, Sir."

***

Friday afternoon, Fourth Classmen were at liberty to check the bulletin boards for their final grades. We were to record our grades and to pass them to our respective flight commanders. Anyone failing a course was to report to Cadet Lt. Col. Jay after evening meal.

As I anxiously scanned the bulletin board to get a look at my grades. *What if I failed a course —which one, math or chemistry? Could I pass a turn out? What if I failed both—I would be out. What if I failed one, would I take a turn back. I don't know . . .*

Finally, I squeezed in. There was the potential dooms day sheet. I quickly scanned the sheet. No grade was below 70. I let out a long, slow breath and smiled. I took my pen and pad out and began writing: Chemistry, 85.6 (*wow!*); English, 84.4 (*gee, I thought that would be better*); Graphics, 81.2 (*not too bad*); Math, 82.4 (*yes!*); Military Studies, 94 (*I knew that!*); Philosophy, 92 (*what a great thinker!*) and Physical Education, 80.1 (*thank you, boxing*).

I turned, consciously undid my smile, and practically triple-timed back to the room. "Say, roomie, how did you do?" I asked Tom as I came into the room.

"All good, except the 80 in English. I would have liked to do better. But, then, you helped a lot. It would have been worse without your tutoring."

"You did even better for me; I dragged down an 82.4 in math."

***

The evening meal was loud, with upper classmen bragging or lamenting about their finals. "Davis, give me your high and low grades; subject, then grade," said C2C Thomas.

"Yes, Sir, I had 94 in Military Studies and an 80.1 in P.E. ah . . . physical education."

Koonce and Gibbons gave their grades.

"Okay, Mister Grey."

"Suh," began Grey, "I had an 83 in math and a 68 in chemistry."

"You had a 68 in Chemistry?"

"Yes, Suh."

"Well, we will have to do something about that. Super Sixth doesn't lose anybody, especially to academics. After you talk with the Squadron Commander, you will get together with Cadet Mays for as much time as you can spare. Cadet Mays is our expert in chem. Is that all right with you, Charley?"

"You bet. If we lose Grey, how will we have a foreign language to study at dinner?" Everyone except Grey snickered.

United States Air Force Academy
Friday, 12 January 1958

Dear Folks,

I'm really happy. I passed all my finals. In fact, even in PE, I had 80s or above. I got a 94 in Military Studies and a 92 in philosophy. I brought the PE grade up with my boxing scores. Speaking of boxing, I did well except for the bout with Jack Lite. I won two, lost one, and had a draw. The draw was really unfair. My coach and the audience thought I clearly won, but I was boxing a Second Classman. All of the judges were Second Classmen and the referee was a squadron mate of my opponent.

I haven't seen Linda for two weeks. Hope her football hero isn't making time with her. I did call twice. She sounded great - and understanding. She said she had cheerleading practice for basketball games and some finals, so she was busy too.

Hope you and Pa are in good health. I know it makes it hard when it is raining a lot there and Pa can't go to work. I was lucky when I was working last summer. It was hotter than the dickens, but we never lost work days because of rain. Of course, I lost some time when that machine ran over my fingers on that Campbell Soup project. That was okay; I didn't like running the jackhammer that much.

I would appreciate it if you would send any income tax forms that come. I should have statements from Weinstock-Lubin. I doubt if I will owe taxes even with our incredible salary here. Yes, Mom, I received the money and newspapers. Thanks for both. I like reading the *Bee*, it feels like home. I like to keep up on Grant High.. I've been looking for that boodle box you promised. Being back on the Fourth Class diet, I could use some supplemental nutrition.

Sarah, Tom's sister, sent us chocolate chip cookies and a nice letter to me. Guess I'll have to make a trip to Long Island with Tom. Of course, Sarah is only a junior in high school, so she is a little young -but nice.

Didn't save much money over Christmas; a lot to do, but it all cost money. The Sanders, of course, gave me a lot of free rides. I used the money you just sent to pay back Tom for some I borrowed. It was no sweat for him because his folks kept giving him money.

Well, Mom, only four months until we'll be out that way. Can't wait. In only 140 more days I will no longer be a lowly Fourth Classman. Hooray. It was nice having a taste of normal during Christmas, but it's really hard getting back into the traces. I don't know how many we lost to academics. We had 280 at the end of Christmas break. Hertz was thinking about flunking out, but he made above 70 (the magic number) in all of his courses. He must have studied hard because he was on the border line in a couple of classes.

I do know of one class mate who purposely failed. His name is Ben Johnson. He is kind of a smart aleck. For the philosophy question: "What is a more?" He answered, "When the moon hits your eye like a big pizza pie, that's amore." We thought it was funny; the instructor didn't. Ben got a 60 on the exam, which was okay because he was carrying an 86 average so he passed the course. Anyway, I'm relieved. I survived my first bout with academics. Guess I won't be coming home early. Whew!

Write and tell my friends to write. I miss the mail.

> God Bless,
> Your loving son,
> Don

Chapter 46

A cadet who is deficient in an Academic . . . course at the end of a semester may be discharged,
turned back to the next succeeding class, or required to repeat the failed course.
Academic Q&A by Superintendent Major General James E. Briggs

Sunday, 26 January, 1958

Monday after finals week was strange. People in all classes were missing from formations. The Academy Board, the advisory board to the Superintendent on deficient cadets, was very busy.

Third Classman John Douglas struggled with Physics all semester. He failed the final and turnout tests. Failing one course, he was given the option of resigning or washing back. He chose to join our class. He'll join us on the field trip after Recognition. He has to take physics again; however, he can validate classes he took and take optional classes in their place.

Tuesday evening, after dinner, Tom, Hertz, Kerr and I sat with John (he said since he was going to be in our class, call him "John") Douglas in the game room and discussed his Monday encounter with the Academy Board.

"First of all, it was intimidating. I mean the Supe, the Commandant, the Dean, and the horse holders; how could it not be intimidating. They had obviously reviewed my academic and military records. Except for physics, my academics are good, mostly in the eighties. I am in the top fifteen percent of military standing in my class. They asked me why I had so much difficulty with physics. I answered as truthfully as I could. I said I didn't have physics in high school and didn't understand my Academy instructor. He was a nuclear physicist R&D at Wright Patterson[108] and talked over our heads."

'Well', the Supe said, 'your final and test scores were in the high fifties, indicating you really didn't understand the subject. Do you think you could repeat the course and pass?' Yes, Sir, I replied. I will get extra instruction from the beginning and have classmates help me.

'Okay, now, do you want to leave or will you take a turn back to the Class of 1961?'

---

[108] Wright-Patterson Air Force Base in Ohio is the home of the Wright Air Development Center which included a Plans and Operations Department (WOO) and Divisions for Aeronautics (WCN), Flight Test (WCT), Research (WCR), Weapons Components (WCE), and Weapons Systems (WCS). It is also the site of the US Air Force Museum.

I was very nervous, but tried to convince the Board I wanted to stay and would take a turn back to the Class of 1961.

After asking the other Board members if they had questions, General Briggs said, 'Cadet Douglas, the Board will consider your situation and give you a determination this afternoon.' True to his word, I got the results of the Board yesterday about 1600. Of course, I am disappointed, but I'm determined to finish. Thank you guys for listening to me."

***

The previous Saturday was business as usual. The room inspection was tough, with Captain Braswell checking laundry bags for clean clothes and desk drawers for contraband. Rumor was Cadet Jay warned the upperclassmen our AOC was going to go through drawers. Before the inspection, the latrines had odors that were not after shave lotion smells.

Tom and I received demerits for "poorly made beds and shoes not properly aligned under the beds." Standing behind Captain Braswell, Cadet Jay shrugged and smirked knowing our beds were some of the best in the Squadron and hardly anyone checked shoe alignments. Our four demerits were low, including upperclassmen demerits. Word was the Commandant thought upperclassmen were getting lax and had not gotten over Christmas leave.

Six inches of snow didn't cancel in-ranks, but the fifteen degree temperature did cut it short. The falling snow measured eighteen inches and led to a cancelled parade.

***

I was worried about Linda traveling in the snow, but she said she'd be with a friend who was dating a classmate and the friend had good snow tires on her car. It promised to be another exciting evening with a show and pizza afterward. But I was anxious to see Linda; it had been a long time.

Linda came into the Fourth Class Club wearing a long, fox collar beige coat and a Russian cap. Her cheeks were red from the cold. Her hair was ruffled. She struck me as being cuter than ever.

"Hi," I said taking her coat. "Did you have any problems on the way?"

"No, the Denver DOT is keeping the roads cleared. It was only 20 minutes from my house. Dad said if it gets worse, call him and he'll bring the four wheel drive jeep. We'd pick up the car tomorrow. Don, this is Janet. She has a date with Ben Wilson. Have you seen him?"

Janet was a petite, well-stacked redhead with hazel eyes and a doll-shaped face. "Yes," I said, directing the two girls toward the dance floor. When he saw us come in, Ben headed our way. "Hey, Ben, this is Janet."

"Wow," said Ben. "Linda said she was going to get me a date with a cute friend, but she didn't say she was bringing the prom queen."

Janet blushed. I smirked at Ben's come-on line. *Janet is cute,* I thought. *But Linda is still the prize.* "Jan, Ben is a New York boy who fancies himself as a ladies' man. But you'll be safe enough with Linda and me as escorts."

Ben grimaced. "Don't listen to him, Janet; he's never gotten over being a Boy Scout."

Since the girls hadn't eaten, we ordered hamburgers and milk shakes.. The snow continued to fall. We decided to skip the movie and let the girls go home early. The jukebox was going continuously, playing mostly slow dancing music. There were probably 30 couples in the club; mostly cadets with steady girlfriends.

"I missed you," Linda said pressing a little closer as we danced to Fats Domino's *Blueberry Hill.* The song reminded me of a strawberry blonde I dated in high school, but being with Linda, the memory was only fleeting. "I'm sorry I couldn't be with you more at Christmas. I know you had a good time, but it would have been much better if we'd been together."

"I agree. I missed you too. It would have been especially nice to be alone with you outside the monastery." I had purchased an Academy pin over the holidays with the intent to get "pinned" to Linda.[109] I decided; however, to see how our reunion went; realizing we had missed a lot during Christmas ,and I was uncertain if her feelings toward me had changed.

"I understand you went out a lot with Tom's sister," Linda said, somewhat accusingly. "Did you have a good time?"

"Yes, I took Sarah to several events, but it was more of a favor to Tom. Just so you know, Tom threatened me with bodily harm if I got too cozy with Sarah. She's a high school junior, and I'll probably never see her again. How do you know so much about my Christmas?"

"Oh, I have my spies," Linda said as she smiled and moved even closer.

The snow continued, increasing in intensity. At 2030, we decided to send the girls home.

---

[109] Being "pinned" was the equivalent of high school's "going steady." A cadet would offer a girl an Academy pin to wear. It was a commitment, but less than an engagement.

"Call my orderly room, Linda, when you get home and tell them to give me a note. I want to make sure you make it home all right."

"That's sweet," Linda said, kissing me on the cheek after checking for upperclassmen.

"Damn, Ben, it's time like this that makes me think about regular college. I don't think I was born to be a monk. I would like to take Linda out on a real date."

"Yeah, by the way, tell Linda thanks for setting me up with Jan. She's nice. Wouldn't mind getting her alone. Well, hell. Hang in there; in 134 more days, we'll be half human again."

***

United States Air Force Academy
Sunday, 26 January 1958

Dear Folks,

Sorry I haven't written. After finals, the upperclassmen began a "buck up," a tightening of the Fourth Class System. Ramp time is worse; now they ask current events—which require research time. Even the academic departments get into the act, increasing homework and pop quizzes.

We've had a flu outbreak. Tom had a slight case. Kerr went back in the hospital; said 80 cadets are in the hospital. Yesterday we had in-ranks inspection with six inches of snow and a temperature of fifteen degrees. The snow was so thick, they canceled the parade.

Captain Braswell was really hard on upperclassmen. He was looking for contraband. One upperclassman joked that before the inspection, the toilets were all drunk from consuming so much alcohol.

I told you I did well on finals; made the Superintendent's List. You have to have 80 in all classes and be in the top third in Military Standing.

After boxing, I was put on the water polo team. I don't swim that well and end up swallowing half he pool. I'm on defense in the shallow end . You are not supposed to touch the bottom, but . . . It's a good thing I didn't go to the Coast Guard Academy; I'd have flunked out on swimming.

The good news is Cadet Thomas, the Varsity Tennis Team Manager, asked me to be his assistant. I'll get to sit at an athletic table. I'll be able to eat. I won't have to worry about my weight since I won't be boxing.

Only 126 days until Recognition. Boy, this has been one of the hardest years of my life. Can't wait to be an upperclassman. The academics will still be hard, maybe even harder, but we won't have the additional pressure of being low on the totem pole. Only 128 days or so until we will be out your way and I get to see the family and my friends again. I'm really looking forward to being with you.

You and Lucille can send more goodies. We can buy some things at the Cadet Store, but it is hard to get there and back because of some of the upperclassmen. The boodle boxes will keep Tom and me from starving.

God Bless,
Your loving son,
Don

Chapter 47

"If I'd only known . . .
Talon Article by C/4C Lee Butler

Sunday, 16 February, 1958

"Davis . . . **DAVIS,** get up your damn alarm is going off."

"Uhhh, Okay, Tom, I got it." Getting up from my comforter, I prepared for sentry duty. *Helluva way to spend your Saturday night.* Frost on the window indicated I was in for my second chilly guard duty night. I slipped on long johns, a Lowry BX[110] skiing purchase; struggled into my fatigues over the insulated underwear, and then wrapped the Artic parka, furnished by the Academy, around my inner layers.

As confirmed by my steamy breath as I exited the dorm, the temperature was an invigorating 15⁰ Fahrenheit. The 14 knot wind whipped the snow around in little eddies. With my gloves on, I re-gripped my M1. C3C Brown, the CCQ, was waiting.

"Okay, Davis, General Orders."

"Sir, General Orders are: I will guard all within the limits of my post and quit my post only when properly relieved. I will obey my special orders and perform all my duties in a military manner. I will report violations of my special orders, emergencies, and anything not covered in my instructions to the Cadet in Charge of Quarters, C3C Brown." *Damn, glad Tom reminded me about General Orders. Hertz got 3 demerits last week for not knowing General Orders.*

"Post, Dumbsquat," said Brown. Dressed only in the regular cadet parka, he quickly turned and headed for the warmth of the dorm.

***

What was that? Did I see a shadow? "Halt, who goes there?"

"Friend," a familiar voice called out.

"Advance and be recognized," I remembered from FASE.

A tall, uniformed figure slipped into the light from the outside building lamps. Recognizing Captain Braswell, I came to a position of rifle salute. "Good evening, Sir."

"Evening, Davis, at ease. Bit nippy tonight, isn't it. Glad to see you're awake; here take this," Captain Braswell said, handing me a steaming cup of hot chocolate.

"Thank you, Sir," I said, relishing the thought of a cup of hot chocolate.

"When's your tour up?"

"At 0200, Sir."

---

[110] BX = Base Exchange. Army military stores are known as Post Exchanges.

"By the way, the cute Fraulein's picture is much better than the dog. Carry on."

I chuckled. I knew Captain Braswell enjoyed Linda's picture. During the last room inspection, he looked at her picture, ran his glove across my bottom book shelf, and didn't even looked at his glove for dust.

***

"Gosh, Linda, it seems like forever since I've seen you."

"I know, Don, I've really missed you. I had to go to those away basketball games, and my folks insisted I go to New Mexico. Dad says I'm not going to be home much longer, and they want to spend time with me. Actually, I'd rather have been with you."

Hmm! She' genuinely sorry we've been apart. I'll give her the pin. "You know what?"

"No, what . . .?"

"I didn't get you a Christmas present," I said, handing her a small colorfully wrapped package.

"Oh, well, I didn't get you anything . . ."

"Actually you did. You gave me that lovely picture I drool over every night."

She opened the package and seemed delighted at the stuffed falcon. "Oh, Don, that's cute. I'll put it up on my dresser. Then when I go to bed I can think of you."

Damn lucky falcon. "I like it you'll be thinking of me when you go to bed. Uh . . . I have something else."

"What?"

I handed her the box with the Academy pin.

She opened the box, took out the pin, and gave me the smile that always melted me. "Oh, Don, I'm not sure I can take this if it means we're pinned—like going steady. I mean, there are going to be times when I want to go out and . . ."

"Yeah, I understand. But I'd like you to wear it. And it doesn't mean you should miss any of your high school events or be unescorted . . . unless it's always with Bill."

"Okay, that's fair. And I understand if you go on trips; you may date . . . as long as it's not serious. Would you put the pin on, please?" she said.

We decided to skip the movie and spent the evening dancing. The Club was crowded, so the jukebox played continuously. As always, Linda's warm body pressing close to me and her enchanting perfume—which she teasingly told me was "seduction" by Shalimar—excited me to the point I had to set out one or two dances, explaining I needed to refresh our cokes.

During a music break, we wandered over to Kerr's table. Beside Art was a striking, tall blonde. "Hi, Davis, Hi Linda," Art greeted us. "Linda, Don, this is my friend, Dagmar."

I couldn't help thinking the slender; healthy bodied, young lady certainly fit her exotic name. "Hi, Dagmar, nice to meet you; presume you've received the standard warnings about Art?"

Dagmar gave me a quizzical look.

"Just kidding. Art's a good fellow, well met. I'm sure you'll enjoy his company."

Frowning, Art said, "Right, Davis, I'll deal with you later."

We spent 20 minutes getting to know Dagmar. A high school senior at Christian Academy; Linda and Dagmar spent the time comparing notes on their schools.

I squeezed Linda's hand as we said good night. I couldn't do more as the Officer in Charge, Captain Ellis, was by the exit observing Fourth Classmen saying good night. Ellis, not a favorite AOC, had written up several of my classmates for PDA.

"Goodnight, Don," Linda said carefully putting her hand on my coat sleeve. "Thank you for the Falcon. I'm really pleased about the pin. I'll wear it, even on dates."

Once again, the wind produced an extra chill as I double-timed to the barracks.

***

In the table shuffle, I saw familiar faces: Tom, Dickson, and Kerr. A new face at the table was Tenny Takahashi. Tenny was from Hawaii, reported to belong to one of the seven most prominent island families. Because of his name and Japanese ancestry, Tenny had more than his share of grief from upperclassmen. Cadet Jay, however, told our upperclassmen to lay off Tenny; to treat him like any other of our classmates. I'd also seen Sixth Squadron upperclassmen shield Tenny from other squadron upperclassmen. The others at the table were all familiar Second and Third Classmen.

"Dickson," purred C3C Bourque, "who's the Fighting Falcons football coach?"

"Sir, the coach of the Fighting Falcons football team is Buck Shaw."

"Really, Mr. Dickson. And is that Shaw's proper name?"

"Ah, no. Sir. But I don't know his proper name."

"Why not?"

"Well, Sir, I've never . . ."

"What, dumbsmack," Bourque said with a mischievous grin.

"No excuse, Sir."

"Right, have it for me by dinner. And you're pulling another Rip Van Winkle. Davis, who's the Falcons football coach?"

Thank goodness Tom and I talked about the new coach. "Sir, the NEW Fighting Falcons football coach is Benjamin S. Martin –whose nickname is Ben."

"Okay, Davis, let's have the rest of it.

"Sir, Coach Martin was the University of Virginia head coach for the past two years. He played football at Princeton before going to Canoe U, where he graduated in

1946. An assistant coach at Annapolis before Virginia. He was born in Prospect Park, Pennsylvania."

"What was his record at Virginia?"

"Sir, his record was 3 and 7 and 3, 6, and 1."

"And why do you think Martin was chosen?"

"Sir, I believe he was chosen because he has a military academy background and will understand cadets and the cadet program. A classmate football player told me Coach Shaw knew football fundamentals, but didn't understand the difficult lives of cadets. It's rumored Coach Shaw and Colonel Simlar, the Athletic Director, had heated discussions because Coach Shaw held players after the scheduled practice time, making them late for formations."

"Wow, Davis," Bourque said smirking. "Good poop, eat!"

***

"Sir, there are five minutes until first period. The uniform is Class B Blues and parka. The uniform for C Flight is flight suits, flight jackets, and boots. Five minutes, Sir." C4C Dickson was minute caller.

"Now what?" said Tom, hanging up his blues and reaching for his flight suit.

"Don't you ever read the schedule, Tom?"

"Yeah, so what?"

"Today we have an airmanship course all day—altitude chamber."

"I heard about that from some B Flight guys. The good news is it takes all day."

***

When we arrived at the buses, I was surprised and pleased to see a brand new Academy bus. Light blue, it had "United States Air Force Academy" in large letters along both sides in silver lettering. On the front was a Peregrine Falcon sitting on a gloved hand. "Fighting Falcons" was written in black letters under the hand.

"Hi," I said to Mr. Jacob, a driver hired for the new buses.

"Hello," said Mr. Jacob, waving and giving me a friendly smile.

Boy, I'm glad they don't indoctrinate support personnel in the Fourth Class System. That would be too much. Seeing Hertz and Kerr near the back of the bus, I went in their direction. "Man, what you think of our new busses. They're neat."

"Yeah, shit hot!" said Kerr.

"Where'd you get that expression, Kerr? The upper classmen will eat you alive if they hear you saying that," I said.

"Maybe. I got it from Captain Miller. He's a fighter pilot and apparently that's a favorite expression of theirs."

"Hi, Hertz," I said, changing the subject. I wasn't sure you were going to be with us. I saw your grades. Not barnburners, but they were all above the magic 70. You stayin' with us?"

"Yeah, I decided to give it a go. I even studied my butt off for finals. After I got the grades, I talked with an airline pilot father of a girlfriend."

"Girlfriend?"

"Yeah, just a friend. Anyway her father convinced me the mature and smart thing to do was finish the program. He says after pilot training and a tour, the airlines will be eager to talk to me. So what the hell; here I am."

As we settled into the rear seats, Kerr asked: "Did you guys hear about Meyers?"

"No, what now?" *I remembered Ken received a Class III after our first open post because he came back smelling like a brewery. He was looking forward to a dismal Christmas because his Class III wasn't going to be forgiven. Then General White absolved everybody…that included Ken. So we thought he would stay.*

"You know everyone likes Ken," Art started. "Anyway, he flunked a math turnout. We thought he'd be "conditioned"—take the course and test again during the summer. Then he turned himself in for drinking on a dining permit during Christmas. Since he was signed out, it would have been an honor violation if he hadn't turned himself in. So the Head Shed gave him the same punishment he received in November. Well, with 80 demerits, they kicked him out on demerits and academics."

"Damn," Hertz said. "If he didn't have bad luck, he wouldn't have any at all."

Art said. "Well, he did it to himself. His last words to me were rather funny though. He said: 'If I'd only known…I wouldn't have come here in the first place.

***

TSgt. Brown escorted us into a warehouse-looking building. Inside, was a large white box with side windows; benches, oxygen masks, pads, and pencils. The inside resembled a trolley car with side benches stretching the length of the box. The oxygen system was arranged with two sets of masks coming out of a center console that contained the regulator with dual controls similar to those found on aircraft.

At the far end of the building, we entered a classroom. On the front wall was a large chalk board. "Welcome, gentlemen," said MSgt. Little. "Welcome to physiological training. You know me and Sergeant Brown. This is Chief Master Sergeant Norman Wells. This is his small kingdom."

"Good morning, gentlemen," said MSgt. Wells.

"Good morning, Chief," we answered in unison.

"Please have a seat. This morning we will learn about the atmosphere, oxygen, and lack of oxygen (hypoxia). We will show you your symptoms of hypoxia and have a refresher on oxygen systems you'll use in your cadet career.

As you know, the atmosphere is made up of gasses—oxygen, carbon dioxide, nitrogen, and a few others. Oxygen makes up approximately 21% of the atmosphere. At 18,000 feet one half of the oxygen is gone. Flying, you must use supplementary oxygen above 10,000 feet."

In the next hour, MSgt. Wells covered hypoxia; its causes and effects; emphasizing the importance of taking quick corrective action in a potential hypoxia situation. The critical first step, he stressed, is donning an oxygen mask or using a walk-around oxygen bottle.

"Okay, gentlemen, it's important to understand the information in this test; anyone not receiving a 90 will have extra instruction and a retake," said TSgt. Little.

The multiple choice test took 20 minutes to complete. Kerr, Dickson, and I got hundreds. Everyone except Tyler and Hertz got 90% or better. While we enjoyed box lunches in the lounge, Tyler and Hertz received special instruction from MSgt. Wells.

As the two of them joined us, I asked: "So, did you finally pass?"

"Yeah," said Hertz, "MSgt. Wells says it's pass or fail test. Everyone passed, and it will show up as a hundred for the course for everyone. That's a gift."

***

The rest of C Flight intently watched Hertz, Kerr, Takahashi, and Dickson through the large side windows. "Ten thousand feet," called MSgt Wells over the public address (PA) system, which transmitted both outside and inside the sealed chamber. MSgt Little and Sergeant Brown sat between the pairs of cadets.

"Twenty-two thousand feet. Okay, gentlemen, masks off. Begin writing your names on the pads. Note your feelings as hypoxia progresses. You may become agitated, have a feeling of euphoria, or begin to feel faint."

Hertz and Kerr—asked to stand and do jumping jacks three times, then sit—lasted eight minutes. Takahashi and Dickson, who merely sat, lasted eleven minutes. Approximately 45 seconds after putting their masks on, all seemed to fully recover.

"Good, gentlemen," said the MSgt. "You all lasted a little longer than average. We attribute that to living at 5,000 feet and acclimating to that altitude. Now, look at your pads, see how your writing deteriorated, and note your symptoms. Next, we're going to 25,000 feet. You will all remain seated. Begin writing your names and continue writing with masks off."

With masks off, all four acted normal until about five minutes. Watching the writing of the cadets, Sergeant Brown quickly helped Hertz and Kerr put on their masks.

MSgt. Little put Takahashi's mask on. When he turned to Dickson, Jim was beginning to shake. As Little tried to help Jim on with his mask, Jim swung at the Sergeant. Sgt. Brown jumped up and held Jim while MSgt. Little put the mask on. Again, all recovered, but in ninety seconds or so this time.

"Crap," I said to Pat Grey, "Jim's going to catch hell for that!"

"Nah, I don't think so. It's like a guy who is real drunk. He doesn't really know what he's doing. I bet they see that all the time."

Takahashi lasted the longest, three minutes at 30,000 feet. The others were masked up at two minutes. It was obvious that individual coordination was affected went much faster at that altitude. Everyone recovered slowly.

"Good," said Wells. "Now we will bring the chamber down slowly. When we reach 10,000 feet, take your masks off. You may ride from there with masks off."

All four cadets took off their masks at 10,000 feet. Strangely, I noticed the instructors left their masks on. When all four had their masks off, they started talking to their partner. Suddenly, there was a loud rushing sound and the chamber filled with condensation.

"MASKS ON, MASKS ON, MASKS ON," Wells called over the PA system. Hertz and Dickson struggled to get their masks on and had to be helped. "That, gentlemen, was a rapid decompression. If that occurs and you don't have your oxygen mask on, you must immediately put it on. A rapid decompression cuts your time of useful conscientiousness (TUC) in half. Okay, hang the masks on the pegs and come out. Next group suit up."

***

"Okay," Wells began. "I left out an important instruction. In addition to hypoxia effects, your bodily gases expand as you go up. If you don't relieve yourselves by flatulating—'farting' in cadet vernacular—you'll feel pain; a pain that can be debilitating. I noticed Mr. Hertz and Mr. Dickson looked pained at 22,000 feet. Mr. Kerr, who has had flight experience, and Mr. Takahashi just did what comes naturally; they performed the proper procedure."

"Yeah, I noticed the place was pretty stinky," interjected Kerr.

"True, Mr. Kerr, makes you appreciate the oxygen masks even more," continued the MSgt. "Now, I want this group to perform the proper exercise, in addition to paying attention to hypoxia. Are there any questions? . . . Yes, Mister Grey?"

"Suh, how do you do this flat u lance maneuver?"
"It's very simple, Mr. Grey. As you go up in altitude, you lift your butt off the bench and let nature take its course. Okay, next four in the box."

***

Having observed the first session, the rest of us did well; including the decompression. Everyone had masks in place within 20 seconds. Our TUC's[111] were comparable with the first four, except Grey who had trouble with his mask at 30,000 feet and had to be helped by MSgt. Little. Each chamber ride took an hour. With fifteen minute breaks and instruction in between, it was 1630 when we finished the chamber.

"How do you feel gentlemen? Who's tired?" asked MSgt. Wells. Eight hands shot up.

"Who has a headache?" Four hands were raised. "Well, those are natural reactions. You should wake up refreshed in the morning. To avoid evening meal, we're will have another box lunch and a 45-minute hypoxia movie. (A mock cheer sounded.)

When you return to your barracks, you are authorized to go directly to your rooms. A note, signed by the Flight Surgeon, will confirm you are confined to quarters for the evening. I hope you have enjoyed your ride in the box (there were groans from my classmates) and learned something important to you throughout your careers."

We applauded and got in line to get our box lunches.

***

"Tom, the MSgt. was right. I'm bone tired and I have a slight headache. I guess it's all right to take the two aspirins they gave us."

"Davis, you're a wimp. Take the aspirin and hit the comforter."

I scowled at Tom and lay down.

---

[111] TUC – time of useful consciousness.

United States Air Force Academy
Sunday, 16 February 1958

Dear Folks,

Sorry I haven't written. We are in "spring funk." The weather is cold, grey, and sometimes snowing. We've had a couple of spring-like days - in the seventies. The days are short and the routine monotonous. The upperclassmen still harass us at meals, but they leave us alone during call to quarters.

Courses are as hard as ever, with lots of pop quizzes and graded reviews. I'm doing all right in the mid to high eighties. I got a 94 in my English speech on the value of high school sports; learning teamwork, making good friends, learning how to compete, and lose.

I had sentry duty on Tuesday. Whenever I have the duty, it's freezing. It was fifteen degrees and snowed. Captain Braswell surprised me about 0100. He was checking on me, but brought me hot chocolate. Guess AOC's never sleep.

How are you and Pa? Are you still looking at that fishing camp up at Clear Lake? Pa likes to fish so much and he is good at smoozing people.

We had a really interesting time Friday. C flight took our physiological training course. We learn all about hypoxia - the lack of oxygen. Then we go in the altitude chamber - it's a big pressurized box (actually, it is a depressurized box) - that simulates going up to altitude.

*You take your oxygen mask off at different altitudes to see how long it takes to get hypoxic. You write your name over and over on a pad. As you get hypoxic, it starts looking like "hen scratching" as Pa would say. We were there
all day, had two box lunches there, and didn't have to go to evening meal.*

I was really tired afterward. Tom and I slept like logs. We lucked out Saturday because it snowed all night (two feet) and it was still snowing Saturday morning. The temperature was fifteen degrees. With all of the flu (80 cadets were in the hospital), there weren't enough cadets for a parade and they cancelled the in-ranks inspections as well.

Linda and I got "pinned" Saturday night, but we agreed she should go to her school functions with a date and that I would probably meet girls on my trips and could have "casual" dates. She is a lovely girl.

Varsity sports are well. Basketball has a 10-3 record, but lost to Loyola of Chicago last week. The fencing team beat Illinois 18-6, but lost to Notre Dame 15-12. Gymnastics lost to Iowa 66-44, but two of our best guys were out. The rifle team, that lost to West Point last year, is undefeated. Swimming and skiing usually come in third in fields of six or seven. The wrestling team just lost its first match.

Well, graded reviews are coming this week, so I'd better get to studying.

God Bless,
Your loving son,
Don

Chapter 48

The light plane crash had quite an effect on cadets in all classes. We were forcefully reminded that the future we planned . . . involved a very dangerous occupation
Comment by Bob Heriza in Man's Flight Through Life

Sunday, 28 February, 1958

The 21st of February was a typical day before upperclassmen went on leave – hard. The occasion was Washington's Birthday. We were at ease after Friday classes. Only upperclassmen on Class III confinement were around; the rest used their weekend privileges.

"Davis," said Cadet DeSantis at Friday noon meal, let's have the poop on Alpha One."

"Sir, Alpha One, or Explorer I, was launched 1 January 1958, at 2248 Eastern Daylight Time. It was the third satellite after Sputniks 1 and 2. Its mission was to study the Van Allen Radiation Belt. A Juno booster launched the satellite. Dr. Werner Von Braun developed the Juno from the World War II V-2."

"And who is Von Braun?"

"Sir, Doctor Von Braun is a captured German rocket scientist brought to the United States to work on our rocket programs."

"Right, and what is the Army doing in space; isn't the Air Force responsible for space?"

"Yes, Sir. I believe the Army is working with rockets because they acquired Dr. Von Braun and were working on the program before the Air Force separated from the Army."

"Okay, but that should be our mission. What about the satellite itself?"

"Sir, the satellite was built for United States participation in the International Geophysical Year. The Jet Propulsion Laboratory (known as JPL) built the satellite. Sir, the satellite weighs nearly 31 pounds, 18 of which is instrumentation."

"What was throw weight of the Soviet's first Sputnik?"

"Sir, Sputnik One weighed 184 pounds."

"So they are still ahead of us. Good job, Davis, eat."

Cadet DeSantis' questioning left me little time to eat. "'I'm starving," I moaned to Tom.

"Oh, suck it up, Davis. Arnold Hall has hamburgers and shakes. You won't starve."

***

I spotted Art and Cindy as I came into Arnold Hall to grab a hamburger.

"Crap, Davis, did you see what happened yesterday morning?" Art said, holding an evening addition of the Denver Post.

"No, I've been studying all afternoon. I didn't leave my room.

"Third Classman Richard Davis bought the farm out at Stapleton."

"Bought the farm?" Cindy asked.

"Oh, I'm sorry," Art said, "that's a pilot's term for getting killed in an airplane crash. Here, let me read you the story." Art unfolded the paper.

DENVER POST
Saturday February 22, 1958

Air Force Academy Cadet Third Class Richard Davis was killed this morning in the crash of a light aircraft at Stapleton Field. Davis and fellow classmate, Willard Johnson, were practicing touch and go landings in a single engine; tandem, open cockpit converted Army aircraft when Davis, who was the pilot in the rear cockpit, overshot the runway and crashed.

According to an eye witness report, Davis overshot the runway and banked sharply to attempt to align with the runway. The aircraft lost speed, stalled, and started to slide sideways, headed toward the ground.

Realizing his predicament, Davis lowered the nose and applied full throttle. The aircraft impacted the ground at one hundred miles an hour.

Reports from the ground indicated Davis broke his seatbelt, hit the instrument panel, and went through the floorboards. He suffered multiple fractures, head, and back injuries. He died at the hospital. Johnson, who is in critical condition, also broke his seat belt, hit the instrument panel, but did not go through the floor.

Davis is the first cadet to die at the Academy, reported the Academy Public Relations Office.

"Oh, that's terrible," said Cindy. Art and I agreed.

We ordered hamburgers and milkshakes and Art and Cindy danced a few dances, but the crash left a pall over the evening's activities.

***

Back at the dorm at 2300, I decided to call Linda. She told me the dance ended at 10:00. She answered on the third ring. "Hi."

"Hi," Linda replied. "Hoping you'd call. I like to hear your voice when I can't see you."

"Yeah, how was the dance and Fred, isn't it?"

"Oh, Fred was fine. He's just a friend. We have a journalism class together."

"Hmmm, Okay. Would you like to go to Glen Eyrie with me next weekend? The Cadet Protestant Choir is having a picnic and Fourth Classmen are invited."

"What is Glen Eyrie?"

"Glen Eyrie is a Tudor style castle built by General William Palmer, the founder of Colorado Springs, in 1903. It's down by the Springs. The Navigators, who own Glen Eyrie, have a picnic ground they are letting the choir use for free."

"How will we get there?"

"Well, Fourth Classmen are being allowed to go on our own. Call to Quarters has been extended. It's only for choir members. I thought we could use your car. Since it's a picnic, I can wear my picnic uniform. So, we could go to the Springs afterward. There is a great ice cream place there. I don't have to be back until call to quarters, ah…2000…ah, eight o'clock."

"Sure, Don, that sounds like fun, and I'll be able to get you away from the monastery."

***

It was 1010. Linda was 10 minutes late. I began to worry she had changed her mind about spending the day with me. I was delighted when her red Bel Air convertible turned onto the road beside the barracks. With a bright sun and 70 degrees, the top was down.

I had not seen Linda's car in the daytime. A Royal Canadian Mountie red, it had ample chrome in front and chrome flashes on the sides. The back fender fins were new for 1957.

"Hi," I said noticing Linda's long sleeve, red plaid cowboy shirt with Levi blue jeans and a red sweater that matched the color of her car draped around her shoulders.

"Hi," she said, getting out and coming around the front end. "Do you want to drive?"

"Not now. Maybe later." I took her hand and escorted her back to the driver's side.

As I got in she asked, "Do you know where we're going?"

"Of course, like any good boy scout, I'm prepared. Actually, someone in the choir made up a map and driving instructions. It'll take us about an forty-five minutes, so we should get there just in time for lunch."

As we left the south Lowry gate, Linda put her hand on mine. "I've missed you."

"I've missed you too," I said.

Linda turned on the radio. Elvis Presley's *All Shook Up* was playing. *Yeah, that fits,* I thought. *Linda does that to me.* Pat Boone came on with *Love Letters in the Sand. Well, that's pretty appropriate for here. There aren't any beaches, but there's a lot of sand to the east.*

Little Darlin' by the Diamonds and *Blueberry Hill* by Fats Domino took me back to Grant High days, but those thoughts vanished when Linda again took my hand and smiled.

Just before we got to route 87, Linda pulled off on a turn out. "Want to drive now?"

"Sure," I said, "but with the top up, just in case we run across an upperclassman."

We put the top up, and I jumped in the driver's seat. *Damn, I hope I remember how to drive—look at this, seat belts. Just like flying a jet. Oh, well, shouldn't be a problem with a four lane until the Springs. I'll have to give her back the car before we get close to Glen Eyrie.*

"Wow," I said as we entered 87 and the car accelerated like the T-33 on my T-Bird ride. "This thing certainly has some juice." I was trying to think what was so different, then realized there was no clutch. The car had an automatic transmission.

"Yes, Daddy wanted me to have the top of the line. We have the same 225 horsepower as a Corvette. You've noticed the automatic transmission; it's a *Turboglide* 3 speed. Dad thought I might have trouble with snow with a stick shift, so he got the *Turboglide.*"

"What are these lights on the dash?"

"Those are for the generator and oil pressure. They took the gauges out."

"Hmmm. That will take some getting used to."

As Sam Cooke began singing *You Send Me*, Linda undid her seat belt, slid closer to me, put her head on my shoulder, and her hand on my thigh. I had some trouble concentrating on the road. We enjoyed the radio and each other until we approached Colorado Springs.

Pulling off on a side road, we switched positons. I navigated through Colorado Springs and on to north 30th Street. Spying the Glen Eyrie sign, we took the unmarked road leading to the castle. From a mile away, we could see the castle silhouetted against the horizon.

***

"Well, hello, Mister Davis. Glad you could make it," said C2C Thomas as Linda and I rounded the castle wall. We walked onto the luscious green grass leading to the picnic area.

"Who is this pretty young lady?"

"Sir, this is Linda Jackson. She lives in Aurora. I met her in dance class."

"Hello, Linda, you can call me Ken."

Damn, did I make a mistake bringing Linda here? Is Cadet Thomas going to hit on her? Oh, wait, he has a fiancée. No sweat."

"Sir, we are thinking of going downtown to Michelle's for desert after the picnic? Is that authorized in picnic uniform?" I asked.

"It's an authorized uniform, isn't it Davis?"

"Yes, sir," I answered.

"Sometimes you have to be inventive," he said, with a slight smirk. "My Dad, who was in the Air Force, told me that 'sometimes it is better to ask forgiveness than permission.'"

***

The picnic was great. Colonel Echelberger and his staff sent a special van with hamburger, hot dogs, buns, and three-bean salad. Team members—Doolies naturally—did the grilling and serving, supervised by C3C Stanley. I jumped in to help my classmates, leaving Linda talking to some of the other dates, including one of her high school friends.

"Nice date," said classmate Larry Shewmate.

"Yeah, hands off," I replied with a grin.

Shewmate, Bill Stackhouse, Carl Rene, and I did the hamburgers and hot dogs and put them on the long table that had the salad and all the fixings. Everyone lined up and helped themselves. At the end of the table were large field containers with iced tea and lemonade.

There were tables for 10 with accompanying chairs. Tables tended to end up by class seating. Jim Stock, a third classman in my squadron, joined us.

"Slumming?" said Shewmate with a smile.

"No, it's just that I'm alone ,and you have the best looking dates. Besides, I thought you all needed some close supervision."

After we cleaned up the picnic area, we met in groups of 10 at the front door of the castle. Waiting for us was a young lady named Christine. A junior at Colorado College in the Springs, she worked as a paid docent at Glen Eyrie.

"Glen Eyrie is an English Tudor-style castle built in 1903 by General William Jackson Palmer, the founder of Colorado Springs," Christine began.

The tour topped an afternoon of comradery among Choir members. The eased social intercourse between classes was a benefits of participating in a mixed class extracurricular activity. The picnic broke up around fifteen hundred hours. As we drove toward 30th avenue, I asked Linda if she had ever visited the Garden of the Gods. "No," she said.

"I've heard it's impressive. Why don't we do a run through? It's a national park, so there's no charge. Besides, I'm full, so it's too early for Michelle's."

We parked in front of a red rock formation called Kissing Camels. The camels, indeed, seemed to be locked in an eternal kiss as they faced each other. "Wow," said Linda, "I'll bet this is really romantic at night." She took off her seat belt and slid over to my side of the car.

We became very involved in each other and our passions were rising. We could not go too far – the place was very public and Linda's jeans ensured nothing beyond heavy petting. She placed my hand on her breasts. I could feel them tightening beneath her shirt.

The sharp rap on the window on the driver's side startled us. Looking up I saw the lower part of a uniform with a "Park Ranger" badge showing on the left hand pocket.

The six-foot-two, 20-something ranger bent over and indicated that Linda should lower the window. "High, folks," he said. "I'm Ranger Stevens. You two looked like you were going at it hot and heavy. I just wanted to remind you that this is a very public place. I didn't want you to be embarrassed."

"Ah, thanks, sir," I said in my best Fourth Class manor. "We were just about to leave."

He smiled. "Okay, hope you enjoyed the park. Come back sometime when it's darker. He winked. "The park's beautiful at night."

***

We parked in front of Michelle's. The red and white awning below the wooden store front set the marvelous ice cream shop apart from the other businesses on the street. On the sides of the large script "Michelle's" were listed the house specialties: Sodas, Sundaes, Tea Room, and homemade Ice Cream, Candies, and Cookies.

As we entered, Linda looked at the array of sweets in the glass-fronted display cases. "Wow," she said, "a person could really get fat on all those goodies."

Several families sat at the booths down both sides of a central corridor. The kids were attacking various ice cream creations that ranged from sundaes to banana splits, and smaller concoctions named "Pike's Peak" and the "Rocket."

The owner, John Michopoulos, a large, olive-skinned Greek wandered up and down the aisle greeting people. "I heard an interesting story about the owner. Mr. Michopoulos was an Army Major in the Greek Army. One night at a night club, Mrs. Michopoulos, Lois, visiting from America, got up and sang. Apparently Mr. Michopoulos was very taken because he chased her back to America and married her."

"That's interesting," said Linda. "Guess military men are determined and persuasive."

"Of course we are. But, we'd better finish our banana split and get me back to the monastery or you will see a lot less of this military man than you normally do."

The ride back was quiet. I took a chance and drove. Linda was snuggled up next to me until we had to change driver positions. All too soon we arrived outside the barracks. I got out of the car and walked around to the driver's side.

"I had a great time, Don. I want to be alone with you again."

"Yeah, I wish I had more time." I looked around and snuck a quick kiss. As I went up the stairs to the dorm, I again had thoughts of giving up the drudgery of being a Doolie.

***

United States Air Force Academy
Sunday, 2 March 1958

Dear Folks,

Yes, I received your last three letters, but after the upperclassmen had a three day weekend over the Washington Birthday holiday. Returning, they were their usual obnoxious selves. We had little time for letters. Then, the academic department wanted to bring us back to reality; I had tests in four of my classes.

Don't know if you read about our tragedy—a Second Classmen crashed a private airplane and killed himself. He had a classmate with him, who was severely injured. The classmate will probably be discharged for violating regulations. The Wing was shocked by the accident—Cadet Davis (the name's ironical, huh!) was the first Academy cadet to die for any reason.

Don't worry, Mom, they say it's more dangerous on the roads than in the air. The only flying we do is T-29s navigation training. Our pilots are very professional and experienced.

Cadet Davis 'memorial was in the theater on Wednesday. General Briggs, General Stillman, many of the staff, and over 700 cadets were there.

I almost got in big trouble. I was out after call to quarters, visiting Art Kerr. Cadet Jay saw me coming out of Kerr's room. He asked if I had marked my card for an authorized absence. I said "no." Had I marked my room card and was in an unauthorized place, it would be an honor violation. Thank goodness I didn't mark the card. Anyway, Jay said, "Okay, Davis, it's still four demerits for visiting during call to quarters. However, the Squadron has been getting too many demerits lately and Captain Braswell 's on my back. You're confined to your room Saturday after the parade until dinner." I can live with that. It's much better than the demerits. I think Cadet Jay is still giving me a break because of Short's maltreatment of me.

Just 93 more days until Recognition. I felt bad after I took Linda to the choir picnic. I really like her and would like to spend more time with her - out of uniform. We went to Michelle's. I think I told you about it before. It is a great ice cream parlor. Tom's folks took us there during Christmas. We also went to the Garden of the Gods, the park with red rock formations. They have a formation there called the Kissing Camels. A park ranger threw us out of the park; he didn't like us imitating the camels.

Well, must close now and get ready for another week of the Colorado inquisition. We were hoping it would let up, but no luck. At least sitting on the Tennis Team training table—even as a manager—I'm getting enough to eat. Write soon and often.

God Bless,
Your loving son,
Don

Chapter 49

"Only twelve weeks to join in our silly little game; get your 10A's now!
Sign on the Squadron Checkpoints Board posted by the Minute Caller

Sunday, 14 March, 1958

"Well, Mister Davis," said Cadet Major King, "who was last year's Wimbledon champ and who was his opponent in the finals?" C2C Robert King was the leading doubles player on the tennis team. His father was in the Air Force and King came to the Academy from Wiesbaden, Germany. He was the table commandant on one of two tennis team tables.

I loved sitting at a varsity athletic table, even if I were a manager and not a legitimate tennis player. *Nice softball toss, Cadet King.* "Sir last year's Wimbledon champion was Mr. Lew Hoad, an Australian, who defeated Mr. Ashley Cooper, also of Australia.

"Okay, who were the Americans in the tournament and how did they do?"

Thank you, Sports Illustrated. "Sir, the two Americans, Mister Vic Seixas and Mister Herbie Flam, were both eliminated in the Quarterfinals."

"Not bad, Davis. Eat!"

The athletic table ambiance consisted of chatter rather than the din at regular tables. We performed table duties, but everything was more relaxed. Occasionally Fourth Class knowledge was asked; more often current event questions, especially sport's. At ease occurred more often also. The "at ease" usually came with team victories.

What a pleasure to enjoy the superb food prepared by Colonel Ike's staff. We had hot dogs or hamburgers on Saturdays. Friday was steak night. Turkey was served twice a month. Staples were beef and pork casseroles, with a variety of vegetables. We had ham three times a week. Deserts ranged from simple puddings to cake, ice cream, or sundaes on special occasions.

***

Friday, the tennis team was on a road trip to Arizona. Coach could only take one manager; naturally I got left home. The worst part; I had to return to my Squadron table. Unfortunately, I landed on C3C Whiteman's table. The Table Commandant, C2C Charley Mays, was also known as a Fourth Class baiter.

"Well, Davis, welcome back to Super Sixth. I see they've fattened you up at the tennis table. Maybe we can help you take off some ugly fat. Give me all versus of the Air Force song."

***

"It's sure going to be a long couple of days until the tennis team gets back," I said.

"Yeah, Don, I saw Whiteman giving you a hard time, " Tom said. "The wrestling team table is near the Sixth. We were at ease for tomorrow's meet. Lot to be said for training tables."

"Am I glad Mom sent the candy and cookies. I think food is going to be a little scarce until I get back to the training table," I said as I took the lid off of the large, tin, potato chip can."

"By the way, tell your Mom I love her cookies much more than the candy bars. I only had a couple of the chocolate chip cookies, because I have to make my weight class tomorrow. Oh, yeah, thank her for the Kool-Aid, too. I'm not crazy about the lemon-lime, but the orange and strawberry are good."

"I'll tell her you like the cookies; she has an inferiority complex about her baking. She's getting smarter at packaging too. That popcorn keeps the cookies from breaking up; of course the popcorn is a little stale to eat."

"Can you ask her to send regular sugar packages for the Kool-Aid? The cubes are hard to melt to put the sugar in the canteens. We need to be careful about cleaning the canteens. I hear Hertz got 3 demerits in the last yellow alert. Capt. Braswell found out Hertz had Kool-Aid in his canteen. Worse, his Fight Commander made Hertz drink the Kool-Aid and wouldn't let anyone give him water. That stuff is great, but not very thirst quenching."

"Come on, Tom, we're going to be late for class."

***

"Cripes, Kerr that was a hell'uva graded review. I studied hard and Tom helped, but I have a hard time grasping calculus. Hope the curve is low," I said as Art and I walked to our Chemistry class.

"Yeah, and I'll bet Captain Stevens has a great GR set up for chemistry. I need a decent grade to stay proficient. Not only that I have to put up with Ron."

Ron Mueller, Art's roommate knew how to work the system. "Now what's he done?"

"He's in the hospital; flu they said. Ron conned somebody into giving him passes. I think he's smoozing the head nurse. He goes out, gets looped, then sneaks back in, jumps in bed."

"How can he drink?"

"He doesn't have to sign out, so he's not on his honor not to drink. Of course, if they catch him, they may just boot him. He's pretty sly, though. I doubt he'll get caught."

Speaking of getting caught; I talked to Cloud yesterday. He drew a bunch of demerits and five tours. He got caught sleeping without pajamas and was wearing red suspenders under his blouse. When he took his blouse off, his instructor, a former ATO, wrote him up. In math class, he didn't put his pencil down at 'cease work.' He said he was just checking his work, but the instructor said there are no exceptions. So, Cloud got three demerits for that."

"He'd better watch out. If the academics don't get him, his military standing will."

"Yeah, and Hertz caught it too. He was minute caller and thought he would be a smart ass—big mistake. He wrote on the minute caller's board: '*Only twelve weeks to join in our silly little game; get your 10A's now!*' The upperclassmen didn't think it was cute or funny and hit him with a serious Form 10a.[112] He had 10 special inspections and five tours."

***

It snowed Thursday, Friday, and Saturday morning. After I told Captain Braswell that Tom was off on a wrestling match, he wandered around my side of the room, looked at the picture of Linda, turned and said, "**Carry on!**"

The freezing temperature resulted in a cursory, 30 minute in-ranks inspection. The snow cancelled the parade. Since Linda was at an away basketball game in Colorado Springs, I decided to spend the afternoon and evening in my room studying, shining shoes and catching up on the latest *Dodo* and *Talon*.[113]

After dinner, a normal evening with upper classmen, I came back to the room and turned on the radio. To my delight, the Air Force – Notre Dame Basketball game was on. Although we played a good game, we lost to the number 10 nationally rated Irish. At dinner, they announced Norte Dame score and then that the rifle team beat Canoe U handily. Since the middies were last year's national champs, the win was somewhat of a coup. They announced the soccer team ended the season undefeated with a win over Colorado College.

I put my hand out at the table after the announcements.

"What you want, Davis?" growled Cadet Mays.

"Sir, in honor of our excellent sports teams and especially a victory over Canoe U, may the Fourth Classmen sit at ease?"

"Davis, you've been sitting at a training table for too long. Sit up, chin in."

---

[112] A form 10A was an upper class derivative of a Form 10, the official write-up form. It didn't include demerits, but the upperclassmen could assess tours and special inspections.

[113] The *Dodo* was the cadets' semi-underground newsletter that spoofed cadet life, the administration, and cadets. The *Talon* was the Cadet Magazine that showcased cadets' literary skills.

That was the end of my meal. Fortunately, I still had some of Mom's cookies left and the popcorn, while stale, was filling.

***

Sunday morning was early for a Sunday. Protestant Choir members had to get up at 0400, eat breakfast, and get on a bus for Colorado Springs. Mister Boyd had scheduled two concerts at the First Presbyterian Church's 0830 and 1030 services. The public was invited; overflowing crowds filled both services. We sang Handel's *Halleluiah Chorus*; *American the Beautiful*, and, of course, *The Air Force Hymn*.

While the acoustics were not as good as Arlington, they were good enough that the last verse of the Air Force Hymn was stirring and sung to a stilled church sanctuary. The words of the last verse were printed in the Church bulletin. As we sang, *O God, protect the men who fly through lonely ways beneath the sky*, the Congregation joined us.

Following the 1030 service, church members provided a pot luck lunch in the Fellowship Hall. Lunch included the presence of a number of pretty Colorado Springs girls.

"Hi, I said to the petite, pert red-head who joined our table. "I'm Cadet Don Davis."

"Hi," she responded. I'm Peggy Johansson. "I really like your uniforms."

"Thanks, these are our winter parade uniforms. They were designed by the movie producer, Cecil B. DeMille. Do you live here?"

"Well, sort of; I'm a freshman at Colorado College, but I'm from Michigan."

"Hmm, that was one of the places they thought about putting the Academy. I'm glad they decided on C Springs. So, will you be here next year?"

"Yes. Three other girls and I rent a four bedroom house."

She's pretty cute. Maybe I should get her telephone number. "Would you like to see the new site when we get down here next year?"

"Yes, I'd like that."

"Can I get your phone number? I'll call you when we get into the new quarters. How do you get to school if you live off campus?"

"Oh, I have a car. It's not much, a 1949 Plymouth. My number is Melrose 1673."

Great, she even has wheels. "Good, then you'd be able to come out to the Academy."

"Sure."

Lunch included fried chicken; turkey, ham, and roast beef sandwiches; potato salad, macaroni and cheese; green beans, and tomato aspic. An abundance of pecan, apple, and cherry pies; two types of chocolate cake, and cheesecake filled the dessert table. The fare reminded me of Lucille's family picnics in William Land Park.

***

"Say," said Cloud, sitting next to me on the bus. "I thought you and Linda are pinned. What are doing getting that sweet, little redhead's number? I saw you."

"True, and don't you mouth off about it to Linda. Peggy goes to Colorado College. I thought it would be good to have a contact in the Springs. I think Linda is going to DU, so I might need a date sometime. She also has a car. It's always good to have reserve resources; that's what they teach in Military Studies."

"Yeah . . . okay, I guess."

"Right, so just cool it and grab your nap, like the rest of us."

***

Monday brought 4 to 6 inches of snow. The storm was too late to cancel the parade, but because of the ice that formed when the weather heated up then plunged again to freezing, Doolies were allowed to walk instead of double-timing everywhere.

Friday was a relief. Flight operations scheduled a night orientation navigation flight for 6th Squadron Fourth Classmen. Sergeant Little, escorting us to the ramp, passed out flight lunches on the bus. What a great night, we would miss evening meal, have two box lunches, and arrive back at the dorms late enough to miss SAMI and in-ranks inspection. If we were late enough or the snow continued, we would also miss a parade.

"All right, gentlemen, buckle up," said Lt. Jensen. I was pleased to see Lt. Jensen again and even happier to see Major Galt as the pilot. "Take out your maps and spread them out on the work table. This is an orientation flight and you're not graded, but you will work a navigation problem; you'll use ADF bearings and ground checkpoints to follow our flight."

We had had classroom instruction on map reading and ADF use to fix positons. We learned how to compute winds to project the aircraft's flight path by dead reckoning. Using cities as checkpoints, you had to know your approximate position, look at your map, and pick out a city on the ground. The pattern and size of the lights indicated the proper city.

The clear night made it easy to pick out the cities to use as checkpoints. The cars traveling the roads between cities were clearly visible. We circled Ponca City, the end of the navigation run, at approximately 2230 local time. Given all the tales we had heard from the upper classmen, the few lights of the 20,000 citizens in the city were disappointing.

Lt. Jensen was all business tonight. He didn't "bomb" Ponca City with boiled eggs. He was very intent on giving actual instruction. He said that even though it was an orientation flight, we should get something out of it other than just a plane ride.

"How'd you do?" asked Art Kerr as we rode the bus back to the barracks.

"Pretty good," I said. Lt. Jensen said I only had one fix that was out of limits. I think I picked the wrong ADF station. I was back on track on the next fix though. Lt. Jensen said I would have received an 88 or 90 if this were a graded mission. This is going to be challenging."

***

United States Air Force Academy
Sunday, 16, March 1958

Dear Folks,

It has been pretty nice, almost spring for several days. At the end of February, we had a lot of snow. In fact, there was so much snow they cancelled the parade the first Saturday in March. Since I was confined, I couldn't see Linda, but I got some studying done and my shoes and boots shined.

Cadet Thomas put me on the tennis training table as I mentioned. The team went to Arizona and the coach couldn't take me . I had to return to a Squadron table. Some of the upperclassmen don't like Fourth Classmen at training tables. They think we're beating the system.

You'll never guess who I was supposed to have a date with, so I'll tell you—Ethel Merman's daughter. She goes to school in Denver. My Element Leader had a date with her and fixed me up. I couldn't go because Cadet Whiteman gave me a confinement on a form 10A. I had to cancel the date. One of my classmates said I didn't miss much because she apparently isn't too attractive.

Even though we had to get up early (0400) this morning, it was worth it. The choir gave two performances at the First Presbyterian Church in Colorado Springs. The crowds at both services were appreciative and friendly.

We wore our new winter parade uniforms. Everyone, including the girls, ooowed and awed over the uniforms. I met a cute redhead named Peggy. Peggy is from Michigan. She has a house with three other girls and a car. I might see her some weekend if Linda can't come down from Denver.

I hope Pa didn't really hurt himself getting hit with that 2x4 on the job. You really should make him go see a doctor. Head wounds or concussions are nothing to mess with.

You didn't tell me that you and Pa were laid off. Hope things aren't too rough. If it will help, I will send you my income tax return.

Glad to hear Lucille and baby are doing all right. That makes seven, right? I have so many nieces and nephews, I won't remember their names.

I may bring two or three fellows with me on my leave in June. One of the guys, Tenny Takahasi, is from Hawaii. He will be trying to catch a military hop out of Travis AFB, over by San Francisco.

Friday we spent the whole day doing an orientation navigation flight. We had classroom instruction, then flew a route to Ponca City, Oklahoma. We used automatic direction finders (essentially radio stations) and checkpoints (spotting places on the ground). I did pretty well; missed one fix. The instructor, our friend, Lt. Jensen said I probably would have received an 88 or 90 on the flight. I think navigation is interesting, but challenging.

I'm enclosing some colored pictures. I have included a picture of the new site. It is going to be fabulous, but hard in the beginning. The activity building won't be finished; just quarters, dining hall, and academic buildings. There won't even be a theater. I feel for the Doolies. It might be good for us, though, because we may get more off base privileges.

Well, it's getting late, so I'd better close. I love and miss all of you. Let me know if you would like me to send you my tax return money.

God Bless,
Your loving son,
Don

Chapter 50
The Dark Ages

Sunday, 30 March, 1958

Monday, I woke with a headache; not improved by a breakfast session with C3C Whiteman. After English class, I threw up in the latrine, just as Major Galt happened in. When he saw me, he took me to the instructors' lounge, got his car, and took me to the clinic.

After an hour, I saw the flight surgeon, who said "Welcome to the flu brigade." He prescribed aspirin and Alka-Seltzer and sent me, with several other cadets, back to the barracks, with instructions to stay in bed and not breathe on my roommate.

When I got to my room I slept from noon until 0700 the next morning. By the end of the week, 80 cadets were hospitalized; 12% of the Wing restricted to their rooms. I figured I got the bug downtown. But since many cadets had the flu, it could have come from anywhere.

Restrictions to quarters came with early, hassle-free meals. Fourth Classmen sat at ease, performing normal serving duties. I didn't feel like eating on Monday. Tuesday and Wednesday I concentrated on soups and soft meals to keep from upsetting my stomach.

Tom survived the epidemic. He gathered homework from my instructors so I could keep up with classes. He even coached me in math. I was careful not to get too close and shared nothing with him. I felt so bad I let him have the last of Mom's cookies.

***

I spent Thursday in bed. Friday, the upperclassmen were gone, so I had a respite from the Fourth Class System. After lunch Friday, I felt better and decided to go to Arnold Hall. Tom, Art, Bob, and Terry were there. Linda and Cindy were going to join Terry and me later.

"Say, Bob," I said, "what's this I hear about you resigning, again?"

"Well, I was pretty damned pissed after the 'Custom's Board'"

"The Custom's Board?"

"Yeah, I put a snide note on the bulletin board which hacked the upperclassmen. They held a "Custom's Board"; a kangaroo court which gave me 10 special inspections and five tours. You know, 10a's aren't in the regulations. I thought it was piss poor they couldn't take a joke, so I asked for some Squadron stationary for a resignation letter.

All of a sudden Whiteman was my best friend; said they were on me because they thought I could do better. Then, I had to meet Jay and DeSantis, my element leader. They said they would cancel the three remaining special inspections and two tours, but I had to show a lot more effort and stop being a smart ass. I heard a rumor the Supe was taking heat for the attrition rate; not only from Headquarters Air Force, but from Congress too.

Anyway, I agreed to try harder. In return, they said they would lay off some and even help me more with my academics."

"Damn," said Art, "maybe we should all threaten to resign."

"Yeah," retorted Terry, "in your case, they'd accept the resignation in a heartbeat."

***

With upperclassmen gone Friday through Monday, we had Arnold Hall to ourselves. Wearing a mid-length, plaid skirt and a peach colored sweater under her suede jacket, Linda brushed off snowflakes as she came through the door. "You look great as always," I said.

She smiled. "I'm glad you have some free time. Did you say we're going out Sunday?"

"Yes, a bunch of us rented a place called 'Chief Hosa Lodge' for the open post. It's up by that restaurant we went to before. We hired a disk jockey and the restaurant is going to have a buffet set up. We don't have to be back until midnight. Can you drive?"

"Sure, Don. Will we be alone?"

"Well, if you don't mind, Tom and his latest, Susan, would like to double date with us."

"Is there going to be drinking?"

"They sell beer, but everyone pledged not to have more than a couple during the evening. We don't want any trouble. It's too close to recognition. The owner is a former Air Force sergeant. He made the guys who made the arrangements promise there would be no heavy drinking. Seems the Sixty guys had a party there ,and it got a little wild."

"Okay, how about tomorrow night. Will I see you?"

"No, I'm afraid I have CCQ . . . ah, Cadet in Charge of Quarters all day tomorrow."

"Drat," said Linda with a disappointed look on her face. "Let's dance."

***

Being CCQ with the upperclassmen gone was easy. I accompanied Captain Braswell to inspect several upper class rooms. He wrote up C3C Whiteman for improper display of record albums. Cadet DeSantis was awarded a Form 10 for "contraband"—a box of cookies from home in his laundry bag.

CCQ Duty

Captain Braswell sampled a cookie and with a grimace, said, "I should write DeSantis up for having stale boodle." As he left, Captain Braswell said, "Make sure everyone is in his room at taps; I may be back."

I assured Captain Braswell I would get the word out.

***

To remind us we are still Fourth Classmen, Captain Braswell had Tom, as acting Squadron Commander, accompany him on room inspections after breakfast on Saturday.

"**Room Attention!**" called out Tom as he trailed Captain Braswell into the room. With a cursory look at Tom's side, he walked over to my side. I was at attention in front of my bed. Captain Braswell flipped a quarter on my bed and smiled. He turned to my bookcase. He ran a white gloved hand along the edge of the top shelf, all the while looking at the picture of Linda.

"Good job, Davis," he said. You finally have a picture of a pretty young lady. Carry on!"

"Wow, Captain Braswell seemed in a pretty good mood," I said to Tom as he returned.

"Yeah, good thing we got the word out he was coming around. Our rooms looked good. He only gave out two demerits. He got Kerr for the wastebasket out of place and Hertz for articles on the top of his desk. He had a pen and paper out – think he was writing a letter."

Throwing my comforter on the floor, I said. "Look, I'm still not feeling red hot. I'm going to get a couple hours rest so I'll be ready for the party tomorrow. If you're staying, try to keep the riff-raff out."

***

Linda looked pert with the checkered cowboy shirt and Levis she wore to the tennis picnic. The Colorado weather was cooperating—no snow or rain, and a temperature in the 60s. Linda had added a denim jacket to deal with the cool temperature. I was a little concerned because the temperature was slated to go down to the fifties. When I mentioned my concern to Linda, she said, "No problem, I have a heavier jacket in the car. Besides I expect you to keep me warm. By way, where's your roommate and his date?"

"Can't wait," I replied. "Oh, Sandy got her dad's car, and she offered to drive. I think she wanted to be alone with Tom. They were going at it pretty heavy at the New Year's party."

"And you?"

"Ah, I told you, Tom was looking after his little sister. Besides she's a junior in high school—a little young for me."

"Oh, and I'm not too young?" Linda said with a little pout on her face.

"Ah, come on, you're almost as old as I am. Besides, I kind of like you."

Given the temperature and Linda's offer to let me drive, we had the top up on the convertible. The ride was similar to the trip to the Springs. Linda slid next to me and dialed in KXOA, which played the latest popular songs. I wondered at the beauty of the Rockies as we climbed to the forest areas still interspersed with snow.

"What are we going to do this summer?" Linda asked casually.

"What do you mean?" I answered.

'Well, you're going on field trips, and you said you're going to go home on leave."

"Yeah, I have to go home on leave to see my folks . . ."

"And old girl friends!"

"Look, I have girls who are friends and write once in a while, but you are my girlfriend. If I come back from leave early, we can be alone, enjoy the Kissing Camels at night."

"You're going to have dates on your field trips and leave. That will be hard for me."

"I probably will have some dates, and you, of course, can do the same. That doesn't mean I will love you any less and want you any less. And I promise I will send letters and postcards."

"Great, post cards are hard to cuddle."

"I don't think the separation will change anything."

"I'm not so sure, but I thought I'd just mention it."

"Okay, you have. But let's just enjoy each other tonight."

Linda put her hand on my thigh and leaned her head on my shoulder. Ironically, the song *See the Pyramids along the Nile* came on the radio as if Linda had called it up. The sentiment was not lost on me.[114]

---

[114] The words of the song included: "See the Pyramids along the Nile; Watch the sun rise on a tropic isle; Just remember darling all the while, you belong to me." Even more appropriate: "Fly the ocean In a silver plane; See the jungle wet with rains; just remember till you're home again...You belong to me."

***

The fading light cast long shadows from the trees. As we pulled into the parking lot, we could see Denver to the east. Lights began popping up like lightening bugs beginning their nightly foray. Advancing shadows turned buildings into dark blocks until electricity magically lit them up again.

"That's amazing," said Linda. "Watching the patterns of light receding from Denver is like watching someone pulling a giant, dark cloak across the city. It's fascinating watching the lights illuminate the city. It's like it's reborn."

"Wow," I said, "that's pretty philosophical. I hope the night's not going to be deep and dark. I could use a little light and warmth to hold me over until Recognition."

"Hmmm, we'll just have to see," she said, giving me one of her melting smiles.

***

Chief Hosa Lodge was big, some 3300 square feet; large enough to easily accommodate the 50 classmates and dates that had signed up for the evening's pleasures. The sign at the entrance of the lodge gave a brief history of the place.

"'The Lodge was designed by architect Jules Jacques Benois Benedict. It opened in 1918," I read. "Timber and stone native to the region were used to blend the lodge into the hillside. Benedict named the lodge after a Southern Arapaho tribal leader who was given the honorary title 'Hosa' by the tribe. Hosa means "peaceful and beautiful" in the Ute language.' Boy, I hope the Chief's spirit isn't around. This beautiful setting won't be peaceful tonight."

Chief Hosa Lodge

The massive stonework in the walls made the building look like a fort. The steep-pitched roof was designed to keep the winter snow falls from collecting on the roof.

Festive decorations promised a great venue for dancing in the large room where the band was warming up.

The roast beef, ham, and turkey sandwiches, potato salad, and bar-b-que beans buffet sat on a table against a wall in a side room. Cakes, pies, candy and cookies, obviously meant to meet cadet cravings, sat on a separate table. Beverages included ice tea, water, and lemonade.

***

Everyone, well, anyway the cadets, dug into the buffet like they hadn't eaten in a week. The young ladies were more demure, but joined the cadets around dining tables. Round tables, seating 10, were scattered around the perimeter of the dance floor. Terry Cloud was sitting with Cindy when Linda and I came into the ballroom.

"May we join you," I asked Terry. "Sure," he said.

"Did you two come alone?"

"Yeah," said Cloud, "we offered Kerr a ride, but he said he was bringing the Dagmar girl and wanted the chance to be alone with her. Can't image why?" he added, with a smirk.

Cindy kicked him under the table. "Right, all you guys are the same!"

"Hey, it's hard," I said, "when you live in a monastery . . ."

"Right," Linda added with an innocent smile. "You boys . . ." noticing the disapproving look on Terry's face . . . "ah, men, are so abused and hard done by."

Just then Tom and Sandy and Hertz and Joanne made their way to our table. "Is this a private party or can any lowly Fourth Classmen and their dates join?"

"Please join us," said Cloud.

Tom and Hertz introduced their dates.

***

The party committee had briefed the DJ on the music to play; plenty of current popular music, with Elvis Presley's *Jail House Rock, All Shook Up, and Hound Dog* featured. As the evening wore on, the DJ mixed in slow songs. When he played *Come Go with Me* by the Vikings and Fat Domino's *Blueberry Hill, I had a flashback to Grant High and dances in the gym.*

However, when the DJ played Tab Hunter's *Young Love* and Linda pressed closer to me and I could smell the enticing aroma of her "Seduction" mixed with a musk-like scent, I was immediately in the present. When the DJ played Elvis' *I want you; I need you; I love you,* Linda sang along with the words.

"Is that you or the song?" I asked.

"What do you think?"

"It's a great sentiment; I think we should explore it more."

348

"Hmmm," she said and pressed closer.

***

Around 2200 couples began drifting off the dance floor and out the front door of the Lodge. Around 2215, Linda said, "Shall we leave?"

"Okay. You know I don't have to be back until midnight. What did you have in mind?"

"Oh, I thought we might go to the bluff and admire the lights of Denver."

Wow, I think she wants to make out. I don't know how much of that I can take.

***

Rising just over the horizon, the full moon intermingled with the star spangled sky and the lights of downtown Denver. "Isn't that gorgeous?" Linda asked taking my hand in hers.

"Yes," I agreed putting my arm around her and pulling her toward me. She willingly responded to my kiss, sending shivers through me.

"Let's go in the back seat," Linda said.

After fifteen minutes of heavy petting, both of our emotions were rising. Linda allowed me to unzip her jacket and unbutton her wool shirt. I could feel her breasts tighten as her breathing became heavier.

"I'd like to make love to you," I said as we paused to catch our breath.

"I'd love for that to happen," she said, "but my father would get upset, and he's not very pleasant when he's angry."

"Yeah, and the back seat of a car is not very romantic . . ."

"That's what my mother says," Linda said, buttoning up her shirt and zipping up her coat. "I'm getting cold, Don."

Looking at my watch, I said, "You know I'm a little hungry. We have time. How about going into Denver and sharing a hamburger and shake at the Red Top?

"Great idea; and, Don . . ."

"Yes?"

"This just wasn't the time and place."

"I know."

As I wrapped my parka more tightly around me and headed toward the room, I knew it was going to be difficult to get to sleep, and when I did, I knew my dreams would be of Linda.

***

United States Air Force Academy

Monday, 31, March 1958

Dear Folks,

The upperclassmen aren't back yet, so I'm still eating well. But, we appreciated the cookies and lemonade. Next time please send regular sugar. We have to melt the cubes in hot water before we can use them.

We had an open post Sunday. About 30 Fourth Classmen and dates rented a place in the mountains called "Chief Hosa Lodge." We had a buffet and a DJ for dancing. I took Linda and had a wonderful time.

Is Pa still having headaches? He should see a doctor; concussions can be serious. That was really careless of that guy to hit him with a 2x4. How are Lu and her tribe? Fine, I hope. I hope Gene stays down in Louisiana. The people he runs with in Sacramento aren't very good. He should look into commercial art; he does very artistic drawings.

The fencing team just returned from California; said it was pretty nice there. The weather here is crazy. One day the sun shines, the next it snows or rains. I like the rain or snow better; when the sun shines you get spring fever and don't feel like doing anything. It was definitely spring today. The sun was shining and it got warm (warm is the high 40's). There are still patches of snow; and I don't think we have seen the last of it.

We were issued our summer blue uniforms. They look like the winter uniform, but are about 20 pounds lighter. Unlike the winter uniform, they even have pockets and belt loops.

Tomorrow starts another month. Only 62 days until recognition; 65 until we will be in California. We got a little more info about the summer field trip. One third of the class will get to fly F102's, a third will fly F-100s, and a third will fly B-47s or KC-135s. The 135 is our latest tanker aircraft. I hope I get to fly one of the fighters. The 102 is an Air Defense fighter and the F-100 a tactical fighter.

I'm looking forward to being home. If you talk to Jim LeDoux, tell him to tell the guys I might get to see them if I get a weekend off on the field trip. If I bring Tom, Jim will have to get him a date. I think Sandy would go out with me.

God Bless
Your loving son,
Don

Chapter 51

Sixtieth Day

On the 60th day before Recognition, the Third and Fourth Classmen change places.
The Third Classmen have to run their chins in; sit at attention for meals, etc.
Letter Home by Terry Storm

Sunday, 13 April, 1958

Tuesday was relatively quiet after the upperclassmen returned. The table conversations, among upperclassmen, of course, were mostly about camping, partying, and bowling. There was some talk about conquests...among the self-imagined Romeos in the group.

Wednesday was a different story. It was as if the Third Classmen had been given shots of adrenalin. From roll call until Call to Quarters, Cadets Whiteman, Bush, and McCarthy were all over us. At dinner, Cadet Whiteman demanded all versus of the Star Spangled Banner and the Air Force Song. I managed only a full serving of mashed potatoes and half of my salad.

That evening Cadet Bourque called a meeting of Sixth Squadron Fourth Classmen. "Okay, men," he began, "tomorrow is 60th day. The roles of Fourth Classmen and Third Classmen will be reversed. Like Cinderella, you will have magical powers from Reveille until Call to Quarters. Short sheeting, water balloons, and shaving cream dispersal might be anticipated on your part. However, no permanent damage; i.e. ink on clothing, etc., will be tolerated. If things get out of hand, you may be subject to disciplinary consequences.

Sixtieth Day is meant to be conducted with good humor. You may impose the Fourth Class System on my classmates. Most, I emphasize most, of my classmates will comply with the spirit of the day. However, you may be subject to counter measures. At no time will real anger be tolerated from any cadet. If tempers flare; the Third Classman will call a 'time out' and go to his room. If you are engaged, cease what you are doing and back away.

Finally, I would remind you there is a 59th day, and it could be a long time until Recognition. I hope I've made the rules clear. Any questions?"

Art Kerr's hand shot up. "Sir, what are the Second Classmen doing tomorrow?"

"Second Classmen are observers. If they see a situation getting out of hand, they will step in and either arbitrate or stop whatever is going on. You will treat them normally...with 'Yes, Sirs' and "No, Sirs;" they will not expect any "No excuse, Sirs! Okay, Davis, what is it? "

"Ah, Sir, can we implement the Doolie diet at the table for Third Classmen?"

"As I said, I think most of my classmates will go along with the program. It worked pretty well with the Second Classmen last year. No one got hurt and there were some funny incidents. But…there is always tomorrow, tomorrow. Enough, go hit the books. The instructors are not part of the game and they may be waiting with pop quizzes."

***

Tom and Art Kerr had organized a class meeting Sunday night. The Cadet Store apparently had been informed of Fourth Classmen needs for 60th Day. The C Store had an ample supply of balloons, shaving cream, and saltine crackers available. Tom and Kerr had collected money from each of us and acquired the necessary supplies.

At 0300 the Sixth Squadron Doolie crew gathered behind Dorm 914 as planned. Vic Apodaca laid down the large brown paper roll he had acquired from the mess hall. "Okay," said Kerr. "Everyone knows their task. Cut a sheet of paper large enough to cover the Third Class doorways. Tape the paper securely over the door. Does everyone have enough shaving cream and crackers and know how to short sheet a bed?"

A number of soft "yeses" responded. "Right, everyone get to it. Avoid the Orderly Rooms, although the CCQs are undoubtedly sleeping. Get back to your beds by 0400."

***

As the last notes of reveille sounded, pairs of Fourth Classmen stood in full uniform outside the papered doors of the Third Classmen. Tom and I had positioned ourselves in front of our favorite cadet's door. Cadet Whiteman and his roommate, John Bush broke through the paper barrier with puzzled looks on their faces.

"Nice of you to join us, Mister Whiteman, hit it for 10," I said.

Whiteman snarled and started to assume his usual Third Class demeanor. "It's 60th Day," said Bush poking his roommate in the ribs and assuming a position of attention.

"Mister Bush," Tom said. "Don't think you have permission to talk. Hit it for 10."

A continuous din rose throughout the dormitory. The exercise lasted 10 minutes. It ended with the faux Doolies instructed to shave, dress, and get in formation by first call.

Breakfast formation was a series of get evens: "Get that chin in, Mister; reach for Colorado, Mister, and hit it for 10."

Breakfast itself was a reversal of demands for Fourth Class knowledge, current events, and naming of staffs and Air Force Commands. Third Classmen ate little. But the constant grilling of Third Classmen left my classmates and me little time to eat as well.

***

While the Administration was silent on 60th Day, it apparently quietly accepted the event as a new Academy tradition. The Dean cancelled the first two periods of Fourth Class classes, leaving us free to conduct raids on Third Class rooms.

Forming two man cadet teams, we set about short-sheeting beds, filling beds with cracker crumbs, putting shaving cream in boots and overshoes, and dumping dirt in waste baskets. Next, we switched all the clothes in the closets between roommates, ensuring articles were not in inspection order. For Whiteman and Bush, we also switched the shorts and tee shirts to the opposite cabinets. Water balloons were stored in the hallway closets for later use in bombarding Third Classmen getting ready for intramurals.

***

Sixtieth Day progressed with interesting interchanges between classes. The Second Classmen reported there were howls from Third Classmen when they discovered switched clothing, shaving cream inserts, and dirty wastebaskets. The balloon bombardment was a tactical success, resulting in extra Third Class physical hits on Fourth Classmen in soccer and basketball games. The Third Classmen levied the hits on their own Doolie squadron mates.

"**Bourque**," I yelled as we conducted a mock shower formation. "**Let's have 10.**" Cadet Bourque pulled out a water gun; squirting, he counted, "One, two three..."

Tom and I were assigned to Bourque. Because of our respect for him, we short sheeted his bed, but did not give him the crackers or shaving cream treatment.

At day's end, a huge water balloon fight broke out in and around the dormitories. Cadet Jay called a halt to the fight when the hallways became part of the battleground. He ordered Fourth AND Third Classmen to bring out mops to clean up the mess.

We dreaded reveille the next morning. Amazingly the Third Classman almost ignored us. The whole day was quiet. We were allowed to finish our meals, almost without interruption. We had a Squadron party just before taps, with cookies and cokes with all classes participating.

***

Friday, after classes, the Third Classmen were occupied straightening out their closets, ridding sheets of cracker crumbs, cleaning shaving cream from their boots, and generally putting their rooms in SAMI order.

***

"Damn, Davis, now why are you getting up in the middle of the night?" Tom said groggily, "did you manage to pull guard duty again?"

Taking my parade uniform out, I said, "No friend, it's Easter. The choir's performing a sunrise concert at Red Rocks. After breakfast, I have to catch the bus for the park."

"What the hell time is it anyway?"

"It's 0430, go back to sleep. Religious Catholic slackers don't have to get up until 0730."

Tom rolled over and grunted, "Have fun and turn out the light on the way out."

***

I loaded up on pancakes, scrambled eggs, and sausage. Except for usual table duties, Fourth Classmen sat at ease. C2C Jay, my Squadron Commander, was the Table Commandant. A tenor in the choir, he directed "at ease" as soon as we were seated.

At ease included being able to converse with classmates, some of whom we didn't see often. A third of the Fourth Class cadets were in the Protestant Choir[115]. Gary Theiler, one of 20 fellow appointees from California, passed me a cup of coffee.

"Hi, Gary. Haven't seen you since summer training. How's it going?"

"I'm doing well. Academics is "no sweat" so far. I'm carrying an 86 average. I'm on the *Contrails* and *Polaris*[116] committees, which are great. How about you?"

"I'm a manager on the tennis team, so I get to go on bus trips to games—Wyoming, Colorado College, Colorado Mines—but not on the great trips—Arizona and New Mexico. The great thing; however, is sitting at a training table. The team guys do some Fourth Class stuff, but mostly interesting things; sports, current events. The bad news is going back to a squadron table. A couple of my Third Class jerks make life miserable again."

"I can relate to that" chimed in Bob Brickey, sitting across from us. The football tables were great. We ate as much as we wanted and Fourth Class Mickey Mouse was minimal. When I went back to First Squadron, two Third Classmen and a Second Classman, Jeff Davis, tried to make up for lost time. I lost five pounds in a week.

I was seriously thinking about an SIE[117] when one of the football team Second Class lineman caught wind of what was going on. He threatened bodily harm to the nerdy upperclassmen if they didn't lay off. When I got on the ski team training table, I regained the five pounds.

---

[115] In addition to the pleasure of singing and "outside events" such as the performance at Red Rocks and Washington, D.C, choir time was time away from the system.

[116] *Contrails* is the Fourth Class information booklet; *Polaris* is the Academy Annual.

[117] SIE – Self initiated elimination.

"All right," said Mr. Boyd at the Command level microphone, "let's go get on the busses and enjoy Easter and Red Rocks."

***

"'Enjoy Red Rocks'; man it's going to be cold. Weather said about 50 degrees. Glad we have the horse blanket coats and gloves."

"You're right," said Kerr sitting next to me. It's going to be colder than Arlington. I thought I was going to freeze to death there."

"Oh, come on, Kerr, you've been here for six months. You should be used to the cold. What are you reading," I asked, noticing a pamphlet Art was thumbing through.

"It's a program Cindy got for me for the sunrise service. Pretty interesting stuff; listen:

Colorado Council of Churches
RED ROCKS EASTER PROGRAM

The Red Rocks Amphitheatre, a rock structure located eight miles west of Denver, in Morrrison, Colorado, seats over 9,000 guests in open air setting. At an altitude of 6,450 feet, it is one of the highest performance venues in the world.

John Brisben Walker envisioned performances in the natural setting used by the Ute Indians in earlier times. Several concerts were held between 1906 and 1910.

The City of Denver purchased the amphitheater and the surrounding 728 acres from Walker in 1928 for 54,133 dollars. The Civilian Conservation Corps (CCC) and the Works Progress Administration (WPA) provided the labor and materials necessary to finally complete the amphitheater structure in June, 1941.

This is the 11th annual sunrise service sponsored by the Colorado Council of Churches. Attendees are advised to wear layered, warm clothing as predawn temperatures can be chilling.

Sunday's Schedule of Events
4:30 am – Doors open
5:30 am – Pre-worship music begins
6:00 am – Worship Service begins
7:30 am – Worship Service ends (approximate)
Chaplain (Colonel, USAF) J.S. Bennet presiding
Music: The Air Force Academy Protestant Choir

"Wow that's interesting. Sounds like we may need oxygen as well as overcoats."

"Did Cindy tell you how many people might attend?" I asked.

"She said the Council told the Supe they expected a full house for the Service."

***

As advertised, the incredible acoustics sounded like the music at Arlington. We sang *Onward Christian Soldiers*, *A Mighty Fortress is Our God*, *The Battle Hymn of the Republic*, and closed with the *Air Force Hymn*. Chaplain Bennet spoke on "One's duty to God and Country." The sermon and music drew applause at the end of the service.

I invited Linda and her parents to the service. Surprised and pleased they decided to attend, we agreed to meet at Saint Paul's Presbyterian Church in Aurora after our performance. Saint Paul's sponsored our Red Rocks performance. Church members arranged a brunch at 0900. Ironically, the Jacksons attended Saint Paul's. Jack was cooking pancakes, and Alice was serving the food. We had to go to Saint Paul's on the buses, but essentially had an open post after the brunch. Call to Quarters was at 2100, which allowed us the afternoon and early evening free.

***

"That was a marvelous service," Alice said. "It was a bit chilly. I was glad to see sunrise at 6:30. It was beautiful with the rays of the sun streaming through the clouds on the horizon." Alice served me a large portion of scrambled eggs, sausage, and pancakes along with orange juice and coffee. "When you finish, we'll take you and Linda downtown to the zoo. Have you seen our zoo, Don?"

"No, Ma'am," I answered. "I haven't had a chance to visit the zoo."

"Alice," she reminded me, "not Ma'am."

Several upperclassmen gave me inquisitive and not necessarily friendly looks when Linda sat beside me. Linda, noticing the attention, got up and helped her mother serve. That seemed to ward off further issues, but I was concerned some of the wolfish upperclassmen would hit on her. They did, but she put them off saying she had to concentrate on serving.

***

When we had finished eating; after a few words from the Saint Paul's minister and a thank you to the volunteers from Chaplain Bennet, we were dismissed. Linda was waiting for me by the kitchen. Her folks were finishing the cleanup.

"Okay," said Jack, "let's go," drying his hands.

"It should be pleasant," Alice said, "the temperature's up to sixty degrees so the animals should be out."

As we approached the car, I noticed it was a new Ford Edsel. "Gee, Mister Jackson, is this an Edsel?" The bright shiny new four door car had a black and red paint job; the front was black with red paneling down the rear quarter and around the rear.

"Yes, Don, it is. We just got delivery in January. Ford thinks it is going to be a best seller that will beat Chrysler and GM. However, I still like my Chevys. Opening the driver's door, he said, "It's got a couple of new features: buttons in the center column change the transmission gears and, as you can see, the speedometer is different."

The speedometer looked like the T-33 standby compass. "Wow, it certainly is different. Is it expensive?"

"Relatively so, this Corsair model is around thirty four hundred dollars."

"That's certainly out of my league," I said as we jumped into the car.

***

The animals in the 80 acre zoo were actively enjoying the temperate weather. The giraffes and hippos, having just been fed, were chowing down. Located City Park in the middle of Denver, the zoo was the first in the United States to use naturalistic enclosures instead of confining cages.

Alice, Jack, Linda, and I had a great time roaming the natural habitats, admiring the tigers, lions, and bears that seemed perfectly content with their environments. Taking a break, we stopped at the small café for a cup of chocolate and a donut.

"I really like the natural settings," Linda said. "I hate to see animals cooped up in cages. It's better, of course, if they're in their native lands and environments, but the zoo does a good job of making them comfortable."

"They certainly look comfortable," I said, "better than the Blue Zoo."

***

Linda's folks dropped us off at the Tabor Theater. The matinee was the *Bridge over the River Kwai*. I appreciated the opportunity to be alone with Linda and her folks being so understanding. Alice said they would come by after the movie and we could have Red Top burgers before they took me back to the base.

I escorted Linda to a mid-row seat. The Tabor was dark, except for several faint emergency lights illuminating the outside aisles. Linda took my hand and put it in her lap as soon as we sat down.

"Thank you for inviting us to the sunrise concert. My folks said they really enjoyed it. I think you made a few brownie points."

"That's great. I've really missed you since last Saturday."

"I've missed you too. That was fun at the Lodge, and after."

"Ssssh," said someone sitting two rows in back of us. The Tabor wasn't crowded, but the acoustics made talking not a good idea.

***

"Did you like the movie, Don?" Jack asked.

"Well, I could sort of see both sides, but I have a hard time siding with Alec Guinness aiding the enemy. While it helped with the morale of his prisoners of war country men, it also could contribute to the deaths of allied soldiers in the Burma Theater. The poetic justice of Guinness actually causing the bridge to blow was a good twist."

"I can't imagine enduring the conditions those men were under," Linda said. "I don't know if I could take that."

"You don't know what you will do until you are faced with the situation, honey," Jack told his daughter. But he didn't elaborate on his experiences in Korea.

The rest of the 20-minute ride back to the base was quiet. Linda was holding my hand. Not knowing the Jacksons well, I felt discretion was in order and did nothing more than hold Linda's hand.

The Jacksons drove me right next to Dormitory 914. I said a very quiet goodnight to Linda and trudged toward the back door of the barracks.

***

Tuesday after the Easter Weekend, I was walking by the Orderly Room when I heard Third Classman Cadet Whiteman shout out, **"Davis, get your butt in here."**

Wondering what grievous crime I'd committed; I did an about face and stood in front of Cadet Whiteman. Whiteman glared at me from his desk. He held a brown paper wrapped package at arm's length. A breeze blew through the open windows.

As he handed me the package I immediately sensed the problem—an awful sulfuric, putrid smell was coming from the package.

"Davis, you trying to asphyxiate the entire Squadron?"

"No, Sir," I replied; wondering how long I'd have to hold the offending package.

"Then why the hell do you have people mail you chemical warfare packages?"

"No excuse, Sir," I said, anticipating at a minimum a special inspection with Cadet Whiteman that evening. Instead, Whiteman almost screeched: **"Get that damn thing out of here—and DON'T dispose of it in the Squadron area."**

Almost gagging, I did an abrupt about face, double timed out the door, and headed for the garbage cans outside the mess hall. As I was double timing, holding the package as far away from me as possible, I read the return address: "Mrs. Violet Ferris, 1492 Grace Avenue, Del Paso Heights, California." *What the devil could Mom have sent me that smells so bad?* I thought. *She wouldn't intentionally send anything that could be this awful.*

"You man, halt!" I recognized the voice of Tom Shores, a Third Classman from 5th Squadron, from a previous run-in with 5th's most notorious Doolie baiter.

Approaching me, he said, "What are you doing, Dumbsquat?"

"Sir, I am disposing of a package."

"Don't want to get caught with contraband, huh? Let me see the package."

Without hesitation, I handed Shore the package. I had to work hard to stifle a laugh as being downwind and thinking there might be boodle in the package, C3C Shores inhaled the full aromatic fumes from the package. I would later enjoy sharing with classmates a description of the utter look of disgust as Shore handed me the package and almost yelled: "**Post.**"

As I resumed my double time, I glanced back. C3C Shores was doubled over and appeared to be at the point of heaving.

As I lifted the lid on the garbage can, I noted the postal stamp with a date two and a half weeks before. I couldn't stand the suspense. I ripped open the package and lifted the lid off a shoe box. The smell was even worse. On top was a plastic bag full of colored hard boiled eggs was a card.

"Happy Easter, Son," the card read. "I know how much you like your Easter eggs, so I thought I would send you a dozen. You can share them with your roommate if you like." *Damn*, I thought, *I'm glad they didn't deliver the package to the room. We would have had a hell of a time getting the smell out. I'm surprised Whiteman didn't think of that.*

***

United States Air Force Academy
Monday, 31, March 1958

Dear Folks,

Thank you for the two letters. I just haven't had a chance to answer until now. It is pouring rain and intramurals have been cancelled, so I have a chance to write.

We have our summer squadron assignments. Tom and I won't be in the same squadron. We really worked together to beat the system. Of course, the "system "should be a lot better next year; At least the military will be easier..

The new Fourth Class will have it tough. There will be 450 or so and they will have three upper classes. I's a ways to downtown Colorado Springs and it'll be harder for the girls to get to the Academy. Our class will have more privileges, but we'll have a transportation problem..

Linda has a car, but she has says maybe we shouldn't be pinned. She thinks I'll be dating on field trips and when I come home. I said it would be better for us next year because I'll be able to get off base. She's going to go to Denver University, so she would be two hours away.

We have our summer leave schedules. I have late July. After the field trip, we come back here for four weeks of training. Then I go to Mariana, Florida, for two weeks of pilot training. We will fly the T-34, the T-37, and T-28 trainers. The T-37 is the newest trainer.

I'll get a weekend in Florida, but won't have time to see Aunt Jean in Louisiana. I think we'll be pretty busy in the flying training. Don't worry, we will always have an instructor with us so it will be very safe.

We had an event called 60th Day - 60 days before Recognition. Third and Fourth Classmen trade places. We subjected them to Fourth Class rules. They sit at attention and perform table duties. We played tricks like short sheeting beds. You fold the sheets halfway and tuck them in. We put cracker crumbs in their beds and shaving cream in their boots. We thought we would be in for it on Friday, but it was unusually quiet and we even got to eat.

On Easter, the Protestant Choir provided music for a sunrise service in Red Rocks. A crowd of 10,.000 attended. We sang Onward Christian Soldiers; A Mighty Fortress is our God, The Battle Hymn of the Republic; and, of course; the Air Force Hymn. Chaplin Bennet conducted gave the sermon.

Thank you for the Easter eggs. Unfortunately the Post Office held them for a couple of weeks. They were really ripe when they got here. The smell got me in trouble. Fortunately, they never got to our room.

Linda and I saw The Bridge over the River Kwai Sunday at the Tabor Theater. Not sure I agree with Alec Guinness's role in aiding the enemy.

Since we had a weekend off, the instructors will probably be waiting with pop quizzes. I'd better do some studying and dress up my shoes. We expect the upperclassmen, especially the Third Classmen to start a "buck up" soon. In a buck up, the

upperclassmen turn up the intensity of the Fourth Class system.
ONLY 50 MORE DAYS UNTIL RECOGNITION!!!!

God Bless,
Your loving son,
Don

Chapter 52
Downwind

There is a definite correlation between a Dooley's academic ability and his mental status . . .
Man's Flight Through Life—Robert Heriza

Sunday, 27 April, 1958

The long weekend for the upper classes had a mellowing effect on them. This was especially true at the tennis team table. Most of the table talk among upperclassmen centered on our trip to Laramie – scheduled for Saturday. Wyoming was expected to be a tough match.

Following wins over Colorado Mines, Regis, and Colorado State, the team felt like it was on a roll and could defeat Wyoming. Singles ace Steve Roberts won his last four meets. He and doubles partner, Ron Parsons, won their last three doubles matches.

I could hardly wait for classes to finish on Friday. In a move usually reserved for the football team, the athletic department paid for a hotel for the tennis team. The team would get a good night's sleep on Friday and be ready for 1000 matches Saturday.

***

We were booked at the Holiday Inn near the University. Everyone met in the restaurant for dinner. Hamburgers and fries were on the menu at an affordable cadet price. We were on per diem, but because box lunches were furnished, dinner was not part of the per diem.

Remembering to bring change, I found a pay phone before dinner and called the Gamma Phi number Susie gave me during our earlier visit. When a girl answered, I asked, "May I speak with Susie Watson, this is Cadet Don Davis calling."

"Just a minute" answered the sweet voice on the other end.

"Hello," Susie said tentatively.

"Hi, Susie, Don Davis. We danced together last October when the team came up."

"Oh, yeah, Don. It's good to hear from you. Where are you?"

"Well, I'm a manager on the Academy tennis team, and we're here for a match. We should be through about 1400 . . . ah, 2:00 o'clock tomorrow afternoon. I was hoping we could get together for an early hamburger and shake. The bus back leaves at 9:00 p.m."

"That would be great, Don. I have my car. Where should I pick you up?"

"We will be having lunch at the student cafeteria. So if you could pick me up outside of the cafeteria about 3:30, maybe you could show me around town."

"Sure. There isn't much to see in Laramie. Still, it'd be nice to see you. I'll be there."

"Great, I'm really looking forward to seeing you again."

***

Tennis did not go well—we lost 7-0. The lunch at the student cafeteria was good, with fried chicken, mashed potatoes, string beans, and cake for dessert. The friendly atmosphere helped sooth the disappointment of the one-sided loss; it's easy to be a gracious host when you win.

***

Susie was waiting in her 1949 Chevy. The pink bottom and cream top reminded me of my car and kindled memories of my senior year. I wondered if Susie would be as great as some of the girls back home.

She certainly looked the part of an exciting afternoon, wearing a blue skirt that outlined her shapely figure and a pink sweater that she filled nicely. She had a black leather jacket lying on the seat beside her to cope with the 50 degrees and the prevailing 35 mile-an-hour wind.

"Wow, you're punctual," I said. "Glad you could come."

"Well, I wasn't sure about the time. Did you have to wait long?"

"No, we had just finished all the niceties at the end of lunch."

"Hop in and we will do the grand tour of Laramie, Wyoming."

***

Susie was right. Laramie had a main street and several side streets that boasted mom and pop stores. Two restaurants, four bars, and two movie theaters made up the town's entertainment inventory. Laramie had the flavor of towns depicted in old western movies.

"Would you like go to a movie, Don? The Laramie Theater has a five o'clock show that gets out about seven. That would give us time to get a hamburger at the Corral Burgers and Brew and get you back to the University by nine."

As if on cue, the movie at the Laramie was a western, *The Big Country,* starring Gregory Peck and Jean Simmons. The cast also included Carroll Baker, Charlton Heston, and Burl Ives. I knew Ives was a country singer, but didn't know he was also an actor.

I was pleased with the 50 cent admission because I didn't have a lot of money with me, and I would surely pay for dinner. As soon as we got comfortable in the back of the darkened theater, Sue took my hand.

Three quarters of the way through the movie, Sue turned and kissed me. Adapted to the dark, I could see very few people were in the theater, and none of them were cadets. I returned her kiss. She lifted my hand and put it on her breast. We made out for 15 minutes.

"Whoa," I said, "I can't take this. You're great, but we're really limited in here."

"I know a place where we could go park," she said.

"I'd really like that," I said, "but I'm in uniform and very conspicuous. Look, come to Denver, and we'll make a night of it. Right now, I think we'd better go get those burgers."

"Hmmm," she said with an obvious pout. "I guess if that's the best we can do, okay. But I'd really like to finish this."

"Ooooh, so would I. It's just not the right time or place. *Hmmm, that sounds familiar.* I hope you're not angry."

"No, a little disappointed but not angry. You're right. I'll really try to get to Denver."

***

The rest of the evening was pleasant, but subdued. Sue asked me if I wanted to drive, but I said "no, it's such a small town and if an upperclassman saw me driving, I might not be able to see you when you get to Denver."

"Wow, that's pretty silly."

"I know, "I said, "but unfortunately those are the rules we have."

We grabbed a hamburger and shake at a little restaurant called the Corral.

At 2045, Sue dropped me off at the bus, which was idling outside the cafeteria.

"I would like to see you again, Don," Sue said.

"And I'd love to see you. Come to Denver." I looked around. Seeing no upperclassmen, I give her a kiss. She rolled up the window and sped away.

***

"Well, roommate, how'd you make out in good old Laramie? I hope it was good because you missed Friday dinner, Saturday meals, SAMI, in-ranks, and a parade. Oh, and I think the blue tags[118] are gearing up for hell week, even though it's 40 days away."

"Yeah, well sort of makes up for the weekend you spent at the AAU Wrestling Tournament. Of course you and the team did better than we did; getting a third place and you getting a second. I remember, however, you bitching about having no free time and no girls. I have you beat there. Remember the blonde, Susie, I told you I met on the football trip?"

"Yeah, and so . . ."

"Well, I called her Friday night, and she met me after lunch. She showed me the town—not much to see—and then we went to a show. Man, she's hot. There weren't any

---

[118] The Class of 60 had blue name tags, the Class of 1959 gold, ours were grey; next year's class would be red. Classes were nicknamed for the color of their name tags.

cadets in the theater, so we made out like mad. I said the seats make it a little hard to do any serious loving so she suggested we go park somewhere . . ."

"And . . ."

"Nothing. Look, the tennis team was all over. I didn't think with would be a good idea to get caught parking. I invited Sue to come visit."

"And what about Linda?"

"Ah, come on. I like Linda a lot, but she's talking about breaking up. I'm not sure she's serious, but it doesn't hurt to have a backup."

***

After lunch, Tom and I decided to go to the Fourth Class Club. Linda was out of town with her folks, so I couldn't see her. Probably just as well, I had a nice dream about Sue last night and we were going to a motel when reveille blasted over the loudspeaker.

Kerr, Cloud, and Hertz were sipping cokes. "Hi, guys, can we join you," I said.

"Sure," Cloud said, "have a seat. We were just trying to console Hertz."

"Why?" Tom asked.

"Did you see the grades on the bulletin board Friday," Hertz moaned. "I'm running a 68 in math and a 69 in chemistry. If I bust both of those, I'm gone. Maybe that wouldn't be so bad." "Come on, Hertz," chided Art. "You pulled it out before; you can do it again. Think about the June field trip. You'll get to go supersonic in a fighter, have the evenings free and, most importantly; you'll have a chance to meet hot chicks."

"Yeah, right. Assuming I can squeak by the finals and don't have to take turnouts."

"Damn, Hertz," Tom said. "Quit whining like a baby. I'll pump you up in math and Sutter can get you square in chem. Not only that, take EI[119] in both of those between now and finals and you'll make it. We need you around for comic relief – although right now you are more like a Shakespeare tragedy."

"Hell, Hertz, get us some cokes and cheer us up," ordered Cloud. "Either that or go back to your room to cry. Not to change the subject, but . . . did you hear about next year's changes?"

"Now what are they going to do to us?" I asked.

"Christmas will be two weeks instead of twelve days like this year . . ."

"Yeah for us; screw the Doolies," said Kerr.

". . . and there will be no spring break …"

"Crap," said three of us simultaneously.

---

[119] EI – extra instruction.

". . . but, we will have a two week field trip to various US bases. Fourth Class summer will be eight weeks instead of nine and academics will start a week earlier. Oh, and finals will be before Christmas break instead of after."

"Well, some good news and some bad," said Tom. "We get the Doolies sooner—bad for them; and we get a better break in the spring. The gold tags say the field trips are a blast—lots of interesting Air Force things, great socializing—namely girls—and lots of free time. Finals before Christmas is a master stroke. Damn, Cloud, where do you get all your info?"

"Ah, remember, Cindy works for the Commandant. She hears and sees a lot."

Refreshed, we headed for our rooms; everyone in a better mood, including Hertz.

***

Back in the room, Tom and I began putting an inspection shine on our shoes, anticipating the dreaded "buck up" leading up to Recognition Day. "Finish all your homework?" I asked.

"Yeah, including my 600 word English essay," Tom said smugly.

"Six hundred words; that's half what Major Galt gives us. But, I'm sure your work will outshine Thoreau."

"Yeah, and what was your trig grade, smart ass?"

"Hey, it was 82.4, but you're right, I'll take your help for the final."

***

Monday was relatively quiet. The upperclassmen at the tennis table were rehashing the matches and their encounters with Wyoming girls. I was glad that none of them saw me with Susie, especially the ones that knew I was going with Linda.

***

As we marched back from afternoon Tuesday English class, the loudspeaker gave its usual warning hiss. **"Attention in the area, attention in the area; this is a Yellow Alert. I say again, attention in the area; this is a Yellow Alert. All personnel take appropriate actions."**

Sutton double timed the section back to the barracks and gave a quick 'dismissed.'

"Here they go again," I said. "We're going to play army. We thought they'd get us in the middle of the night last weekend . . ."

"Yeah, we had to go through all that crap: packing the field gear, getting our combat uniform ready, making sure the M1 was polished and clean. The upperclassmen sure had that wrong. So here it's after class and they are going to ruin our Tuesday afternoon."

I dug my field pack out of the closet, grabbed shorts and T-shirts, and recovered the fatigue set stored in my laundry bag. "No sense ruining a new set of fatigues. If I know the upperclassmen, we'll be doing calisthenics in addition to inspecting all the field gear."

"Whiteman is great for inspecting and giving out demerits. I thought this is meant to be military training, not harass the Fourth Classmen."

"Boy, this really torques me," said Tom. "I need the wrestling practice time. Colorado is coming up and they are tough. Zaleski, the team captain, is going to be pissed. He said we need every minute we can get to practice."

"Zaleski, is that the football player?"

"Right, he's a heavyweight; really good."

"This is going to mess up Tennis practice too. This is only the second nice day we've had in a week. Practicing outside is tough when the weather doesn't cooperate."

***

"**Sixth Squadron**," Cadet Jay's command voice called out. "**Fall out on the double**; four minutes until roll call. Make sure you have your gear and water in your canteens."

"Oh, crap," Tom said. "Give me your canteen; we still have Kool-Aid in them."

Tom ran down the hall into the latrine and returned in two minutes. "Here, Davis, you owe me. Fortunately, the upperclassmen are behind, so there weren't any in the hallway. Of course, Bourque was in the bathroom emptying and rinsing his canteen."

"Good catch, Tom. Remember last time, we didn't get it done. Hot Kool-Aid was terrible when Cadet Thomas made us drink it. And after three hours, it got mighty thirsty out."

Rushing out the door, we slid into formation 30 seconds ahead a couple of upperclassmen. "**Squadron . . . Atten . . . shun**," Cadet Jay sang out.

"**Sixth Squadron all present and accounted for, Sir,**" Jay reported to the Group Commander. Orders cascaded from Wing to Group to Squadrons, Cadet Jay ordered, "**Right Shoulder . . . Arms . . . Column of Flights, A Flight . . . Forward March.**"

***

The Yellow Alert was meant to simulate a real life emergency. But, of course, if it were a nuclear attack—which some feared—being in the field we'd all be fried due to exposure to radiation. While cadets, including upperclassmen, considered the exercise one of futility and another attempt to make us feel military, the Commandant and his staff considered the exercise important. Some heard the Dean thought it was a waste of time.

We marched five miles along a circular route that ended on the safe area of the Lowry bombing range. Each squadron set up tents and unpacked their gear for field inspection.

The norm was to make positive corrections, treating the exercise as a training session. Captain Braswell had an unusual quirk: he gave out one demerit to upperclassmen for not including paper clips and rubber bands in their gear. No one could figure out his reasoning.

When a cadet tried to beat the system, by not packing the proper equipment—some upperclassmen had paper stuffed in their backpacks—he earned five demerits. Tom and I had seen that happen and made an honest effort to play the game straight.

Once rifles were stacked, tents set up, and field equipment checked, we went by squadron to a field mess. We used mess kits, but the kitchen provided plastic forks and knives, napkins, and beverages. As usual, Lt. Col. Echelberger fed the troops well. The menu consisted of barbeque pork, red beans, macaroni and cheese, and a three bean salad. Chocolate cake and vanilla ice cream completed the menu. The best part—Fourth Classmen were at ease.

After dinner, squadrons assembled for lectures on escape and evasion, survival techniques, and the meaning of the code of conduct. The sun approached the peaks of the Rockies as squadrons formed up and marched back to the quarters. We arrived shortly before call to quarters—the Dean insisted study time was inviolate.

"Well, that was fun," I told Tom as I sat down to study.

"Yeah, I think they want to make sure we don't want to go in the Army. At least I can add another merit badge to my Eagle Scout vest."

United States Air Force Academy
Sunday, 27 April 1958

Dear Folks,

Received two letters yesterday. Thanks. My other letters have been sparse. Guess everyone's getting ready for graduation (like Walt).

Being with the tennis team, I don't have intramurals. The tennis team lost a match to Wyoming—7 to 0. But, I had a date with a cute blond named Susie. She showed me Laramie; not much to see. We had hamburgers and shakes at a place called the Corral.

We had a "Yellow Alert" this week. We play Army and go to the field, set up tents, and have lectures on survival and escape and evasion. The Dean thinks it is a waste of time, but it does remind us that this is a military school.

There are only 36 days until Recognition and 38 until San Francisco. We have some good things happening. There is a Glenn Miller concert and we're going to the Tabor Theater to see *South Pacific.*

The Squadron, the Protestant Choir, and the Tennis Team have picnics next month. The Squadron's going to the new site. The Tennis Team has the picnic grounds at Fitzsimons Army Hospital. The Choir's going to Glen Erie.

Hope Pa and Gene are working. Construction work can be iffy. I was lucky when I worked summer before my senior year. The weather was hot—which made digging ditches a bear—but we never got rained out.

I can't wait to see you in June. Tell LeDoux and Walt to let everyone know I'm coming. Well, must close and hit the books and shine the shoes.

God Bless,
Your loving son,
Don

Chapter 53
Base Leg

A cadet's life is different from that of a civilian college student in many ways.
For example, his daily schedule is more exacting . . .
At the Ramparts

Sunday, 4 May, 1958

"Now I remember, Tom, why I don't like khakis," I said, fastening the blue garter belts from my shirt bottom to the inside top of my socks and carefully putting my leg in the highly starched pants."

"What's that, Davis?"

"Well, you have to be so careful getting into the pants so you don't mess up the starched legs or get the cuffs dirty. And the gig line is always a pain. That's one of Whiteman's favorite gigs; that along with 'crooked nametag.'"

"Yeah, and Whiteman's likely to be ready and waiting with the form 10's. Glad your sister sent brownies and little sister Sarah sent chocolate chip cookies. It may be slim pickings at the table the rest of this month."

"I'm still good for two more weeks until after the last game. Too bad wrestling finished so soon. You can have most of the boodle until I get back on a Squadron table."

"Great, thanks, come on let's go face the storm."

***

It was if May Day was the signal to begin the pre-Recognition buck up. Cadet Whiteman wrote me up for crooked gig line and name tag not properly aligned. Cadet John Bush wrote Tom up for improper tie and crooked hat. Unfortunately, we didn't know Captain Braswell had declared demerits would only be awarded for legitimate violations—buck up demerits would not count. Captain Braswell did not want cadets' military standings impacted by fallacious write-ups. The noise in the quadrangle was reminiscent of that first day in July.

Friday was a repeat of Thursday. The dining hall din brought memories of summer training. Training tables were more moderate, but I had to recite "four verses of the Air Force Song" as well as having to recap the last five Wimbledon winners in singles and doubles. I was stumped until the Information Desk Librarian, Mary Jones, researched the names for me.

***

Saturday brought another rude awakening—literally—when the Squadron Third Classmen, dressed in gym gear, woke us at 0430, directed us to dress in combat uniforms, and report to the quadrangle. Tom and I looked at each other in dismay.

"Dumb Smacks, doesn't combat gear mean with M1s and back packs?" shouted Whiteman at Tom and me. "Get your butts in there and bring out your full gear."

In flight formation, we double-timed for five miles, ending up at the obstacle course. Visions of past runs came to mind. *Oh, crap,* I thought, *here comes that damn wall again. How are we going to run the obstacle course with rifles?*

"Okay, men," sang out Cadet Bourque, who seemed to be in charge. "Stack rifles. Be sure you can identify yours when we get back. A Flight, form in front of the starting point."

The obstacle course was as gruesome as I remembered. I did Cadet Javier's trick of dumping my back pack at the front of the wall. My lack of physical conditioning from being the Tennis Team Manger showed. I was blowing hard by the time I reached the wall. Fortunately, Tom was beside me. Seeing my struggle, he offered his hands for a leg up on the wall. I thanked him and struggled over my nemesis, the monster wall.

Thankfully, the run back was only a mile. I staggered into the room. "Damn, Tom. I'm really out of shape. That almost killed me. I'm going to have to do some running. I can do that while the team is practicing." I shoved my dirty fatigues into the laundry bag and polished the stock of my rifle. We still had SAMI looming.

"Yeah, I noticed you were a little ragged. Wrestling conditioning payed off for me. We do five miles and sprints every practice. If we do the obstacle course again, I'll stick with you. But, you'd better get in shape. I think we're in for more fun before Recognition."

"Right, thanks."

Captain Braswell breezed in and out of the room, only looking up at Linda's picture on my side, leading us to believe he was aware of the fun and games going on. Being a West Pointer, he probably empathized with our Doolie plight.

Several of my classmates in the other squadrons took a knee during the hot, clear blue- sky parade. They had also endured the morning exercise. Word came to us in the afternoon that the Commandant decreed there could a "spirit" or obstacle course run, but not both. Exercise time was also limited to 35 minutes.

***

We were so beat that Tom and I decided to stay in the room instead of going to the Fourth Class Club. We'd eat brownies and go to bed early. Much as I hated to, I called Linda and said I couldn't make it to the club, but looked forward to seeing her at the Glenn Miller concert Sunday.

She sounded a little miffed but said "Okay, what time should I be there?"

"The program starts at 3:00 o'clock. Meet me at the theater at 20 of to get good seats."

The theater was packed. A lot of cadets had invited dates. Linda showed up looking pert as usual. She had on a form fitting bright yellow summer dress. It reminded me of the song we sang during formations *Nellie wore a New Dress*. Even though there were 15 minutes until the show began, we found seats about four rows down from the back.

Mr. McKinley began the program with a rendition of *The Star Spangled Banner*. Following the National Anthem, the band played many of Miller's well-known arrangements. The audience was delighted when the band played *In the Mood, Moonlight Serenade, Pennsylvania 6-5000, and A String of Pearls*. Everyone applauded enthusiastically when the show closed with *American Patrol* with Air Force war planes on the screen behind the band.

"Wow that was great. I really like Glen Miller's music," I said.

"Yes," agreed Linda. "Too bad they didn't have them at the Club. We could have danced to their music. It's very smooth and romantic."

Walking to her car I said, "Linda, we have to get back for the evening meal, so I can't see you at the Club. But the Tennis Team's picnic is next Saturday after the parade at Fitzsimons Hospital picnic grounds. Can you drive to the picnic after the parade? They are letting us get our own transportation."

"I'm sorry, Don, I won't be able to make it. We are having a cheerleader competition in Colorado Springs, and I won't be back until about eight in the evening."

"Oh," I said, hoping I didn't look too disappointed. "Well, how about the 25th? The Protestant Choir is having its picnic in Glen Eyrie where we went before. Cloud's date said she would drive. We have to go on the bus."

"I don't know, Don, call me after next weekend. I'll know better then. I think I can make it. It depends on what my folks have planned."

"Oh, okay. I hope you can make it. I miss seeing you."

"I miss seeing you, too," she said as she slid into the driver's seat of her Bel Air. She rolled down the window. Not seeing any upperclassmen, I gave her a quick kiss. She rolled up the window, waved, and drove away.

***

It rained steadily for four days. Because spirit and obstacle course runs would track mud into the barracks, Cadet Jay ruled them out. We'd have preferred the runs; however, to morning shower formations at 0500. We were grilled incessantly on Fourth Class Knowledge and alternated between doing pushups and sit-ups.

On the fourth morning, I challenged Cadet Bourque and his classmates in our dorm to a pushup contest. Expecting only more pushups, I was surprised when Cadet Bourque accepted the challenge on behalf of all Third Classmen. The losers would forfeit desserts for a week. We knew this was a losing proposition even if we won because we did not expect a full meal until Recognition. Each Third Class cadet was paired with a Fourth Classman.

Cadet Bourque stood in front of me. In a low voice he said, "Good show, Davis." Then in a louder voice he commanded: "**Assume the position** . . . **ready** . . . **begin**!

"Fifty four . . . fifty five . . . fifty six . . ." I could see cadets on both sides of the hallway giving out. Cadet Bourque and I gave out at the same time. The contest was tied at 10 apiece, with only Tom and C3C Danny Fey still doing pushups. We all gathered around the two. Both were wrestlers—accounting for their outstanding conditioning.

"Come on, Tom," I encouraged.

"**Get him, Fey**, said Bourque in a loud voice.

"Seventy six . . . seventy seven," Bourque picked up the count. "Seventy eiiiight . . . seventy niiiine . . . both struggled to get to the top; both collapsed at the same time.

"A tie, a **TIE**!" I proclaimed.

"Okay, Doolies, hit the wall, "sputtered Cadet Whiteman.

***

Thursday evening Cadet Bourque arranged for Third and Fourth Classmen from Dormitory 914 to sit together. The story of our bravado in challenging Third Classmen to a push up contest spread throughout the Squadron. Cadet Jay, when he heard the story, told Bourque to sit the contestants at the same table for dinner. The inquisition could be continued during the meal, but when the desserts were served, Fourth Classmen would be allowed to eat their desserts without interruption. What a treat; the dessert was make-your-own sundaes.

***

Friday resumed the morning five mile runs. Per the Commandant's instructions, the obstacle course was not included. Sixth Squadron reserved the obstacle course for Friday. Rain limited tennis practice to the gym. I ran five miles within the gym all week. When Friday came, I kept up with Tom and felt great at the end of the run. The conditioning also helped with the obstacle course on Saturday, but I still accepted Tom's help with the wall.

***

After a hellacious breakfast inquisition—I was now on the "salt mine" table with C3C Whiteman and C/2C Mays. I got three bites of scrambled eggs and half a biscuit, sans butter or jam; we were dismissed to our rooms to put on our summer white parade uniform.

Bless you Armed Forces Day. Instead of SAMI, in-ranks inspection and the regular parade, the Academy buses loaded us up after breakfast and took us to the ops side of Lowry.

Following a concert by the Academy Band, featuring the Army, Navy, Air Force, and Coast Guard songs, Superintendent Briggs gave a short (thank goodness) talk on the role of the armed forces in preserving liberty and freedom. It was a clear, blue-sky Denver morning with a hint of warming quickly.

As scheduled at 1045 hours, the Wing paraded in front of the bleachers along the taxi way. The crowd numbered several thousand with a mix of civilians and uniformed military personnel. We passed in review in front of the Academy Staff, The Lowry Wing Commander, and Navy Officers from Buckley Field. The crowd gave us a standing ovation.

Bussed back to the barracks, we were released until call to quarters. While not technically an open post, the upperclassmen were allowed to leave the base. For those who desired, the noon meal was served in the dining hall. Fourth Classmen skipped going to the dining hall; most opted to go to the Fourth Class Club for a hamburger and a milk shake.

***

"Where're you going?" Tom asked as I got into my grey pants, white shirt picnic outfit.

"The Tennis Team picnic is this afternoon. We're taking the buses to the Fitzsimons picnic area. Starts at 1500 and we don't come back until 1900 . . ."

"After dinner—sneaky."

"Right, the upperclassmen take care of us. Isn't the Wrestling Team's picnic next weekend at Red Rocks?" I'm sure you'll manage to get back after dinner."

"True. You taking or meeting Linda?"

"Nah, she has a cheer leading competition in the Springs."

"Are you going to meet her at the Club tonight?"

"She won't be back. Her folks and the other parents are taking a bunch of the girls to dinner at the Broadmoor."

"You sure she isn't meeting Billy Boy. Your romance seems to have cooled."

"It's okay. I'm sure she will be with her folks." *Hmmm, I wonder. She didn't say who all was going for dinner.*" I'll just come back to the room and study. Finals aren't that far away."

***

The Tennis Team picnic was relaxed. A Country and Western Band performed for an hour or so; then played dancing music for the couples. Cadet Thomas introduced me to his finance, Shirley. She was pretty and pleasant and had flown in from New York on Friday. She was only staying for the weekend.

Colonel Ike's steak, corn on the cob, and salad; topped off with chocolate cake and ice cream made missing the evening meal all the better.

***

Sunday was quiet. Upperclassmen, as usual, were cordial during the practice and service. The theater held mostly cadets. Visitors were sparse. *The new chapel will be nice. Acoustics are supposed to be great. But Mr. Boyd said last week chapel construction is behind schedule. Our Class may not get to use it.*

***

I wandered over to the Fourth Class Club when we arrived back in the cadet area.

"Hi, Davis, where's Linda? asked Cloud.

"She's in C Springs with her folks. She's in a cheer leading contest. Schools from all over the state are competing. It's a two day event, and Linda won't be home until tonight some time. I thought I'd come over and have a milkshake and get away from the terror squad."

"Know what you mean. It's getting pretty nasty. Ah, well, only three weeks and a wake up until we're human again. Have you seen Hertz?"

"He's in his room. He's studying hard. He says he doesn't' give a damn whether he passes or not, but I don't believe him. He might leave, but it will be because he wants to; not because he has to."

"Yeah, he said Tom is helping with the math, and he has been taking extra instruction in chemistry. I think he'll squeak by."

"By the way, where's Cindy?"

"She went down to C Springs with some girlfriends. They were going to stop by the new site. Think the Commandant wanted an informal look at the progress."

"Well, Cloud; I've got to get back to the books. I'm not as pessimistic as Hertz, and I think I've got a shot at the Supe's list[120] again so it's study time.

Purgatory continued on Monday. Added to the morning run or obstacle course, the Third Classmen conducted field pack inspections; repeated after dinner before call to quarters. Anything out of order required a "special inspection" with one of the Third

---

[120] Having all grade averages above 80 per cent and being in the top third of your class military rating put you on the Superintendent's list. The big incentive was extra privileges above the norm for your class.

Classmen. Tom and I suffered along with the rest of our classmates. Toward the end of the week, we were all exhausted and wondering why we were still putting up with all the crap.

The rest of the week was a repeat of Monday, but a funny thing happened on Thursday. After dinner, C3C Bourque inspected our packs in front of our room. "Well, if those aren't two of the sorriest pieces of military equipment I've ever seen. You'll report to my room in five minutes with full field packs and helmets."

"Damn, Tom," I said entering the room and grabbing my helmet, "that's not like Bourque at all. Normally he's such a decent guy."

"Yeah, guess that he's just got the fever. Let's go."

***

"Sir, Cadets Davis and Sanders reporting as ordered," Tom and I said simultaneously.

Cadet Bourque was standing beside his bed. His roommate, Jon McCartney, was sitting at his desk, his radio playing the *Ride of the Valkyries* at high volume.

"Davis and Sanders, I've been watching you two. I'm not sure you two are taking this seriously. Okay. Starting with Davis give me all verses of the Star Spangled Banner."

"Ohh say can you see . . . " I started.

"Hey, Jon," Bourque said, "these Doolies interfering with you listening to your music?"

"Yes, they are Val, why don't you have them knock it off."

"Right, okay, knock it off. At ease."

Tom and I looked at each other, perplexed.

"What's the matter, Dumbsmacks, don't you know what 'at ease' means?"

Cadet Bourque and his roommate told us to take off our helmets and backpacks and to sit on the beds. They brought out several pints of ice cream, packed in bags of ice —no doubt pilfered from the mess hall.

***

"Okay, Dumbsmacks, back to the grind. You have seventeen days left. We'll leave you alone during the week prior to finals and finals week, so you really only have about three terror days left. Hang in there. *Non illegitmus caborumdum!*. DISMISSED."

Tom and I saluted and quickly backed out of the room.

***

United States Air Force Academy
Sunday, 18 May, 1958

Dear Mom and Dad,

Tomorrow we have 14 days left as Doolies. Third Classmen have been all over us. We either run five miles or do the obstacle course before breakfast. I've lost five pounds in the last two weeks .

Actually, the physical part has been good. Being Tennis Team manager made me soft. The mental stuff is no fun. It's really noisy in the dining hall during meals. Reminds me of summer training. Some upperclassmen are really immature. We have shower formations like during summer. Although we did get to the Third Classmen; I challenged them to a push up competition. It was a tie. Cadet Jay, the Squadron Commander let us eat our entire dessert one night - the bet on the contest was desserts.

Oh yes, we don't double time; now we triple time. So, it's good to get back in shape. I will have to bring some running clothes with me on our field trip so I can run every once in a while.

When we're not doing anything (Ha, Ha!), we have to pack up everything to send to the permanent site. We have a large uniform wardrobe box. It is four feet tall with a bar across the top. We hang uniforms on hangers on the bar; tape the hangers to the bar so the uniforms don't fall and get all scrunched up. Then we have a large and a small box to put everything else in. I think they are doing this like a military operation and having the troops move everything. We'll see how it comes out.

We had a Glen Miller Band program last Sunday. Glen Miller, of course, was killed in WWII in Europe. Some band members were from his Army Air Force Band. Ray McKinley, the current conductor, gave a brief history of Miller's life. They played favorites including *In the Mood, String of Pearls,* and *Moonlight Serenade.*

Saturday we paraded at Lowry for Armed Forces Day - for the first time in our white parade uniforms - big hit with the crowd. The Tennis Team picnic was at Fitzsimons Hospital picnic grounds Saturday. Wasn't much fun without Linda. She was in C Springs with her folks. They served steak, corn on the cob, and a salad. The weather was nice; the sun shining, the temperature in the 70's, and a slight breeze. We missed evening meal, one less inquisition.

Val Bourque, our favorite Third Classman, and his roommate, Jon McCartney stunned us Thursday. Bourque ordered Tom and me to his room. We thought it was for a special inspection - with Forth Class knowledge and physical things like pushups. Instead, Bourque broke out a quart of ice cream and offered it to Tom and me. Then he sent us back to our room with a "hang in there." I think things are going to improve a lot after Recognition.

We now have two sets of bunk beds in our room; anticipating the expansion with the new class of over 400. Cadet Jay said we could sleep on the bottom bunk; so naturally that's what we do. Thank goodness we don't have to make the upper beds. It is hard enough just trying to make the bottom bed.

One of the Third Classmen has offered to take movies of Recognition for Tom and me. I can get a roll of color film from the Cadet Story for $1.63. It would be great to have a movie of the Recognition ceremony and the parade.

God Bless,
Your loving son,
Don

Chapter 54
On Final
The daily life of a [Fourth Class] cadet is long and arduous
At the Ramparts

Sunday, 23 May, 1958

"Wow, it was quiet at the table this morning. Like the upperclassmen had forgotten about us," Tom said, as we got back to the room and picked up our things for class.

"Oh, yeah, well if there's a truce, Whiteman and Mays haven't got the word. I had MacArthur's quote and the Superintendent's staff. Whiteman said MacArthur's quote is important. With intramural finals coming up, the Squadron can win some championships. Mays was just Mays. The spirit run this morning didn't do anything for my studies."

"Ah, quit griping, Davis, there are only two more weeks. I heard Bourque talking to McCartney after breakfast. Bourque said the runs will continue, but no obstacle course. He said Jay didn't want anyone to get hurt. They can hassle you at breakfast, but not at lunch; and evenings are olly, olly, oxen free."

"Where'd you get that dumb expression?"

"Geeez, Davis, didn't you ever play kick the can? Come on, we'll be late for class."

***

Tom was tutoring in math. Sutter and I were holding study sessions on advanced English. Our guess was the final would focus on *Atlas Shrugged;* the novel studied most during the past semester. Math and Chemistry were my greatest worries, but with Tom's help and extra instruction in chemistry, I felt comfortable about next week's exams. I was excused from the Military Studies test with a 98 average. I had a 91 in philosophy. Graphics was a "no sweat" test as it was open book and multiple choice. My PE grade was now 81 with the two good bouts in boxing. And I can make the Superintendent's list again if I don't bust any finals.

Friday afternoon was great because all of the squadrons were competing in final intramural games or matches. Tom and I watched the cross-country race, with four squadrons competing – any of which could take first place. Sixth Squadron was nosed out when Tenny Takahasi, my classmate, lost to a Second Class Cadet Faye from 1st Squadron. It was about 1500 and time for the softball game between 6th and 3d for the championship.

"Think we can win?" I asked Tom as we took seats in the bleachers.

"Of course, what kind of squadron spirit is that? Bourque is really sharp on the mound. And McCartney, Brooks, and Willis are all hitting over 300."

Most of our squadron cadets were in the stands. So we had a good cheering section. The game was tied three runs apiece after five innings. In the top of the sixth inning, Bourque walked the first batter. The next batter, Ken Johnson, 3d Squadron, put the ball over the left field fence to take the lead at 5 to 3.

The game stayed that way until the bottom of the seventh. John Stackhouse, a Doolie, struck out the first two batters, Brooks and Willis. Then he walked the next two batters. With two out and two on, McCartney was up. He was 0 for 3. Stackhouse got McCartney on a curve for the first strike, threw two balls to make the count 2 and 1. The next pitch was a fast ball that McCartney blasted over the center field fence. Sixth walked off with 6 to 5 win and the intramural championship.

***

SAMI and in-ranks inspection on Saturday went well. Captain Braswell did the SAMI and the in-ranks. He was whistling and smiling. He came in our room looked at Tom, stepped to my side looked at Linda's picture, gave me a thumbs up and strode out of the room.

"What was that?" I asked Tom.

"Jay told me at the ball game yesterday that Captain Braswell is on the majors' promotion list. Think he is going to announce it at the Squadron Picnic."

***

Saturday afternoon, after breakfast, the Squadron loaded up on three Academy buses for the two and a half-hour trip to the new site and the Squadron picnic. As usual the bus was segregated, with the upperclassmen in front and Doolies in the back of the bus.

"Is Cindy coming down?" I asked Cloud who was sitting next to me.

"Yes, she is driving down with three other girls. How about Linda?"

"No, she's going to a church dinner with her folks. Said she couldn't get out of it."

"How are you two getting along? Seems she's missing a lot with you lately."

"Yeah, I know. What'd you think the new site will look like? They only have a year to get the basics—quarters, mess hall, and academic area ready," I said changing the subject.

***

The upperclassmen weren't hostile, but not overly friendly. Tom and I believed it was because they planned on making the time after finals brutal. Nonetheless, the atmosphere was suitable for a picnic. The fact that many had dates softened the interactions.

The girls were allowed on the buses for the tour of the new site. On each bus was an officer from the Base Civil Engineering Office. They were the ones charged with overseeing the site construction. Captain Dave Brooks was our guide.

We disembarked on the observation area north of the campus off the road from the North Entrance. It was a beautiful setting to get an overview of the new site.

"As you see, they're working on the athletic fields down below us. In the construction area, the Skidmore, Owings, and Merrill design is taking shape. Emphasis is on the cadet quarters – the horizontal buildings nearest us – the dining hall – the square building in the background – and the academic buildings –the buildings on the left of the campus. Still to come are the chapel, the recreational area – which will contain Arnold Hall; the cadet club, the theater/auditorium, and the social area for dances/receptions – and the headquarters building. What you cannot see is the housing areas, the exchange and commissary, and the schools for children of Academy personnel. Those are in valleys or ridges to the south of the campus area.

Construction is on schedule to be able to bring the Wing, including the classes of 1959, 1960, 1961, and 1962, to the new site in August. Are there any questions?"

Art Kerr's hand went up. "Sir, Cadet Fourth Class Kerr, I have had friends come here after a rain storm. They said the area was a sea of mud. Will the area be finished enough so we won't be sloshing through the mud?" There was a ripple of snickers throughout the group.

"Mister Kerr, I wouldn't worry about that. We're taking whatever measures necessary to get to the dining hall and academic areas and back to the quarters without messing up your shoe shines. Okay, let's get back on the bus and have a picnic."

***

Picnic tables were on the area cleared for the tennis courts. The weather was cooperating, with sunshine and blue skies. The Base Recreation Section set up several volleyball and horse shoe courts. They also provided bases, balls, and bats for softball games.

"Where's your date, Davis?" Cadet Bourque asked.

"Ah, she could not make it. She is with her folks today at a church function."

"Yeah, I'll bet, Anyway, too bad. I was looking forward to seeing Linda."

Damn, he remembers her name. I wonder if he is going to hit on her. Probably. I guess he can't get his own dates. Well, Linda is cute.

***

At 1300, Colonel Ike and his staff dished out fried chicken, macaroni salad, baked beans, and rolls. Desert was chocolate cake. In addition to lemonade, water and coffee were available.

Around 1500, after everyone had eaten, Captain Braswell announced he was on the promotion list to major. We gave him a loud round of applause.

"In recognition of my promotion and the part you all have played in making that happen, there will be no SAMI or in-ranks inspection next week. On Monday, Fourth Classmen will sit at ease all day. Cheerfully, we got on the buses for the trip back to Lowry. Most cadets, having stuffed themselves, took up their favorite pastime—napping.

***

"Want to go over to the Club?" Tom asked as we got back to the room. "That was a great picnic, but I could use a hot dog or a burger to tide me over."

"I'm not hungry. I have some cookies Mom sent me. Think I'll hit the books."

"Why didn't you ask Linda to come over?"

"Ah, I wasn't sure what time we'd get back. I'll see her tomorrow at the Choir Picnic."

"Damn, Davis, you've escaped part of the inquisition again. Where are you going?"

"We're going back to Glen Eyrie. I have to go on the bus, so Linda's going to meet me."

***

For the second day in a row, the Colorado weather was beautiful. Blue skies and sunshine a temperature in the mid-seventies, up from a frosty morning 40 degrees. I was in good spirits anticipating spending the day with Linda. I was sure the food would, as always, be outstanding. Rumor was Colonel Ike had prepared bar-b-que beef and pork, along with the usual trimmings.

"Hi, I said," as I met Linda who was waiting as the buses pulled up. "I didn't expect to see you when we got here."

Linda was dressed in her Levi jeans and jacket, with a light, white sweater under the jacket. She came prepared for hiking with tennis shoes. Fortunately we were allowed to wear tennis shoes with our picnic uniform and I had chosen to do so.

"Well, I came down with Cindy. She doesn't pay much attention to speed limits. Fortunately, the highway patrol wasn't out today. It's good to see you."

"It's great to see you. How did the cheerleading contest go?"

Linda beamed. "We took first place in the varsity competition. The junior varsity squad was third. So we got first place ribbons for the overall completion."

"That's great. I'm proud of you."

We were free to explore Glen Eyrie and the surrounding grounds until lunch time. Since Linda and I had seen the Castle, we decided to explore the grounds. We passed along a small creek with a foot or two of rushing water.

"Look," said Linda, "there's a bridge over the creek. Looks like the path that goes into the woods toward the Red Rocks. Let's go explore."

"Okay," I replied, "let's see what we can see."

We crossed the bridge and followed the path between the towering pines. About a mile down the path the trail split; one part leading deeper into the forest; the other reaching toward the red rock formations.

"Which way do you want to go?" I asked.

"Oh, let's take the one to the Red Rocks," Linda answered. "That looks like the road less traveled." She took my hand.

I chuckled at Linda's reference to a Robert Frost poem. *Damn she's not only cute; she's smart, an achiever, and even intellectual.* "Okay, let's go."

A mile and a half down the path, it opened up and we encountered the beginnings of rock formations. We traveled until we came to a place where we could climb the rocks.

"Be careful," I said. "There are rattlesnakes around. Although it's probably a little early for them since the mornings are still in the forties."

"I know. I'll watch where I'm going." She started climbing, dragging me behind her. When she reached a flat rock about eight feet wide, she sat down.

I sat beside her. She took off her jacket and laid it on the rock. She reached over and kissed me. I could feel excitement pulsing through my body. I put my arm around her and returned the kiss. Linda lay back upon her jacket.

I felt her breath quicken as I put my hand on her breast and we French kissed.

"Don't, Don," she said as I dropped my hand to the top button on her jeans. "This is too uncomfortable . . . and besides, what if a rattlesnake or an upperclassman came along. That would be embarrassing."

"You're right," I said getting up and pulling her beside me. *Damn, she's going to drive me crazy. Oh, for a motel room.* "Oh, oh, it's 1:15, we'd better get back. They'll have eaten all the food."

As we walked along the path back toward Glen Eyrie, Linda said: "Are you excited about your field trip and leave at home?"

"Sure. The upperclassmen say field trips are great. We learn a lot about the Air Force, have great dinners . . ."

"And meet girls."

"Well, they do have dances and receptions with girls, and we are expected to mingle."

"And have you contacted your old flames and let them know you are coming back?"

"Well, I don't have any old flames. I told Mom to tell a couple of my buddies I'm coming home so they can set up a party or two. Why all the questions?"

"Just wondering how much I'll see you this summer. You're going to be gone a lot."

"Yeah, I know, But I will call you as soon as I'm back. Being a Third Classman, I'll be able to get off base a lot more."

"That'll be nice," she said as we crossed the bridge and walked toward the picnic area.

***

The ride back to the Academy was long. I couldn't take my usual nap. I was thinking about my conversation with Linda. I wasn't sure what it was all about, but I wasn't having pleasant thoughts about our relationship.

The dorms were very quiet that evening. You could almost hear pages turning as everyone was doing last minute cramming for finals.

***

The agony began Monday morning with my first final – chemistry. Eighty percent of the final was derived from a standard college general chemistry curriculum given to students all over the country. I was sure this was done so the Dean could compare our results with the national averages. The other part (20 percent) was a problem written by the chemistry department. The chemistry department problem was hard and probably a curve setter.

The first part was basically taught in class, with the instructor emphasizing important theories and formulas. The second part was material we'd seen, but was not highlighted in class. I was comfortable with the first part and thought I might have aced it. I struggled with the second part, but got most of the formulas done even though I didn't get the final answer.

From the groans of my classmates, I think the test was a challenge for everyone. Thank goodness for partial credit and the curve.

The graphics final Tuesday morning was a 100 question multiple-choice test. Most questions had an obvious answer identified, with only one other answers even close. Think I aced it. Philosophy scheduled their test for Tuesday afternoon. It too was an easy exam. I finished in two hours of the allotted three. No chance of busting this one.

Wednesday was open for me since my grade in Military Studies allowed me to skip the final. A couple of guys, also eligible to skip the test, took it anyway hoping to up their average. I spent the day concentrating on math and studying Tom's notes.

The math test was as hard as I anticipated. Guess my lower grade in the SATs was legitimate. The test covered the spectrum of topics in Rees and Sparks *College Algebra –*

Third Edition from definitions, such as integer to rational numbers to irrational numbers, to quadratic equations to linear and fractional equations. Ten challenging problems tested knowledge, problem solving skill, and the ability to quickly solve problems. I was all right with the definitions and did some work on all of the problems. I had solutions for six of the problems, but only partial work on the rest. As with chemistry, I was counting on credit for partial work and the curve. I didn't have much hope for help with the curve because so many of my class had solid foundations in math.

The final I was most comfortable with was English. It was a class I enjoyed and, with Sutter, had put in a lot of study time. Friday morning was overcast. The temperature was a comfortable 65 degrees. I had a good night's sleep and was ready for Major Galt's challenges.

"Room, attention," called out Sutter.

"Take seats, gentlemen. Good morning. Glad you could join us this morning," said Major Galt. "I hope you enjoy our little exercise. You have three hours." Passing out the exams and blue books, he said, "Begin," and left the room.

The test was pretty much as Sutter and I had guessed. The first question was "Who is John Galt?" I began: "John Galt is an industrialist intent on saving the US Society from an ever encroaching and malevolent government. He is the protagonist, although he shares the role of protagonist with Dagny Taggart. Dagny initially views Galt as an enemy rather than seeing him as an ally in her efforts to counter the oppressive government."

The second question was: Who was Ayn Rand: I explained: "Alisa Rosenbaum (Ayn Rand) was born in St. Petersburg, Russia. She immigrated to the US in 1926 with her family. In addition to her best-selling book, *Atlas Shrugged*, she wrote *The Fountain Head.*

The third question was: What was the theme of the book. My response was: "Because of her background, Ayn strongly believed in 'Objectivism—a philosophy that champions capitalism and pre-eminence of the individual.' In *Atlas Shrugged*, she builds her beliefs in objectivism into the underlying theme of the book. The fight of her protagonists is to counter a government that is attempting to destroy both capitalism and individualism."

Asked to define three characters, I chose Dagny Taggart, the female protagonist and Vice President of Taggart Transcontinental Railways; John Galt, the mysterious organizer of the rebellion against the corrupt government; and Francisco d'Anconia, a cohort of Galt and an energetic recruiter of the "disappearing businessmen."

I was exhausted but satisfied I'd done a good job on the exam and might even add a point or two to my final average.

When I finished, I triple-timed to the room and threw the blue comforter on the floor.

***

"Come on, Davis, wake up, Tom said nudging me with his foot. "The tormentors are on open post and we have the run of the place. I understand Colonel Ike has laid on steaks, mashed potatoes, and sundaes for dessert. We can go over to the club after dinner. Did you call Linda?"

"Uh, yes I did. She is going to meet me about 1830. I heard Mrs. McComas has scheduled a combo for dancing."

***

Dressed in a short, blue skirt, a white blouse, and a peach colored sweater that had a falcon embroidered on the pocket, she was as smart looking as ever. Her page boy neatly outlined her cherubic face.

"Hi," I said. "Long time since Sunday, which was really great by the way. Glad you could make it tonight."

Giving me a coy smile, she said, "Hi. I thought I'd better see you before you go traveling around the country. Can we get a coke, I'm thirsty."

We walked over to the table with Cloud, Hertz—who was sitting with a cute redhead—and Tom, also with his friend from Denver University. "Hi, guys . . . and, of course, girls."

Everyone said "hi." Hertz introduced his date, Gloria, and Tom reintroduced Sandy.

"How'd you do?" said Cloud asking the question on all of our minds.

"I did all right. How about you?"

"I'm sure I squeaked by."

"Hertz, what's your story? You still with us?"

"Damned if I know. I did ask about my math score. That was a 76 ,so I'm safe there. I'll have to see what happens in Chem. They were going to post the grades by Sunday, right?

"Yeah, that's what I heard," I said. "I have to get cokes. Anybody want anything?'

As I returned with the cokes, I looked at Linda and said, "Let's dance."

The evening was spent talking about grades and the field trip, enthralling the girls, I'm sure. I danced almost every dance with Linda. She was warm and her perfume was intoxicating as ever. Yet she seemed a little distant.

Just before call to quarters, at 2200, I walked Linda to the door. "You seem a little bit distracted tonight; what is it?"

"Well, Don, I have been thinking a lot about this summer. I don't think it is going to work for us." With that she handed me the box with my Academy pin in it.

Wow, I wasn't expecting this. I really like Linda. But maybe she's right. "Look, I still feel the same about you; guess you could call it love. But, I understand what you are saying. Keep the pin. Put it on Freddy the Falcon. I'll call you when I get back. We'll have to get together. Okay?"

Linda smiled slightly. A tear ran down her cheek. "Good night," she said quietly.

Without looking around, I said "Good night," and kissed her. The night seemed particularly dark as I made my way back to the room.

***

The next two days were hellacious. It began Saturday morning with a 0400 wakeup and a five mile run. Breakfast was worse than the first day of summer. Each Third Classman at the table concentrated on a particular Fourth Classman. No Doolie got a bite to eat.

In-room inspections were conducted by the Third Classmen. Cadet Whiteman, of course, inspected our room. Not only did he call out discrepancies to his cohort, Cadet Phil Brooks, he tore up the beds, took things from the shelves and threw them on the floor, and dumped the contents of our laundry bags.

"Damn, Tom, that was worse than any ATO treated us."

"Yeah, some of these jokers are really immature; can't see them as Air Force officers, much less as commanders. I hope our class is better as upperclassmen."

In-ranks inspection began as a new ordeal. Cadet Whiteman was in front of Tom and me. "Okay Davis, chin in. Nice gig line. Hit it for ten."

As I was finishing the push-ups, Cadet Jay was walking by monitoring the inspection. "Whiteman, knock it off. We have a parade to go and we don't want any of our cadets to have messed up uniforms. I'll have a word with you in my room after the parade."

As the in-ranks was ending, a huge thunderstorm moved in from the west. Just as we were dismissed, the rain began coming down in a torrent. Within minutes, three inches of water flooded the quad. The rain continued as the storm seemed to be stalled over the base.

"Attention in the area, attention in the area. This morning's parade is cancelled," announced Command Post.

Cheers rang out from the dormitories. "How lucky can we get?" I asked Tom.

"Right. And with rain we can't do spirit runs. So we don't have anything until lunch formation. They can't come in our rooms. It's blue comforter time."

***

The inquisition continued for lunch, dinner, and Sunday breakfast. Tom and I had run out of boodle, so the lack of food was beginning to tell. Choir practice and Sunday chapel provided a welcome break from the continual harassment.

Lunch was suspiciously quiet. We were allowed to eat our fill while performing our normal table duties. Rumor was that the chaplains had ordered that Fourth Classmen would get a full meal at lunch time. Whatever the reason, we were thankful for the respite.

We were also left in peace Sunday afternoon and allowed to visit the bulletin boards where our grades were posted. I was delighted with my grades; they were: chemistry: 85.6; math: 83.4; graphics: 87.2; English: 87.4 (with a 97 on the final); philosophy: 89, military studies: 98; and PE: 81. Best of all, I made the Superintendent's Merit List. I quickly glanced at Hertz's grades. Great, everyone was over 70. Hertz was still a classmate.

Since the storms passed, Sunday afternoon brought spirit runs both before and after dinner. Sunday night was quiet after call to quarters. I had no trouble getting to sleep as soon as I hit my comforter.

United States Air Force Academy
Sunday, 1 June 1958

Dear Mom and Dad,

Well tomorrow is the magic day, Recognition. I wasn't sure I was going to make it this far. The past two days have been horrific. We were treated worse by the upperclassmen than we ever were by Air Training Officers. We had little to eat. Tom and I survived on the boodle you and his sister sent. Even so, I lost eight pounds between running and the Doolie diet. Oh, well. I'll look good when I see you.

We did well in intramurals. Won the softball championship and placed second or third in the other sports. I'll get an Academy letter for Assistant Tennis Team Manager.

We had three picnics the last couple of weeks. That was good because we got something to eat. The Squadron Picnic was at the new site. It's coming together. They're working on the dormitories, the academic area, and the dining hall. But, a lot of construction isn't finished.

The open areas are going to be giant mud puddles. We won't have any recreational facilities or chapel. Don't know how they are going to manage with mandatory chapel. Good news is we will probably get more off base privileges.

I took Linda to the Choir picnic. We had a good time. However, when I saw her after finals were over, she broke up with me. She's worried I am going to see old girl friends when I come home and have dates on the field trips. We are still friends, I guess. I will try to call her when I get back here. I really do like her.

Must close. I'm beat. Want to be nice and fresh for tomorrow.

God Bless.

Your loving son,

Don

Chapter 55
Recognition

For a full year, we have known the punishment, both physical and mental,
that befalls any entrant in any military academy .
Dennis Dillon, June, 1958 Talon

2 June, 1958

I was awake at 0400, anticipating a knock on the door. None came. My fatigues were on top of the laundry bag in anticipation of an assembly call for a five mile run.

When no call came, I sat and read *Contrails* from front to back. I had been through every item in the book the past two days. I could not believe this day had arrived.

"You awake, Tom."

"Yeah, can't sleep. What're you doing up?"

"I couldn't sleep either. What do you think they'll do to us today?"

"Have no idea. What more could they do?"

***

My classmates and I formed up at first call for breakfast. No upperclassmen were present. At one minute to final call, the upperclassmen came out and took their assigned places.

As we marched to breakfast, the Academy Band was playing Sousa marches. The Squadron cadence was in perfect time to the music. I glanced sideways; a straight line stretched to the end of the formation.

"Okay, Mister Dickson," said Cadet Thomas, "give me the lowest rank in the Air Force. When he finishes, Mister Davis, you give me the next rank in the Air Force. Begin."

Crap, I thought, *they are going to keep this up until the last minute.*

"Sir, the lowest rank in the Air Force is a second lieutenant."

"Davis, did I say the officers' ranks."

"No, sir." *Damn, bet the President's cabinet is next. What is the lowest rank . . . oh, yeah.*

"Then start with the lowest rank."

"Sir, the lowest rank in the Air Force is airman basic."

"Dickson . . ."

"Sir, the next rank in the Air Force is an airman third class."

Tom described four star general as the top Air Force rank. Thomas simply said, "Eat."

***

As we stood at attention, the upperclassmen began coming out of the building. Without a word, they again took their positions.

"Squadron, **Atten...shun,**" called out Cadet Lieutenant Colonel Jay. Upperclassman, fall out and perform your duties."

Crap, I thought again as C2C Thomas slid in front of me.

"Well, C3C Davis, congratulations. I've enjoyed having you in my flight and on the tennis team." Taking a pair of Third Class shoulder boards from his pocket, he fastened them on my uniform.

The next person who stepped in front of me was C3C Whiteman. "Good show, Don. I'm Ed. Sorry for all the hassle. At first I was pissed at you for outing Short. Later I thought you were courageous to stand up to him. He didn't belong here. I don't think we are in the same squadron next year. But let's go have a drink some open post."

Cadet Jay appeared in front of me. "Davis, when you first got in the Squadron, I didn't think you were going to make it. Then, when I figured out what Short was doing, I talked with Captain Braswell. We decided you needed a chance with a clean slate. I watched you not only in the Squadron, but with the choir. You're a good cadet. Keep it up." With that, he pinned the prop and wings on my collar.

Cadets Bourque and McCartney stood on either side of me. "Good show, Davis, you did a good job of playing the game. It's Val, by the Way."

"And I'm Jon. You're a credit to your class. I hope we can do some things together, like double date maybe. Of course, only if you bring that cutie Linda along," said Bourque.

Well, Val, I haven't decided what to do about Linda yet. But you and Jon have been great. I just might give you her phone number. "That would be great. I'll look you two up when we get back from the field trip."

After all the upperclassman had trooped the line, Cadet Jay announced: "In honor of you receiving your prop and wings, the Superintendent has declared the uniform for the parade is Class A Khakis. You don't have to change. Don't forget your white gloves. **Dismissed.**"

***

The perfect day continued. Blue skies and a 70 degree temperature were ideal for a parade. The march on and the officers front and center were flawless. The Superintendent, the Commandant, and the Dean all sat on the reviewing stand. The bleachers were full of guests, most wearing colorful red, white, and blue clothing.

After the officers' front and center, the Superintendent walked to the podium.

"Members of the Class of 1961, now Third Classmen at this, the newest of our military Academies. Congratulations. You are part of the tradition that will become the

'Long Blue Line'. You have been sorely tested in what *Newsweek* has described as 'The Toughest School in America.' You bade farewell to our Air Training Officers, who by the way, were high in their praise of your class. You have trained the upperclassmen to be upperclassmen.

You must now apply yourselves for the rest of the program so that you may graduate as second lieutenants in the finest Air Force in the world. You also have the distinction of being the last class to graduate as navigators. Most of you will go on to pilot training and on to flying careers. But you will also have been prepared to assume ever increasing responsibilities in the Air Force. We expect most of you to provide the future leadership in the Air Force.

You have reached a very important plateau in your lives and careers. There are many difficult stairs left for you to climb. You have been tested, so I know you will succeed in whatever endeavors you undertake. Good luck and God's Speed."

As the Superintendent finished his remarks, the sky over the parade ground was

filled with the USAF Thunderbirds formation. The rolling thunder of their F-100s boomed as they flew over us. I looked up as the sleek aircraft roared overhead. I saw the red, white, and blue Thunderbird emblem of their underbellies flash by.

Wow. I have not felt this much exhilaration since I received that telegram from Congressman Moss. I believe I can do whatever I set my mind to do. I know there are more challenges, but the walls will not stop me. I know why I endured the torment of Doolie year. I will proudly serve our country as a United States Air Force Officer.

AF photo by Staff Sgt. Larry Reid Jr.
http://afthunderbirds.com/site/2012/12/20/delta-burst-2/

Epilogue

Part One

Having completed the toughest year in the toughest school in America, the survivors began the journey to graduation, three years hence. There were challenges and obstacles to meet and overcome, but also some educational, entertaining, and enjoyable activities.

Seventeen percent (51 Fourth Classmen) of the Class did not finish the first year. The losses were from a lack of desire or ability, lack of skills to consistently achieve the 70% academic requirement, self-initiated-eliminations, and medical dismissals. The first year Class of Sixty-One loses were similar to losses of the Class of 1960 and less than those of 1959.

The giant elephant in the room was academics. Studies included collegiate, military, and airmanship programs. All three areas of studies were administered throughout the summer periods as well as during the academic year.

The curriculum, never easy, became more difficult as we advanced from Fourth to First Class Cadets. The regular academic year classes first semester, 1957, were as follows:

Fourth Class Year

Course	Number	Title	Credits
Chemistry	101	General	3
English	105	Composition, Speech, Semantics, Literature	3
Geography	101	Physical and Cultural	3
Graphics	101	Engineering Drawing	2
Mathematics	101	Algebra, Plane Trig, Spherical Trig, Anal. Geometry Intro to Calculus	5
Physical Education	101	Handball, Judo, Boxing, Basketball, Gymnastics Tests, Intermural Sports	N
Fly Tng	101	Equip Orientation, Physiology of Flight	3/4
Military Studies	101	Airpower & National Security	¾

N* - Continuous - Courses are in addition to weekly room, in-ranks inspections, parades, and extra duties such as mail distributor. These are academic year only and do not include summer term courses.

Academics were a shock to most cadets entering the Academy after high school. Even those with a year or two of regular college courses found the Academy's program challenging. Math courses were the most challenging for Fourth Classmen. The continuing pressure of the Fourth Class System was a burden not found in normal colleges and tested "Doolie" stamina.

Third Class Year

Course	Number	Title	Credits
Hist	102	US History	3
Math	202	Calculus & Intro to Differential Equations	3
Physics	202	Basic & Modern Physics	3
Pol Sci	202	Contemporary Foreign Governments	2 ½
Physical Education	202	Unarmed Combat	1/8
Nav	202	Celestial Navigation & Meteorology	2 ½
Military Studies	202	Airpower II	2 ½
Military Studies	204	Field Studies: Army, Navy /USAF	2 ½

Weekly room, in-ranks inspections, parades, and extra duties were still imposed. Navigation training required bus trips to/from Lowry. Field Studies: A visit to Pensacola, Florida, provided an introduction to Navy equipment and missions. The Army units at Fort Benning, Georgia, staged an all-out combat scenario. Air Force logistics and research and development were highlighted at Tinker AFB, Oklahoma, and Wright Patterson AFB, Ohio respectively. Formal dances featuring dates with local girls occurred at every stop.

Summer courses by class. The Second Class courses are reflective of the mix of academic subjects and military requirements. For instance, Instructor training and Duty with Basic Cadets are military requirements and specific to the Second Class. Duty with an Air Force Unit (Operation Third Lieutenant) was only offered the Second Class summer. Other summer events included Flight Orientation Training in the T-34, T-37, and the T-28. Some chose to give up leave for options such as Army Parachute Training.

Second Class Year (Summer)

Course	Number	Title – May 1960 Term	Credits
Ldr Stu	203	Instructor Training	1 ¼
Ldr Stu	400	Duty with Basic Cadets	3
Mil Stu	410	Contemporary Military Thought	1
Nav	400	Advanced Navigational Techniques	¾

Second Class Year (Summer II)

Course	Number	Title – Summer Term	Credits
Ldr Stu	400	Duty with Basic Cadets	3
Ldr Stu	410	Duty Air Force Unit*	1 ½
Nav	400	Advanced Navigational Techniques	¾

Second Class Year

Course	Number	Title	Credits
Econ	301	Economic Principles and Problems	2 ½
El Engr	301	Circuits and Machinery	3 ¾
Hist	201	Recent World History	3
Ldr Stu	301	Psychology of Adjustment	2 ½
Thermo	301	Fundamental Thermodynamics	3
Mech	301	Mechanical Engineering	3
Nav	301	Radar Navigation	1 7/8
Phy Ed	301	Swimming	1/8
Phy Ed	305	Intramurals/Intercollegiate Sports	1

In addition to the regular duties, leadership/wing support roles demanded extra time. Navigation missions from Lowry took one or two days from academics. The missions, employing advanced techniques, required study and good performance on the flights.

First Class courses in Aerodynamics and Astronautics kept academic pressure on. First Classmen were responsible for administration of the Wing including Squadron, Group, and Wing Staff positions. Privileges were broadened and some demands, such as Call to Quarters were lessened. Of course car purchases and graduation planning were new burdens.

First Class Year

Course	Number	Title	Credits
Aeronaut	401	Basic Aerodynamics	3
Astro	401	Elements of Astronautics	3
Engl	401	Masterworks of Western Literature	3
Law	311	Introduction to Law	2 ½
Pol Sci	401	International Relations	2 ½
Nav	202	Celestial Navigation & Meteorology	2 ½
Span*	211	Elementary Spoken Spanish	2 ½
Phy Ed	405	Competitive Athletics	2

Span* In addition to Spanish; French, German, and Russian were offered. First Classmen "ran the Wing." Navigation was still a time consumer. Graduation preparations: Buying/tailoring Air Force uniforms; choosing a pilot training base/non-flying assignment; buying a car, arranging a wedding (some), passing the navigation check ride (resulting in a navigator rating), and ensuring all grades remained above 70 percent all required additional efforts.

Proficiency and Cadet Life

Proficiency was defined as above a 70% average in all courses. Failure to maintain the average resulted in being "deficient." A deficient cadet could not participate in intercollegiate athletics, go on optional field trips – such as the Protestant Choir trip to DC – and, worst of all, not enjoy stress relieving privileges afforded to a cadet based on his class. Academic achievement – on the Dean's/ the Superintendent's List – meant extra privileges.

In July, 1958, the Superintendent, General James E. Briggs, informed parents of the status of the Wing in a "Dear Parents" letter. In it, he outlined the "privileges" which "are contingent upon maintaining a high standard of cadet performance."[121]

Cadet Privileges at the New Site

Class	Off Base Privilege	Week End Leave	Call to Quarters	Civilian Clothes
First	Unlimited	1 a Month	Not required	On leave/off base
Second*	1 a Week	1 Fall/2 Spring	Required	No
Third**	1 Month	1 Spring	Required	No
Fourth	None	None	Required	No

Second* Second Classmen on the Superintendent's List: 2 Fall Semester Weekend Leaves and 3 in the Spring; also not required to observe evening Call to Quarters. **Third****Third Classmen on Superintendent's List; Off Base Privileges once a week; a Weekend Leave Fall Semester and two Spring Semester. **Fourth Classmen** Fourth Classmen would have a tough beginning at the new site. Recreational facilities were not finished, Colorado Springs was 15 miles away, with no established transportation to the City. Dates would have to provide their own transportation. Actually, all cadets, except First Classmen when they received their cars, would require their dates to have cars.

---

[121] High standards included academic proficiency and no awarded confinements and/or tours.

Deficiency at semester end (or doing summer studies) meant an opportunity to take a "turn-out" (make-up) exam. Failure of the exam meant meeting an Officer Academic Board.

Depending on the degree of failure, motivation of the cadet, and the cadet's willingness to accept the Board's decision, a cadet might be allowed to repeat the courses while being "turned back" to the following class. The Class of 1961 had seven turn backs, six of whom graduated with the Class. Failure of two or more classes resulted in a "turn out;" that is, dismissal. Dismissal, however, for the first three classes held no military consequence except eligibility for the draft. We were the last class not faced with serving in the Air Force Reserve if released from the Academy.[122]

Academics accounted for only 5% (15) of Class losses for the first year; and six of those washed back to the Class of 1962. However, many classmates struggled with the Deficiency Demon. After initial summer training, the big challenge was academics. Chemistry and math kept several classmates dancing along the 70% line; sweating quizzes, graded reviews, and finals our first year.

The Navigation Program proved a challenge to some. There was always a worry factor after a mission, especially if there was bad weather and a questionable performance. One of the more notable episodes involved football star, Bob Brickey. Following a particularly difficult mission, Brickey was uncertain about his performance. This occurred after the team's unbeaten football season and a zero to zero tie with Texas Christian University in the Cotton Bowl.

Hoping to positively influence his score., Brickey wrote at the bottom of his navigation log: AFA – 0, TCU -- 0. Several days later, Brickey log was returned. At the bottom of the paper was the annotation: AFA – 0, TCU –0, Brickey –0 in red ink.

In the Third Class year, Physics and Math (with calculus and differential equations) were the worries. In our Second Class year, Mechanics, Thermodynamics, and Electrical Engineering gave humanities students headaches and sleepless nights. Astronautics and Aerodynamics worried First Classman concerned about graduating.

New Academy Academics

All Classes benefited from the initiative, innovation, perseverance, and leadership of the first permanent Dean, Colonel (later Brigadier General) Robert F. McDermott.

---

[122] Beginning with the Class of 1962, cadets who separated would be transferred to the Air Force Reserve as enlisted personnel with a six year military obligation.

Appointed as Dean in 1959 by President Eisenhower, McDermott has been called "The Father of Modern Military Education."

General McDermott believed cadets should be prepared to be problem solvers and educated to be future Air Force leaders; as opposed to West Point and Annapolis, which prepared their students for their first assignment after graduation. Determined to create a new "military mind,' McDermott's efforts drove West Point and Annapolis to grudgingly follow suit. His curriculum balanced the sciences, social sciences, and military education.

Our class was admitted under a "whole man" concept; meaning applicants were evaluated on academic achievement, proven leadership, athletic abilities, and eligibility for pilot training upon graduation. While Congressmen could nominate candidates, applicant selection was based on a competitive basis; considering the factors listed and various entry exams. Using measures of a candidate's moral and leadership attributes, as well as physical and mental qualifications, for selection was introduced in 1956, for the first time at any service academy.

In his curriculum enrichment program, cadets could get credit for previous college work, take on extra or special courses for extra credit, and work toward various course majors. McDermott was instrumental in having the Academy accredited before the first class, 1959, graduated; a first in the American academia world at the time.[123]

Tragedies

Later we would become accustomed to losing classmates in Vietnam. But, like all college students, we were invincible. So, the loss of two classmates before graduation was traumatic. Sid Abbot fell from the wall at Arnold Hall the night of our ring dance. No one witnessed the incident. The Class, however, was moved by the loss. Bill Gibbons, as a First Classman, crashed his car on his way back to the Academy from Denver. He died in the crash. Again, there was a great sense of loss.

1958 The Undefeated Football Team

In just the fourth year of football competition, the 1958 football team went undefeated. It was a feat that has not repeated. This was somewhat of a national

---

[123]See McDermott's story in *Battling Tradition: Robert F. McDermott and Shaping the US Air Force Academy* by Paul T. Rigenbach.

sensation. The Academy had only three classes on the football team. It was Coach Ben Martin's firs year at the helm.

Twelve of the 36 varsity players were from the Class of 1961. Brock Strom, a 59er, was named as an All-American. Cadets who traveled to the Cotton Bowl on leave brought their uniforms and marched onto the field. They were reimbursed $10 for attending. The 1958 football scheduled was as follows:

The 1958 Football Schedule

Team	Score	Team	Score
Academy	37	Detroit	6
Academy	13	Iowa	13
Academy	36	Colorado State	6
Academy	16	Stanford	0
Academy	16	Utah	14
Academy	33	Oklahoma State	29
Academy	10	Denver	7
Academy	21	Wyoming	6
Academy	45	New Mexico	7
Academy	20	Colorado	14
Academy	0	TCU/Cotton Bowl	0

First year coach, Ben Martin led his team to an undefeated season. Icing on the cake was the zero to zero tie with Texas Christian University in the Cotton Bowl. Another highlight was a tie with Iowa University during the regular season.. The Cadet Wing arrived in Iowa City at half time after a 12 hour bus ride. The 13 to 13 tie brought Iowa's ranking from 8th to 9th nationally and the Academy's highest ranking in its short history to 14th in the nation.

The Great West Point Mule Raid

In anticipation of the Academy's first game with West Point, a daring squad of USAFA cadets went on a spirit mission to try to kidnap the Army's mule mascot. According to Classmate Brice Jones, it was intricately planned, but failed due to runaway asses (mules).

Preparation included walkie-talkies, a primary and backup truck, and use of a C-130 reserve aircraft to transport the mule from West Point to the Academy or near-by grounds. Of the eleven raiders, only Tom Pattie, Brice Jones, Wayne Whalen, Marty

Fricks, Ken MacAulay, Dick Cooper, and Bill Foster are named. A Doolie living near West Point provided his family's residence as the Operation's Headquarters. The Cadet Wing Commander, Tony Burshnick, was complicit in the plot and, conveniently, did not report the team AWOL (absent without leave).

Although Pattie infiltrated the Corps, including marching and eating a meal with the West Point Cadets, he garnered little information about the mules. In fact, lack of intelligence and stubborn mules doomed the mission.

At 0100 on 27 September 1959, the raid began. West Point had won a resounding victory against Boston College. The entire campus was in a celebratory mood; including staff and support personnel. Many support personnel (read security) overindulged, causing lax security.

The raiders entered the stables and found the presence of seven stalls somewhat perplexing. Nevertheless, Whalen seized the initiative and the largest mule. He guided the mule to the nearest truck. At the gangplank to the truck, Marty Fricks applied his homemade 400 volt, battery charged prod to the mule's rear. The mule reared, bolted toward open pasture, and drug Whalen with him.

All the while, sirens were sounding, lights were glaring, and mules were everywhere. In the confusion, the team slipped into the darkness and fled back to their headquarters; all except Ken MacAulay. Sitting in the backup truck, Ken was captured by a Military Policeman. After lengthy negotiations, MacAulay was liberated, in exchange for the names of the rest of the team.

Defeated, but not subdued, the raiders returned to the Academy with several mementos, including West Point uniforms. Disciplinary measures were not meted out to the raiders.

The game was scheduled at Yankee Stadium on Saturday, October 31st. Four hundred upper-class cadets flew to New York in military and chartered airplanes. Emerging from a bus convoy, the Wing representatives marched into the stadium in front of the Army Corp. During game march-on George Luck, Class of 1960, entered with the Corp, stripped off his West Point overcoat and ran triumphantly to the USFA stands. The game ended in a 13-13 tie.

The Annapolis KIDnapping[124]

In late summer of 1960, with Air Force scheduled to play the Naval Academy in football in the fall, the Falcon Raider Team (FRT) was once again assembled under the leadership of Tom Pattie. Learning from their aborted Mule Hoist, the team, now consisting of Pattie, Wayne Whalen and Brice Jones, ditched the radios, trucks, hot sticks, and extraneous members (minimizing communications problems and lessening capture opportunities for the Middies).

Navy's "Billie" & Friends at USAF

Capitalizing on Pattie's residence in Virginia, the raid was set for August. Plans were to use the Patty family car, a four-door Dodge as transport. Analyzing the intelligence shortcomings of the Army mission, the team surveilled the dairy farm where the Navy mascot was located. This was accomplished in the summer morning at 3 am, the day before the actual mission. Realizing the farm was active during the day, the team planned a night operation.

Using stealth and surprise the team entered the farm at 11 p.m. Billy was captured on an August night before the start of the academic semester and the return of all Middies.

Billy spent the night in the trunk of the Dodge. The team, was uncertain how to transfer Billy to Colorado Springs. Brice Jones remembered that Colonel Smith, the Base Commander at Andrews Air Force Base was a former neighbor in Alaska. Brice took the team to Andrews and asked for an appointment with Colonel Smith.

"Hi, Brice, how are you? I understand you're at the Academy? What can I do for you?"

"Sir, I have the Navy goat in the parking lot; we need to get him to Colorado Springs."

After he came down from the ceiling, Colonel Smith said, "Be on the flightline in an hour with your guest."

---

[124] Or: "Who's got your goat?

Arriving at the flight line, the team found a B-26, two pilots and a vet with a huge hypodermic needle. Billie was sedated by a cooperating vet, strapped into the aircraft's bomb bay, and accompanied by the FRT to Colorado Springs.

Arriving in Colorado, Billie was sent to the "farm" of MSgt William Coultrin, USAFA's Cadet Wing Command NCOIC.[125] Recovering from his comatose state, Billie found his accommodations acceptable and enjoyed his four week stay. Despite efforts of Navy's Pentagon Intelligence to locate Billy—even satellite imagery did not locate the errant goat, the mission was a success.

Eventually, the raiders were identified. Cadet Pattie was summoned to Commandant Sullivan's office. In desperation, the Navy agreed to non-punishment of the FRT members in exchange for return of the goat. The prisoner parade at USAFA and the "hostage exchange ceremony" made the pages of *Life Magazine.* Billy was sporting Air Force blue horns.

Air Force cadets were not the only ones with mission spirit. When the Navy Goat was delivered to Peterson Field for his return, he as detained. Enlisted men at Peterson substituted a ragged-looking granny goat for the pride of Annapolis. Enraged when the imposter arrived, Annapolis leadership called upon higher military authority, who in turn ordered the Air Force Academy personnel to return Billy. With a feigned apologetic attitude, and the assistance of MSGT Coultrin, the Academy complied.

The Navy game was played on October 15th in Baltimore Memorial Stadium, home of the Baltimore Colts. The Cadet Wing flew into Friendship Airport in a fleet of US Air Force planes. Quartered in Fort Meade, the cadets were treated to no electricity, no heat, and no bedding. Because of the cold, cadets slept in uniforms on mattresses with overcoats as blankets.

The Navy graciously placed smoke bombs in the Air Force seats. The bombs were set off following the USAFA march-on. Quick thinking Air Force cadets grabbed the smoke bombs and tossed them into the Middie stands.

Contrary to the Army Mule episode, the kidnapping of the USNA mascot was successful; the football team was not. USAFA lost the football game, 35 to 3.

Seeing Europe on $5 a Day

While military field trips were interesting and informative, they could not compare with the Second Class summer field trip to Europe. Visiting Europe as an

---

[125] NCOIC – Non Commissioned Officer in Charge

eighteen or nineteen-year old cadet on per diem and with free transportation was exciting, exhilarating, and just plain fun.

The Asian trip which the Class of 1959 had enjoyed was cancelled for the Class of 1960. We were concerned because of expense, our European trip might also be cancelled. Not only would it not be cancelled, it became mandatory for members of our Class.

The European itinerary included Spain, England, France, and Germany. Treated like adults, we were released from 1600 after a day's activities until 0700 the next morning.

One of our first information briefings was conducted by our accompanying flight surgeon. After advising to be careful about the food and water and being sensible while drinking, he finished with: "Now remember, flies breed disease; keep yours closed."

***

Spain was the first stop. We visited the Spanish Air Force Academy near Murcia, Spain on the country's Southern coast. At dinner with the Spanish cadets, we were introduced to Spanish cognac. Despite the language differences, the evening was interesting and educational.

We transferred to Madrid where we attended a reception in honor of Generalissimo Francisco Franco. Included in the stay was a side trip to Toledo and attendance at a bull fight.

Two classmates and I were caught in the language barrier. We spent forty-five minutes on a Madrid street corner trying to find our way to a restaurant. English was not common in Spain at the time and none of us spoke Spanish. Our pleading gestures finally got us directed to a restaurant, where we enjoyed paella and wine.

Two of our classmates suffered a different and unpleasant experience. On the night of our arrival, 6 June, two classmates named Bob decided to do a night on the town. In the words of one they were "slumming" in old Madrid. Bob One related: "I drank five cognacs. The fifth one must have had a 'mickey' in it. I was out cold a few minutes later and got robbed of 650 pesetas ($12). Bob (2) put me in a cab and sent me back to the hotel. He went on alone, got mugged and robbed of about $15. Other than that, we had a great time in Madrid." So much for sophisticated travelers who had just spent a year in a very sheltered environment.

We arrived at Rheine Main AB, a US operated base, following the flight from Madrid. Our first dinner included pilots from the reconstituted Luftwaffe; several were veterans of WWII action. Fascinated by the war stories, we listened intently. A conversation stopper was a question asked of a veteran fighter pilot: "What was it like flying against the B-17 formations?"

Without hesitation, Gunther answered: "Well, have you ever tried to take a shower without getting wet?" Our group applauded.

In addition to visits to Bonn, the Capital, the Hofbrauhaus in Munich, the Olympic City of Garmish; the highlight was a trip to West Berlin and an excursion into East Berlin.

The night we arrived in Berlin, Dick McMonigal and I took in a restaurant and were strolling the streets of the City. A Volkswagen bug with an older couple in the front seats pulled up beside us. "Are you American, the driver asked?" With crew cuts, sport coats, and ties, it was hard to disguise we were Americans.

"Yes," we replied. "We're visiting cadets from the United States Air Force Academy."

"Well, we appreciate what you Americans have done. I worked with the crews that supported the Berlin Airlift. We would have starved and frozen to death if it were not for you.

We'd like to show you the City and buy you a drink. Would you join us?"

Dick and I were delighted. We jumped into the somewhat restricted back seat of the bug. True to their word, the couple showed us all around the city. After the tour, we were escorted to an elegant nightclub called the Resi. The club was full of young people. We watched a magnificent water show put on by Club and designed by the owner.

A telephone on each table and a Rohrpoststation (a pneumatic tube system) just above the table allowed communication between tables. The phones were on a red post with a rotary dial and a table number on the post.

We were fascinated watching the young people talking on the phones and sending notes through the tubes. Our hosts explained there were some 135 "gifts" that could be purchased and sent to other tables. Given our limited German language abilities and in deference to our hosts, we did not try to start up a conversation with any of the pretty frauleins in the nearby tables.

Since we had eaten, we declined our host's offer to order food. We readily agreed, however, to share beers. We spent a fascinating two hours in the Resi. Our gracious hosts dropped us off at the hotel. Although we thanked the couple, I regret I did not get their name and address to send an appreciative thank you note.

The following day began with a bus tour of East Berlin. On the main avenue, we were amazed at the condition of the buildings. Looking like a surreal scene from Hollywood, the building fronts were rebuilt. Behind the fronts were ravaged remnants of the War, in stark contrast to the facades.

We next visited a war memorial park honoring the Soviet dead. The park was immaculately cared for. The landscaping was beautiful. Our guide pointed out there were six guards patrolling the park. The first pair was watched by a second pair. The second pair of guards was watched by a pair of non-commissioned officers. This arrangement, he said, showed the Soviets' concern the guards might join the many East Berliners fleeing to West Berlin.

The last stop was at a point where we could observe the ongoing destruction of Hitler's bunker. The thick concrete walls that were part of the "The Fuhrer's" last residing place lay in heaps in the middle of a large excavation.

***

The looseness of discipline on the trip was illustrated when two classmates showed up for a morning formation in Wiesbaden somewhat inebriated. The Major Officer-in-Charge (OIC) noted the two's condition and said he would speak with them after the day's NATO[126] briefings. Bob and Pat sweated out the day, desperately trying to stay awake and fearing the hammer that would fall during their meeting with the OIC. When Bob and Pat met with the Major, he said their behavior was not acceptable . . . they were putting themselves at risk. "You are on restriction for 24 hours . . . you need to get some rest."

Following their restriction the next night, the duo ended up in a *Brau Haus* drinking cognac – with their favorite OIC.

***

A brief visit was made to the French Air Force Academy, the Ecole de l'Air at Salon–de-Provence Air Base. We also had briefings at NATO Headquarters. But, of course, the main lure in France was Paris. We were told to avoid the Left Bank because there were rumors of riots there. Naturally a group of cadets ventured there, but returned without incident.

The real awesome event for eighteen and nineteen-year old young men visiting Paris was the fabulous dinner and cabaret show at the Lido Nightclub. The chorus-line dances and minimal costumes had the cadets paying much more attention to show than to dinner. We were amazed to find out the beautiful dancers were mostly English, not French.

Several cadets ventured into the Pigalle area of Paris, but did not write home to their parents about their adventures there. To be able to say we'd seen the Eifel Tower, several of us took a cab to the Tower. At two in the morning, access to the Tower was closed. Four of us lay down in the grass below the Tower and wondered at its beauty from that viewpoint.

***

---

[126] NATO – North Atlantic Treaty Organization

Joining the cadets at the British Air Force Academy, Cranwell, for a dinning-in and the after dinner party, we learned first-hand the traditions the US Air Force had adopted as its own. After many toasts to the leaders of each country and numerous trips to the grog bowl, we were all set for the Cranwell parlor games.

We fully participated in the bicycle jousts and jump-the-rug games. Fortunately, there were no serious injuries; just a few bumps and bruises.

In London, we took in usual tourist sites: London Bridge, the Parliament Building, the Tower of London. Of course, we also did some pub hopping. Some even enhanced their culture by attending a performance at the Drury Lane Royal Theater.

A once-in-a-lifetime event occurred when we observed the parade and ceremonies celebrating the Queen's official 31st birthday. On June 13th we were bussed to St. James Park to observe the proceedings. Queen Elizabeth II was escorted by an English Infantry Regiment of over 500 men. The soldiers wore traditional Red Coats and tall fur-like hats. The Queen passed in her royal carriage preceded by the British Grenadiers Band. As the parade concluded a "flyby" of the British demonstration team streaked overhead.

***

The scheduled stop in New York City on the return leg was cancelled. It was just as well because most of the cadets needed to return to the Academy to recuperate. None-the-less, class members had memories and "war stories" enough to last a life time. Many of the stories were not publically told nor shared with parents, but would be shared among classmates in our remaining time at the Academy and, certainly, in the many reunions of following years.

Life at the New Site

Life at the new site south of Colorado Springs, despite the majesty and beauty of surrounding forests and mountains, was challenging. The Class of 1962 marched from the north gate to the quarters. The "Red Tags"[127] were in for a difficult year. The quarters, terrazzo, partial academic buildings, and the dining hall were complete; the recreational facilities and chapel were not. Athletic facilities, including expansive football and soccer fields, were available to conduct the physical education programs, intermurals, and intercollegiate football practices.

The Red Tags would enjoy all the trials and tribulations of the Fourth Class System without some of the amenities that made it somewhat tolerable. The distance of the

---

[127] Each class was known by their name tag colors. The Class of 1962 had red name tags.

Academy from Colorado Springs (or even greater to Denver) and the weather conditions made it more difficult for young ladies to interact with the Fourth Classmen.

When it rained, mud was everywhere. The "diggers" and "fillers"[128] were still working on the air gardens and other landscaping. The completed terrazzo allowed travel to and from classes and eating. When not in formation, the Doolies were required to double time across the terrazzo; making them, of course, susceptible to upper class supervision.

The modernistic quarters were incredible. The two-man rooms had closets, beds, desks, and wash basins. Large windows, depending on your location, could provide spectacular views of the mountains to the west. While community latrines were still the norm, shaving could now be accomplished in the room. Minute callers were still the bane of the Doolies, but there was an overhead light panel in the hallways indicating the current required uniform.

Snow and cold weather were a challenge, overcome with proper clothing and a functioning, comfortable heating system. A major design flaw, however, caused problems. The long, narrow dormitory shape created a venturi effect. The winds, sometimes formidable, increased in velocity as it passed through the corridors of the buildings. The winds rushing past the windows created a vacuum that "popped" windows out. There were no known reports of cadet injuries due to window malfunctions, but a considerable amount of time, effort, and money went into window replacement.

Little by little, the campus took shape. When our class became First Classmen, Arnold Hall was an excellent facility for entertaining. A large ballroom provided a setting for dances and other activities. A theater, including a performance stage, allowed first run movie dates and special events, such as the Bob Hope Show. The only structure not completed was the Chapel.

Presidential Inauguration

On the 18th of January, 1961, a convoy of 32 air planes carrying the entire USAFA Cadet Wing left Colorado headed for Washington, D.C. The Wing was to march in President John F. Kennedy's inaugural parade. Bad Washington weather caused 15 of the aircraft to abort and divert to alternates.

The "successful" cadet contingent marched five miles in five degree, snow and icy weather. The Middies, marching in front of the AFA group, lost low-quarter galoshes and

---

[128] Workers completing site landscape features were called . "Diggers and fillers" When workers filled an open spot, a crew the next day would open up the same spot. The process seemed never-ending.

even regular shoes as they marched. Following an opportunity to thaw out at Bolling Air Force Base, the cadets dressed in formal uniforms to attend the inaugural ball at the DC National Armory.

The aborted group flew to Fort Campbell, Kentucky, where we were put up in contingency Army barracks. After dinner in the Army mess, we returned to our quarters – not realizing that, despite missing an historical event, we probably got the best end of the deal. My roommate, Jim, and I found two others and played bridge until three in the morning.

Graduation

June Week was a flurry of activities. The 4th of June featured Catholic and Protestant Baccalaureate Services. Parents, relatives, and friends gathered from all over the country. Fairchild Hall, Mitchell Hall (Dining Hall), Vandenberg Hall (Academic Area), Arnold Hall (Social Center).the Planetarium, and the Air Gardens were open to cadets and their guests.

June 5th highlighted an Individual Awards Ceremony, a Thunderbirds[129] show, a parade review, and a Superintendent's Reception for the Class of 1961. John Sullivan, the number one graduate, walked off with 13 awards, including the Harmon Award recognizing his achievement as the top graduate.

At 0900 on 6 June, the Commandant, Major General Henry R. Sullivan, presented Class members their USAF Navigator wings, signifying their status as rated navigators. Most would hold their wings and have parents, finances, or girlfriends pin-on[130] the wings following graduation ceremonies. The graduation parade (First Classmen's last) and Thunderbirds demonstration followed the wings presentation.

The magic day, June 7, 1961, arrived with beautiful Colorado blue skies and moderate temperatures. We marched in, sat in the rows of fold up seats on the parade ground facing the temporary reviewing stand. Following the invocation, we heard Secretary of the Air Force, the Honorable Eugene M. Zuckert, tell the Class: "There is no greater need in our democracy than an ever-growing number of those who are willing to devote themselves to the many tasks of promoting our security and forwarding our programs throughout the world. . . . You who have dedicated yourself to your Country's

---

[129] The USAF Aerial Demonstration Team

[130] Traditionally, someone close to the recipient pins-on wings and/or rank insignia. In an active unit, a commander will normally pin-on one shoulder insignia and the spouse/friend will pin-on the other.

service will find the Air Force an organization clearly worthy of your high purpose and fine training here. "

The Secretary presented Commissions and Diplomas. We rose together with a rousing cheer as Wayne Arthur Haring, the last man in order of merit, received his diploma;

Major General Sullivan administered the oath of office. Following the Benediction and Dismissal, 217 hats flew in the air to culminate our cadet lives. We would now pursue our Class Motto: *Pro Nobis Astra*, for us the stars.

POSTSCRIPT: Most of the Class went to pilot training, some pursued careers as navigators; several received additional honors: John Sullivan: Rhodes Scholar; George Lee Butler, John Kohout, John Wolcott, Darrell Koerner: Olmstead Scholars; Ron Muller: German Federal Government Fellowship in Economics and Sociology. Bob Brickey and Richie Mayo were football All Americans.

Epilogue
Part Two

Vietnam was waiting for the Class of 1961. Seventy-six percent of our graduates became pilots. Sixty percent served in Southeast Asia, the designation for areas directly supporting the United States conduct of the Vietnam War. While many were significant achievers during their careers, the early focus was on combat and combat support involving Viet Nam.

Officers of the Class of 1961 served as fighter pilots, rescue pilots, transport pilots (strategic and tactical), strategic bomber pilots, combat navigators, and in various staff and leadership positions. Nine gave their lives in performing their mission.

The nine on the Academy Memorial Wall, designating those who fell in combat, are:

Classmate	Killed in Combat
Maj. Victor Joe Apodoca	8 Jun 67: Air Mission, N. Vietnam, Plt. 389th TFS*
Capt. Robert George Bull, Jr.	26 Aug 68: Air Mission, S. Vietnam, Plt. 475th TAS.**
Capt. Lee Chris Dixon	7 Jan 66: Air Mission, Laos, Plt. 774th TCS***
Lt. Col. Terry Treloar Koonce	25 Dec 67: Air Mission, Laos, Plt. Unit Not Listed
Capt. Monte Larue Moorberg	2 Dec 66: Air Msn, N. Vietnam, Plt. Unit Not Listed
Maj. Burke H. Morgan	4 Jun 67: Air Mission, Laos, Nav., Unit Not Listed
1/Lt. Thomas Andrew Sanders	7 Jul 65: Acft. Accident, S Vietnam, Plt., 33d ABS****.
Capt. John Earnest Stackhouse	13 Sep 66: Acft. Accndt, Ubon, Thailand, P497th TFS
Capt. Thomas Tyler Walker	7 Apr 66; Air Mission, Laos Nav, Unit Not Listed

TFS*: TAC Fighter Squadron; TAS**: TAC Airlift Squadron; TCS***: Troop Carrier Squadron; ABS****: Air Base Squadron.

Two Class members were prisoners of war (POWs) in North Vietnam; Kenneth Richard Johnson 1971 to 1973. Hayden James Lockhart, Jr. was detained 1965 to 1973.

Two vignettes are associated with those lost in combat and POWs. Robert Apodoca, the son of Victor, escorted his father's remains from Vietnam to the Air Force Academy for interment, with honors, at the Academy. Half way to his destination, Robert's commercial aircraft was grounded along with all other air traffic. The date was September 11, 2001.

Fortunately on the other side of the airport was an Air Force Reserve C-130 airlift unit. Arrangements were made for Robert to continue his special mission. With changing fighter escorts, the C-130 flew to Peterson Field, Colorado, where Victor could be returned to his final resting place. Robert was the only civilian passenger in the air on 9-11, after the terrorist attacks.

The other vignette involves my son, living with his mother in San Clemente, California, while I was stationed in Taiwan, Chris was concerned with the plight of our POWs. At age seven, he stood in front of the local grocery store and collected money to send to a POW oriented organization. In return for donations, the organization sent donors bracelets inscribed with a POW's name. Chris received a bracelet with Classmate Hayden Lockhart's name. Some year's later, at a Class reunion, Chris met Hayden and told him of his experiences as a young boy concerned with the welfare of our troops.

It is apparent 61ers had a positive impact on the Viet Nam air war: Fifteen received Silver Stars; three had two Silver Stars. Ninety-one earned Distinguished Flying Crosses; several had multiple awards. The awards were across the spectrum of aviation operations in the region.

Fighter pilot missions included Air to Air Combat, Troop Ground Support, Bombing of North Vietnam, Forward Air Controller, Wild Weasel (jamming of radar/SAM[131] sites), Search and Rescue and Reconnaissance Flights. North Vietnam, Laos, and, of course, South Vietnam were all areas of operation.

Flying an F-4 Phantom II in March 1967, Captain Earl Aman's aircraft suffered damage from antiaircraft fire over North Vietnam. Flying as wingman to Captain Bob Pardo, Aman suffered a ruptured fuel tank; it appeared Aman's crew was destined to bail out over the North, with the undesirable probability of capture by the Vietnamese.

Unwilling to let his teammates crash in enemy territory, Pardo maneuvered his aircraft behind Aman's. He eventually was able to literally push Aman's aircraft by

---

[131] SAM – Surface to Air Missiles

placing the tail hook of the crippled aircraft against his own windshield. Unable to maintain altitude, the two Phantoms, nonetheless, edged toward friendly air space.

Eighty-eight miles after the maneuver began, the two aircraft reached Laotian airspace. Pardo's aircraft was out of fuel. The two crews safely ejected, evaded capture, and were rescued by helicopters. Pardo and Aman received Silver Stars for what is known as "Pardo's Push."

Other air ops included Strategic Bombing, Strategic and Tactical Airlift, Jungle Defoliation[132], Flare Ship missions, Gun Ship missions[133], Search and Rescue (SAR, and Aerial Refueling both for strategic bomber aircraft and a variety of fighter aircraft.

B-52 Bombers flying from Guam conducted interdiction, ground support, and eventually, strategic bombing missions. Operation "Arc Light," from 1965 to 1973 was primarily interdiction and ground support missions. B-52 sorties are credited with breaking the siege of Khe Sanh, the Marine Forward Base Camp under attack by overwhelming North Vietnamese forces. Operations "Linebacker" and "Linebacker II" bombed North Vietnam as President Richard Nixon's instrument to bring the North Vietnamese leaders to the negotiating table.

Strategic Airlift brought critical materials and troops to prime airports: Cam Rahn Bay, Danang, and Tan San Nhut. Missions were also flown into lessor fields. "Operation Blue Light" in December, 1965, employed 12 C-41s and 4 C-133[134]s on 225 missions to deploy 4,000 troops and 4,700 tons of cargo of the 25th Infantry Division, from Hawaii to Pleiku, Vietnam. Blue Light, at the time, was the largest and longest airlift of personnel and cargo into a combat zone in military history.

C-7, C-123, and C-130A/E aircraft conducted tactical airlift missions. The C-130 was the workhorse, carrying cargo, troops, ammunition, and even fruits and vegetables from one part of Vietnam to another. It is estimated 7 trillion tons of passengers and cargo were moved in Vietnam from 1962 to 1973. The C-7, C-123, and the C-130A could all use shorter airfields than the C-130E, but the E model had a higher load capacity.

Modified C-123s were the primary aircraft used in defoliation operations. The aircraft flew in formation, several abreast, to spray defoliant over large areas. The purpose

[132] Operation "Ranch Hand:," specially equipped C-123s defoliated large areas of jungle
[133] C-47, C123, and C-130 aircraft performed flare missions, lighting up areas for American troops under attack. Designated AC-47s and AC-130s, these aircraft could deliver devastating firepower to an area.
[134] The C-141, an all jet transport, began operational service in April, 1965, replacing the C-124 piston-driven aircraft in the Military Airlift Command inventory. The C-133, a large turbo-prop aircraft, was still in use because it could carry out size loads and 110,000 pounds of cargo verses 68,500 for the C-124.

of the operations was to deny the enemy the camouflage of jungle growth. Without the coverage, exposed areas were then subject to air strikes.

Forward Air Controllers (FACs) played a key role in Viet Nam air operations, almost all in the South and Laos. FACs flew in light aircraft, the O-1, O-2, and, later, the OV-10. Subject to ground fire and anti-craft fire, the mission was exceptionally hazardous. Later, "Fast Movers," flying F-100s and F-4s, had better survivability.

FACs gathered intelligence, marked targets, directed air strikes, and served as on-scene-commanders for search and rescue missions. FACs could deliver light ordnance, but were most valuable to the ground forces calling in air strikes, including fighters and gunships.

Gunships, originally modified C-47s and later C-130s served the ground forces by providing flares to light up the night and concentrated firepower on a specific combat zone. The AC-47 had 7.62mm miniguns directed out the side of the aircraft. The C-130, originally armed with Gatling Guns and later with 20mm and 40mm cannons, aimed its weapons out the side of the fuselage. The aircraft circled over a battle field and laid down a devastating barrage of fire.

Air Force helicopters and fixed wing aircraft conducted search and rescue operations. Often mission fighter aircraft would loiter in the area of a downed wingman until search and rescue (SAR) aircraft could be on scene. SAR missions flew in all the combat zones of the Vietnam Conflict.

Aerial Refueling was an important element in the Vietnam War. KC-135 aircraft refueling was available to the B-52s in an emergency, but more importantly, were an integral part of fighter operations. F-4s and F-105s on North Vietnam missions were able to carry heavier bomb loads, have increased loiter time for reconnaissance and air to air operations, and have a margin of error on their fuel returning to base.

There were several instances of aircraft with damaged fuel systems hooking up with tankers until within safe gliding distance of a suitable airfield. Search and rescue operations were often extended through the availability of aerial refueling

Class of 1961 officers were involved in virtually all of these operations. Many started as basic crew members and advanced to leadership positions; from leading strike forces to directing overall operations from headquarters. One hundred and thirty served in South East Asia (SEA), a term designated for the region providing direct support for the War in Vietnam. Of those in SEA, 19 (14%) received Silver Stars, the third highest combat decoration.

Ninety-one (70%) of grads in SEA were decorated with the Distinguished Flying Cross. Class Members received 1,359 Air Medals (AMs). Air Medals could, and probably were, awarded for excellence in aerial flight other than Vietnam. Therefore, the number of AMs received for combat support may be less. Different units used varying criteria for the medal – for instance, number of flights or type of flights.

The level and amount of decorations presented to 61ers indicates the valor and combat contributions of the warriors who served.

Military Service

Class of Sixty-One Classmates served in many capacities in the military. Seven received the Distinguished Service Medal, 26 the Defense Superior Service Medal, and 73 the Legion of Merit. These decorations, the highest recognition of significant acts and/or sustained superior service, reflect the contributions made throughout the Defense Department or the Air Force in various commands and levels of responsibility.

Excluding those killed in combat or under other circumstances, 120 or 55.3 per cent of the Class completed military careers. Nineteen reached the rank of general while a third of the Class (56) was promoted to the rank of full colonel.

George Lee Butler was the Four Star Commander of Strategic Command, the Nation's nuclear deterrent force. Marcus Anderson, in addition to serving as Commandant at the Air Force Academy, served several years as the Inspector General of the Air Force. He retired as a Lieutenant General. Norm Campbell, Thomas LaPlante, Kenneth Staten, and Frank Willis all attained the rank of Major General. Norm was a Tactical Officer at West Point and an Air Officer Commanding at USAFA.

The Air Force almost didn't have the service of General Butler. When taking his physical examination for entry into the Academy, Butler was underweight and failed the exam. The Med Tech, noting Butler's dilemma, suggested Butler drink a lot of chocolate milk, then come back later for a reweigh in. Butler did as recommended and later successfully passed the exam.

Education and Training Contributions

Many graduates served in education and training in the Air Force and civilian positions. Twenty-six returned to the Academy in positions ranging from Commandant of Cadets to sports assistants. One served as Dean and four others were professors. Four were on the Commandant's staff as Air Officers Commanding, the military department's inter-face with cadets. One, Norman Campbell, served in the same capacity at both USAFA and West Point.

Additionally, graduates were professors/instructors at Embry University, Arizona; Maryville College, Tennessee; North Texas State, Texas; and Clemson.

Several served in leadership positions at various institutes to include:

1961 Leadership Positions at Educational Institutions

Name	Position	Institute
Marcus Anderson	Commandant of Cadets	USAF Academy
Don Box	Commandant (Director)	Defense Language Institute
Ruben Cubero	Dean	USAF Academy
Gene Davis	Commandant (Director)	Inter-American Air Forces Academy[135]
John May	President	Atlantic Community College
Richard Milnes	Commandant (Director)	Inter-American Defense College[136]
Charles Stebbins	Provost/Dean	University of Charleston
Dale Tabor	Commander	Sheppard Technical Training Center

Diverse Occupations

Those who left the military were involved in various endeavors. The military-industrial complex, naturally, benefited from the expertise, management, and leadership skills of graduates. A natural transition for pilots was into commercial aviation. Twenty-seven graduates flew in commercial aviation. But classmate ventured into many varied occupations.

Brice Cutrer Jones traveled to France, educated himself on the wine business, and developed the successful Sonoma Cutrer Chardonnay brand of wines. Moreover, Brice, like many others, contributed to social causes as well. Hosting an international croquette tournament and associated wine auction benefitting the *Make a Wish Foundation*,[137] Brice contributed millions of dollars to the Foundation through his events.

---

[135] The Inter-American Air Force Academy (IAAFA) is a USAF Tech Training Center benefiting Latin American countries. Begun in the mid-forties, the school initially offered pilot training (primarily for Brazilians) and courses in aviation support; later courses focused on maintenance and logistics.

[136] Under the Organization of American States, the Inter-American Defense College (IADC), is a senior military school for Latin American and US officers. The Commanding Officer is a US general or Admiral.

[137] The Make-a-Wish Foundation grants the wishes to critically ill children between the ages of 2 and 17. It is nation-wide and international. The first child involved, Christopher Grecicius, wanted to be a police officer. Through individual efforts, he was made an honorary officer of the Arizona Department of Public Safety; given a tailor-made uniform, "sworn in," and received a police helicopter ride. Christopher died soon after his experience.

Sam Hardage, became deeply involved in the hotel business. With over 30 years in the business, he was Chairman and CEO of Hardage Hospitality. Sam built the Embassy Suites hotel chain. His efforts included 74 projects in 16 states, including the Woodfin Suite and Chase Suite Hotels. Sam was an outstanding player on the 1958 undefeated football team.

On a smaller scale, Carl Cranberry assumed the presidency of the Brother's Manufacturing Company. The Company is located in Winona, Texas, and has been a producer of brooms. The Company is now engaged in metal manufacturing and employs four people.

Several members chose professional careers: nine are attorneys, three are doctors, and one is a pastor. Of the lawyers, Weldon Bates was the Assistant Attorney General for Oregon; Phillip Lane a US Magistrate Judge in Texas; and Russell Cash a District Attorney in California.

Richard Arnold, Virgil McCullum, and James Wild are doctors; Thomas Schutt a pastor.

Graduates often interacted with foreign governments. NATO, the State Department, and Military Advisory Groups were all assignments involving working with foreign counterparts, often including high level government officials.

Pat Buckley, after retirement from the Air Force, lived in Albania for five years. Employed by Lockheed Martin Global; Pat, as the Managing Director of Albania Air Traffic Improvements, was instrumental in helping to establish and operate a national Air Traffic Control System. His efforts brought kudos from Albanian Government Officials.

While on assignment as the Political Advisor to the Commander, US Forces Azores, I was the principle negotiator for the use of the Portuguese base at Lajes Field, Azores. Working with my Portuguese counterpart, I secured US airfield landing rights and resolved other issues, including labor relations with the Azorean work force. At the time, the Base Rights negotiations were the only ones in the Air Force completed at a local level.

From cattle ranchers to educators to airline pilots to military and industry leaders, Air Force Academy graduates of the Class of 1961 have contributed to the American military and society in significant ways. A chronicle of all their achievements as individuals and as a group would fill a book. That book would begin in 1957 with an accounting of our shared experiences as Doolies in the third class of cadets to enter the Air Force Academy—the toughest school in the United States.

About the Author

Colonel Gene Davis (USAF Retired) is a member of the third class to graduate from the USAF Academy. Following pilot training, he flew C-133 aircraft at Dover Air Force Base, completing over 4,000 hours on airlift missions world-wide.

With over 1,000 hours (600 combat support hours) in the C -130 in Southeast Asia, Gene was awarded the Distinguished Flying Cross.

In the Air Force, he was the Chief of the Western Hemisphere Division; Political Advisor to the Commander, US Forces, Azores; Assistant Deputy for Operations, Travis AFB; US Mission Advisor the Argentine Air Force; and Commandant of the Inter-American Air Forces Academy, which he moved from Panama to the US.

Gene was the Assistant Supervisor of Elections for Brevard County, Florida, during the 2000 Bush-Gore Presidential contest. He was the Assistant Program Manager for the State Department's anti-narcotics program in Latin America and the Phase-in Manager for DynCorp in the International Police Force effort in Hatti during the return of President Aristide.

He wrote various professional papers for the Air Force and the Department of Defense. As Past President of the Space Coast Writer's Guild, he has authored two poetry books (*Words Unspoken* and *Silver Memories*), a children's book (*The Kissing Camels*) and a murder mystery (*Murder at the Blue Ridge BBQ Festival*). He wrote for and edited the Guild's magazine, *Literary Liftoff*. He authored and edited segments of the Guild' children's serial *A Summer Storm* published in the *Florida Today* newspaper.

Judy is Gene's wife of 57 years. They have two children and seven grandchildren. Judy and Gene live in Melbourne, Florida.

Made in the USA
Coppell, TX
13 December 2020